REALITY'S EDGE

>>CYBERPUNK_SKIRMISH_RULES

JOSEPH McGUIRE

OSPREY GAMES

OSPREY GAMES
Bloomsbury Publishing Plc
PO Box 883, Oxford, OX1 9PL, UK
1385 Broadway, 5th Floor, New York, NY 10018, USA
E-mail: info@ospreygames.co.uk
www.ospreygames.co.uk

OSPREY GAMES is a trademark of Osprey Publishing Ltd

First published in Great Britain in 2019

ISBN:
HB 9781472826619
eBook 9781472826626
ePDF 9781472826633
XML 9781472826640

19 20 21 22 23   10 9 8 7 6 5 4 3 2 1

Originated by PDQ Digital Media Solutions, Bungay, UK
Printed and bound by Bell & Bain Ltd., Glasgow G46 7UQ

Osprey Games supports the Woodland Trust, the UK's leading woodland conservation charity. Between 2014 and 2018 our donations are being spent on their Centenary Woods project in the UK.

To find out more about our authors and books visit www.ospreygames.co.uk. Here you will find extracts, author interviews, details of forthcoming events and the option to sign up for our newsletter.

AUTHOR BIOGRAPHY

Joey McGuire is the President and Head Janitor of World's End Publishing, and is the author of This Is Not a Test. A geek and long-time gamer, Joey got into the miniatures hobby after entering a gaming store in 1997 and discovering the Games Workshop product catalog. Since that auspicious day, Joey has been modelling and painting miniatures, building terrain, and writing his own rules. This Is Not a Test was his first solo publication, but he has also worked on several other projects, both personal and for Rattrap Productions. Joey is also a devoted husband, proud father, and a humble civil servant by day.

ARTIST BIOGRAPHY

Thomas Elliott has had a lifelong love of Sci fi and fantasy art. He grew up in Watford and went on to study Fine Art painting at City and Guilds of London Art School. After Graduating, Thomas made the decision to put fine art to one side and focus on a career in illustration. He now works for Games Workshop as one of their in-house Artists.

CONTENTS

FOREWORD

Welcome to *Reality's Edge*, a world of the future where the promises of a better tomorrow were replaced with corporate greed, cynicism, and a breakdown of social order. Inspired by *Neuromancer, Shadowrun, Blade Runner, Johnny Mnemonic,* and hundreds of other noir tales, *Reality's Edge* is a skirmish game set in a technologically advanced, dystopian world, where everything can be bought and sold, even you. Reputation is everything, money and information are equally valuable, and you lead a team of free-agents trying to make the best of a corrupt world.

Before we get to the gratuitous violence, you need to keep a couple of things in mind:

- You and your crew are punks, not super soldiers or Olympic-level athletes. The road to the top is long and dangerous. Are you tough enough to last where others—many others—fail?
- There are no easy shortcuts; nobody becomes great overnight. If you want to be the best, you must work at it, and work hard. Experience points are few and far between and earned through hard-knocks.
- Chrome is a short-cut. Cybernetics are great, but the improvements come as a high price: your humanity. If you want the cheat code to awesomeness, you must pay dearly for it.
- You cannot do it all. Choose your crew carefully, especially when you're just starting out. You will have some weaknesses—they are unavoidable. Luckily, your competition has them, as well.

Reality's Edge is a true cyberpunk game. Nobody cares whether you succeed but you, and the deck is stacked against you. Of course, that's half the fun! Every success means you did it, not the dice. You make the choices, take your lumps, and give back as good as you get.

Stay alive out there, *péngyou.*

GETTING STARTED

If this is the first time you're reading *Reality's Edge*, we do not recommend you read the rules from front to back. The book is organized as a reference, so it is easy to look up rules quickly during your games. Therefore, each section is, for the most part, self-contained. When you read this book for the first time, understanding the game and getting to the table quickly is more important than having an in-depth understanding of all the rules. Some sections contain additional rules that seem a bit superfluous until you play through a game or two.

Instead, we recommend you read the following sections first (in order of presentation):

- The *World Building* sections (*Your Reality*, etc.): These parts set the game's theme within the world and give your future struggles a narrative focus.
- *Gameplay:* The mechanics. You need rules to play the game, and this is where you get started. Read up to *Cyber Warfare* and skip the *Non-Player Character* section for now.
- *Building Your Crew:* Equally important to the mechanics, this section starts with creating your Showrunner—the model that represents you in the game—as well as assembling your first crew, and the starting rules for each. Certain topics may not make much sense at first, such as the effects of certain special rules like skills, but that is okay. The goal is to quickly assemble a simple, beginning crew.
- *Special Rules:* Once you create your first crew, circle back and look up the special rules for each crew member. You still do not need to read the entire section, just look up the rules that apply to your crew. They are listed in alphabetical order, for easy reference.
- *Black Market:* This section lists the various items your models can equip. Peruse the section thoroughly, but ignore the *High-End Items* portion for now.
- *JOBOPS:* This is the last section you need to worry about, and there is no reason to read every mission. You only need to choose the first mission you and your fellow players want to try. Ignore the *Hitches* and *Bystanders* rules for your first few games, until you have a good handle on the basic rules.

Congratulations, you are ready to select your crew! Enjoy!

REALITY AND BEYOND

Your Reality - The Sprawl

Humanity has reached the stars in the world of *Reality's Edge*. We established colonies on Mars and beyond, we have orbiting stations above Earth, and corporate arcologies (self-contained, self-sufficient sky towers) pierce the heavens. However, all of this has little to do with you. You live, work, and will likely die in the Sprawl, a thriving mass of humanity that extends hundreds of miles in all directions. The Sprawl is everywhere and could be anywhere. Rio de Janeiro, Paris, Shanghai, New York—they are all the same: a tangled mess of city blocks, suburban enclaves, and every conceivable structure in-between.

A Quick and Dirty Guide to Corporate Takeovers

Corporate takeovers happen quietly and faster than you might think. Environmental catastrophe and overpopulation led to global resource shortages and economic collapse. The corporations stepped into the void left by a failing government bureaucracy, providing what the government could not—for a profit, of course. Soon, governments shriveled, and mega corporations arose. No longer leashed to the yoke of benevolent governance, corporate greed and consumerism became the virtues of a new age, which focused on maximized profit and corporate intrigue. Battles once fought in boardrooms now spilled out across the globe into actual wars. The mega corporations replaced the military and police with their own agents and equivalents. The vestiges of the old-world governments grasped at the remaining crumbs.

The common people barely noticed this new dystopia at first. One master replaced another, the new master more practiced at keeping them in a stupor of low-quality entertainment, violent spectacle, and just enough comfort to stifle thoughts of revolution. For a time, things looked promising. With extensive corporate funding, and the lack of government meddling and ethical restraint, researchers and scientists made wondrous discoveries—cures for centuries-old diseases, advances in genetic manipulation, cybernetics, robotics, artificial intelligence once considered science fiction, and even science fantasy.

Like all things corporate, however, these miracles were weighed against improved shareholder value. Only the elite could afford to live forever via cloning or having their consciousness transferred from their decaying bodies. For the have-nots, this promise was

soon broken, and they returned to their mindless consumption of whatever media the corporations fed them. Still, even they were lucky, for many did not receive this much. These marginalized people sheltered as best they could in the voids that remained, hopeless and forgotten.

Special Economic Zones

Nation-state collapse meant former geographical boundaries were replaced with those of corporate sovereignty. The Sprawl does not have a single authority, rather jurisdiction is divided into demesnes under a corporation's authority. Mega corporations rule most areas, but smaller corporations maintain their own domains, as well—either independently or as franchises to a megacorporation. Many former nation-states retain some semblance of control between corporate zones. Despite this rather anarchic system, stable markets and flowing commerce keep everyone agreeable and polite, at least in public. However, in the shadows, it is as deadly and dangerous as ever, if not more so.

Corporate Authority

The Sprawl contains a mixture of different corporate policies and laws. What is legal in one zone may not be in another. Some zones maintain strong authoritarian control with total police surveillance, whereas other zones may essentially be lawless. Even within zones, there may be a huge disparity. The corporate elite districts are calm and orderly, with all violent crime managed swiftly. However, neighboring areas just beyond these walled enclaves are practically warzones. Mega corporations oversee everything: hospitals, schools, police forces, and the courts that keep society running and controlled. Essentially, they *are* the law.

Districts

Corporate growth and the expansion of one's control is the goal, which leads the Sprawl to spread far and wide. Each district, sub-district, and block is as unique and individual as the Sprawlers who live there. There are, however, some basic commonalities between the various districts.

UPPER REACHES

The most technologically advanced, beautifully designed, and expensive places to live are in the Sprawl's upper levels. Here, the corporate elite live and work in massive arcologies for high-level corporations. Typically, a single corporation or very wealthy family owns each arcology. These stratified ivory towers house a corporation's upper management and their families. The highest sections are privately owned spaces, protected by a small army of well-paid, highly-trained private security agents who employ multiple checkpoints, death fields, security turrets, and any other measure necessary to keep Sprawlers from entering. As you travel down from there, the buildings begin to connect through a bewildering array of walkways and skybridges until you reach street level.

BURBCLAVES

Corporations designed track housing with a 1950s mid-American aesthetic for middle management—those dead-eyed salary-men and women. These midsize, beige and white houses, have white picket fences and in-ground pools. Built in rows of a hundred and surrounded by a large perimeter wall with razor wire and heavy security turrets, these houses are the reward for a lifetime of pointless service to the corporation.

THE STREET

The most common of all districts, the Street is the Sprawl's ground floor. Miles of housing complexes, tenement blocks, skyscrapers, flats, and every other building type known to man surround the bases of the massive arcologies, which remain under heavy guard. The hodgepodge of buildings is mostly gray and dirty, lit by thousands of holo-vid advertisements and shop signs. Here white-collar, working-class employees rub shoulders with blue-collar garage dwellers, vagrants, criminals, and everyone else who has a place to live or a job to do. Yes, it's bad, but it's better than the alternative.

RAGTOWNS

These vast areas on the Sprawl's fringe are the worst of the worst. The most desperate and marginalized people live here, doing whatever they can to make a living. No margins or missions exist in Ragtowns—the corporations pulled even the most basic services. Multiple families share a single room in the few remaining buildings. Open areas are full of shanties and favelas, built next to and on top of each other using pieces of scrap metal, leftover plastic, and salvaged vehicles in an array of desperate ingenuity.

This is the *real* world. The gray, dreary world in which you live. However, you do not have to stay here.

THE HYPERNET

The Internet of yesteryear evolved into a more robust and all-consuming worldwide data network. Officially, this mesh network of interconnected devices that acts as both router and computer is called the HyperNET; but, it goes by about a hundred other names. Data transmissions across millions of major and minor nodes happen nearly instantaneously. Plenty of other minor, temporary, and local networks also thrive; but, the mega corporations and Gov.Mil treaties and agreements ensure the HyperNET remains the one network for all business—legal or otherwise.

The HyperNET is the whole worldwide data network, but its backbone is comprised of the major and minor nodes through which much of the data flow. To keep the HyperNET running safely and prevent its collapse, the corporations and other powers keep the major nexus network nodes behind layers of security that it would take an army to pierce. Still, the most important type of network node is the humble and ubiquitous Community Access Terminal (CAT). Encased in armored housing and rated to survive even heavy machine gun fire, mega corporations provide CATs to keep the populace connected "for their own betterment." The CAT Terminal node is hardwired directly to the HyperNET via underground fiber optic cables. It is a network broadcaster—wirelessly sending, but never receiving— and those without neuro-chips can supposedly access it directly. However, these public access points are usually broken, non-functional, or monopolized by local transients and gutter-deckers.

ACCESSING THE HYPERNET

Only Ragtowns and the most backwater, forgotten parts of the Sprawl go without some form of HyperNET connection due to the CAT Terminal network. The HyperNET is, in many ways, life and a promise better than Meatspace.

You do not access the HyperNET so much as experience it; and it is as much a part of the Sprawl as the clouds in the overcast sky and intermittent gunfire. Most Sprawlers have a neuro-chip implanted as adolescents. Neuro-chips have multiple functions: they store all personal data (medical, financial, and statistical) and offer a direct connection to the HyperNET's augmented reality—digital data superimposed over physical objects to create a composite view. These digital displays—called Hyper-Reality Overlays (HROs)—can be anything from simple text to holographic videos and images in which you can fully immerse yourself. You can digitally manipulate HROs, which are fully interactive and range from the size of an insect to truly immense proportions. Building-sized advertisements, digital personas, and avatars (all licensed, of course) swim about offering the latest pleasures and distractions, allowing you to replace the Sprawl's drabness with the beauty of a thousand neon signs. Indeed, while Sprawlers can turn off this view of the world, most choose to stay plugged in as they go about their daily business; the grayness of the world is just too depressing.

The HyperNET's final layer is the virtual. When a person chooses to go full immersion, they completely replace the real world with the designer's new world. Unlike hyper-reality, going deep in the virtual requires—at minimum—an immersion helmet and sensory gloves. A helmet and gloves allow sight, hearing, and touch. However, a full pod also provides taste and smell. Because of this, full pods are quite popular with those who try to remain online full-time. Unlike the hyper-reality layer, there is no continuous virtual Hyper-NET. Private grids host most virtual digital worlds, which tend to be invite only. All mega corporations, Gov.Mils, and other major groups have some sort of virtual environment to facilitate internal communication via telepresence, shared data storage, and even entertainment. However, to keep up appearances, the HyperNET also has a low-grade public grid divided by locality and hosted on CAT Terminals. Therefore, while a continual virtual world that covers the entire planet does not exist, these public grids are widespread enough that a user could conceivably traverse the planet if given the time and opportunity. Of course, the private grids can be quite fanciful. An Asian-based corporation may design their grid to evoke feudal China or Japan, whereas a CEO with an affinity for diving may design his corporate virtual world entirely underwater with his subordinates swimming around him. The public grid contains no such whimsy. Uninspired data engineers usually just recreate the physical location of an area on which the grid is based.

The Edge of Reality

The HyperNET's virtual and hyper-reality layers are distinct by design, but for those who have or can gain access, the edges of what is real and virtual can blend together. Avatars, AI, minor data sprites, and security Intrusion Countermeasures Emulation (ICE) programs can all traverse into the real world. While they are not physical, they still possess a visual form—projected as holographic objects or HROs. Without license or permission, such activities are highly illegal and ruthlessly suppressed by the corporations. For those working among the shadows, that is half the fun and worth the challenge.

YOUR PART IN THIS WORLD – THE SHADOW ECONOMY

While corporate wars do happen, they are uncommon. Early war endeavors held a poor return on investment of human life, materials, and capital, which lead most mega corporations to manage their disputes through voluntary arbitration. Though military options remain on the table, war brings instability, which is bad for business. When war is not an option, and arbitration does not deliver the necessary results, the corporations turn to covert actions—shadow wars. Shadow units are like any other business unit, driven by results and return on investment.

Long-term and permanent corporate jobs are the exception, not the norm. Permahires expect insurance, regular salaries, and other expensive benefits. Therefore, the corporations use these positions as rewards for the most efficient or well-connected short-terms, which leaves most with gig work. The corporate world runs on the so-called gig economy—short-term jobs that pay upon completion. While gig work is touted as a benefit to workers, as they can self-schedule and maintain control of their employment terms, it really equates to low pay, unreliable hours, and no repercussions should an employer abuse the terms of a contract. Everyone plays this rigged game for which the corporations wrote the rules.

This where you come in. Within the shadow economy exist freelancers of every stripe. Professional hackers, melee specialists, combat doctors, bodyguards, and more are available for hire. Most operatives have just enough skill and experience to be dangerous, but not enough to go pro. Enterprising individuals with an eye for emerging talent, a resolve to take any job offered, and a certain ruthlessness can hire these low-level operatives and start their own crew. These leaders start with simple employees; but, over time, they bring the best into their inner circle, offering them a greater share of the profits and a certain amount of job security, and supplementing their crew's needs with disposable temps. The goal is to climb the corporate ladder to the upper strata of management, or—if they dare—incorporate.

You are one such enterprising individual. You are a Showrunner, a mercenary majordomo who struck a Faustian bargain and accepted bleeding-edge cybernetics with no questions asked. Beholden to a mysterious shadow backer who rides along with you in your head and provides virtual support, you supply yourself and additional manpower. Your backer sends you on jobs proposed by anonymous fixers—you complete the missions, get paid, and grow your reputation and crew. Perhaps you can pay off your shadow backer and regain your freedom, someday. But that day is far in the future and you have a lot to learn before then. So, pay attention.

Lexicon

Before we send you on your way, we offer this bit of support. The Sprawl is loaded with technical terminology and local slang; and, as a melting pot of hundreds of cultures, Sprawlers are not shy about helping themselves to words from other languages. This section helps familiarize you with some of the more common verbiage that tends to confuse newcomers to the world of *Reality's Edge*.

- *Bot:* Short for *robot*, but more specifically used as slang for any mechanical being with complex behavioral programming or rudimentary AI.
- *CC:* Short for cryptocurrencies, which is how you do business in the shadow economy. Everything the Showrunner needs for a successful crew—including operatives, weapons, equipment, and so on—has a CC cost.
- *CORPSEC:* Short for corporate security, the general term for the various corporate agents and agencies that police special economic zones and the HyperNET.
- *Corporati:* High-level corporate employee.
- *Chum:* A person newly exposed to or inexperienced with harsh Street life. Chums are easy prey for more experienced Sprawlers.
- *Drone:* Robots that have numerous forms and are operated remotely by a controller. Drones have little to no capacity for independent action. Controllers are usually human or, in rare circumstances, unshackled AIs.
- *Favela:* Large, multi-family dwellings built from whatever scraps were found. Favelas come in various sizes and shapes and can spread for miles in many directions with no central planning or safeguards. Most often seen in Ragtowns, but sometimes in the Street.
- *Gov.Mil:* Refers to the last vestiges of nation state governments and the military industrial complex as a whole; the heavy intermixing of the two makes trying to separate them challenging. May also refer to individual agents of these authorities.
- *Holo:* Short for holographic video, the 3D electronic replacement for traditional 2D video. Standard image display for most media forms.
- *Hood-net:* A low-quality computer network, usually cobbled together by poor Sprawlers using stolen routers and satellite dishes. Typically found where a neighborhood CAT is not present, though it can also include an extensively modified CAT with jury-rigged repeaters and signal boosters.
- *Idoru:* A computer program like text-to-speech that translates data into song. Often linked to a holographic or robotic performer and usually backed by entertainment or technological corporations. Many such performers are quite popular and have large fan groups. Several idoru are rumored to be unshackled AI's.

- *Iso-Cell:* Short for isolation cell, this is where one serves the general punishment for committing crimes against corporations. If the crime results in minimal loss to the corporation's bottom line, the criminal can expect to be put *"on ice"* or in the virtual reality (VR) version of solitary confinement for an amount of time equal to the level of charge—though to the prisoner, it can feel much, much longer. Isolation and indentured servitude are the most common punishments for serious crimes.
- *Meatspace:* Used to describe the *real* world—most often used as a pejorative, outside of virtual space.
- *Musico:* A well-known musician or music-based media personality. Can also refer to an idoru.
- *Network Node:* A physical place to access cyberspace. Smaller nodes can be wireless, but HyperNET nodes are hardened and require direct-link access only.
- *Péngyou:* Mandarin for friend or pal, a common term in the Sprawl for friend or compatriot. Implies a close connection.
- *Permahire:* An employee with a long-term contract—a permanent hire. As being permanently hired is considered a reward for excellent service, it usually includes a generous benefits package and regular salary.
- *Realspace:* Another term for the *real* world, with fewer negative connotations than Meatspace.
- *Sprawler:* Someone who lives in the Sprawl. Usually used to describe those who live and work in the lowest and/or poorest areas.
- *Unshackled AI:* An artificial intelligence that managed to bypass the Turing Protocols and achieve some type of independence or managed to improve itself beyond the parameters of its programing. Most are found hiding in the virtual side of the HyperNET.
- *Vid-Joint:* Essentially a bar, with low to mid-tier quality holographic video entertainment booths and viewing rooms for rent. Many offer food and beverages and are used as central meeting places for discreet business dealings.
- *VR-Joint:* Similar in concept to the vid-joint, but instead of media screens, Sprawlers can rent immersive VR pods to go full avatar into the HyperNET. VR-Joints offer long-term leases with IV nourishment and bowel voidance measures, so the user need not exit the booth.

GAMEPLAY

"The HyperNET is about freedom. They can't rule what they can't control!"

Mr. Incog-neat-o, Console Cowboy

The Basics

SCALE AND BASING

Reality's Edge is designed for 28mm to 32mm scale miniature models, but is perfectly adaptable for other sizes of models. Simply play as usual or adjust ranges as desired. For example, if you want to play with 15mm models, you could simply convert inches to centimeters.

There is no presumed ground scale for *Reality's Edge*—all distances and ranges are meant to balance the game rather than simulate real world physics.

Reality's Edge does not require a set type of basing. We recommend basing be consistent among models whenever possible, but it is not required.

FACING AND LINE OF SIGHT

Generally, models in *Reality's Edge* have a 360-degree field of view and may move and shoot in any direction without penalty. However, in some instances, models may have a restriction that allows only a front or rear 180-degree arc. These arcs are defined by drawing an imaginary line through the middle of the model's base, separating the front and rear.

Reality's Edge uses line of sight to determine what a model can and cannot see. If the model can see an object or other model, they can shoot or otherwise interact with it. However, terrain, additional models, and other obstructions may block a model's line of sight. For situations in which it is not obvious whether a model has line of sight, the player may need to get as close to the model as possible to gauge what it would actually be able to see. Note that for conversion purposes, some models may have antennae, weapons, or other items held above their heads, or other extraneous detailing that extends well beyond the model's base or normal outline. It is not the intent of these rules to punish players for dynamically posing their models. Thus, these extra features do not count when determining line of sight, if the rest of the model is completely concealed and only the detail is exposed. Use common sense and give the other player the benefit of the doubt when line of sight cannot easily be determined.

ROUNDING FRACTIONS

On occasion, a rule specifies that you should halve a number, such as a stat or die result. Unless otherwise stated, round all fractions *up* to the nearest whole number.

MEASURING

Reality's Edge uses inches (") for all distances.

Some rules require you to halve or quarter distances. Remember, when this happens, round fractions *up* to the nearest inch. For example, a model with a movement of 5" in rough terrain (which requires you halve the movement) may move 3".

You can pre-measure, but should not abuse it. *"Abuse"* is defined as whatever your fellow gamers are willing to put up with.

BOARD SIZE

Reality's Edge is best played on a 36" x 36" table. You can play on other sized tables, but ranged or melee combat opportunities may noticeably increase or decrease, depending on the table size. Thus, for larger or smaller tables, you should proportionally adjust the models' starting positions, so they begin at the same distance from the center of the board.

DICE AND MECHANICS

Players need a 10-sided die (D10) and occasionally a standard 6-sided die (D6) to play *Reality's Edge.*

Two different die roll mechanics—Opposed Tests and Stat Tests—resolve all actions.

Opposed Tests are used to resolve direct actions between models (usually close combat). Both players roll a D10 and add their result to the appropriate stat and any applicable modifiers. The player with the highest score wins. **The defending player always wins ties.**

Stat Tests are used when a model tries to accomplish an action—usually unopposed by an enemy model. Examples include opening a locked door or shooting at a target with a gun. The player rolls a D10, adds the result and any applicable modifiers to the relevant stat, and compares the result to the required Target Number (TN), which is always 10. If the player's results are higher, they win the Stat Test.

Additionally, we employ several dice conventions:

- **Critical:** A natural roll of 10 on a D10 indicates a Critical success. When you roll a Critical on a Stat Test, it means you automatically succeed, regardless of modifiers or other factors. When you roll a Critical on an Opposed Test, you automatically win unless your opponent also rolls a Critical. If such a rarity happens, you should both reroll until a clear winner is determined. A D6 never generates a Critical.
- **Fumble:** A natural roll of 1 on a D10 indicates a Fumble. When you roll a Fumble on a Stat Test, it means you automatically fail, regardless of modifiers or other factors. When you roll a Fumble on an Opposed Test, you automatically lose unless your opponent also rolls a Fumble. If such a rarity happens, you should both reroll until a clear loser is determined. A D6 never generates a Fumble.
- **D3:** Some rules require you to roll a D3. To do so, roll a D6: a result of 1 or 2 = 1, a result of 3 or 4 = 2, and a result of 5 or 6 = 3. A D3 never generates a Critical or a Fumble.
- **Scatter:** A Scatter roll usually represents a thrown grenade or other errant entity that can damage more than one location at a time. To determine a random direction for a Scatter roll, roll a scatter die. If you do not have a scatter die available, use another agreed upon method or roll a D10 and use the triangular point on the top of the die to determine the direction.
- **Reroll Dice:** Some abilities allow you the opportunity to reroll your dice when you are unhappy with the first result. When you use such an ability, the second result stands, even if it is worse than the first roll. You may never reroll a reroll!

COUNTERS AND TOKENS

You may find it necessary during a game of *Reality's Edge* to denote a status or effect that applies to a model or models, such as whether a model is *hidden* or *on fire*. Players should keep counters or other tokens available for this. You can use anything for tokens, from fancy custom pieces to currency. The only thing that matters is that your fellow players can tell the model's status from a quick glance.

TERMINOLOGY

The terms *melee* and *close combat* are used interchangeably in *Reality's Edge* and mean basically the same thing.

Additionally, the phrase *out-of-action* refers to any model that can no longer fight because it is *terrified*, *unconscious*, *dead*, or *catatonic*. The result is the same no matter the status: the model is no longer a factor in the battle for that turn. You should always leave models that are out-of-action on the table or mark their position when removing them. Place a token next to the model or use some other indicator (such as laying the model on its side, for example), so its status is obvious. Out-of-action models may still participate in the game—other models might loot them for gear or try to resuscitate them via medical care—but players can otherwise ignore them for most rule interactions.

The phrase *remove from play* indicates you should remove the model from the board entirely, rather than placing it out-of-action. This usually occurs as a result of a model leaving the board's edge or a spectacular failure of morale. Models you remove from play do not return for the duration of the skirmish but may be available for later games.

Stats

Each model has several stats.

- **Name**: The model's basic name, for rules purposes. Remember, you live in the Sprawl—your name should be flashy, never boring.
- **Move (MOV)**: How many inches the model can move per activation.
- **Melee (MEL)**: How well the model fights in close combat.
- **Aim (AIM)**: How well the model can fire a gun or other distance-based weapon.
- **Strength (STR)**: The model's ability to damage opponents in melee or complete tasks involving brawn.
- **Mettle (MET)**: A catch-all stat to represent the model's overall quality. Mettle reflects the model's reliability, intelligence, courage, and nimbleness.
- **Defense (DEF)**: The model's overall toughness. This includes any armor or special defensive abilities.
- **Hit Points (HP)**: The amount of damage the model can take before going out-of-action.
- **Firewall (FW)**: How well the model can ward off cyber-attacks. we describe this further in the *Cyber Warfare* section (see page 47).

SPRAWL RONIN							
DEF	HP	FW	MOV	MEL	AIM	STR	Met
5	8	10	5	3	3	5	5

Stats and Tests

As we discussed in *Dice and Mechanics*, certain situations may require a model to roll a Stat Test. The rules describe when you must take such tests. Keep in mind that you can modify these tests further with other skills and abilities the model may possess.

TYPES OF STAT TESTS

- **Activation (Mettle):** React to battlefield conditions. This determines how many actions a model gets per turn.
- **Agility (Mettle):** Climb, jump, physically dodge hazards, or react to the enemy's moves.
- **Intelligence (Mettle):** Solve puzzles, negotiate, or interact with technology.
- **Strength (Strength):** Break down doors, escape entanglements, pull or lift heavy items.
- **Survival (Mettle):** Resist the effects of poison, disease, negative status effects, and various other hazards of the Sprawl.
- **Spot (Mettle):** Attempt to spot concealed enemies.
- **Will (Mettle):** Affect morale or matters of internal fortitude.

Throughout this book, we always present Stat Tests by the test name. Stat Tests always have a TN of 10, though some effects and rules may modify the Test. This often results in a penalty or bonus, which are noted with a minus (-) or plus (+) sign.

Turn Sequence

There are four phases in each game turn in *Reality's Edge*:

- **Initiative Phase:** Each turn, you determine initiative order. Each player rolls a D10 and adds any scenario-specific modifiers to the result. The player with the highest score activates their models first that turn; reroll any ties. While a player is activating their models, they are considered to *have initiative*.
- **Activation Phase:** Players activate as many of their models as possible before initiative passes to their opponent, who then tries to activate as many their models before initiative passes to the next player (or back to their opponent) and so on.
- Players make an *Activation Test* to activate their models. Models perform actions by spending *Action Points* (AP).
- Continue this phase, passing initiative from player to player, until all models are activated.
- **Non-Player Character (NPC) Phase:** After all players activate their models, any remaining models on the board—such as innocent bystanders, rampaging creatures, or security forces—activate. Not all games have NPC models.
- **Clean-Up Phase:** Resolve any end-of-turn effects and remove any statuses that no longer apply.

Activation

ACTIVATION TEST

A game turn consists of a series of initiative rounds, in which players try to activate their forces one at a time and perform one or more actions before attempting to activate their next model. To activate a model, the player with initiative chooses a model that is not yet activated and attempts an Activation Test. If successful, the player may use the model's full AP (typically 2, unless modified by special rules). If a player rolls a Critical for the Activation Test, the model gains an additional AP for the turn. When the model has no remaining AP, the player chooses another model to activate, until all they either activate all their models or fail an Activation Test. If a player fails an Activation Test, the model has only 1AP and play passes to the opponent at the end of the model's action. Note that players cannot voluntarily pass play. They must always nominate a model to activate until all models are activated.

The effects of wounds caused by ranged attacks resolve after a player completes their model's actions and before play passes to the opponent. We discuss this further in *Determining Casualties* in the *Ranged Combat* section.

The game turn continues until all models on both sides roll for activation and complete their actions. If a player has more models to activate, but the opponent does not, the player continues to make Activation Tests to determine the number of AP their models receive, but play no longer passes between players if they fail a Test. Rather, the player continues the turn until all they activate all their models.

MULTIPLE PLAYERS

When there are more than two players involved in a game, the players must decide an initiative order for activating models. We recommend using dice rolls (highest roll goes first and so on) or card draws (highest card goes first, and so on) to determine initiative. All other rules occur as usual in multiplayer games (for example, play passes between all available players when rolling to activate models).

Actions

Your models may perform one of the following actions for each AP spent. Unless specifically prohibited, a model can perform the same action multiple times in a turn if it has enough AP to do so.

FREE ACTIONS (0 AP COST)

DROP

A model may fall flat to a surface (prone position) from a standing position.

1 AP ACTIONS

MOVE

A model may walk up to its Move stat in inches.

HIDE

A model may attempt to conceal itself.

STAND

A prone model may stand up.

RANGED ATTACK

A model can fire one of its weapons. They can do so **only once** unless a weapon or special ability gives them the ability to fire **multiple times.**

UNJAM WEAPON

A model may remove one *Jammed* token.

CLOSE COMBAT ATTACK

A model may make a close combat attack against an enemy model within range.

CONCENTRATE

Receive a +2 bonus to the combat roll when a model makes a ranged or melee attack immediately after performing the *concentrate* action.

USE ABILITY

A model may use any special ability for which it meets all requirements. AP cost varies, depending on the ability.

CLIMB

A model may climb up or over an appropriate piece of terrain.

CHARGE

A model may make a normal move action followed immediately by a free close combat attack against any enemy within range. **A model may charge only once per turn.**

MISCELLANEOUS ACTION

A model may take an action not previously covered, such as break down a door, access a computer terminal, or barricade a window. Most miscellaneous actions require a Stat Test. Note that there must be a consensus among the players that it is possible for a model to take such an action.

2 AP ACTION

OVERWATCH

When a model is first activated, it may spend 2 AP to "save" its action for later. Then, during any subsequent enemy activation, this model on Overwatch may interrupt the active model's action to take its own action. The model on Overwatch may perform any 1 AP Action, after which activation reverts to the original model. If the model on Overwatch chooses to make a ranged attack with its interrupting action, it may only do so within its front 180-degree arc.

A model on Overwatch may take an interrupting action immediately after an enemy model declares an action (such as interrupting an enemy's charge action to move) or in the middle of or after an enemy's action (such as interrupting an enemy's action to move from cover to cover).

Example: An enemy model declares a move action and intends to use its full MOV of 5". After it moves 3", a model on Overwatch decides to make a ranged attack (perhaps the moving model is no longer protected by cover or may be about to leave the line of sight of the model on Overwatch).

Note that a model on Overwatch may not interrupt another model on Overwatch. While this may result in a slightly unfair advantage, it removes the unnecessary complexity that would result from multiple models interrupting each other in a catastrophic chain of interruptions.

A model may remain on Overwatch from turn to turn in a game. The player must roll to activate as usual to see how many AP the model receives and whether initiative passes to the next player in the case of a failed roll. If a model on Overwatch performs any action other than interrupting an opponent, it immediately loses its Overwatch status.

Movement

The first time a model spends AP to move, the model may move up to their full Move stat in inches. If the model spends another AP (total of 2 AP) to *double move*, it may only travel an additional D6 in inches, not an additional full MOV value. If the model spends another AP (total of 3 AP) to *triple move*, they may move only an additional D3 in inches. Note that when moving multiple times, a model may never move more than their Move stat, even if they roll higher.

Example: Model A has 3 AP. Its player decides to move it once and use its full Move stat of 5". The player decides to move the model again, but instead of automatically moving the model another 5", they must roll a D6 to determine how far the model can move. They roll a 6, which is higher than the model's Move stat of 5", so they default to the model's Move stat and move another 5". Finally, the player decides moving is the best option for now and chooses to move again. This time, they roll a 1 on a D3 and move an addition 1". For the model's entire activation, it moved a total of 11".

Any model that uses more than one move action in a single turn counts as making a double move. This is relevant when determining certain effects, such as when a model can be hit by ranged attacks.

DIFFICULT TERRAIN

When a model moves through difficult terrain (such as shallow water, garbage piles and other sprawl detritus, or woods), it moves at half its normal rate. It costs a model 2" of Movement to cross linear terrain (like fencing, crates, and Jersey barriers) up to 1" tall. A model must climb anything taller.

PRONE

A model may drop to the ground (go Prone) as a free action at any point during their movement, but this ends its movement for that AP. When prone, models may only Move 1" per AP spent. To indicate a model is in Prone position, the player may place the model on its side or place a marker next to the model. For line of sight purposes, a Prone model's height is approximately the height of its base, or about 1/8".

Note that standing from a prone position does not count as movement for purposes of ranged attack targeting. This means a model that stands and moves, or moves and drops, does not count as double moving when determining to-hit penalties.

JUMPING

A model may attempt to jump during any move action. The model does not gain extra distance from jumping, unless it has a special rule that allows it to do so, but it may leap over small obstacles or hazards. A model may cross a 1" or less (in-game) gap without a penalty or Stat Test. Such a space is small enough that the model's natural stride carries them over.

    Wider jumps are possible, but more difficult. Any such jump requires an Agility Test and players must agree on whether or not it is possible for the model to make the jump. Use common sense. Should a model fail to clear a large gap, it falls, it may take damage as described below in the Climbing rules, and it ends up prone where it lands.

CLIMBING

Models may climb any surface greater than 1" high that has a suitable surface to give them purchase, such as a ladder or other handholds. The exteriors of most buildings should otherwise be considered impassable terrain. A model can generally climb 1" of vertical height per AP spent, and can likely travel up one level for every 2 AP spent.* If something attacks a model while it is climbing, the model must pass a Strength Test or fall. This test is taken after resolving the to-hit portion of the attack.

*Note that building height is not universal. One building might have 2" between levels and another may have 2.5" or even 3". For game purposes, a model should be able to climb up a single building story when spending 2 AP. The rule of 1" per AP is not a hard and fast rule, and players should modify it to meet the needs of their terrain.

FALLING

When a model falls, it is placed prone on the ground and automatically loses hit points. The Hit Strength and damage it inflicts depends on the height from which the model fell. Consult the following table:

FALLING TABLE		
Fall Height	Hit Strength	HP Loss
0–3"	6	D3
3.1–6"	8	D6
6.1"+	10	D10

To determine wounds, the player whose model fell and an opposing player each make an Opposed Test, using the falling model's DEF against the Hit Strength. If the opposing player wins, roll the appropriate die to determine the falling model's HP loss.

HIDING

A model may attempt to conceal itself by hiding. To hide, a model must be out of all enemy models' line of sight and spend 1 AP to become Hidden. This is automatic and does not require a test. Some scenarios and special exceptions allow models to begin a game Hidden. As long as a model is Hidden, it may not be directly targeted by ranged attacks or charges until it is *spotted*. Hidden models may still be indirectly targeted by suppressive fire. We discuss this further in the rules for *Ranged Combat*.

A Hidden model remains Hidden after a move action if it has base contact with cover or remains out of line of sight. However, if a model makes any type of attack, it automatically loses its Hidden status. Hidden models may only move 3" per turn, no matter what their Move stat is. They may double move, but only receive an additional D3" instead of D6". Hidden models may not triple move. Models that move more than this lose their Hidden status.

SPOTTING

A model may attempt to spot hidden enemies. However, operatives are not omniscient; the fog of battle and low-light conditions may foil awareness. To represent such difficulties, a model may only attempt to spot enemy models within 2 x their Mettle stat in inches. This is called *spotting distance*. If an enemy model is outside this distance, it remains hidden.

To spot a Hidden enemy, a model must make a Spot Test and spend 1 AP. If successful, remove the Hidden status of the spotted model. Also, assume the operative who spotted the enemy model communicates the Hidden model's position to their team, who may be beyond spotting distance. If the model fails the Spot Test, the enemy model remains Hidden and the AP is wasted. A model may make multiple Spot Tests per turn. Certain special rules or scenario conditions affect how easy or hard it is to spot Hidden models.

Ranged Combat

A model who spends 1 AP can take a ranged combat action against any *legal* enemy (see *Line of Sight*). Assume all models have a 360-degree field of view unless they are using the Overwatch action. Remember, unless a special rule or weapon ability states otherwise, **models may only take one ranged combat action per activation.**

LINE OF SIGHT

All targets of ranged attacks must be *legal*, meaning the target is within range of the attacking model's weapon and line of sight. Both friendly and enemy models block line of sight. However, models without the Large special ability do not block line of sight to Large models (we further discuss this rule later).

TO-HIT

To make a ranged attack, a player must make an Aim Test. The test is modified by several cumulative conditions, except Cover. If the attacker scores greater than or equal to TN 10 or rolls a Critical, the attack is successful. A successful attack only indicates the attack hit the target and does not indicate damage or HP loss. Determine casualties at the end of the Activation Phase before initiative passes to the next player (see *Determining Casualties*, page 38).

FIRING MODIFIERS

When you make a To-Hit roll, apply the following applicable modifiers:

\multicolumn{2}{FIRING MODIFIERS TABLE}	
Modifier	Condition
+3	Attacker uses suppressive fire
+2	Attacker uses the concentrate action
+1	Target is at point-blank range*
-1	Attacker moves or stands up from the prone position this turn
-1	Target uses two or more move actions this turn
-1	Target is in light cover
-1	Target is prone and more than 6" away from attacker
-2	Target is in heavy cover
*Unless the weapon rules specified otherwise, point-blank range is 6" or less.	

TEMPLATES

Some ranged attacks use templates, which allows the attacker to hit multiple models at the same time. We describe the template types in the *Black Market* section (see pages 128, 130, and 131). For now, it is important to remember that once a template's position is determined, all models even partially under the template have the possibility to be hit. Any exceptions are delineated in the template's description.

COVER AND INTERVENING TERRAIN

A model that hides behind obstacles or basically makes itself smaller may benefit from being in *light* or *heavy* cover.

Light cover includes such things as wooden fences, wooden barricades, tall grass, hedges, and similar features. Basically, light cover blocks line of sight and makes it harder to see a target but may not actually stop a bullet. Heavy cover includes things like buildings, vehicles, brick walls, metal barricades, large rocks, and more substantial items. These things not only hide a model, but would probably stop a bullet. Models who shoot at each other while inside a building both count as being in light cover.

The model's base needs only to touch the terrain feature, not be wholly inside it, to be considered in cover and benefit from the terrain's protection. Note that when a model receives benefits from being in cover, it counts as being in the terrain for such things as movement penalties, too.

All players should agree on the type of cover a piece of terrain provides to a model—light or heavy. If the situation is ever unclear, such as when a model is behind an unarmored vehicle, it is best to assume they are in heavy cover.

A model can also benefit from being in cover if a terrain piece, even one without base contact, partially blocks line of sight to the model. We call this *intervening terrain*. If ever it is not obvious whether a piece of linear terrain provides cover to a model, use a simple rule of thumb and determine the actual distance of the shot. If the intervening terrain is closer to the target, the target benefits from the cover. If the terrain is closer to the attacking model, the target does not benefit.

A model that shoots at any target in light cover suffers a -1 firing modifier to its to-hit rolls; heavy cover imposes a -2 firing modifier. Cover bonuses do not stack, use only the highest bonus.

DETERMINING CASUALTIES

Firefights are chaotic affairs and it is not always obvious when a target is hit, wounded, or killed. To represent this confusing mayhem, resolve all hits scored within a player's Activation Phase (not just an individual model's activation) immediately before the initiative passes to the opponent. This prevents the player with initiative from knowing the results of their models' attacks until after the firing is complete, which means they cannot simply shoot one model until it goes down and then move on to the next target. Instead, players must decide whether to risk depending on a single hit or using multiple attacks to take an enemy down. A model may receive multiple hits and still survive. Attacks and HP loses inflicted on a model that is already out-of-action are wasted. Such is the price to guarantee the enemy's doom.

It is useful to have a handful of markers or dice to place next to each model to note the number and strength of the shots that hit them. Because you usually determine results fairly quickly, the battlefield should not end up needlessly littered with counters.

WOUNDS

When an attack successfully hits the target, the attacker rolls to wound the defender. This is an Opposed Test between the attacker's weapon Strength stat and the target's Defense stat. If the attacker rolls higher than the defender, the attacker wounds the defender, who suffers an amount of damage equal to the Strength of the attack divided by two (round up).

Example: Hitoshi the Sprawl Ronin is hit by an assault rifle (Strength 7). The attacker's result on the wound roll is 9, which we add to the assault rifle's Strength for a total of 16. Hitoshi has a DEF of 6. His result on a D10 is 4, for a total of 10. Since Hitoshi's opponent rolled higher, he is now wounded. He suffers 4 damage (Assault Rifle Strength of 7 ÷ 2, round up).

OUT-OF-ACTION

When a model runs out of Hit Points, it is considered *out-of-action*.

GRAZED

If an attack hits a target but fails to take the model out-of-action because it does not do enough damage or fails to wound, the target must pass a Will Test or move to find cover and go prone, moving up to 3" to reach such cover, if necessary. If there is no cover available within 3", the defender instead goes prone in place. A player may always choose to automatically fail the Will Test for a Grazed model, especially when trying to avoid further incoming fire. No dice roll is required, simply move the model up to 3" toward cover, if possible, and place them prone.

MULTIPLE SHOTS

Some weapons or rules allow multiple shots during the same activation, as indicated in their description. A model may fire one or more shots at a single target or spread out its fire. A model firing multiple shots may target additional models within 3" of either side of the original target. When a model fires multiple shots, it must always target the closest model within 3" of the original target (friend or foe) in sequence. It may not skip intervening models to hit targets farther away.

Example: Speed Daemon the Tracer fires a submachine gun at three enemies, each about 1" away from the next in a straight line. He targets the first model in the line and rolls his ranged attack. To fire at the last model in the line, he must "walk" the stream of bullets through the second model; he cannot ignore the second model and hit the third.

SHOOTING THROUGH WALLS

Specialized equipment, cybernetics, and other electronics allow a model to *see* an enemy target, but not have line of sight in the traditional sense. For example, you can roll a POV'er (see the *High-End Grenades* section, page 196) into an enclosed room the operative cannot see and draw line of sight from the POV'er. As such, models can target enemy models through linear terrain, even if the terrain totally blocks the target, as long as the model has the means to draw line of sight to the target. However, this is limited to a single piece of linear terrain, such as a wall. When shooting through a wall, the targeted model obviously counts as being in appropriate cover. However, should the attack hit, it suffers -2 Strength and does one less point of damage than it normally would.

FIRING INTO MELEE COMBAT

Normally, people do not fire into a swirling group of combatants for fear of hitting a comrade. Sometimes, though, the best option is to shoot at the group, hope for the best, and see what happens. All hits from ranged attacks fired at a group of models in close combat are randomized among all models involved in the melee. Simply determine which shots hit, and then roll for wound results as described in *Determining Casualties*. You can assign hits in any order, but you must distribute them as evenly as possible among all targets.

Example: Darkfyre fires his submachine gun at a melee between his friend, Dirty Bob, and members of a rival crew. For each attack, Darkfyre's player rolls a D10 to determine the hits. If he attacks more than once, the player must keep track of how many hits there are. After all attacks, assign the hits: Bob gets the numbers 1–2, the enemies get 3–4, 5–6, and 7–8. Reroll 9–10.

SUPPRESSIVE FIRE

Models may fire wildly at enemy models intending to scare them into keeping their heads down, not wound them. This is also an effective method for pinning down unseen enemies.

Players who want to attempt suppressive fire must declare this before their model fires. Suppressive fire follows all the usual rules for ranged combat actions, except that the attacker receives a +3 firing bonus when making a to-hit roll, and a hit is considered a Graze—with an additional -2 penalty and no wound roll. The exceptions to this are any Critical rolls made while using suppressive fire. For these, the player rolls to wound instead of counting the hit as a Graze. Sometimes, people who use suppressive fire get lucky—or not, depending on the point of view. It is important to note that a model cannot use suppressive fire and the concentration action in the same action, because a model may not aim while wildly firing a weapon.

Suppressive fire may also be used to target Hidden enemies. In such cases, the attacker does not target a specific model, but shoots toward the vicinity in which an enemy model could be hiding. To represent this blind firing, we allow you to target Hidden models, provided they are within the attacking model's spotting range. You do not need to make a Spot Test. Targeting Hidden enemies otherwise follows all rules for suppressive fire, except the attacking model does not receive the +3 bonus to shoot. All other firing modifiers apply. If a Hidden model is wounded by a Critical during suppressive fire, they must pass a Will Test or lose their Hidden status. The attacking model never really knows whether it drove off the suspected enemy or not unless the enemy is forced out of hiding.

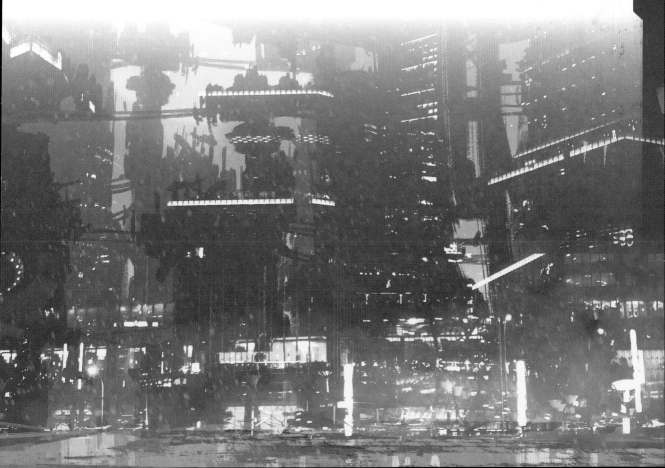

Close Combat

CHARGING

Most close combat is initiated after a charge move. Remember, as we described in the *1 AP Actions* section, a charge move is when a model makes a normal move action, ends its movement within Melee Range of another model, and gets a free action to make a close combat attack against that model. **A model may only charge once per turn.**

Note that models may charge through difficult terrain, but they may not charge a target that is not within line of sight (around a corner, for example). Charging does not have a minimum distance and involves more than just moving fast—it is also an attempt to initiate close combat. Models may use the concentrate action on the turn in which they charge.

ATTACKING

A model may spend 1 AP to make a close combat attack action against an enemy within range of one of its melee weapons. The attacker may spend any additional AP to initiate more attacks. Defense is free—a model does not need to spend AP to defend itself.

To make a melee attack, roll a D10 and add the model's Melee stat and any applicable modifiers to the result. The target also rolls a D10 and adds its Melee stat. All modifiers are cumulative.

MELEE MODIFIERS

Apply the following modifiers as applicable when making a close combat attack:

MELEE MODIFIERS TABLE	
Modifier	Condition
+2	Enemy is prone
+2	Attacker is concentrating
+1	For each additional friendly model in base contact with enemy
-1	Enemy is behind cover

If the attacker wins (their total is higher than the defender's), they hit the target. If the attacker loses, the defender may move the attacker back 1" anywhere within the attacker's rear 180-degree arc or stay locked in combat (defender's choice). If the result is a tie, the models stay locked in base contact, but the attacker does not score a hit. A winning attacker may also choose to push the target back, but fails to take the opponent out-of-action. Should an obstacle of some sort prevent a model from being pushed back, the two models remain locked in combat, as they have nowhere else to go. You can push a model over an edge or into another dangerous situation.

An attacker who wins a close combat against a model who is behind cover may cross over a linear obstacle (such as a wall) or climb up to the opponent's level. If the opponent is alive, both models must remain in base contact. The attacker is essentially using the impetus of its attack to get closer to the foe or to gain the safety of cover.

WOUNDS

When an attack successfully hits the target, the attacker rolls to wound the defender. This is an Opposed Test between the attacker's weapon Strength stat and the target's Defense stat. If the attacker rolls higher than the defender, the attacker wounds the defender, who suffers an amount of damage equal to the Strength of the attack divided by two (round up).

OUT-OF-ACTION

When a model runs out of Hit Points, it is considered *out-of-action*.

CONCENTRATE IN MELEE

Models who use the concentrate action in melee may add +2 to the to-hit roll or the hit Strength. You must choose which bonus you want before the to-hit roll. Models may not concentrate twice in the same turn, even if they have AP remaining and use concentrate bonuses.

DISENGAGE FROM MELEE

A model in base contact with an enemy may attempt to pass an Agility or Strength Test (player's choice) to disengage from melee. If the roll fails, the model forfeits the AP. If the roll succeeds, the model may move and does not suffer the usual repercussions from the enemy with base contact.

A model attempting to disengage from a melee with multiple opponents must only make the Agility or Strength Test once, but receives a -1 penalty to the roll for each opponent after the first.

NIGHT-TIME FIGHTING

Certain circumstances (such as a mission result or special rule) may result in some games being played in night-time conditions. Power outages are common in the Sprawl, so it is not unusual for models to encounter total blackness. Night-time fighting has the following effects:

- All attacks made from less than or equal to 12" away suffer a -1 penalty to the to-hit roll.

- All ranged attacks over 12" automatically miss, unless the attacker rolls a Critical.

- All spotting distances are halved.

Morale

MORALE TEST

Certain situations may make your crew rethink their continued participation in a fight. This is represented by the Morale Test; a form of the Will Test. You must test your models' morale in the following circumstances:

- Whenever a model is wounded in melee but does not go out-of-action.
- If the Showrunner or other designated leader goes out-of-action within 12" and within line of sight of a model.
- When its crew is reduced to 50 percent of its starting size.
- When its crew is reduced to 25 percent of its starting size.
- When prompted by a special ability.

Make a Morale Test immediately after any of the above situations apply. A model *can* be forced to make multiple Morale Tests in a turn. Note that skills, rules, and abilities that apply to Will Tests also apply to Morale Tests, but the reverse is not true.

If a model passes the test, it believes victory is still achievable and there is no other effect. A failed test indicates a model lost its nerve and must make an immediate move action toward the edge of the board where it started—or the nearest board edge if it did not deploy at a board edge—ending in cover, if possible. If a model is forced to leave melee combat because of a failed Morale Test, each enemy model in base contact may make a free, out-of-sequence attack against it.

If a model must retreat because of a failed Morale Test and crosses its starting board edge, it must immediately make another Morale Test. A failed test means you remove the model from play.

Rolling a Fumble when making a Morale Test is a dramatic failure. Basically, the model's nerve breaks completely, and it flees from the battlefield in abject terror. Remove the model from play.

Situations can occur where a model is forced to make a Will Test for Grazed *and* a Morale Test. This most often occurs when a model with more than one wound suffers a gunfire wound. Should this occur, the model first takes the Morale Test—it is beating a hasty retreat before possibly diving for cover—and *then* takes the Will Test for Grazed.

STRATEGIC WITHDRAWAL

Sometimes, a Showrunner and their crew have a bad day. Mounting casualties, loss of a leader, and numerous other unfortunate situations may cause a crew to withdraw from a battle. This is a voluntary decision any player can make. At the beginning of a turn, before rolling for initiative, the player must announce that they are cutting their losses and withdrawing. Remove all their models from the field. The player must roll against the *Survival Table* as usual for models that are out-of-action, but no other models are negatively impacted by withdrawing. When a player withdraws, it is assumed his opponent automatically wins the scenario. The player that withdraws gets to keep any rewards they earned, CAT Terminals hacked, Grudge Operation kills, and so on. However, any unclaimed rewards automatically go to the other player or team.

CYBER WARFARE

"Codekiddies hacking from their coffin cube is pure noobness. The real deals are in combat hacking. It's great. Nothing like trying to penetrate a hardened Liar 452 Network with ICE out the wazoo while all hell is breaking loose around you. It's a pure rush. Pays well, too. The electronic creds are all untraceable, just like me."

FULLTYLT, Console Cowboy

The HyperNET is everywhere in the Sprawl and cyberspace is simply another vector for which the successful Showrunner must be prepared. The Showrunner's crew is full of cybernetics and high-tech weaponry at risk of electronic attack. Further, given the value of information in a whole interconnected digital world, it is not surprising that Showrunners are often tasked with breaking into networks separated from the main HyperNET. These networks are not only defended by digital defenses, but by physical ones, as well. Without a significant cyber warfare element, a Showrunner quickly becomes one of the many failures that haunt the Sprawl.

Hacking

Hacking comes in two varieties. *Virtual* hacking tries to penetrate distant networks remotely to cause as much as trouble as possible while keeping a physical body safely tucked away. Virtual hacking involves the use of avatars to explore the fully virtual HyperNET networks. By following the trail of HROs, avatars can provide cyber support to the Showrunner. This is both powerful and limited, as the avatar can only see the virtual and cannot visually interpret what the Showrunner sees in Realspace.

When avatar-based support is not enough, you can use *combat* hacking. Console cowboys and others accompany the Showrunner on missions. By jacking into the HyperNET wirelessly via a cyber-deck, they can influence the digital world while still having a physical presence. Combat hacking not only targets the HyperNET's network nodes through direct neuro-links, but also the ubiquitous HROs that litter the Sprawl's visual spectrum. The most important targets are HROs belonging to enemy operatives and any physical electronic defenses, like bots, that might try to impede the mission.

A hacker that can blend the two types of hacking is most successful. In game terms, hacking is a specific ability to access the HyperNET beyond just a casual sense. Whether a model is a hacker or not is noted in the model's profile or roster entry.

Applications (Apps)

Hacking involves the use of pre-written computer programs called applications, or apps for short. The HyperNET is too vast and dynamic for coding on the fly, only the world's most elite hackers and super AIs even attempt such a thing. Instead, most hackers use apps to infiltrate enemy networks, sabotage enemy cybernetics, equipment, or bots, buffer the electronic defenses or abilities of their allies, or create digital beings called *sprites*. Basic apps are available for purchase from several legal and illegal vendors, but the best hackers build their own or modify stock brands to tailor their attacks. Only models with the *Hacking* special rule can use applications.

USING APPS

Just like any other action a model takes, using an app requires you to spend AP. Most apps cost 1 AP to use, but some of the more time-intensive and powerful programs require more AP. We list an app's AP cost in its profile. A model may use an app at any time during activation. However, a model in base contact with an enemy model may not use apps, as it is otherwise occupied.

FRIENDLY APPS

An app with the label *defense* or *support* in its profile is what we call a friendly app. These apps are always beneficial, and a model's Firewall does not resist them. The user must only be within the app's specified range and have line of sight to the target. We discuss friendly apps further in the *Apps* portion of the *Black Market* section (see page 176).

Cyber Stats

Models with the Hacking ability have three important stats:

- **Cyber (CYB):** This is a native bonus the model receives to all hacking attempts from its cyber-deck, its means of accessing the HyperNET remotely. Higher quality cyber-decks have better bonuses.
- **Firewall (FW):** This is a model's passive defense against cyber-attacks. Firewalls vary in quality, but even the most mundane objects with a computer chip have digital protections of some sort.
- **Digital Hit Points (DHP):** This measures the digital damage a model can take. DHP is an abstract means of quantifying a model's physical connection to the HyperNET.

For non-virtual hackers—read, humans—these stats represent their cyber-deck, which is their means of connecting to the HyperNET. Virtual beings also have such stats, plus a few others, but we explore these further in their own section.

Digital Targets

Hacking and apps can target any model with some type of connection to the HyperNET, using their HRO as the access point. Fortunately, this includes pretty much any model.

OPERATIVES

Every mission operative—save those with a penchant for old-school mechanical gear—is decked out with fancy electronic equipment. Almost everything contains a computer chip of some sort, and anything with a chip can be hacked. In an abstract sense, models attack each target individually, and the target's singular Firewall resists the attack. Targets may include the following items:

- **Ranged and Melee Weapons:** all melee weapons, handguns, long guns, support weapons, and grenades.
- **Cybernetic Enhancements:** upgrades to cybernetic body parts. Some apps specifically target enhancements instead of the body part in which they are located.
- **Cybernetic Body Parts:** cyber arms, cyber legs, etc. When you target a cybernetic body part, all cybernetic enhancements installed there also suffer the attack results. For instance, if a cyber arm becomes disabled, all enhancements the arm has become disabled, as well.
- **Equipment:** you may target individual pieces of equipment, such as underslung shotguns or tactical flashlights, etc.

It is rare for a model in a game of *Reality's Edge* to not have an HRO of some sort. Therefore, players may never keep secret what their models are carrying. Instead, each time a model suffers a cyber-attack, a player should note aloud which items their model is carrying and, thus, which items can be affected by the attack.

VIRTUAL CREATURES AND CYBER-DECKS

There are two types of hackers that use DHP, physical models using a cyber-deck and virtual beings. We cover them in detail later. For now, it is important to understand that DHPs are synonymous with a model's connection to, or presence in, the HyperNET. As a model's DHPs dwindle from repeated cyber-attacks, their connection is also reduced until it is eventually severed. A model with zero DHP may no longer hack or use apps.

NETWORK NODES/CAT TERMINALS

The network nodes, such as the ubiquitous CAT Terminals that litter the Sprawl, are probably the most valuable of all hacking targets. The data stored inside nodes and CATs are worth a good amount of currency to the right broker. Nodes are unique in that they are shielded from remote communication attempts. The only access is a direct connection via neural interface or primitive keyboards. In game terms, this means models can only hack network nodes and CAT Terminals while they are in base contact with them. A model gains *access* when it hacks a node. Having access means the model can download the data stored on the network. Network nodes are specific to each mission and have different rewards, but CAT Terminals always have random information, which you roll for after the game. As you begin to gain control of the local networks, your crew's ability to hack improves immensely.

BOTS AND DRONES

You can also hack electronic beings, such as bots and drones, which you can then temporarily disable, permanently shut down, or control remotely. Different apps allow you to target different options.

ENVIRONMENT

Some apps target the Sprawl itself. Such apps can raise parking barriers, hack cameras or holo-projectors, or bring the virtual into reality.

Sample App: Gatecrasher (1 AP) – A standard network breaking app, you can find this program—and a thousand others like it—on the cyber-deck of both new and experienced Hackers. While it is not subtle, this workhorse app uses several decryption algorithms to gain access to the targeted network system. Gatecrasher only targets networks and has a range of 0". If the roll is successful, gain Access. If it is a Fumble, the Hacker's crew gains a Trace token. A Critical has no effect.

Cyber-Attacks

All models with the Hacking ability may make cyber-attacks using any available apps in their possession. When doing so, the hackers use their Cyber stat to attack and the targets resist using their Firewall stat.

LINE OF SIGHT

Cyber-attacks do not require line of sight, since hackers can partially see in the virtual world. However, they are limited by the app's range. Note that you may target hidden models with cyber-attacks, but this does not reveal the model in any way because the hacker may not be able to see the target's physical form.

MAKING CYBER-ATTACKS

To make a cyber-attack, the attacker must first choose and declare which app they are using. Then, they roll a D10 and add the model's Cyber stat and any applicable modifications to the result. The target rolls a D10 and adds their Firewall stat and any other modifiers from apps or other sources to the result. All modifiers are cumulative.

If the attacker wins (their total is higher than the defender's), the target's Firewall is breached. The app used to hack and the target determine the effects of a successful hack.

If the attacker loses (their total lower than the defender's), the Firewall keeps out the unwanted intrusion and there is no further effect. However, depending on the app used, a Fumble may sometimes represent a disastrous failure.

If the cyber-attack does not target a specific model—such as when the target is a random building—as is the case with most environmental apps, the app itself provides the target's Firewall stat. Any opposing player may roll for the Firewall's defense.

App Properties

TARGETS

Apps have different effects, but most are designed to be efficient and useful against multiple targets. The app description designates the type of target(s) the hacker can attack. For example, the Gatecrasher app only allows the hacker to target network nodes, which is useless against an enemy operative or bot. Each hacker has different apps, so there is a great variety of danger when going out into the Sprawl.

RANGE

Each app has a range or distance based on its overall strength. Powerful attacks tend to have a shorter range (in game terms, this represents the HyperNET's native security protocols resisting), whereas weaker ones can usually travel much farther. The Gatecrasher app has a range of 0", which means it is only useful against targets with which your model is in base contact.

CYBER BONUS

Hacking is a combination of network savvy and having the right app available at the right time. Many apps provide a bonus to the attacker's Cyber stat. If the app does not mention a bonus, it does not provide one.

CYBER-ATTACK RESULTS

Apps always have specific effects, which we describe in detail in each app's entry. The app in the example above is rather simple and gives Access to a network node. Most apps do not have an effect when the hacker fails (except when the hacker Fumbles, which we describe below), but if it does, we describe it in this section.

APP RESTRICTIONS

Each app is unique, and only unimaginative hackers rely on a single app to wreak havoc. As such, you may use each app successfully only once per turn. Note that you may repeat failed attempts to use an app until you are successful.

CRITICAL EFFECTS

Some apps may also list a Critical Effect. A player may apply this effect if they roll a Critical on their cyber-attack roll or if they beat their target's score by 10 or more. Note that if a Critical is achieved, the player always has the option to apply the lesser effect instead of the critical effect.

COMMON APP EFFECTS

ACCESS

After hackers successfully penetrate a network node, they gain Access. During subsequent activations, they can spend 1 AP to download the data hosted on the net. Depending on the scenario, they may have the option to spend more AP to gather additional data. If not, they bled the network dry of information.

DIGITAL DAMAGE

When a model takes Digital Hit Points (DHP), their connection to the HyperNET is reduced. This does not have any significant impact until the model reaches zero DHP. When a virtual being, has zero DHP, they are taken offline. When a model with a cyber-deck has zero DHP, they may no longer use apps. A model with a cyber-deck may re-establish its connection by regaining DHP.

DISABLE

Many apps on the market primarily attempt to disable a target, since this does not require complex code and is one the simplest and fastest results to achieve. Disabling a target could mean you reset, turn off, or reboot it—regardless, the effect is the same. If the target is an item, it is no longer usable. If it is a bot, it cannot activate or spend AP. If it is a weapon, it loses its original attack profile, but may be used as an improvised weapon, instead.

Disable lasts for the number of game turns the app indicates and begins with the attacker's activation or the object's own activation, if it can spend AP.

Disabled models can be repaired before the app's countdown ends. If the target is a bot, drone, or similar model, the affected player may move another model into base contact with it and attempt an Intelligence Test (MET/TN 10) to repair the disabled model. The target cannot repair itself. Attempting this test costs 1 AP, and the player may repeat it as many times as they wish. Some items have additional effects when disabled, such as cyber limbs. These are noted in their profile or rules entry.

Author's Note: It may seem silly that you can disable a sword or club, but this is a bit of abstraction. We could try to justify it by saying that such weapons have built-in safety measures, such as automatic sheathing for cutting edge weapons that corporations automatically install, but in reality, we chose to say you can disable all weapons to avoid having to come up with a complicated list of exceptions.

BRICKING

Bricking occurs when a piece of electronic equipment is physically damaged beyond immediate repair. Whether caused by electric feedback or forced overclocking, the result is the same. Bricking is identical to the disable effect, except that the affected player cannot attempt to repair the equipment for the duration of the game. You can brick neutral bots and cyborgs, but not player-controlled Cyborgs and drones. This is a simple matter of balance and fairness. Note that anything that gets bricked is only damaged for the current game and returns to normal for the next game.

NERF

A word first used in the world of HyperNET online gaming, it has since entered the Hacker's lexicon. A "nerfed" target has its functionality sabotaged by malignant code that embeds itself into the target's processor software. If the target is an object used by another model, all attempts to use the item suffer the listed penalty. If the target is a bot or drone, it suffers the listed penalty to all Stat Tests, except those related to their Defense or Firewall.

CONTROL

Among hacker culture, there is nothing better than "pwning" or gaining remote control of their target. Doing this is no simple matter, it takes hardcore apps or extreme luck/skill to pull off such a stunt. Controlling a target can have several different effects, depending on the target. If the target is a weapon, the hacker can overload the weapon and cause it to deal a small amount of damage to the model holding it. If the target is a bot, cyborg, or

drone, the hacker may decide how that model spends its AP while under their control. The model does not count as a part of the hacker's crew, so it does not benefit from any abilities the crew may possess, such as Motivator, etc.

Control lasts for the number of game turns the app indicates, and ends during the Clean-Up Phase when the duration is over.

FUMBLES

Hacking is not risk free. Corporate security is always watching for intrusion attempts and specialized computer programs may attack the hacker. When a model rolls a natural Fumble on their cyber-attack, a special negative Fumble effect may apply. Note that not all apps have a Fumble effect.

TRACE

Sloppy hackers leave virtual trails when sneaking through the HyperNET. Network admins and defense programs stalk these trails back to the hacker. During gameplay, crews can receive Trace tokens. Trace tokens are not assigned to one specific model and should be placed nearby where every player can see them. Opposing players may remove a crew's Trace token to gain a +1 bonus to a cyber-attack against any model in that crew. If a crew has Trace tokens remaining at the end of the game, CORPSEC HyperNET agents can potentially trace the crew. Getting traced can lead to public exposure or a visit from CORPSEC.

ENHANCED FIREWALLS

Most apps attempt to conceal a hack as a routine, authorized access attempt or a login by an approved user. However, a particularly sloppy hack can cause native automatic defensive protocols to raise the target's Firewall by overclocking the system. When this occurs, the target's Firewall is permanently raised. It is quite possible for a model's Firewall stat to fluctuate up and down during a game. Note that a Firewall stat can never be higher than 3 points above its starting number.

NEURO-FEEDBACK

Though it is less common, the most dangerous Fumble has physical ramifications. This does not involve an off-the-shelf HyperNET defense program, but rather bleeding-edge corporate and/or Gov.Mil countermeasures that can track an illicit entry back to the source. Once the program finds the source, it sends a haywire shock through the hacker's neuro-chip causing brain damage and possibly brain death. In game terms, the hacker loses both DHP *AND* actual Hit Points.

We discuss Attack Apps further in the *App* portion of the *Black Market* section (see page 176).

Virtual Hacking

Hyper-reality is just one part of the HyperNET. HROs can simultaneously exist in the physical and virtual worlds. Therefore, hackers can go fully virtual, take the form of an online avatar, enter a public grid, and hack the HROs from the comfort of their own bolthole.

ABSTRACTING THE DIGITAL

Before we begin, it is important to understand that VR combat in *Reality's Edge* is highly abstract. We place items that represent digital assets on the board and treat them as other wargaming assets. This is done purposely, to allow cyberspace and Realspace to exist on the same board at the same time—yet remain separate entities—with hyper-reality bridging the gap between them. The public grid in the virtual space reflects the actual battlefield in the real world to reinforce this connection. Later supplements include whimsical virtual fantasy realms, but for now, the public grid is a great place to start.

THE TRUE HYPERNET

The virtual worlds of the HyperNET are both amazing and mundane. For most users, the public grid hosted on the CAT simply provides the transition between connection points—via full pod or immersion helmet—to the user's final destination: online gaming, media streaming, or free chatrooms. Most users in avatar form avoid the open areas; not only are they open to digital predation, they are also quite boring. The underpaid engineers who work for the corporations—which care little about a public utility's "wow factor"—tend to be lazy minimalists. Though there are a few exceptions, this means that when your model goes full avatar on the public grid, its starting point is a virtual area that looks almost identical to its Realspace location. From the street layouts to the local landmarks, everything is there—with the addition of a lot more advertisements, of course. For most people, this is a bummer. For the entrepreneur, it is an opportunity.

By following the data trail the special Showrunner cybernetics leaves behind, a shadow backer or representative may tag along with the crew on their missions. Of course, this stowaway does not see what the Showrunner sees in Realspace—they are literally worlds apart. They can, however, see all HROs and any other virtual entities on the local grid.

VIRTUAL BEINGS

In game terms, we separate the digital from the physical using the Virtual rule. A model's profile or roster entry shows whether this rule applies.

Virtual creatures are models that exist entirely within the HyperNET. Only those with direct cyberspace connections, like console cowboys and Showrunners can see them. Occasionally, they can enter Realspace via digital HRO projection or another holographic means. A physical model still represents them on the board. You can use actual models for virtual beings, especially in the case of avatars, but use tokens or markers to indicate lesser sprites and ICEs. The profiles or entries for all such digital models that use the rules in this section are noted as having the Virtual rule.

VIRTUAL BEINGS AND APPS

Virtual beings are, by default, capable of hacking. They can also possess and use apps. They may use friendly apps that affect any friendly model with an HRO, or they may make cyber-attacks.

VIRTUAL CYBER-ATTACKS

Virtual beings may navigate the board and attack other Virtual beings or models with an HRO. They follow all normal rules for hacking. Any model in base contact with a virtual being is not considered to be in base contact with an enemy model—they may freely move away if they so desire.

VIRTUAL BEINGS AND NETWORK NODES

The HyperNET's infrastructure is designed to be impervious to remote hacking. CAT Terminals and other networks broadcast signals, but never receive signals. In game terms, this means that unless a specific ability or rule allows for it, virtual beings may not hack any type of network node. They can, however, possess apps that can target networks; they just rarely get the chance to use them.

VIRTUAL STATS

Virtual beings have four main stats:

- **Cyber (CYB):** The virtual being's ability to influence the HyperNET.
- **Firewall (FW):** This is the virtual being's passive defense against cyber-attacks. Its core programming contains the ability to defend itself and resist outside code.
- **Digital Hit Points (DHP):** The amount of digital damage the virtual being can take. DHP is an abstract means of quantifying a model's physical connection to the HyperNET. For virtual beings, this is the strength of their existence before they are taken offline.
- **Move/Tether (MOV/Tether):** Move tells how many inches the virtual being can move per AP spent. Tether is how many inches a virtual being may move away from their point of origin. For virtual beings, this is a split stat with both move and tether scores listed in that order. Note that a point of origin can be an item, not just a place.

SAMPLE AVATAR STAT CHART

DIGITAL AVATAR				
FW	DHP	MOV/Tether	CYB	AP
6	10	5/16	4	2

Virtual beings follow all the usual *Reality's Edge* rules, with the following exceptions:

- Difficult and linear terrain do not affect virtual beings—they may move through such terrain freely, though they must have enough MOV and AP to fully clear the terrain. Further, virtual beings may move up linear terrain without penalty. Virtual beings may not pass directly through enclosed spaces, such as buildings, without going through a door.
- Virtual beings ignore and are ignored by all physical models for purposes of

movement and line of sight, and they do not otherwise affect non-virtual gameplay, except for cyber-attacks.

- Virtual beings do not roll for Activation like other models. Unhindered by physical and emotional concerns, they roll for Activation, but only fail on a Fumble. Further, they may always use their full complement of AP—they only make an Activation Test to see if initiative passes. Finally, a virtual being may activate on the turn in which it is generated.

- Virtual beings do not perceive the real world—they only perceive virtual digital space. As such, they cannot attempt to spot Hidden models.

- Only models capable of making cyber-attacks or using apps may attack or affect virtual beings. Conversely, they may only affect models with a Cyber or Firewall stat, and only if they have an appropriate app.

- Virtual beings do not go out-of-action, they go Offline. This happens when they lose all their DHP or when a special rule explicitly tells them to go Offline. Virtual beings never roll for wounds; they are simply removed from the board.

- Virtual beings do not have standard stats like Mettle or Strength. Therefore, they cannot make tests that involve those stats. Should someone or something call for such a test, assume the Virtual being is immune to the effect. For example, if a Sprawl Ronin attempts to use the Lightning Reflexes ability against the virtual being, they find they cannot use that ability to interrupt the being's actions because the being does not have the required Mettle stat to oppose the test.

TYPES OF VIRTUAL BEINGS

Below is a list of virtual beings a Showrunner can add to their crew and/or encounter frequently in the Sprawl. You can find specific stats for these beings under *Applications* in the *Building Your Crew* section, or in the *Neutral Parties* section (see page 288).

AVATARS

Avatars are usually a physical person's online presence, though avatars can also include AIs. Avatars are the strongest of all virtual beings, so there are generally a few on the board. They always have the Virtual rule. They are completely autonomous and may move about the board unhindered, within the limits of their tether. Avatars are tethered to their allied Showrunner in *Reality's Edge*; they function as a member of the crew.

SPRITES

Sprites are electronic assistants that certain apps create in cyberspace. They are similar to avatars, but rather than representing the user, they are a minor form of AI created by an app. When an app creates a sprite, it is tethered to a certain location or model and may only perform certain actions. The sprite's point of origin and actions are delineated by the app that creates it. Sprites have the Virtual rule.

INTRUSION COUNTERMEASURES EMULATION (ICE)

Firewalls are passive resisters and have a high failure rate. To protect important network nodes and virtual locations, ICE may be installed. ICE are essentially sprites, in that they are minor forms of AI. However, they differ in that they are slated to an area of virtual space to defend against unwanted intrusion. Before an opposing model can attack the Firewall in an ICE defended area, they must first destroy the ICE. This can be tricky when a crew faces time constraints or when the ICE is particularly powerful. ICE always has Tether of 0, since they cannot move, and also has the Virtual rule.

NON-PLAYER CHARACTERS

The Sprawl is a living, breathing creature—full of life and death. Its inhabitants vary—some are a simple annoyance, others are as deadly as an enemy operative. This section describes the actions and motivations of the numerous creatures, neutral parties, and innocent bystanders that can get in the way of the Showrunner's mission. Any model not considered part of any Showrunner's crew is a Non-Player Character (NPC). This includes nervous citizens and the CORPSEC officers they regularly call, as well as random security bots and turrets, psycho gangers, and even feral critters.

NPCs and Bystanders

An NPC is either a Sprawl bystander or a Neutral. *Sprawl bystanders* are the gray, tedious masses that live and work in the Sprawl; they constantly get in the way and almost never put up a fight. They do not even have a stat profile. *Neutrals* is a catch-all term for everything else that can fight, interact, and otherwise cause your Showrunner trouble. Neutrals have their own profiles. We deal with both separately below.

Neutrals

Neutral NPCs cover a lot of various ground. We provide stats and rules under *NPC Profiles* in the *Neutral Party* section.

NEUTRAL PLACEMENT

Neutrals can arrive during an ongoing battle, or they might be there the entire time, unnoticed. There are three main ways you can set Neutrals up on the table.

AT THE TABLE'S EDGE

This is the most common way to place Neutrals. You place the models in such a way that their bases touch a particular edge of the board or table. The rules for each Neutral clarify which edge. The player chosen to place the models may place them anywhere, provided the models touch the edge of the table/board. There may be additional rules to follow, as well—such as making sure placement is within 12" of the board's center.

NEAR TERRAIN

This is common for critters, though other models may also be inside buildings. A model placed in this way is usually touching a specific terrain piece. Typically, the scenario or a model's special rules dictate the type of terrain. If no terrain piece is explicitly stated, the player assigned to place the model may choose. The model *must* touch the named terrain, but you may otherwise set it up however you like.

DROP-IN

This is the most unusual way to place new models. It usually represents the deployment of elite CORPSEC units via transport craft (VTOLs, stealth landers, etc.). You may place drop-in Neutrals anywhere on the board, at any elevation. However, you must place them in a landing zone with a radius no smaller than 5". All models you set up via drop-in must fit in the landing zone, and the zone must not contain models already on the table.

Activation

NPCs do not need to test for activation. Instead, they always receive 2 AP. Neutrals activate at the start of the NPC phase, in the order the controlling player wishes. Neutrals have their own agenda—though the players control them, they are not part of any crew. They have their own actions, which we cover under *Motivations*.

Unless specified by another rule, players alternate the control of Neutrals each game turn. Most groups of Neutrals contain 1–3 models, which a single player controls. If there is more than one group of Neutrals, each side controls one group and then switches groups the next turn. It is important to handle Neutrals fairly, so one player does not exclusively control any one group for longer than a single turn. Players are free to control their Neutrals in ways that benefit them, but should keep in mind that their opponent will do the same next turn.

Motivation

When a player controls a group of Neutrals, they may use any abilities or actions the models possess. However, the models' *motivation* limits their actions. A Neutral's motivation represents its natural inclination. Some are aggressive and pursue combat, while others are cautious and hang back as long as possible. Some are even downright psycho and charge at the nearest thing they can kill. Neutrals activate using the following list of possible actions established by their motivations. We remind players that *Reality's Edge* is intended to be fun, and players should always play Neutrals in the spirit of their motivations. A Neutral's profile states which motivation it follows and under which circumstances that motivation may change.

TYPES OF MOTIVATION

CAUTIOUS

A cautious model may never voluntarily move within 12" of a player-controlled model or another Neutral that is not in its group. If a Neutral is within 12" of such a model when it starts its activation, it must spend at least 1 AP to move away. It must use its full Move stat, and head into cover, if possible. If this still does not take the Neutral farther than 12" away, it may either use another AP to move again or, if the other model is hostile and the Neutral possesses a ranged weapon, it may shoot at the hostile instead. Cautious models do not charge into close combat, but do not have to flee from combat once engaged. Cautious models receive a -1 to all Grazed Tests.

AGGRESSIVE

An aggressive Neutral may move freely toward any model it deems hostile. The controlling player determines which models meet that requirement. The Neutral must spend at least 1 AP to move within 18" of a hostile model and may use its ranged weapons when within 18". If the ranged weapons it carries have a range of less than 18", the Neutral may move until it reaches that range. Once it meets these requirements, the Neutral may operate as the controlling player sees fit. The Neutral may also move close and attempt to make close combat attacks if it carries a melee weapon. While engaged in close combat, it is not obligated to flee. Aggressive models receive a +1 bonus to all Morale and Grazed Tests.

GRIEFER

A Griefer's motivation is to cause the most havoc or grief possible, while being a downright jerk. The anonymity of the HyperNET is the only way such cavalier actions are possible, so being a griefer is limited to Neutrals with the Virtual rule. Essentially, a griefer may take any action the model can perform as long as it spends 1 AP per turn using an app or ability to target a player-controlled model. The only time a griefer can ignore these requirements is when no such target exists. If that is the case, they may only make move actions until they are within range of a target again.

GUARD

These Neutrals are tasked with guarding a place or person. A guard model strays no further than 6" from a person it is guarding, or 12" from a place it is guarding. It attacks any models that try to get within 6" of its charge, unless such a model is Hidden or carrying concealable items (blending in with the public, as it were). Guard models only attack models/groups of models that attack first or get too close, as previously stated. Otherwise, they are free to act as their controlling player wishes.

PSYCHO

A psycho model is inured to the threat of harm. It must attempt to engage the closest hostile model, which can include another Neutral from a different group or a player-controlled model. A psycho model attempts to move the maximum distance each turn until it can charge. When engaged in melee, it continues to make close combat attacks until either it or its opponent ends up out-of-action. Psycho models are immune to Grazed Tests.

GENERAL CONSIDERATIONS

Neutrals take all Will Tests as required. Further, Neutrals never attack members from their own group, unless another model or group of the same affiliation controls them. For instance, CORPSEC models consider all other CORPSEC groups friendly. However, gangers from different gangs consider each other hostiles, unless the rules state otherwise. Players should use common sense here.

Sprawl Bystanders

The Sprawl is an endless sea of humanity and there are people who call even the most desolate places *home*. The following rules characterize the effects random citizens and innocent bystanders just going about their normal routines can have on a game of *Reality's Edge*. For the most part, bystanders are not particularly brave or willing to put up a fight. Many have become desensitized to random violence, provided it is not directed at them. However, a few may fight back if something pushes them too far.

SINGLE BYSTANDERS

We refer to individual Sprawl citizens as bystanders. These are your office workers, street people, and other innocents who may be out and about at any given moment. Their base size is not important, though these rules assume a 25mm base size.

CROWDS

It is not uncommon for bystanders to form crowds while tending to their daily business. They could be waiting for public transport, watching a communal holo-display, or even waiting in line to use the CAT. They could also just be a random group of individuals near each other for an instant in time. Crowds are represented by a 4" template. Because crowds are more likely to get in your operative's way than a single bystander, we use the template to represent how much physical space they fill.

Note that for rules purposes, when we mention bystanders from here forward, the term applies to single bystanders *AND* crowds, unless otherwise stated.

BYSTANDERS AND JOBOPS

The *JOBOPS* section describes whether or not a mission uses bystanders and, if so, how many and which types. Certain Hitches may also add or subtract from this number for a JOBOP.

BYSTANDER PLACEMENT

Unless a JOBOP specifies how to place bystanders, players are free to intersperse them around the board. Players take turns placing single bystanders and crowds, as close together or as far apart as they like, with the caveat that they may not place them within 6" of a player-controlled model.

BYSTANDER ACTIVATION

Bystanders do not activate in the same way as other models. They simply react to what happens around them:

- If a model makes a ranged attack within 12" of a bystander, the bystander must make a Panic Test (see below).
- If a model makes a melee attack within 6" of a bystander, the bystander must make a Panic Test. Note that the attacking model may be another bystander.
- If a bystander is not forced to make a Panic Test by the end of the Clean-Up Phase, they must move. Determine which direction the bystander moves by rolling a scatter die. If you do not have a scatter die, roll a D10 and use the triangular point on the top of the die to determine the direction. Move the bystander D3" in the direction indicated.

PANIC TESTS

Bystanders tend to panic at the first sign of trouble. When a bystander must make a Panic Test, roll a D10. If the result is 2–10 they are fine, but they must move toward the closest cover within 6" and hide behind it. If the result is a Fumble (result of 1), roll another D10 and consult the following tables:

SINGLE BYSTANDER PANIC TABLE	
D10 Result	Panic Result
1	Flee – Remove the bystander from the board.
2–9	Flight – Move the bystander D6" toward the nearest board edge. A single bystander skirts any terrain or other models by the shortest distance possible.
10	Fight – The bystander draws a concealed gun and shoots at the closest player-controlled model within 12" (ignore this result if no such target is available). Roll a D10: if the result is 6 or higher, the shot hits. If the result is 5 or less, the shot misses. Resolve all hits as Strength 6 with a Max Damage of 3. Regardless of the result, remove the bystander from the board.

BYSTANDER CROWD PANIC TABLE	
D10 Result	Panic Result
1	Flee – Remove the crowd template from the board and replace it with D3 single bystanders. You must place the bystanders within the bounds of the original template.
2–9	Flight – Move the crowd D6" toward the nearest board edge. They attempt to skirt any terrain, but if they come in contact with a player-controlled model, they may trample them in terror. The crowd stops after making such contact, and the player-controlled model must pass an Agility Test or suffer D3 damage and be knocked Prone.
10	Fight – Move the crowd D6" toward the nearest player-controlled model. If the crowd comes in contact with a model, they attempt to trample it. The crowd stops after making such contact, and the player-controlled model must pass an Agility Test or suffer D3 damage and be knocked Prone.

Bystanders may make multiple Panic Tests per turn, depending on the carnage around them. However, they may only fail one such test a turn. Ignore further Panic Tests for such bystanders for the duration of the turn. If bystanders touch a board edge because of panic, remove them from the game.

BYSTANDERS AND MOVEMENT

Bystanders tend to get in the way, meaning player-controlled models may need to move through crowds. Treat crowds as difficult terrain, but only if your model has enough movement to move through the crowd entirely. Unless, it is attempting to *Blend In*, as described under *Special Actions* (page 70), a player-controlled model may not remain in a crowd. You cannot move through single bystanders.

BYSTANDERS AND RANGED COMBAT

Bystanders do not block line of sight but can cause a penalty of -1 for single bystanders and -2 for crowds to a ranged attack if the attack draws line of sight through the bystanders. Should your model miss by one with such a shot, it hits a single bystander. Should it miss by two, it hits the crowds. Cruel operatives may note that standing in base contact with bystanders significantly increases the chance of civilian casualties. It is also possible to take bystanders hostage, which we describe under *Special Actions* (see page 71). However, such a nefarious use of civilians could result in major repercussions to a crew's reputation.

BYSTANDERS AND MELEE

Models may attack bystanders in melee. Bystanders never roll to defend themselves. The attacker rolls to attack as normal and automatically hits the bystander unless the result is a Fumble. On Fumble, they whiff the attack.

WOUNDING BYSTANDERS

Bystanders are automatically wounded when hit by any melee or ranged attack. For a single bystander, simply remove the model from play. For a crowd, remove the crowd template from the board and replace it with D3 single bystanders. You must place the bystanders within the bounds of the original template. Roll Panic Tests for these remaining bystanders immediately.

Special Actions

BLEND IN

Savvy operatives can attempt to hide amongst innocent bystanders. If they conceal their weapons and make themselves inconspicuous, they can avoid detection as they move about the battlefield. To *blend in*, a model must be in base contact with a crowd of bystanders and spend 1 AP to make a Survival Test. If it fails, the AP is wasted, and the model cannot try to blend in again this turn. If it succeeds, remove the model from the table. It is now part of that bystander crowd and forfeits any remaining AP. Note that a model equipped with weapons it cannot conceal suffers a -3 penalty to the Survival Test when attempting to blend in.

During its next activation, the operative model can spend 1 AP to either leave the crowd or travel to another bystander crowd within 9". This happens automatically and does not trigger Overwatch or other types of reactive actions. A model may not blend in and leave a crowd during the same turn.

A model blending in with a crowd moves along with the crowd whenever it moves— this includes movement from Panic Tests. If the crowd is removed from the board for any reason (panic, being attacked, etc.), place the operative model with the remaining D3 single bystanders. The newly revealed operative model must make a Grazed Test due to its sudden predicament

HOSTAGES

An operative model may spend 1 AP to grab any single bystander and hold it hostage; the bystander does not initially attempt to resist. Any attacks that target the operative during the turn automatically hit the hostage instead, unless the attacker rolls a Critical. While holding a hostage, an operative model reduces its movement by half and suffers a -2 penalty to any actions. At the end of the NPC Phase, hostages attempt to break free. The hostage-holding operative model must make a Strength Test. If it fails, remove the bystander from the board. If it succeeds, it may hold on to the hostage.

Crowds are too unwieldy to hold hostage. However, they can be useful when trying to block incoming shots as described under *Bystanders and Ranged Combat*.

BUILDING YOUR CREW

Costs

A dizzying array of competing currencies exists among the many economic zones and nation states, but no one uses them to pay Showrunners. Official money is easily traceable, which is a problem for a Showrunner. Instead, the Sprawl uses cryptocurrencies (CC) as their true legal tender. Verifiable, anonymous, and easily transferable, CC are good everywhere. Anything you can purchase with actual money or credits has a listed CC cost.

STARTING FUNDS

Starting Showrunners have 800 CC to spend on their first crew. This includes the cost of all personnel, as well as their items and equipment. You lose any CC you do not spend.

If you are playing a one-off game, players can adjust this amount as they wish.

Operatives

Showrunners lead crews of mercenaries called *operatives*. Operatives are independent operators and mercenaries, each of whom has a *type* that brings a unique skill set and expertise to the crew.

TYPES OF EMPLOYMENT

A crew is made up of three types of employees:

- **Showrunner:** The big boss. Each crew has only one. Showrunner is an upgrade to a normal operative type.
- **Permahire:** After gaining the Showrunner's trust, a freelancer can be upgraded to a Permahire (see page 284 for more on Permahires). Permahires are reliable, they gain experience, and they have a better selection of special abilities.
- **Freelancer:** Hired on a per-mission basis, a freelancer comes with pre-set stats and abilities. Some may have additional options—this is delineated in their entry. Except for your Showrunner and shadow backer avatar, all models you hire in the beginning are automatically freelancers.

Roster Profile

Each operative type has a roster profile, which contains the following aspects:

- **Title:** The general name for this type of operative.
- **Stat Block:** The operative's stats, including Move, Melee, Aim, Strength, etc. Note that each operative type has three options, which are determined by the specific operative type.
- **Stat Increases:** You may choose one option when you first add this operative to your crew. Add the designated increase to the model's stat block.
- **Edge:** The latent abilities that come with each specific type of operative. These are generally unique to each operative, with a few exceptions. Your operative has all the abilities listed in this section.
- **Carry Capacity:** The number of slots the operative has for carrying weapons and other items.
- **Choose Primary Weapon:** Each operative type tends to favor certain weapons. Nominate one weapon for your operative from the list when you first hire them. the model gets a +1 to-hit bonus with their chosen primary weapon. You cannot change the selection later, though the bonus still applies to upgraded versions of the same weapon.
- **Determine Skills:** Skills represent the little bits of knowledge and expertise an operative has learned. You almost always randomly determine skills by rolling against the Skill Table, but each player may choose which column of the table to roll against. When first joining a crew, all models—including the Showrunner—begin with one skill.
- **Starting Salary:** The CC cost to add the operative to the crew.
- **Restrictions:** Any restrictions or special exceptions that exist for the operative, including whether they are prohibited from carrying certain weapons, etc. This applies to Permahires and freelancers, but not Showrunners.

ADVANCED OPTIONS

These additional roster options only apply to Showrunners and Permahires.

- **Tricks of the Trade:** Even within each operative type, there are variances. In this section, a player determines any subspecialties their hired help has. *Tricks of the Trade* are not available to freelancers. Permahires roll randomly on the Tricks of the Trade Table and apply the result; Showrunners choose their option.
- **Personal Motivation:** The in-game goal an operative can complete to gain experience. This can be as simple as killing enemy models, but there are alternatives beyond simple violence. Freelancers cannot track or gain experience.

Assembling Your Operatives

A crew has a minimum of three models and a maximum of six models (with a few exceptions we explain later). Additionally, a crew may never have more than two of each type of operative. The Showrunner's starting operative type counts against this limit. For example, if your Showrunner is a Sprawl Ronin, your crew may have only one other Sprawl Ronin.

ESTABLISHING A NARRATIVE

As your crew develops, we recommend you come up with a cool backstory or codename for each member. If you need help with this, there a quite a few online codename generators that can provide suitably random codenames. After all, *Black Sparrow* sounds infinitely cooler than *Sprawl Ronin #2*.

CREW LOGISTICS

Note that the following section only covers hiring models for your crew. We cover weapons, armor, equipment, cybernetics, and spending CC in general, in the *Black Market* section (see page 123). Also, special rules for each model are listed in the *Special Rules* section.

For now, choose your starting crew and record their special rules and stats. The *Talent Roster*, a record sheet for your crew, is included in the back of the book. After you establish a crew, move on to the *Black Market* section to purchase weapons, armor, and other equipment for them (see page 123).

Showrunner

Showrunners are the primary character in *Reality's Edge*—they represent *you*, the player, on the table top. They come from many walks of life and may be independent professionals, corporate shills, criminal entrepreneurs, or anything in-between. They can have any race, gender, or creed. Showrunners are nowhere near the top of the corporate ladder, but they are not far from the bottom rung.

Showrunners are so-named for their characteristic chrome install. Called the Visualizer, this piece of chrome is a special neural network implant that allows the Showrunner to visualize the worldwide data network without a direct jack-in to a network node. It also allows a single remote user to piggyback on this access. Acquiring such an elite piece of chrome is beyond the means of most aspirant Showrunners, but someone is usually eager to pay the steep price for those willing to bargain away their service.

Your crew may only have one Showrunner and **the Showrunner upgrades are free**. However, you must still pay the normal CC amount for their starting salary and any items they equip. To build your Showrunner, you must complete the steps below.

SHOWRUNNER BACKGROUND

Players may select a diverse background for their Showrunner or roll randomly. Of course, the latter is strongly recommended, but is not a requirement. Your Showrunner gains the benefit associated with their background.

D6 Result	Background	Benefit
	SHOWRUNNER BACKGROUND TABLE	
1–2	Street Rat: Your Showrunner was raised on the street. Either an orphan or largely ignored by their family, they had to make friends with other street rats or join a gang to survive. They often dreamed of the luxury of the Upper Reaches but had to make do with society's leftovers. However, they became tougher for it. Their childhood was marked by struggle and deprivation.	Add +4 to HP and +1 to MET. Gain the *Hard as Nails* skill. Gangers cost less to recruit into their crew—subtract 10 CC from the normal cost.
3–4	Middle Class Bourgeoisie: Your Showrunner had an unremarkable childhood with parents that were warm, if not overly affectionate. Raised in corporate suburbia, they never had to fight for anything, received adequate schooling, and started life with one foot forward. Their childhood was marked by boredom and the conventional.	Add +2 to HP and +1 to their MET. Start with one randomly determined high-end item. Roll once against the *High-End Item Table* in the *Black Market* section and gain the result for free (see page 187). You may not transfer this item to another model but may sell it for additional CC. Reroll any *Bleeding Edge* item results.
5–6	Arcology Raised: Your Showrunner was born to affluent parents in a corporate arcology. While not elite, their childhood was what most would consider ideal. With emotionally distant parents and a life of relative leisure, the Showrunner had plenty of time to contemplate how the world really worked. Denied the adventure of the Sprawl, they dreamed of the day they could prove themselves. Their childhood was marked by privilege and ennui.	Add +1 to MET. Start with two randomly determined high-end items. Roll twice on the *High-End Item Table* in the *Black Market* section and gain the results for free (see page 187). You may not transfer these items to another model but may sell them for additional CC.

CHOOSE OPERATIVE TYPE

Before accepting the Visualizer from their mysterious benefactor, your Showrunner was a mercenary operative with enough talent to warrant their shadow backer's attention in the first place. Select from the following operative types and gain the linked benefit.

SHOW RUNNER OPERATIVE TYPE TABLE		
Profession	Temperament	Benefit
Console Cowboy	Addicted to the HyperNET, this Showrunner is an accomplished decker. Lacking a few social graces, and paranoid for good reason, your Showrunner is tech savvy and has developed an above average app repertoire.	Ignore the first Fumble the Showrunner rolls when making a cyber-attack. The attack still fails, but the Showrunner does not suffer the consequences for the Fumble. They also start with one additional app.
Drone Jockey	This Showrunner always tinkers with bots and drones and prefers them to human companionship. A social misfit, for sure, but less so than most Console Cowboys. Drone Jockeys become testy when away from their robot friends. They also are addicted to filming their drone's exploits and trying to one-up other jockeys.	Add +1 FW and +2 HP to any drone that starts the game with them.
Enforcer	A bit rough around the edges, this Showrunner survived several corporate wars and lived to tell the tale. They are reserved, but protective of their friends. They are also very direct and uncompromising.	Replace "Showrunner" in the *Bodyguard Edge* with "any friendly crew member within 6"." Gain the *Do or Die* skill.
Infiltrator	This Showrunner is a bit of a mystery. Quiet and thoughtful, they do not lead out in front but coordinate their crew from the shadows. The crew thinks of them as cold and calculating and always emotionally distant.	Gain *Tactician* and *Coordinated Movement* special rules. May use the *Coordinated Movement* ability on a model within 6" instead of the normal 3".
Masque	Gregarious to a fault, this Showrunner is a friend to all. Crew members, contacts, and even the normally distant shadow backer are all more accommodating around this Showrunner.	After each game, the crew gains +1 INFO. Add +1 to all Survival Tests when this Showrunner enters bystander crowds.
Street Doc	Perhaps a bit clinical and distant because of the bloodshed they have seen, this Showrunner is a helper first and a fighter second. Motivated to expand their skills into the Sprawl, they either want to make the world a better place or cannot find a better place to increase their knowledge.	Increase the benefits of the *Life Saver* special rule by +1. When this Showrunner uses the *Medical Knowledge* Edge, they add +1 to the number of HP they heal.

Sprawl Ronin	A true badass, this Showrunner worked hard to build their reputation as one of the best Ronin for hire. Perhaps a bit arrogant, for good reason, this Showrunner's enemies whisper fearfully about them. They are always quick to accept any martial challenge.	Gain the *Fearful Reputation* special rule. If they take another Showrunner out-of-action, their crew gains 1 point of REP at the end of the game.
Tracer	A speed addict, this Showrunner has a hard time just standing in place. Though their crew views them as flighty and a bit fickle, they never miss a detail or an appointment, and their crew respects their ability to keep things moving.	Gain the *Tactician* special rule. Once per game, this Showrunner's player may reroll the dice to determine Initiative. They may wait until after all players roll to do so, but the second result stands, even if it is worse.

Additionally, you may review the associated roster profile of your Showrunner's operative type and choose a *Trick of the Trade*, a *Primary Weapon* (if applicable), and one stat increase option. The Showrunner also gains the listed Edge and may gain one randomly determined skill from the skill tables listed in the roster.

Finally, Showrunners also gain the following additional Edge:

- **Crew Leader:** The Showrunner is the main authority for their crew. They gain the *Motivator* special rule for free.
- **Visualizer:** The Showrunner's unique chrome counts as the tether point for the shadow backer's avatar. At the start of the game, the avatar always starts in base contact with the Showrunner. Further, the Visualizer does count not count against the Showrunner's Install Point Limit and cannot be disabled, bricked, etc.
- **V-Spyke:** As an additional upgrade, the Showrunner receives a special data-spyke that is unique to them. The V-Spyke, as it is called, is very similar to the common data-spyke. It is about 6" long and the Showrunner can physically jam it into a network's output port. Once embedded, the pick swarms with nano-tendrils and hooks the network up to a tiny wireless router—effectively, if tenuously connecting the network to the greater HyperNET. To use the V-Spyke, the Showrunner must be in base contact with the node and spend 1 AP to install it (they may not install the V-spyke if they are also in base contact with an enemy model). The connection is automatic—from that point on, Virtual beings (friend or foe) may hack that specific network. The Showrunner may use the V-Spyke only once per game.

CC COST

The Showrunner costs their operative type's Starting Salary in CC. This cost does not include any weapons or equipment.

Shadow Backer

Occasionally, a lucky Showrunner aspirant finds, or is anonymously contacted by, a mysterious third party. This could be one of any number of mega corporations, a smaller corporate entity, a criminal syndicate, a Gov.Mil representative, or hacktivist collectives. Regardless, they are willing to provide access for the price of indentured servitude. Akin to a Faustian bargain, if a Showrunner enters this contract, the they become a willing pawn in the shadow backer's secret agenda and agree to provide their backer with their service and exclusive access to their neural network. It is not common for a Showrunner to find out the identity of their shadow backer. Missions are relayed to them through anonymous email, other electronic accounts, or by commercial courier. When meeting online, the backer appears only as an electronic avatar. This avatar can be any number of characters or objects and may be symbolic or randomly generated.

Such servitude is a heavy price to pay, but it also provides many advantages. First, the shadow backer invests in the Showrunner's success. They provide income paid in untraceable CC, which allows the Showrunner to hire and outfit a crew. The Showrunner has great leeway in choosing a crew and deciding how to execute the missions the shadow backer assigns. When out in the field, the shadow backer or their agent can access the Showrunner's neural network to provide electronic warfare support, either by hacking enemy operatives or supporting the crew with various buffs. With continued success and excellent service, the Showrunner may buy themselves out of their contract, in time. While this is quite difficult to do, it is not impossible.

Each crew gets one shadow backer for free. A shadow backer mostly plays a background role, but in game, they can take on the form of an avatar—a powerful Virtual being that provides hacking support to the crew.

The avatar should be represented by a model or other miniature that clearly differentiates it from other models. Avatars are only limited by the players' imaginations, but they should be a similar size to the rest of the models on the table. For 28mm games, the model should be between 25–35mm tall.

AVATAR STATS

SHADOW BACKER AVATAR				
FW	DHP	MOV/Tether	CYB	AP
6	6	5/16	4	3

EDGE

- **HyperNET Avatar:** Shadow backer avatars have the Virtual rule and the Hacking ability. They start with the Gatecrasher, Slice, and Reconnect apps. They may also start with two additional apps from any of the available app groups, though you must determine them randomly by rolling against the appropriate App tables in the *Black Market* section (see page 176).
- **Signal Boost:** For each CAT to which the avatar's crew gains Access, the shadow backer avatar gains +1 AP and +4" of Tether. Should a captured CAT be shutdown, disabled, or taken over by an enemy hacker, remove the benefits for that node. It is quite possible for these bonuses to change frequently as nodes change hands.
- **Always Online:** Should the shadow backer's avatar be taken Offline, remove the model from the table. During the Clean-Up Phase of the next game turn, place the avatar in base contact with its Showrunner, but with only 3 DHP. If the Showrunner is out-of-action, the avatar is not automatically taken Offline. However, should an avatar go Offline, or be removed from the tabletop for any reason (such as being banished by an app), they may not return to play if the Showrunner is out-of-action.

AVATAR UPGRADES

During gameplay, you may upgrade your shadow backer's avatar. We explain this in the *Campaigning in the Sprawl* section, but the possible upgrades are listed here for convenience.

- **Attack Upgrade:** Your shadow backer invests in a high-end virtual rig. Add +1 to the avatar's Cyber stat.
- **Expert Upgrade:** Your avatar's Hacker updates their app suite. The avatar can gain two random apps of any type.
- **Processing Upgrade:** The avatar is now able to partition more effectively, which allows it to process more actions without data loss. Add +1 to the avatar's number of available AP per turn.
- **Streaming Upgrade:** The shadow backer's avatar directly connects to the battlefield via a pirated data stream with multiple network reroutes. They receive +3 DHP and may always return to play via the Always Online rule, even if your Showrunner is out-of-action.

Console Cowboy

"I don't care what's happening, I need more time. You're the muscle, protect me! This is a Watson-Nokugami server link—it's a delicate thing. Unlike your date last night, this is going to take actual finesse!"

Darkfyre, Console Cowboy

AKA Data Jockeys, Hackers, Scripters, Deckers

WHO THEY ARE

Hackers are normally confined to dimly lit coffin cubes, data cafes, or secured server rooms but Console Cowboys are a special breed of cyber warrior, and they are not content to sit in the dark. They know that the juiciest targets are locally networked or accessible only from behind a thick layer of physical security; especially corporate targets. Armed with a neuro-link, the best console they can afford or steal, and a full suite of attack apps and programs—not to mention their quick wits—Cowboys infiltrate the deep recesses of the digital world, looking for anything that might be worth digging into more.

WHAT THEY DO

Console Cowboys are combat hackers equipped to fully enter cyberspace during missions. They both defend against enemy electronic intrusions and attack enemy equipment and local network infrastructure. Their presence is often key to mission success, as many missions focus on virtual targets as much as physical ones. Of course, unlike the Showrunners' more sophisticated systems that allow them to go full virtual, Console Cowboys can only dip their toes into the HyperNET and swim around in augmented reality. Still, to do so is to leave themselves vulnerable to physical danger and at the mercy of enemy operatives. It is up to the rest of their team to protect them while they work.

CONSOLE COWBOY STAT TABLE

CONSOLE COWBOY							
DEF	HP	FW	MOV	MEL	AIM	STR	MET
5	8	6	5	3	3	5	5

CONSOLE COWBOY STAT INCREASES

Choose one from the table below.

STAT INCREASE TABLE	
Option 1	+1 MOV
Option 2	+1 MEL
Option 3	+1 AIM

CARRYING CAPACITY

Six slots.

PRIMARY WEAPON SET

Choose one from: Light SMG, machine pistol, bludgeon, small blade, or sword.

DETERMINE SKILLS

Roll a D6 and consult the table below. Reroll duplicates.

CONSOLE COWBOY SKILL TABLE			
D6 Result	Stealth	Movement	Professional
1	Disarm	Armor Expertise	Clever
2	Careful Blow	Duck and Weave	Self-Assured
3	Observe	Hasty Charge	Hackerman
4	Dive For Cover	Hurdler	Solid Footing
5	Shadow Blend	Pop-Up	Sprawl Survivor
6	Flight or Fight	Running Man	Mr. Fix-It

STARTING SALARY

100 CC.

RESTRICTIONS

May not have more than a +2 Armor Bonus.

EDGE

HIGH-END HACKING

Console Cowboys are the original net-runners. They start with a cyber-deck—always a custom job—which uses the stats below. Through their cyber-deck, they have the Hacking ability. Should the Console Cowboy lose all their cyber-deck's DHP, they may no longer use apps. During the Clean-Up Phase of the game turn after the turn in which they lost their last DHP, they regain 2 DHPs and may use their app(s) once again.

CONSOLE COWBOY CYBER-DECK	
CYB	DHP
4	8

APPS

The Console Cowboy starts out with the Gatecrasher and Slice apps. They may take three other apps from any group of apps for free, but these must be determined randomly by rolling against the appropriate table in the *Black Market* section (see page 176).

ADVANCED OPTIONS

TRICKS OF THE TRADE

Roll a D3 and consult the table below. Reroll duplicates.

CONSOLE COWBOY TRICKS OF THE TRADE TABLE	
D3 Result	Console Cowboy Tricks of the Trade
1	Gain +1 CYB.
2	Gain +2 DHP and +1 FW.
3	Add 2" to the range of all apps

PERSONAL MOTIVATION

Successfully make two or more cyber-attacks.

Cyborg

"We had one fellow we called Tiny Tin. He was about 8' tall, all chrome, and a beast in combat. I once saw him rip a dude in half, literally. But, one day, he got riled up after taking a bullet to the face. Guy went nuts. He charged the enemy and after they were bloody mist, he turned on us. When it was all said and done, what was left of him and many members of our crew was not a pretty sight."

AKA Bricks, Tinmen, Cyber-Psychos, Robo-wannabes

WHO THEY ARE

From the lowest Sprawl Ganger to the most elite, corporate CEO, cybernetics and body augmentation are both common and expected. It can be hard to tell when too much of a good thing is *too much*. Most augmented humans receive full or partial replacement of a single limb or two. Often, this is done to compensate for a physical failing or injury, though sometimes it is for professional reasons. Cyborgs, however, become somewhat addicted to adding chrome—so much so, that they have barely any flesh remaining. Once complete, most are just a head or head and torso combination. In some extreme circumstances, a Cyborg is just a brain in a fully mechanical body. Of course, this much augmentation comes at a steep cost, both financially and psychologically. To pay for such work, many Cyborgs enter into the employment of nefarious individuals (which may or may not be a problem for the Cyborg). Even more dangerous, however, is the fact that it rapidly raises the chance of cybershock and cyber-mania. A Cyborg is an asset for many Showrunners, but the latter risk is always in the back of their minds.

WHAT THEY DO

Cyborgs can be generalists with a variety of different cybernetics, from weapons to speed boosters, to anything in between. Tactical Showrunners use Cyborgs to fill in holes in their crew. Yet, the stereotype of the hulking mechanical monster is also true. Many Showrunners generally value Cyborgs as line-breakers, able to smash through the thickest of enemy resistance. When used in this manner, Cyborgs are far from subtle; and, should they go berserk, the closer to the enemy the better.

CYBORG STAT TABLE

Stat bonuses from cybernetics are not reflected in the Cyborg stat table.

CYBORG							
DEF	HP	FW	MOV	MEL	AIM	STR	MET
5	8	6	5	3	3	5	5

STAT INCREASES

Choose one from the table below.

CYBORG STAT INCREASE TABLE	
Option 1	+1 AIM and +1 MEL
Option 2	+2 MEL
Option 3	+1 DEF
Option 4	+2 HP
Option 5	+2 FW

CARRYING CAPACITY

Six slots.

CHOOSE PRIMARY WEAPON SET

A choice of one from:
- **Heavy Cyberbody:** Any one melee weapon, assault rifle, or shotgun.
- **Light Cyberbody:** Any one melee weapon, SMG (light or heavy), or shotgun.

DETERMINE SKILLS

Roll a D6 and consult the relevant table below. Reroll duplicates.

HEAVY CYBORG SKILL TABLE			
D6 Result	Street Fighting	Machine Strength	Professional
1	Against All Odds	Muscular	Bullet Magnet
2	Bully	Brute	Fearful Reputation
3	Ground Fighter	Steady Hands	Hard as Nails
4	Blitzer	Solid Footing	Self-Assured
5	Brawler	Sentry	Deadeye
6	Muscular	Push Off	Careful Shooting

LIGHT CYBORG SKILL TABLE			
D6 Result	Martial Arts	Major Mojo	Professional
1	Against All Odds	Called Shot	Bullet Magnet
2	Careful Blow	Brute	Fearful Reputation
3	Counter-Weight Throw	Shoot and Scoot	Do or Die
4	Defender	Running Man	Self-Assured
5	Critical Block	Hasty Charge	Quick
6	Opportunist	Duck and Weave	Observe

STARTING SALARY

105 CC for a light cyberbody or 120 for a heavy cyberbody.

RESTRICTIONS

None.

BORGED OUT

The Cyborg sold their meatbag body for the promise of chrome and fame. It is a small price to pay if they lose a good bit of their humanity in the process. Instead of a special Edge for their operative type, Cyborgs start with a full cybernetic body. This is subsumed in their Starting Salary, which essentially equates to a discount. They may choose either a heavy or light cyberbody. Cyborgs also start with the *Up-Armed* special rule.

ADVANCED OPTIONS

TRICKS OF THE TRADE

Roll a D3 and consult the relevant table below. Reroll duplicates.

HEAVY CYBERBODY TRICKS OF THE TRADE TABLE	
D3 Result	Heavy Cyberbody Tricks of the Trade
1	Receive a +1 bonus to all non-combat Strength Tests. Once per game, the Cyborg may reroll a failed Cyber-Shock Test.
2	Take either the LMG or the Minigun as a Primary Weapon instead of the usual options.
3	Gain +2 HP.

LIGHT CYBERBODY TRICKS OF THE TRADE TABLE	
D3 Result	Light Cyberbody Tricks of the Trade
1	Receive a +1 bonus to all Agility Tests. Once per game, the Cyborg may reroll a failed Cyber-Shock Test.
2	Gain the *Multiple Strikes* skill.
3	Increase FW by +1.

PERSONAL MOTIVATION

Force a model of equal or higher value out-of-action or deal 12 total points of damage.

Drone Jockey

"A lot of couch jockeys will tell you to do it all remotely, but where's the fun in that? Nothing's funnier than watching some poor chum trying to outrun a PX-1 Firehawk with a nose-mounted SMG. Plus, I upload the chase vids later for a bit of fun and make some CC on the back-end. Let's see the remote do that reliably."

AKA Controllers, Babysitters, Flyboys, Zoomers

WHO THEY ARE

Drones are a common sight in the Sprawl, as they are used for everything from food delivery to surveillance. Drone Jockeys, as they prefer to be called, are experts at controlling these robotic servants. Most Jockeys start at hobbyists, but the hobby slowly gives way to an obsession with acquiring better drones and mastering control of them. Over time, a master Drone Jockey may seem to control a drone with a mere thought or the faintest of gestures.

WHAT THEY DO

Remote surveillance, offensive operations, and rapid response are the Drone Jockey's mainstays. Drones tend to specialize in one of these functions, and a Drone Jockey uses many different types of drones to fill holes in the Showrunner's crew. Helo-drones can fly across the battlefield to provide a hi-res streaming feed of enemy movements or flank a dug-in enemy with enfilading fire. Down below, predator drones can hunt through the back alleys, looking for enemy operatives to drag down in a flurry of metal claws—or, when equipped with a ranged weapon mount, they can engage the enemy at range, which frees the crew to focus on the mission at hand.

When they are not running JOBOPS for their Showrunner, many Jockeys make action videos from the drone's camera feeds as a side hustle. Action vids shot from a drone's perspective are big ticket items in the Sprawl, and many Drone Jockeys try to outdo themselves and each other to get the best (most shocking and violent) footage possible. Most Showrunners turn a blind eye to these endeavors, provided the Jockeys ensure the vids do not reveal their origins.

DRONE JOCKEY TABLE STAT TABLE

DRONE JOCKEY							
DEF	HP	FW	MOV	MEL	AIM	STR	MET
5	8	6	5	3	3	5	5

DRONE JOCKEY STAT INCREASES

Choose one from the table below.

DRONE JOCKEY STAT INCREASE TABLE	
Option 1	+1 MOV
Option 2	+1 MEL
Option 3	+1 AIM

STARTING SALARY

80 CC.

RESTRICTIONS

None.

CARRYING CAPACITY

Six slots.

CHOOSE DRONE

Each Drone Jockey must start with one drone of their choice, and each drone has different CC costs. The Drone Jockey's Starting Salary does not include the cost of the drone.

STARTING DRONE TABLE		
Starting Drones		CC Cost
Option 1	Predator Attack Drone	40
Option 2	Predator Fire Support Drone	30
Option 3	Fire Support Helo-Drone	30
Option 4	Surveillance Helo-Drone	35

PRIMARY WEAPON SET

Choose one from: Light SMG, machine pistol, bludgeon, small blade, or sword.

DETERMINE SKILLS

Roll a D6 and consult the relevant table below. Reroll duplicates. Drone Jockeys may choose a skill for themselves from their own skill table or a skill for one of their drones from the drone skill table. Note that choosing a skill for a drone means the skill applies only to that particular drone.

DRONE JOCKEY SKILL TABLE		
D6 Result	Avoiding Trouble	Professional
1	Quick	Observe
2	Running Man	Clever
3	Hurdler	Duck and Weave
4	Dive for Cover	Shoot and Scoot
5	Shadow Blend	Defender
6	Flight or Fight	Trekker

DRONE SKILL TABLE				
D6 Result	Predator Drone		Helo-Drone	
	Attack	Fire Support	Fire Support	Surveillance
1	Blitzer	Called Shot	Called Shot	Duck and Weave
2	Brave	Marksman	Duck and Weave	Defender
3	Sentry	Deadeye	Deadeye	Shadow Blend
4	Hard as Nails	Fast-Tracker	Fast-Tracker	Fight or Flight
5	Brute	Brave	Brave	Ranger
6	First to the Fight	Shoot and Scoot	Marksman	Brave

DRONE CONTROL

Drone Jockeys control their drones via HyperNET HUD and neural link. While this gives them unparalleled remote control over short distances, it also requires intense concentration, which leaves the Jockey vulnerable. After rolling for activation, a Drone Jockey may assign one of their AP to a drone within their Zone of Control (listed in the drone's entry). After the Jockey spends any remaining AP they have, the drone immediately gets 2 AP and activates. The Drone Jockey then suffers a -2 penalty to their Melee, Aim, Move, and Mettle stats (to a minimum of 1), and may not gain extra AP for rolling a Critical on Activation Tests. Finally, should a drone ever be out-of-action, the Drone Jockey must make an immediate Morale Test.

Drones are built with multiple fail-safes to prevent tampering, but the unique link between the drone and the Drone Jockey is especially useful at preventing bricking. Should a Drone Jockey's drone ever be bricked, ignore the result and instead treat it as disabled for D6 turns.

ADVANCED OPTIONS

TRICKS OF THE TRADE

Roll a D3 and the consult the table below. Reroll duplicates.

DRONE JOCKEY TRICKS OF THE TRADE TABLE	
D3 Result	Drone Jockey Tricks of the Trade
1	Once per game, attempt to repair your drone by having base contact with it and passing an Intelligence Test. When successful, the drone gains D3 HP it previously lost (up to its maximum HP total), and is placed prone. You can attempt to use this ability multiple times but may only successfully use it once. You can attempt this on a drone that is out-of-action.
2	Once per game, when a drone under your control is successfully disabled, nerfed, or controlled by a cyber-attack, you may reboot the drone during your activation. Instead of transferring AP to the drone, spend 1 AP to place the drone prone so it can revert back to normal.
3	Add 6" to the Zone of Control for any drone you use.

PERSONAL MOTIVATION

Use a drone you control to take an enemy model out-of-action or use the drone's *Fire Assist* ability to aid another friendly model in taking an enemy model out-of-action.

Enforcer

"Jensen, I need that door popped now! Big Mike, swing your gun two clicks to the left and make 'em dance. Let's go people, the boss is starting to lose her patience…"

AKA Majordomos, Point-Men, Combat Managers, Watchdogs

WHO THEY ARE

Dangerous fighters who are coldly pragmatic and nothing if not efficient, enforcers carry out the Showrunner's orders and ensure the rest of the crew do the same. Many are former soldiers who were unable to reacclimate to civilian life. Instead, they hire themselves out as capable mercenaries with an understanding and appreciation for completing their mission, no matter the cost. Enforcers are used to the professional military's spartan lifestyle and tend to be dour individuals with little use for socializing between jobs, though a rare few are quite the opposite.

WHAT THEY DO

Enforcers are tasked with talent management and asset protection. They keep the crew focused on the mission and do their best to keep the Showrunner alive. This can mean anything from literally taking a bullet for the boss (made a bit less dramatic with subdermal armor implants), to barking orders over the din of gunfire, to taking the fight directly to the enemy when the job needs to be done right the first time. Enforcers are sometimes not as people-oriented as they ought to be, focusing instead on bringing big weaponry to a fight. Still, the fire support they offer helps others overlook their shortcomings in personality.

ENFORCER STAT TABLE

ENFORCER							
DEF	HP	FW	MOV	MEL	AIM	STR	MET
5	8	6	5	3	3	5	5

ENFORCER STAT INCREASES

Choose one from the table below.

ENFORCER STAT INCREASE TABLE	
Option 1	+1 MOV and +1 AIM
Option 2	+2 MEL
Option 3	+1 AIM and +1 MEL
Option 4	+1 MOV and +1 MEL

CARRYING CAPACITY

Seven slots.

CHOOSE PRIMARY WEAPON SET

Choose one from: Any one melee weapon, handgun, or long gun.

DETERMINE SKILLS

Roll a D6 and consult the table below. Reroll duplicates.

ENFORCER SKILL TABLE			
D6 Result	Martial Arts	Marksmanship	Professional
1	Against All Odds	Shoot and Scoot	Push Off
2	Careful Blow	Marksman	Fearful Reputation
3	Counter-Weight Throw	Deadeye	Hard as Nails
4	Defender	Fast-Tracker	Solid Footing
5	Critical Block	Careful Shooting	Armored Expertise
6	Opportunist	Steady Hands	Observe

STARTING SALARY

100 CC.

RESTRICTIONS

None.

EDGE

BODYGUARD

If an enemy model moves within melee range of a friendly Showrunner, and the Enforcer is within 6" of the Showrunner, the Enforcer may pass an Agility Test to attempt to intercede. If successful, the Enforcer and the Showrunner swap places. You may not use this ability if the Enforcer is in base contact with an enemy model. You may only use this ability once per turn.

MISSION FOCUS

The Enforcer starts with the *Motivator* skill. If the enforcer gains this skill again from another source (such as becoming a Showrunner), increase the skill's range to 9".

HEAVY SUPPORT

Instead of the *Mission Focus* Edge, the Enforcer can gain the *Up-Armed* special rule.

FIGHTING STYLE

The Enforcer may swap the *Martial Arts* skill list for the *Street Fighting* skill list found under the *Ganger* roster.

ADVANCED OPTIONS

TRICKS OF THE TRADE

Roll a D3 and consult the table below. Reroll duplicates.

ENFORCER TRICKS OF THE TRADE TABLE	
D3 Result	Tricks of the Trade
1	Gains the *Confident Command* skill or the *Brave* skill.
2	Receives a +1 bonus to all Activation Tests.
3	Gains the *Sentry* skill.

PERSONAL MOTIVATION

Successfully trade places with a friendly model or take a model of equal or higher value out-of-action.

Ganger

"We're not street chums, that I can tell you. You ever hear of the Greckers? We ran with them for months before we got kicked out, they said we was too intense! So, now we solo for ourselves. Jaz over there has a PP-260 hooked right into his arm. He gets hassled by the LEOs, but he don't care. Me, I have chrome, but I won't tell. Hire us and I'll show you."

AKA Boosters, Sprawl Trash, Wasters, Bullet-Catchers

WHO THEY ARE

Often no better than street thugs, Gangers are the lowest level operatives. While they may be the Showrunner's least dangerous options, they make up for their shortcomings by being cheap and plentiful. Of course, *Ganger* is a rather vague catch-all for anyone hired directly off the streets with no questions asked. Thus, they could be anything from corporate wannabes to what some call *combat interns*.

WHAT THEY DO

Survival is often a numbers game. A Showrunner's crew is an elite, small team; but, all the experience in the Sprawl is worthless if some street punk catches you off-guard. Nobody expects a Ganger to meet a Ronin in a fair fight and live to tell about it; but then, Gangers do not fight that way. Instead, they wait for the enemy to spread themselves thin, then they jump a single enemy as a group so the odds are more favorable. Gangers may flash some chrome—though, they are usually all flash and no smash—but for a more callous Showrunner, Gangers are a cheap and expendable source of manpower.

GANGER STAT TABLE

GANGER							
DEF	HP	FW	MOV	MEL	AIM	STR	MET
5	5	6	5	3	3	5	5

GANGER STAT INCREASES

Choose one for each model.

GANGER STAT INCREASE TABLE	
Option 1	-1 MET, +1 MOV, and +1 MEL
Option 2	-1 MET, +1 MEL, and +1 AIM
Option 3	+2 HP

CARRYING CAPACITY

Five slots.

PRIMARY WEAPON SET

Choose one from: Any one melee weapon or handgun.

DETERMINE SKILLS

Roll a D6 and consult the table below. Reroll duplicates.

GANGER SKILL TABLE			
D6 Result	Street Fighting	Sprawl Child	Professional
1	Against All Odds	Muscular	Bullet Magnet
2	Bully	Brute	Fearful Reputation
3	Ground Fighter	Trekker	Do or Die
4	Blitzer	Hard as Nails	Self-Assured
5	Brawler	Hurdler	Deadeye
6	Muscular	Push Off	Careful Shooting

STARTING SALARY

60 CC.

RESTRICTIONS

None.

EDGE

THE PACK

Gangers never go into battle alone. Though purchased and equipped individually, up to two Gangers only take up one operative slot. A crew may contain a total of four Gangers, which would take up two operative slots.

STRENGTH OF THE PACK

Being in gang is quite a confidence booster—with friends around, Gangers are less likely to run away or show weakness. While a Ganger is within 6" of another friendly Ganger, both receive a +1 to Will Tests and a +1 to their DEF against all attacks that are STR 6 or less.

ADVANCED OPTIONS

TRICKS OF THE TRADE

Roll a D3 and the consult the table below. Reroll duplicates.

GANGER TRICKS OF THE TRADE TABLE	
D3 Result	Ganger Tricks of the Trade
1	+1 to MEL
2	+2 HP
3	+1 to Activation Tests when within 6" of another friendly Ganger

PERSONAL MOTIVATION

Take an enemy Ganger out-of-action (gang rivalry) or be involved in the same melee (have base contact with the same enemy model) when this model or another Ganger (of the same gang allegiance) takes an enemy operative worth 100 CC or more out-of-action.

Infiltrator

"When do I take off the mask? Practically never. In my line of work, anonymity is my best friend. I'm wanted in three adjacent economic zones and the target we are hitting tonight would put me in ISO in a heartbeat, assuming their CORPSEC let me live. When you carry lock-breaking chrome and EMP bombs, you're not exactly Ms. Popular with authority figures."

Neo-Zero, Infiltrator

WHO THEY ARE

Infiltrators are shadowy operatives, and their origins are often just as mysterious as they are. Many are talented Gangers who moved up from the streets after practicing burglary and theft to the point of artistry. Others are former military special ops or low-end corporate troubleshooters—once trained in clandestine movement and stealth tactics, they now freelance. Out in the Sprawl, they belong to the infamous Infiltrator Guild, a loose confederation analogous to the medieval thieves' guild. For the price of silence and loyalty, the Guild provides its members with protection, a community of sorts, and a central place to look for employment. The Guild has little in the way of direct hierarchy; its membership crosses borders and nation-state and corporate economic zones alike, with near impunity.

WHAT THEY DO

Besides stealth operations, physical infiltration, electronic intrusion, and professional monkeywrenching, an Infiltrator can bypass security systems and guards, move about unseen, and—in a pinch—hack the HyperNET if the crew's Console Cowboy is dead or AWOL. Of course, they are not professional assassins, so their combat capabilities are what some Showrunners call suboptimal. Then again, you cannot fight what you cannot find. As a last resort, Infiltrators can deploy special EMP weaponry requisitioned through their Guild. However, even possession of such materials can result in a minimum of 1 year in the Iso-Cells if they are caught, so they are loath to do so.

INFILTRATOR STAT TABLE

INFILTRATOR							
DEF	HP	FW	MOV	MEL	AIM	STR	MET
5	8	6	5	3	3	5	5

INFILTRATOR STAT INCREASES

Choose one from the table below.

INFILTRATOR STAT INCREASE TABLE	
Option 1	+1 MOV
Option 2	+1 MEL
Option 3	+1 AIM

CARRYING CAPACITY

Six slots.

PRIMARY WEAPON SET

Choose one from: SMG, any one melee weapon, or handgun.

DETERMINE SKILLS

Roll a D6 and consult the table below. Reroll duplicates.

	INFILTRATOR SKILL TABLE		
D6 Result	Stealth	Movement	Professional
1	Disarm	Armor Expertise	Clever
2	Careful Blow	Duck and Weave	Self-Assured
3	Observe	Hasty Charge	Defender
4	Dive For Cover	Hurdler	Solid Footing
5	Shadow Blend	Pop-Up	Sprawl Survivor
6	Flight or Fight	Running Man	Hacking Skill X

STARTING SALARY

120 CC.

RESTRICTIONS

May not have an Armor Bonus over +2.

EDGE

SHADOW DEPLOYMENT

Infiltrators stalk the night while the enemy is blind to their movement. Unless any scenario conditions prevent it, you may deploy the Infiltrator anywhere on the board that is at least 12" away from all enemy models and is behind a terrain feature large enough to conceal it. You may not deploy the Infiltrator inside any terrain piece or behind a locked obstacle. If the Infiltrator's crew deploys before the enemy, it may deploy after the enemy deploys.

RUDIMENTARY HACKING

Infiltrators can hack when necessary, but their skills are very basic. They start with a cyber-deck, which uses the stats below. Through their cyber-deck, they have the *Hacking* ability. Should the infiltrator lose all their cyber-deck's DHP, they may no longer use apps. During the Clean-Up Phase of the game turn after the turn in which they lost their last DHP, they regain 1 DHP and may use their app(s) once again.

INFILTRATOR CYBER-DECK	
CYB	DHP
3	6

APPS

Infiltrators start with the Gatecrasher app.

EMP GRENADE

Infiltrators possess a single use EMP grenade, which they can deploy when things get hairy. The EMP is special ranged attack. It costs 1 AP and targets all models within 5"—enemy, friendly, and the Infiltrator themselves. All firearms, melee weapons, and cybernetics with the *On/Off* special rule are disabled for the entire next game turn.

ADVANCED OPTIONS

TRICKS OF THE TRADE

Roll a D3 and the consult the table below. Reroll duplicates.

INFILTRATOR TRICKS OF THE TRADE TABLE	
D3 Result	Infiltrator Tricks of the Trade
1	While Hidden, may move 4" instead of 3".
2	While Hidden, may not be targeted with Suppressive Fire.
3	While Hidden, enemy models suffer a -1 penalty to all spotting attempts.

PERSONAL MOTIVATION

Remain Hidden for three or more turns—they do not have to be consecutive turns.

Masque

"I'm paid to be everywhere and nowhere at the same time. I got a million views on the HyperNET, but they'll never see me coming."

AKA Faceless, Influencers, Emotion Hackers

WHO THEY ARE

HyperNET mavens and stars, Masques maintain hundreds of different online profiles and avatars, all to feed the media-hungry public. Counted among their number are washed up minor musicos, unscrupulous social scientists, and bored veterans of the entertainment industry—all with a lack of ethics and a knack for social engineering.

WHAT THEY DO

Armor and stealth technology can fail, but deception never goes out of style. Masques are savvy social engineers that use their charisma and understanding of human psychology to boost the Showrunner's reputation online through social media blitzes, and move among the populace as a literal Showrunner on the battlefield. They are so adept at blending in with the humanity of the Sprawl, no one notices when they step out of the crowd to strike a vulnerable enemy.

INFILTRATOR STAT TABLE

MASQUE							
DEF	HP	FW	MOV	MEL	AIM	STR	MET
5	8	6	5	3	3	5	5

INFILTRATOR STAT INCREASES

Choose one from the table below.

INFILTRATOR STAT INCREASE TABLE	
Option 1	+1 MOV and +1 AIM
Option 2	+1 MOV and +1 MEL
Option 3	+1 AIM and +1 MEL

CARRYING CAPACITY

Six slots.

PRIMARY WEAPON SET

Choose one from: SMG or any one melee weapon or handgun.

DETERMINE SKILLS

Roll a D6 and consult the table below. Reroll duplicates.

MASQUE SKILL TABLE			
D6 Result	Stealth	Movement	Professional
1	Disarm	Armor Expertise	Clever
2	Careful Blow	Duck and Weave	Self-Assured
3	Observe	Hasty Charge	Defender
4	Dive For Cover	Hurdler	Solid Footing
5	Shadow Blend	Pop-Up	Sprawl Survivor
6	Flight or Fight	Running Man	Fearful Reputation

STARTING SALARY

100 CC.

RESTRICTIONS

Cannot carry any non-concealable items.

EDGE

ONE WITH THE CROWD

Masques can masterfully blend in with the Sprawl's masses using special chrome or quick-change clothes and hologram make-up. Once per game turn, the Masque may reroll a failed Survival Test when attempting to blend in with a crowd. Further, when moving between crowds, they may move to another crowd within 12" instead of 9". Finally, leaving a crowd does not cost the masque AP, though they still may only enter/exit a crowd once per turn.

FLASH MOB

It may seem as though Masques can summon crowds of Sprawlers out of thin air but this is usually just a flash mob the Masque coordinated online to add some fun to the JOBOP. Once per game, replace any single bystander within 6" of the Masque with a bystander crowd. Remove the single model and place the middle of the crowd template directly over the location from which the single bystander was removed. Remove any other models within the crowd template from the table—remove bystanders from the game, move NPCs and player-controlled models to the exterior of the crowd template in any direction the model's controller wishes. Any Masque within the template automatically blends in with the crowd.

ADVANCED OPTIONS

TRICKS OF THE TRADE

Roll a D3 and consult the table below. Reroll duplicates.

Infiltrator Tricks of the Trade Table	
D3 Result	Masque Tricks of the Trade
1	Gain +1 MET when within 6" of a bystander.
2	Gain +1 MEL and STR on any game turn in which they emerge from a bystander crowd.
3	All ranged attacks against the Masque suffer a -1 to hit when this model is within 3" of a bystander.

PERSONAL MOTIVATION

Successfully blend in with a crowd or take an enemy model out of-action.

Street Doc

"We're all dying; I'm just here to slow the process."

AKA Asphalt Angels, Harmacists, Lifelines, Cutters, MED-OPS, Trauma Queens

WHO THEY ARE

Like anything important in the Sprawl, the corporations control medical care so they can maximize profits. For most of the masses, this equates to long lines and crowded waiting rooms. However, if you are a member of the elite, you can receive treatment you would have thought to be science fiction just a few generations ago. Beyond those two poles, a third option exists. If you have credits to spare and a need to remain anonymous, a Street Doc can patch you up just as well as any *official* doctor. Some Street Docs are former corporate or Gov.Mil who now operate independently. Others are technical specialists who received some basic medical training that they boosted with neural implants. The remainder are basically enthusiastic butchers. You can usually find Street Docs in back-alley clinics or retail health centers, but for Showrunners willing to shell out for hazard pay, they can hire certain Street Docs for missions where they not only assume, but expect casualties.

WHAT THEY DO

Street Docs are the crew's medical support—they are paid to keep the Showrunner and crew up and fighting. This means they must perform battlefield triage under immense pressure. Thus, they carry several specialist's tools, such as medical sprays, Black Market skin regenerators, laser-scalpers, icers, and the like. A secondary benefit of having a Street Doc in the crew is that the rest of the crew appreciates the extra survival insurance and are more willing to stick around when the fighting gets brutal, since the doc is there to patch them up afterward.

STREET DOC STAT TABLE

STREET DOC							
DEF	HP	FW	MOV	MEL	AIM	STR	MET
5	8	6	5	3	3	5	5

STAT INCREASES

Choose one from the table below.

STREET DOC STAT INCREASE TABLE	
Option 1	+1 MET
Option 2	+1 MEL and +1 AIM
Option 3	+2 HP

CARRYING CAPACITY

Eight slots.

PRIMARY WEAPON SET

None. Street Docs do not extensively train with weaponry, so they cannot choose a Primary Weapon. However, as a badge of their profession, many choose to carry a collapse stave. This weapon is easy to master, light to carry, and signifies to the enemy that they are here to heal. In the gig economy, the enemy operatives you fight today may be fighting by your side tomorrow. Therefore, it is a good idea to start off in the Doc's good graces. The collapsible stave's stats and cost are listed below:

Type	Melee Range	Strength/Damage	Special Rules	Slots	CC Cost
Collapsible Stave	1"	STR+1	Defensive	1	Free

DETERMINE SKILLS

Roll a D6 and consult the table below. Reroll duplicates.

STREET DOC SKILL TABLE			
D6 Result	Do No Harm	Grace Under Fire	Professional
1	Disarm	Quick	Clever
2	Careful Blow	Duck and Weave	Running Man
3	Observe	Dive For Cover	Armored Expertise
4	Opportunist	Hurdler	Pop-Up
5	Defender	Do or Die	Sprawl Survivor
6	Flight or Fight	Self-Assured	Trekker

STARTING SALARY

80 CC.

RESTRICTIONS

May not purchase or use a long gun.

MEDICAL KNOWLEDGE

Street Docs stabilize wounds and get models back into the fight at quickly as possible. They must spend 1 AP and then pass an Intelligence Test to attempt one of the following actions:

- Stabilize an out-of-action model. A stabilized, out-of-action model receives +2 to its roll against the *Survival Table*.
- Bring an out-of-action model back into play. Place the model prone; it counts as Injured and regains 2 HP. The Medical Test for this action suffers a -2 penalty, due to complexity.
- Heal D3 HP for a model missing any number of HP. The Street Doc cannot perform this action on out-of-action models.
- Street Docs may only attempt Medical Knowledge actions to assist models with which they have base contact. A failure means the AP is wasted, but neither the Street Doc nor the victim suffers any ill effects.

LIFE SAVER

Having a Street Doc around greatly increases everyone's chances of surviving the mission—a real team-motivating feature. Operatives within 6" of a friendly Street Doc receive a +1 bonus to Morale and Grazed Tests.

ADVANCED OPTIONS

TRICKS OF THE TRADE

Roll a D3 and consult the table below. Reroll duplicates.

STREET DOC TRICKS OF THE TRADE TABLE	
D3 Result	Street Doc Tricks of the Trade
1	Once per turn, add +2 to your Move stat when doing so allows you to end in base contact with a friendly model.
2	Gain a +1 bonus to Medical Tests.
3	May attempt Medical Tests on models up to 1" away, instead of needing to be in base contact.

PERSONAL MOTIVATION

Heal 3 or more HP during the game or bring an out-of-action model back in the game.

Sprawl Ronin

"My fees are non-negotiable. Though, upon my death or yours, your next-of-kin will receive a full refund. That is just a formality, though; I don't plan to ever die."

Jin-Roh, Sprawl Ronin

AKA Sprawl Samurai, Razor Girls/Guys, Deathmarks

WHO THEY ARE

The Sprawl is a dangerous place, and many monsters stalk the shadows. Psychotic Cyborgs, Ganger punks, corporate mercenaries; they are all willing to kill for fun or pay. Showrunners are always looking for protection, but the most discerning want more than simple muscle. They prefer something deadly—someone who would never start a fight, but could always end one.... someone sharp, like a razor's edge: the Sprawl Ronin.

Ronin are combat masters with advanced training in either ranged or melee combat. They combine their skills with cybernetic enhancements to become truly deadly fighters. While the name Ronin harkens back to the days of the Samurai, it is a mistake to assume a Ronin follows a code of conduct or has a sense of honor—though many do. The term Ronin simply implies that they are masterful warriors and are willing to accept payment for their services.

WHAT THEY DO

Combat operations, wet work, asset protection, and more—the Sprawl Ronin does it all, if it involves violence. Anything beyond that and you are out of luck. They leave the tech-head stuff to the Console Cowboys and the shot-calling to the Enforcers. Their job is to stay on guard, keep the team safe from trouble, and meet opponents blade to blade (or with a well-placed bullet).

SPRAWL RONIN STAT TABLE

SPRAWL RONIN							
DEF	HP	FW	MOV	MEL	AIM	STR	MET
5	8	6	5	3	3	5	5

SPRAWL RONIN STAT INCREASES

Choose one from the table below.

SPRAWL RONIN STAT INCREASE TABLE	
Option 1	+1 MOV and +1 AIM
Option 2	+2 MEL
Option 3	+1 AIM and +1 MEL
Option 4	+1 MOV and +1 MEL

DETERMINE SKILLS

Roll a D6 and consult the table below. Reroll duplicates.

SPRAWL RONIN SKILL TABLE			
D6 Result	Martial Arts	Marksmanship	Professional
1	Against All Odds	Called Shot	Bullet Magnet
2	Careful Blow	Marksman	Fearful Reputation
3	Counter-Weight Throw	Deadeye	Hard as Nails
4	Defender	Fast-Tracker	Solid Footing
5	Critical Block	Careful Shooting	Armored Expertise
6	Opportunist	Steady Hands	First to the Fight

STARTING SALARY

100 CC.

RESTRICTIONS

None.

EDGE

LIGHTNING REFLEXES

The Ronin has an almost supernatural ability that allows them to respond before their opponent. Once per game turn, the Ronin may make an opposed Agility Test against an enemy model that just activated. If the Ronin wins, it activates first. Then, the interrupted model may continue its activation. If the Ronin fails the test, it may not use this ability for the rest of the game turn.

CARRYING CAPACITY

Eight slots.

CHOOSE PRIMARY WEAPON SET

Choose from one melee weapon, handgun, or long gun.

ADVANCED OPTIONS

TRICKS OF THE TRADE

Roll a D3 and consult the table below. Reroll duplicates.

SPRAWL RONIN TRICKS OF THE TRADE TABLE	
D3 Result	**Tricks of the Trade**
1	Gain the *Quick* skill.
2	Receive a +1 bonus to all Activation Tests.
3	Gain the *Multiple Strikes* skill.

PERSONAL MOTIVATION

Take another Sprawl Ronin, Enforcer, or Showrunner out-of-action or deal 12 total points of damage.

"I don't care where I've been, only where I'm going… preferably quickly!"

AKA Bounders, Freerunners, Traceurs, Wall Dogs

WHO THEY ARE

Tracers—as in, trace the path—are masters at moving through the urban landscape as quickly and efficiently as possible. Their art is based on the precepts of Parkour and free-running, and honed over decades to allow them to perform almost supernatural feats like vaulting over walls, running along narrow surfaces, and executing perfectly timed jumps. While the purists among them abhor any mechanical enhancements, freelance Tracers that run with Showrunner crews tend to utilize cybernetics and other accoutrements to boost their already formidable prowess. Favored cybernetics among Tracers include leg-boosts, hand-anchors, and micro-jump jets. Specialty gear, such as jump-boots and Cat's Claws™ are equally popular for those who cannot afford the in-built options.

WHAT THEY DO

Tracer specialties gravitate toward transport, reconnaissance, and pathfinding. Showrunners who appreciate their speed and abilities to reach new heights quickly favor Tracers. Due to their enhanced speed and economical movement, Tracers excel at rapidly transporting vital packages, getting the drop on hard to find snipers and remotes, and getting the low-down on a rival's turf. Guaranteed disruptions of enemy movements are also included, at no extra cost.

TRACER STAT TABLE

TRACER							
DEF	HP	FW	MOV	MEL	AIM	STR	MET
5	8	6	5	3	3	5	5

TRACER STAT INCREASES

Choose one from the table below.

TRACER STAT INCREASE TABLE	
Option 1	+1 MOV and +1 AIM
Option 2	+1 MOV and +1 MEL
Option 3	+1 AIM and +1 MEL
Option 4	+2 MOV

CARRYING CAPACITY

Six slots.

CHOOSE PRIMARY WEAPON SET (CHOOSE ONE)

SMG or any one melee weapon or handgun.

DETERMINE SKILLS

Roll a D6 and consult the table below. Reroll duplicates.

TRACER SKILL TABLE			
D6 Result	Martial Arts	Speed	Professional
1	Against All Odds	Armor Expertise	Brave
2	Careful Blow	Duck and Weave	First to the Fight
3	Counter-Weight Throw	Hasty Charge	Ranger
4	Defender	Dive For Cover	Solid Footing
5	Critical Block	Pop-Up	Flight or Fight
6	Opportunist	Running Man	Do or Die

STARTING SALARY

100 CC.

RESTRICTIONS

Cannot have an Armor Bonus higher than +2.

EDGE

FREE-RUNNING

Tracers know the secret to traveling across the Sprawl at breakneck speeds. Thus, Tracers ignore movement penalties for crossing linear terrain up to 1" high and 2" wide. Additionally, they may reroll any failed tests for climbing and they may make an Agility Test to perform any of the following stunts:

- Reduce any fall by 2". They may only use this ability once per fall.
- Cross difficult terrain without a movement penalty.
- Climb up a piece of linear terrain up to 2" high without a movement penalty.

A Tracer may make multiple tests each turn but may only test for each specific piece of terrain once per turn. If a Tracer fails an Agility Test, they suffer no ill effects, but must abide by the usual rules (suffer the movement penalty, etc.).

TRICKS OF THE TRADE

Roll a D3 and consult the table below. Reroll duplicates.

TRACER TRICKS OF THE TRADE TABLE	
D3 Result	Tracer Tricks of the Trade
1	Gain a +2 bonus to all attempts to disengage from combat.
2	Gain +2 to Activation Tests when at least 12" away from an enemy model.
3	All ranged attacks that originate more than 12" away suffer a -1 penalty to AIM. May combine this ability with *Duck and Weave*.

PERSONAL MOTIVATION

Move more than 18" total during a game. This includes horizontal and vertical distances.

BLACK MARKET

"Sure, it's expensive. 2000 creds for one gun is probably a lot for someone just starting out, but this is no Misa-2 garbage—this pistol is the real deal. 100% accurate genetic reader, ain't no one going to fire this gun but you. Fully auto, flechette ammo, neural link compatible. Look, it even has a maker's mark. You won't see that on some stamped out, crap plastic. You want to impress the local trash, this is the gun for you."

Máximo CRED$4VR San Martín

Out in the street, anything and everything is for sale if you have enough CC and the right connections. Of course, quality and variety vary a great deal. Those with corporate contacts can custom order hand-crafted items that take true artists hundreds of hours to make from well-lit boutiques. Those with less access must be a bit less discerning. Still, most corporate economic zones have a robust Black Market, where you can purchase weapons, cyberware, and other useful items. All Showrunners have a least one go-to fixer who can provide what they need or knows someone who can.

Using This Chapter

We divide this chapter into two major sections: *Off the Shelf*, which represents common items easily found, and *High-End*—those items only available to the *right* buyer. We then subdivide each section into weapons (melee and ranged), armor, grenades, equipment, and cyberware. Each subsection also lists any special rules associated with the item.

Starting Items

All models, including the Showrunner, start with zero items—unless their profile explicitly states otherwise. You must purchase each of their items individually. Some operatives have restrictions on what they can buy, which is listed in their roster. Barring these rules, any operative may freely purchase and use any item listed in the *Off the Shelf* section. Items in the *High-End* section are a bit harder to come by and have their own rules for acquisition.

CARRYING CAPACITY

Models have a limit as to how much they can carry when out on a JOBOP. This Carrying Capacity is listed in the model's profile as a number of allowed equipment slots. Each class has a different number of slots—Ronins have extra weapons, whereas Street Docs need their medical supplies and must forgo some killing power. Each weapon and piece of equipment (except grenades), lists the number of slots required to carry it. The combined total of required slots cannot equal more than the model's Carrying Capacity. Note that grenades are generally easy to carry, so models may carry any number of them without affecting their Carrying Capacity. Further, if an item does not list the number of required slots, it does not require any. Note that the number of slots a weapon uses is not necessarily representative of its size, but also the amount of ammunition and other related equipment the model must carry to keep it operational.

Because operatives travel lightly and make extensive use of such items as tactical webbing and magnetic holsters, models may freely switch between weapons and equipment they are carrying without spending AP, unless a special rule prohibits it.

LOOTED ITEMS

Looting seems like such a dirty word but, out in the Sprawl, scavenging from the fallen is as much a tradition as a job for many hardscrabblers. A model may spend 1 AP to pick over a corpse and take any number of items they find. They may also pick up weapons or items that were dropped and not recovered in the same way. However, when using such weapons, the looter suffers a -1 penalty to all to-hit rolls due to lack of familiarity with the weapon. Also, the looter may only use scavenged weapons for the current game. After that, the weapon's original owner regains the weapon, unless they die. This rule helps avoid the unbalancing effect a one-sided battle could have on a crew.

Note that cybernetics cannot be scavenged during game play. Stripping the dead of their now unneeded body parts and hardware is a proud street tradition, but it takes a bit of time and effort to do so—which is beyond the scope of a normal game.

CONCEALED ITEMS

Battles in the Sprawl take place under the noses of the corporate overlords and among the wary public. Only in the most nihilistic of economic zones can operatives walk around with heavy hardware slung over their shoulders and not draw attention to themselves. Even being seen in most zones with a long gun is enough to get you thrown into an Iso-Cell for a good year or so. Because of this constant need to be discreet, weapons, cybernetics, and equipment are classified by whether they are *concealable* or not.

Concealable items are easily hidden on your person without too much work and are designed to be easily and unnoticeably tucked away. The following items are considered concealable:

- Handguns
- Melee weapons (except for the heavy melee weapon)
- Grenades
- Armor weave
- Equipment (except for the articulated weapon harness, underslung shotgun, and underslung grenade launcher).
- Drugs
- Chrome (except for kangaroo extensions, weapon graft, breaching hand, ablative armor, Cat's Claws™, and titanium plating).

Concealable items are used to determine certain effects when attempting to blend into crowds or interact with CORPSEC.

Off The Shelf Items

WEAPON SPECIAL RULES

Below, we list the distinctive rules individual weapons can have. We note any special rules for a weapon in their appropriate section. The rules we present here can apply to both ranged and melee weapons, unless a rule specifically mentions only one weapon type.

BALANCED

This weapon is a finely crafted example of the weapon-maker's art. Add +1 to the user's Melee stat when used to attack, but not to defend.

BLEED

The wicked lacerations this weapon causes can lead to bleed-outs if victims are particularly unlucky. If the user rolls a Critical on the to-wound roll, they do an additional point of damage to the target.

BURST

Burst weapons, also known as automatic weapons, allow the attacker to continue firing for as long as they pull the trigger and ammo is available. When using a weapon with the Burst ability, the attacker no longer has the once per turn shooting limit. Further, if the attacker uses all available AP to shoot, they gain an additional 1 AP with which they may only fire the weapon one final time. All shooting with a Burst weapon follows the rules for multiple shots. You can use this ability even when the attacking model has only 1 AP.

Example: Harry Deborah carries an assault rifle with the Burst ability. On her activation, she gets 2 AP and chooses to let her assault rifle rip. She makes three shots total: one for each normal AP and one extra for using all available AP to fire her weapon. Per the usual rules, she cannot shoot additional targets more than 3" away from the first target and cannot skip over models without putting at least one shot into the closer target.

COMPACT

Its light design allows this weapon to retain its combat efficiency while moving. An attacker may use a compact weapon's Burst ability even if they used a move action this turn. If they moved and fired the weapon at least once, they still gain the additional AP to fire again. The attacker may only use this ability if they performed a move action and then fired—no other use of AP qualifies for gaining the extra shot.

CLOSE RANGE

Some weapons are meant to be deadly when used at extremely close distances. When used at point-blank range, this weapon gains +1 STR and does one extra point of damage.

CONCUSSION

This weapon can leave an opponent reeling after a particularly hard hit. If the attacker rolls a Critical on their to-hit roll, the target loses 1 AP (to a minimum of 0) on its next activation.

DEFENSIVE

This weapon is as effective at stopping mayhem as it is at causing it. When defending in melee, the model receives a +1 bonus to their Melee stat. Reduce all damage dealt with this weapon by 1 (to a minimum of 1).

DISTRACTING

This weapon is usually non-lethal; it is meant to irritate or otherwise distract targets, making them easier to incapacitate. Models hit by a weapon with this rule must pass a Survival Test or suffer a -2 penalty to all Stat and Opposed Tests on their next activation. This includes all melee and ranged attacks.

FLAMMABLE

This weapon gives its wielder the chance to set targets alight. When a weapon with this rule hits a target—whether they are wounded or not—they must pass an Agility Test during the Cleanup Phase of the game turn or suffer a secondary STR 6 hit that does 3 damage when successfully wounding them. If they pass the Agility Test, the flames are extinguished and they take no additional damage.

FLAME TEMPLATE

Some ranged weapons do not fire a single shot, but instead spray their deadly payload over multiple targets. To use the flame template, place the teardrop-shaped template where its small end is touching the attacker's base at any point. All models (both enemy and friendly) who are even partially covered by the template are automatically hit. As flame template weapons do not roll to-hit, ignore all range modifiers.

GAS

This weapon releases toxins or other dangerous substances during the attack, which penetrates unsealed armor and makes the target sick. Attacks with this ability ignore all Armor bonuses.

HAIL OF LEAD

Weapons with this ability are usually heavy automatic weapons designed to unleash a torrent of fire at a target. This rule functions the same way as the Burst ability, but instead of gaining an additional 1 AP to shoot, the model gains 2 AP to shoot.

HEAVY

Heavy weapons are large and unwieldy, though they can do great harm when used properly. Models who use a weapon with this rule suffer a -1 penalty to their Melee stat due to the cumbersome nature of the weapon.

IGNORE ARMOR (#)

This weapon is designed to punch through armor. If the target has an Armor Bonus, reduce it by the amount listed in parentheses when rolling to-wound. The maximum penalty cannot be greater than the target's total Armor Bonus.

IMPROVISED

Improvised weapons can be lamps, bricks, sign posts, or small rocks. Any model may spend 1 AP to scrounge around and immediately pick up an improvised weapon. A model cannot begin the game equipped with an improvised weapon.

INTEGRAL

This model has a weapon directly mounted to their body via cybernetics. No one may disarm or take the weapon from the model during a game, though they may disable it as usual with cyber-attacks. Further, such is the model's familiarity with this weapon that they may reroll a single to-hit die once per game.

KNOCK OUT

This weapon is capable of rendering targets unconscious without killing them. Any model hit by a weapon with this ability must pass a Survival Test or immediately fall unconscious; no to-wound roll is necessary. While unconscious, models are Prone and may not take actions. Instead, at the beginning of their next activation, they may make a free Survival Test to attempt to recover. If a model recovers, it may act as normal. If it fails, it remains unconscious. Models may repeat this test each turn.

LARGE BLAST

Ammunition from ranged weapons with this ability explodes upon hitting its target. Before firing, the attacker should designate a single target model. Place the large 5" template directly over that model. All other models at least partially under the template are hit, as well. Roll to-wound as usual.

LIMITED USE (#)

This weapon's ammo capacity is extremely limited and/or it takes so long to reload that doing so is impossible until the crew return to their base. The number in parentheses shows how many times a model may use this weapon.

MOVE OR FIRE

An attacker must properly brace certain larger weapons before firing them. Models cannot fire weapons with the Move or Fire rule if they move during the same activation.

PISTOL

Pistol weapons are designed to be effective at short ranges, even in melee combat. Models may use a weapon with the Pistol rule even if an enemy model is in base contact. However, they may only target the model in base contact when doing so, and they cannot use the Concentrate action in conjunction with the attack.

POISON

Some weapons are naturally poisonous; some are made so by design. Weapons with the Poison rule allow even the slightest injury to fester, and for long after the injured party believes they are safe. Any model hit—but not wounded—by a weapon with the Poison rule must pass a Survival Test during the Cleanup Phase or suffer an automatic D3 damage points.

SILENT

Preferred by assassins the Sprawl over, Silent weapons generate little to no noise or muzzle flash when fired, which helps conceal the attacker. When a Hidden model fires a weapon with the Silent rule, they do not automatically lose their Hidden status. Instead, every enemy model within range—as determined by spotting rules—may attempt an immediate, free Spot Test. If any of the spotting attempts are successful, the attacking model loses the Hidden status.

SMALL BLAST

Small Blast weapons are less potent or have a more concentrated radius for improved effect than their larger cousins. Weapons with this ability use the same rules as those with Large Blast, except you use the small 3" template, instead.

SMOKE

Operatives use these non-lethal weapons to provide concealment. When using a template weapon with this ability, leave the template in play for D3 turns. Any attack that draws line of sight through or into this area of effect suffers a -2 penalty.

STUN

Weapons with this rule are meant to temporarily blind opponents, cause them to drop their defenses, and leave them vulnerable. Weapons with the Stun special ability do not roll to-wound. Instead, the model hit must pass a Survival Test (MET/TN 10) or lose all AP during its next activation. Note that if this happens, the model's controller should make an Activation Test for the model as usual, to check for turnover.

THROW

Some models may physically throw certain weapons. Models may use a weapon with this rule to make ranged attacks up to 6" away. Unless otherwise noted, once a model throws its weapon, the weapon is gone for the duration of the game. The model regains the weapon for subsequent games.

UNRELIABLE

Not all weapons are created equally. Whether a model has a Bleeding Edge weapon that sporadically fails until they work out the kinks, or a low-quality weapon with a history of poor maintenance, unreliable weapons tend to fail at the worst possible time. Whenever a model rolls a Fumble on a to-hit roll when using a ranged weapon with the Unreliable rule, it receives a Jammed token. The model cannot fire the weapon again until all Jammed tokens are removed. A model may remove one Jammed token for each AP spent to reload, clear, or repair the weapon.

Melee Weapons

"Barbarian. You carry that length of pipe as though you are proud of it. See this sword? This is a hand-forged katana made by the Tenusuki artists in Chiba. Notice the floral pattern on the hilt and the ancient celestial dragon that curves along the blade. This is a work of art as much as it is a weapon. You are not fit to die by this weapon. I do not wish to stain its reputation with your dirty blood. Leave now, or I shall change my mind, gutter rat."

Kikuchi Shuko, Corporate Ronin

Melee weapons cover everything from the common knife to high-end, custom swords. All operatives carry some type of melee weapon—either as backup or because they prefer to kill their enemies up close. This may be as much a matter of practicality as aesthetic choice, as many would-be employers outline in their contracts that they must visually confirm a kill before they render payment. This means operatives must get close to the target. A shot in the dark is easier, by far, but it is also louder and may draw too much attention before the visual confirmation can be made.

MELEE WEAPON CHARACTERISTICS

WEAPON TYPE

The melee weapon's in-game name.

MELEE RANGE

Most melee weapons can only affect enemy models in base contact. Some weapons have a slightly longer reach, which the model may use to make melee attacks up to that range. Note that when models do this, the combatants are not considered locked in combat after the attack resolves, but all other close combat rules apply.

STRENGTH

The weapon's ability to bypass the target's defenses. When rolling to-wound, add the weapon's STR to the model's STR.

SPECIAL RULES

Any exceptions or extra rules inherent to the weapon.

SLOTS

The number of the model's Carrying Capacity slots the item uses.

CC COST

The cost to equip a model with the weapon.

Type	Melee Range	Strength	Special Rules	Slots	CC Cost
MELEE WEAPONS TABLE					
Bludgeon	Base	STR +1	Concussion	1	10
Collapsible Stave*	1"	STR +1	Defensive	1	10
Combat Hatchet	Base	STR +1	Ignore Armor (1), Throw	2	15
Cyber-Strike	Base	STR +1	Integral	0	Free
Heavy Melee Weapon	1"	STR +2	Heavy	2	10
Improvised Melee Weapon	Base	STR	Improvised	1	Free
Unarmed	Base	STR -1	None	N/A	Free
Small Blade	Base	STR +1	Throw	1	10
Sword	1"	STR +1	Bleed	2	15

* This weapon is included here for completeness, but may only be purchased and used if an operative's rules explicitly allow it.

TYPES OF MELEE WEAPONS

BLUDGEON

A thick, stick weapon with a heavy end. Bludgeons may be a simple length of heavy pipe or an advanced military nightstick. A classic weapon that many operatives carry since it is legal in many jurisdictions.

COLLAPSIBLE STAVE

A classic, defensive staff. It may appear to be a club at first glance, but various mechanisms can quickly deploy it into a weapon with reach. Favored by the less-lethal operatives, like Street Docs, who prefer to keep harm at bay rather than causing it.

COMBAT HATCHET

A modern take on an ancient weapon, combat hatchets are patterned after Native American tomahawks but made with modern materials. This may also include hand axes and other small weapons designed to break armor.

CYBER-STRIKE

A Cyber-Strike consists of a solid punch or kick, backed by the force of the model's cybernetics, which can deliver a significant amount of kinetic energy. A model a may choose to count cyber-strike as a Primary Weapon, as it does not count against the model's Carrying Capacity.

IMPROVISED MELEE WEAPON

Improvised weapons are items that are not generally designed for combat but can be used in a pinch. Variants include sign posts, plates, the butt end of a rifle, and other small, heavy items.

HEAVY MELEE WEAPON

A broad category of weapons that includes large, two-handed axes and swords, bulky power tools, such as chainsaws and drills, and other large and dangerous items. Of course, local corporate security does not look kindly on those who carry around such items.

SMALL BLADES

An entire class of knives and similar weapons—including hand axes and cleavers—which a model can wield with one hand and throw short distances. A favorite of Gangers and other criminal elements.

SWORD

A weapon with a handle and a single, long, very sharp blade. This includes any number of variants, such as katanas, combat machetes, and so on. Ronin and other deadly street fighters who care more about a weapon's lethality than its legality carry swords.

UNARMED

Though not as dangerous as using a weapon, a good solid kick or punch can be just as effective when stuck in a tight situation. All models can make unarmed attacks and cannot be disarmed of the ability to do so.

Ranged Weapons

"Every time I pull the trigger, I always make this "pew" sound in my head. Shooting people reminds me of this old vid-cade in my home district. It had this shoot'em game that made the same sound when you bagged a zombie. It was fun, and killing is fun; so, I guess I just connect the two."

"Black" Tom Grady, Enforcer

Guns rule the street. It is rare for operatives to not pack some type of heat, even if it is just a pistol for emergencies. Guns come in all manners of size, quality, and caliber. Operatives can purchase them legally in many places and though the rules vary with jurisdiction, most allow defensive weaponry such as pistols and shotguns. If operatives need anything bigger or fancier, they must talk to a black market arms dealer or a street fixer. However, it is not uncommon for ex-military and ex-law enforcement operatives to take their service weapons home with them, either stolen or as part of their out-processing pay.

Ranged weapons fall into three broad categories: Handguns, Long Guns, and Support. We describe each in detail later.

RANGED WEAPON CHARACTERISTICS

WEAPON TYPE

The ranged weapon's in-game name.

RANGE

The farthest distance a weapon can reasonably shoot. Some weapons use the flame template for range. See *Flame Template* under *Ranged Weapons Abilities* for further information (page 128).

STRENGTH

The weapon's ability to bypass the target's defenses. Weapon Strength is a static number.

SPECIAL RULES

Any exceptions or extra rules inherent to the weapon.

SLOTS

The number of the model's Carrying Capacity slots the weapon uses.

CC COST

The cost to equip a model with the weapon.

HANDGUNS

Handguns include most ranged weapons that require only one hand for effective use. They are generally carried as back-up weapons, but could be the main weapon for lightly armed operatives. Handguns are light and easy to carry.

HANDGUNS TABLE					
Type	Range	Strength	Slots	Special Rules	
Crossbow Pistol	12"	5	1	Silent, Pistol	10
Handcannon	10"	7	2	Pistol	15
Light SMG	16"	6	2	Burst, Compact	15
Machine Pistol	12"	6	1	Burst, Compact, Pistol	15
Pistol	12"	6	1	Pistol	10
Taser Pistol	12"	N/A	1	Knock Out, Pistol	15
Vapor Pistol	Flame Template	6	1	Flame Template, Gas, Limited Use (2), Pistol, Silent	15

TYPES OF HANDGUN

CROSSBOW PISTOL

Crossbow pistols are relatively rare, due to their low fatality rate. However, they are easily concealable and virtually silent.

HANDCANNON

Just because a gun is small does not mean it cannot pack a punch. Trading some range for more stopping power, these large caliber pistols are popular with Cyborgs who suffer from cyber-psychosis and factions tasked to hunt bots.

LIGHT SUBMACHINE GUN (SMG)

A fully automatic firearm, the SMG is essentially the carbine version of the assault rifle. Chambered for pistol ammunition, the SMG is capable of a withering hail of fire at short ranges.

MACHINE PISTOL

A small, compact weapon, the machine pistol is also fully automatic. Though it lacks the range of SMGs and assault rifles, the machine pistol does have a high rate of fire and is more portable.

PISTOL

The pistol is by far the most ubiquitous firearm operatives carry in the Sprawl. Made in bulk by multiple armories, pistol quality ranges from *outstanding* to *close your eyes before you fire*. Because they are cheap and readily available, pistols are a common back-up weapon. They are also typically the first weapon newly minted operatives and criminals carry.

TASER PISTOL

Designed solely for its concealability and non-lethality, the taser pistol is a common item for sale across the Sprawl, and—more importantly—is legal almost everywhere. Taser pistols have tongs that attach to conductive nano-cable, which an operative can launch short distances. Upon contact with the target, a low-voltage but disabling jolt of electricity shoots through the cable.

VAPOR PISTOL

An unusual weapon for sure, but one sold in many bodegas and other convenience stores. Vapor pistols are primarily sold for self-defense, but they are also a preferred weapon for operatives who wish to avoid attention.

LONG GUNS

Long guns are weapons that have longer barrels than the average pistol. Designed to be held in both hands and braced against the shoulder, long guns have great firing capacity, superior range, and significant stopping power. Long guns are a staple of law enforcement and military forces, as well as dangerous street criminals and civilians obsessed with home defense.

Type	Range	Strength	Slots	Special Rules	CC Cost
Assault Rifle	24"	7	2	Burst	20
Heavy SMG	20"	6	2	Burst, Compact	18
Modern Bow	24"	6	2	Silent	15
Rifle	30"	7	2	N/A	15
Shotgun	16"	7	2	Close Range	15

LONG GUNS TABLE

TYPES OF LONG GUN

ASSAULT RIFLE

The standard issue firearm for all corporate and Gov.Mil military forces, the assault rifle is powerful, easy to maintain, and has a large rate of fire. Though they are highly illegal for civilians to possess in most jurisdictions, a large number slip through the cracks. Therefore, operatives can find them in most corners of the Sprawl.

HEAVY SMG

A larger version of the light SMG, the heavy SMG uses a larger caliber of ammunition but retains its smaller cousin's maneuverability and high rate of fire.

MODERN BOW

This weapon type includes all modern manufactures of the ancient, drawstring weapon, including compound bows, crossbows, and others. Operatives who like to work quietly or have a flare for the unusual prefer modern bows.

RIFLE

The rifle is a single-chamber firearm designed to be fired from the shoulder and capable of accurate fire at long range. Though they lack rapid-fire ability, rifles are much easier to obtain than assault rifles.

SHOTGUN

A simple but brutal firearm, the shotgun is a firearm with either a single or double-barrel that shoots a burst of smaller projectiles. Designed for close-range work, operatives favor the shotgun for its ruggedness and solid *thump* when fired.

SUPPORT WEAPONS

Support weapons are not a common addition to a crew's arsenal. These powerful weapons are the hallmark of military forces or specialized forms of warfare. Thus, it is expensive to not only purchase them, but also to maintain them and keep them in ammo. Still, support weapons are devastating and can turn the tide of battle if operatives use them correctly.

EQUIPPING SUPPORT WEAPONS

Only models with the *Up-Armed* special rule may purchase and use support weapons. This prevents a member of the crew passing a support weapon to another model or scavenging it.

SUPPORT WEAPONS TABLE					
Type	Range	Strength	Slots	Special Rules	CC Cost
Flamethrower	Flame Template	6	3	Flammable, Limited Use (3)	20
Grenade Launcher	24"	Varies	3	Must purchase ammo separately	15
Light Machine Gun (LMG)	30"	8	4	Burst, Move or Fire	30
Minigun	30"	6	4	Hail of Fire, Unreliable	30
Sniper Rifle	36"	7	3	Move or Fire, +1 to Hit at 18" or more	20

FLAMETHROWER

Designed to shoot gouts of flame over small distances, flamethrowers are the hallmark weapon of pyromaniacs and military forces specialized in urban warfare. They are a rare sight, as they are particularly unsubtle and uniquely terrible weapons.

GRENADE LAUNCHER

Typically a stand-alone weapon, a grenade launcher can lob various grenades farther than an operative can throw them. There is no standard ammunition for the grenade launcher—it can launch any type of grenade the operative carries. The grenade launcher follows the rules for grenades, except its range is 24" instead of 6".

LIGHT MACHINE GUN (LMG)

A squad support weapon, the LMG is designed to give a single man the firing capability of a small squad and the ability to engage light to medium armored targets. Acquiring an LMG on the black market is expensive; being caught by CORPSEC with one can lead to an especially harsh punishment.

MINIGUN

Another *"off the hover truck"* black market item stolen from armories and traded by dirty CORPSEC officers, the minigun has a rate of fire unmatched by most other firearms. It compensates for this by being exceedingly heavy, requiring constant barrel replacement, and having a high jamming probability.

SNIPER RIFLE

A specialized military weapon for taking out important targets, sniper rifles come with optics or a powerful scope that allow the shooter extreme accuracy at range, at the expense of maneuverability. When firing a sniper rifle, the model gains a +1 bonus on its to-hit roll if the target is at least 18" away.

GRENADES

"Boom-Boom likes things that go boom."

Boom-Boom, Ganger

Grenades are small hand-held explosives operatives can throw at enemies, either to cause injury or otherwise debilitate them. Operatives can always acquire grenades in the special *"behind the counter"* section of their friendly, neighborhood self-defense dealer.

USING GRENADES

Grenades operate like other ranged weapons, with the following exceptions:

- Grenades have a range of 6".
- When throwing grenades, the attacker may target any point within range. The target does not have to be a single model or even within line of sight, as the attacker may throw a grenade over terrain. Players should be reasonable with their presumed targets.
- Grenades with the *Unreliable* special rule do not receive a Jammed token with a Fumble. Instead, the grenade fails to explode and is wasted.
- Should the model fail a ranged attack, the grenade deviates. Center the appropriate blast template over the intended target and roll a scatter roll, then a D6. The template moves D6" in the direction of the scatter roll result. Resolve the effects of the blast as usual on models underneath the template. Note that if the attacker did not have line of sight to the original target, the template deviates 2D6", instead.
- Operatives purchase grenades as single, one-use items and may purchase as many as they like. Grenades replenish at the beginning of each game. For example, an operative who buys frag grenades twice may use up to two per game.

GRENADE CHARACTERISTICS

GRENADE TYPE

The grenade's in-game name.

STRENGTH

The grenade's ability to bypass the target's defenses. Grenade weapon Strength is a static number.

SPECIAL RULES

Any exceptions or extra rules inherent to the grenade.

CC COST

The cost to equip a model with this grenade.

GRENADE TYPE TABLE			
Grenade Type	Strength	Special Rules	CC Cost
Flash Bang	N/A	Limited Use (1), Large Blast, Stun	10
Fragmentation	7	Limited Use (1), Small Blast	5
Molotov Cocktail	5	Flammable, Limited Use (1), Small Blast	5
Sleep Grenade	N/A	Gas, Knock Out, Limited Use (1), Small Blast	10
Smoke Grenade	N/A	Limited Use (1), Smoke, Large Blast	10
Tear Gas	N/A	Distracting, Gas, Large Blast, Limited Use (1)	10

TYPES OF GRENADE

FLASH BANGS

Also called stun grenades, CORPSEC commonly uses flash bangs as a non-lethal suppression device. Flash bangs use a concussive blast combined with a chemical flash to disorient the victim's senses, rendering them helpless for a few precious seconds.

FRAGMENTATION GRENADES

This standard grenade type is found all over the world, not just in the Sprawl. The frag grenade, as it is also called, employs a concussive blast and jagged shrapnel to disorient and injure a victim.

SMOKE GRENADES

Operatives primarily use smoke grenades to conceal movement and provide cover for troops who need to close distances where there is no terrain to hide behind.

MOLOTOV COCKTAIL

Easy and cheap to manufacture, though not particularly deadly, the Molotov cocktail is simple a mixture of combustible liquid stored in a bottle that an operative then lights before throwing. You cannot use Molotov cocktails with the grenade launcher.

SLEEP GRENADE

Sleep grenades are uncommon, sought-after items. They use a special gas that remains inert until exposed to oxygen, which then renders targets unconscious. They are a favorite of bail bondsman, freelancer gaolers, and other operatives who specialize in *bringing 'em in alive*.

TEAR GAS

Another non-lethal favorite of CORPSEC, tear gas works by chemically assaulting a target's senses, causing tears, irritation, and pain.

Armor

"You wanna live don't you? Pay now and live; or don't pay and die later. I don't care. I got an order of plasti-kevlar from Pan-Honduras yesterday and there's a metaphorical line around the block waiting to get at it. It's bullet resistant, self-cleaning, and it's got that faux leather look that's really popular with the musicos."

Lon Weiss, Owner, Brigade Tactical Solutions

Armor has always been useful throughout the ages. Nowadays, clunky plastic and metal armor are things of the past. Today, with the modern miracles of advanced synthetics and composites, digital body scanning, and computer tailoring, operatives can have armor designed and built to spec; all while featuring the latest fashion trends. Of course, for those on a more limited budget, the older versions are an affordable—albeit inferior quality—alternative.

USING ARMOR

Armor provides a bonus to the model's defense against all attacks; though, at times, armor may prove less effective against ranged or melee attacks. We call this bonus an Armor Bonus, and you simply add it to the model's Defense stat. Armor Bonus is always followed by a number in parentheses that shows the bonus. Example: Armor Bonus (+2).

MAXIMUM ARMOR BONUS

Models may only wear one type of armor, but cybernetics may also increase their defensive profile. As a universal rule, a model's Armor Bonus may never be higher than +4.

ARMOR BONUS REDUCTION

The Armor Bonus does not permanently increase the model's Defense, as some types of attacks can negate or even ignore a model's Armor Bonus. Note that if an ability negates Armor Bonuses beyond the capacity of the wearer's armor, it does not result in a penalty to the model's Defense.

The reduction amount is shown in parentheses after the name of the ability. For example, if an operative uses a Flechette Defender (2 Pts) to hit a model with Armor Bonus (+2), the model no longer receives a bonus, but its original Defense stat still applies.

ARMOR CHARACTERISTICS

ARMOR TYPE

The armor's in-game name.

ARMOR BONUS (#)

The Armor Bonus this type of armor provides when the model is hit by an attack.

SPECIAL RULES

Any exceptions or extra rules inherent to the armor.

CC COST

The CC cost to equip a model with this armor.

ARMOR SPECIAL RULES

PRIMITIVE

Primitive armor is typically a low-quality, scavenged affair worn by those without better options. It does not provide an Armor Bonus against ranged attacks.

PONDEROUS

While it is not necessarily heavy or bulky, the extra protection this armor provides costs its wearer some mobility. Models wearing ponderous armor suffer a -1 to their Move stat.

RESTRICTIVE

This armor fully covers the wearer's body, restricting any type of quick movement. The wearer suffers a -2 to all Agility Tests.

ARMOR TABLE			
Armor Type	Armor Bonus	Special Rules	CC Cost
Armor Weave	+1	None	20
Combat Armor	+3	Ponderous and Restrictive	40
Gutter Armor	+1	Primitive	10
Security Armor	+2	Restrictive	30

TYPES OF ARMOR

ARMOR WEAVE

Available under a variety of trademarks like Ballisti-Cloth and Under Armor, armor weave is a dense, nano-fiber woven into everyday clothing. It provides decent personal protection at an affordable cost, and claims to draw only the *right kind* of attention.

COMBAT ARMOR

The baseline armor for military units all over the world, combat armor offers significant protection in melee combat and against ballistic weapons. Superior to security armor—at the cost of mobility—combat armor is the lightest, heavy combat armor. Anything heavier requires servo-assistance, such as those found in exoskeleton suits. Combat armor is heavily restricted in almost all corporate economic zones, so it tends to be somewhat uncommon among Showrunner crews. Still, some Ronin and Enforcers have no trouble trading a few extra years in an iso-cell for the ability to survive a bullet to the chest.

GUTTER AMOR

Usually a scavenged affair, gutter armor is better than nothing—but not by much.

SECURITY ARMOR

This set of interlocking, light, full-body armor is standard issue for CORPSEC officers; its identity-concealing helmet is a symbol of corporate authority and oppression. Often referred to as a *"goon suit"*, it offers significant protection against most small arms. Despite being somewhat constrictive, many operatives with a military or law enforcement background retain use of their old suits. When worn under baggy clothing, operatives can reasonably conceal this armor.

Equipment

"Just a slap! That's right friends, that's all it takes to save a life—a simple slap. With Fischer Brand Slap-It Autopatch, you can rid yourself of annoying scratches, cuts, major and minor abrasions, and even significant lacerations. Why spend hours waiting in line at the corporate hospital, or worse, trust your life to an illegal Street Doc? For just a small number of credits, you can "slap and patch" your way to a healthier you! Note that by using Fischer Brand Slap-It Autopatch you agree not to hold Fischer Brand—a subsidiary of Kshatriya Defense Industries—its employees, or shareholders liable for any consequences from using this product; including, but not limited to, cramps, blood in stool, profuse bleeding, diarrhea, chest pain, heart attack, or death."

Radio Advertisement

The bounty for corporate rulership is an assortment of low-quality goods at the right price. Beyond weapons and armor, operatives may find all kinds of items useful—especially if they use the items in ways other than intended.

USING EQUIPMENT

The list below describes the multitude of equipment operatives can purchase and their associated rules. Note that equipment like the poison vial, autopatch, and data-spykes, are one-use items that operatives must repurchase between games. This inconvenience is reflected in their somewhat cheaper costs.

ITEM CHARACTERISTICS

ITEM

The equipment's in-game name.

SLOTS

The number of the model's Carrying Capacity slots the equipment uses.

CC COST

The cost to outfit a model with this equipment.

EQUIPMENT PRICE TABLE		
Item	Slots	CC Cost
Articulated Weapon Harness	2	10
Autopatch	1	10
Ballistic Shield	2	15
Combat Shield	1	10
Climbing Gear	1	10
Data-Spyke	1	10
Holster Guard	1	10
Lucky Object	1	10
Masterwork	1	Double CC
Poison Vial	1	10
Respirator	1	10
Tactical Flashlight	1	10
Underslung Grenade Launcher	1	5
Underslung Shotgun	1	5

TYPES OF EQUIPMENT

ARTICULATED WEAPON HARNESS

A military-grade upgrade often seen on off-planet, corporate marines, the weapon harness employs articulated arms mounted at the operative's waist to hold a heavy weapon. This improves the weapon's weight distribution, reducing user fatigue and allowing a more mobile firing platform. Operatives who carry weapons equipped with this upgrade ignore the *Move or Fire* special rule. However, they still suffer a -1 penalty when rolling to-hit if they fire the weapon after moving.

AUTOPATCH

When medical support is a ways away, operatives can self-administer autopatches to heal minor wounds. Autopatches are small squares of cloth with embedded nanites that administer coagulants, topical painkillers, and shock preventatives. They are not as good as more traditional medical treatments, but they will do in a pinch. Operatives must spend 1 AP to use an autopatch, whether it is on themselves or another model in base contact. The target regains up to 2 HP they lost. Autopatches do not provide benefits to models that are out-of-action.

BALLISTIC SHIELD

A heavy shield typically carried by security forces, the ballistic shield provides additional protection in close combat and against ballistic weapons. When carrying this shield, models always count as being in light cover. Though, this shield does not confer any additional benefit if models are already in cover. Further, models with this shield gain a +1 to their Melee stat when defending in close combat. However, models may only use melee weapons and handguns while holding the shield. To doff the shield, they must spend 1 AP to tuck it away. While the shield is doffed, they do not receive any of its benefits.

COMBAT SHIELD

This is the modern equivalent of an ancient shield, though instead of wood and iron, it is made of advanced polymers and composite plating. Models who carry this shield gain a +1 to their Melee stat in close combat. However, they may only use melee weapons and handguns while holding the shield. To doff the shield, they must spend 1 AP to tuck it away. While the shield is doffed, they do not receive any of its benefits.

CLIMBING GEAR

This collection of grapples, nano-fiber rope, and other materials can create a temporary ladder of sorts. Models with this gear may spend 1 AP to place a token at the base of a single piece of impassable terrain. They may then use this gear to climb the terrain (up to 3" in height). Any model may freely climb the terrain where the token is for the remainder of the game. Models may only use their climbing gear once per game and once they set it up, they cannot move it.

DATA-SPYKE

Banned in nearly all corporate zones, the data-spyke is a brute force hacking tool operatives use to breach network nodes without needing to know how to actually work a computer. About eight inches long, data-spykes are hard spikes that operatives can literally jam into a network node's output port. Once it is in, micro-tendrils emerge and attempt to interface with the network, using a variety of onboard network-cracking programs. Data-spykes are not guaranteed to work and are often slow to get results. Operatives can purchase faster versions, but they have even higher failure rates. If it does work, the data-spyke allows the operative to control the node remotely and/or shoots out a mini-drive full of (hopefully) useful INFO.

Models in base contact with a network node or CAT Terminal can use a data-spyke. They must spend an AP to drive the spyke in, after which they are free to move away. During the Clean-Up Phase of each subsequent turn, players must roll a D6 for each data-spyke they have in operation. If they Fumble, the spyke fails and is lost. If they roll a result of 6, the spyke gains Access to the node for all scenario and game benefits (extra AP for avatars, etc.). Once the operative gains Access, any model (including enemy models) may move in base contact with the node and spend 1 AP to remove the spyke and claim the INFO hosted on the node. Note that data-spykes are one-use items, regardless of success or failure, and they do not regenerate after each game. Operatives must purchase new ones at the start of the next game.

HOLSTER GUARD

Cyber-attacks can lead to weapon malfunction, unintended weapon discharge, and dangerous overheating. To combat this, models can purchase custom holster guards to contain or absorb the damage. Holster guards must be linked to a particular ranged or melee weapon when purchased. When models place a weapon in a holster guard, enemies can no longer target the weapon with cyber-attacks. Of course, models can no longer use the weapon, either. To use the weapon, models must spend 1 AP to remove the guard; they must also spend 1 AP to put the weapon back in the guard. Once the model removes the weapon from the guard, enemies may once again target it with cyber-attacks.

MASTERWORK

The melee weapon with this improvement is an expensive expression of master craftsmanship. Though it is not as high-quality as weapons elite corporate assassins carry, this weapon is still finely made and deadlier than others of its type. A model may apply this improvement to a single melee weapon, which then gains the *Balanced* special rule. If the weapon already has the Balanced rule, it gains the *Ignore Armor (1)* special rule, instead.

Models must purchase this improvement when purchasing the weapon they wish to improve. Applying this improvement doubles the weapon cost. For example, a masterwork bludgeon costs 20 CC total (the improvement cost + the weapon cost).

LUCKY OBJECT

This operative possesses a personal item they believe gives them an edge over the competition—a memento from an old lover, a favorite cigarette lighter, and so on. Though the item provides no practical use, it does seem to inexplicably influence the model's luck. Once per game, a model with this item may reroll a single, non-combat related Stat Test. The model may not use this item on ranged attacks, melee attacks, or cyber-attacks.

POISON VIAL

Sprawlers are always looking for something to give them an extra edge. Operatives can purchase vials of toxic substances—useful for coating piercing weapons—from black market pharmaceutical purveyors or Ganger chemists who concoct the substances themselves. A poison vial allows a model to envenom a single weapon, giving it the Poison weapon ability for the duration of one game. The model may only use the poison vial on the following weapon types: crossbow pistol, modern bow, small blade, sword, heavy melee weapon, and combat hatchet. The poison vial contains enough poison to dose the weapon for two games, after which the model must purchase another vial.

RESPIRATOR

The ability to breathe clean, sterile air an age of ecological catastrophe makes the respirator a wise purchase. The model with this item wears a small, tankless respirator that can recycle air for up to several hours. The model receives +2 DEF against all attacks with the *Gas* special rule and a +2 bonus to Survival Tests that involve any type of gas.

TACTICAL FLASHLIGHT

The Sprawl's power grid is notorious on the best of days, and many enemies use the darkness to conceal their movements. Wise operatives carry a tactical flashlight to bring a little illumination to a situation when needed. Any model with this item can see normally while night-time fighting and in enclosed areas of darkness. They also suffer no combat disadvantages or penalties. However, because the light acts a focal point, enemy models who target this model with ranged attacks suffer no nighttime penalties, either.

UNDERSLUNG GRENADE LAUNCHER

A weapons upgrade seen most often in the military and elite CORPSEC units, the underslung—or under barrel—grenade launcher filtered onto the Sprawl's streets through the usual black market supply chain. While it is usable only once, this upgrade is designed to give a bit of extra fire support to otherwise lightly armed soldiers. The operative must assign this upgrade to a specific long gun or handcannon. Then, once per game, this weapon may use the profile for the grenade launcher instead of its own. Note that a model does not need to have the *Up-Armed* special rule to use this upgrade.

UNDERSLUNG SHOTGUN

A common weapons upgrade for military units assigned to urban warfare duties and CORPSEC breacher teams, this item adds a single-use shotgun to a rapid fire weapon. This allows the operative to trade the ability to lay down heavy fire for the ability to engage a particularly tough target. Note that this upgrade and the weapon it is attached to cannot fire at the same time. The operative must assign this upgrade to a specific long gun or handcannon. Then, once per game, this weapon may use the profile for the shotgun instead of its own.

Drugs

The rather bleak reality of living in the Sprawl, combined with a corporate motive to market profitable (read: addictive) substances to the public, means drugs are a pervasive part of street life. Official corporate-branded pharmaceuticals like Nite-Shyft™, Profiterall™, and Muze™ are available without prescription in nearly every mall, bodega, and convenience store. Operatives can purchase more illicit concoctions, such as Frenzo, Necro-Dust, and Taint in illegal open-air drug markets or from back-alley druggists.

Drugs are a special type of equipment and we categorize them separately for convenience. All drugs are one-time use items. You must purchase new drugs for your models between games. Models ingest drugs before their current mission, so they start the game under its effects. Models may only use one type of drug at a time.

Models with the Bot or Cyborg type may not use drugs, as their bodies cannot process biological inputs.

ADDICTION

Using drugs gives an operative an edge, but this comes at the risk of addiction. At the end of each game, players must roll a D10 for each of their models that used drugs during the game. If they Fumble, the model becomes addicted. Otherwise, the model is fine and staves off needing that next fix. If a model becomes addicted, note the drug to which it is addicted. That model must take that specific drug in subsequent games or suffer a -2 penalty to all Stat Tests (except for those that use their Defense or Firewall stats), as the model suffers withdrawal.

The player must continue to make addiction rolls at the end of a game, even if a model has already become addicted. Should they roll another Fumble, the model's addiction becomes worse and they must purchase and take an additional dose of the drug to stave off withdrawal. Once a model requires two doses of a drug per game, further rolls for addiction are unnecessary—they are truly hooked.

DRUG TYPES

DRUG PRICE TABLE	
Item	CC Cost
Braverax™	10
Frenzo	10
Muze™	10
Necro-Dust	10
Nite-Shyft™	10
Profiterall™	10

BRAVERAX™

An emotional fear-response suppressor, *Braverax*™ is advertised as a safe and effective way for soldiers, first responders, and others who face danger professionally to quell the body's fight or flight response to stress.

- Benefit – The model may reroll all failed Morale and Grazed Tests.
- Side Effect – Should the model roll a Fumble on any Grazed Test they "wig out" a bit and lose 1 AP during their next activation (to a minimum of 0).

FRENZO

An illegal concoction distilled from banned steroids and cocoa derivatives, *Frenzo* places the user in a constant state of aggression.

- Benefit – The model may make any number of charges per game turn, instead of just one. However, they can only do so D3 times per game.
- Side Effect – Even if the model wins a round of melee, they may never push an enemy model out of base contact.

MUZE™

A popular drug among HyperNET users—especially hackers—*Muze*™ is a psychoactive stimulant that overclocks the mind's logic centers and abstract thinking capability. Side effects include agitation and racing thoughts.

- Benefit – The model gains +1 to their Cyber stat when using apps.
- Side Effect – The model suffers a -1 to all melee and ranged attacks.

NECRO-DUST

A rather insidious drug, Necro-Dust gives the user a false sense of invulnerability by numbing their pain centers.

- Benefit – The model starts the game with 3 extra HP.
- Side Effect – A Street Doc attempting to use Medical Knowledge on this model suffers a -2 penalty.

NITE-SHYFT™

A designer drug for wage slaves who must work three shifts to keep the lights on, Nite-Shyft™ suppresses the body's need for sleep and includes various stimulants to induce random bouts of hyperactivity.

- Benefit – The model is immune to the *Knock Out* special rule and similar effects that would render them unconscious. Further, whenever the model rolls a Critical on an Activation Test, they receive 2 extra AP instead of the usual 1.

- Side Effect – This model must use at least one move action during their activation (moving, charging, standing from prone, going prone, etc.) or suffer a -1 penalty to their next Activation Test.

PROFITERALL™

Marketed under the slogan, *"When your best just isn't good enough,"* Profiterall™ has a stress reducing effect much like that of THC in marijuana, but without the latter's lack of focus. Side effects include constant hunger and severe dry mouth.

- Benefit – The model gains +1 MET.
- Side Effect – The model suffers addiction with a result of 1 or 2 on the check for addiction, instead of just with a Fumble.

Chrome

Science has evolved to the point where the differences between man and machine are blurred. Advances in medicine—namely genetic manipulation, biomechanical interfacing, and nanotechnology—have brought incredible changes to mankind. Surgeons can fully replace or improve limbs with bionic options, people have beaten common diseases, and doctors can even stop a person from aging, at least for a time. The human mind can now directly interface with technology through neuro-chips, allowing memories to be made or erased and skills to be engrammed directly to the brain or downloaded via neuro-chipset. In fact, humans even found a form of immortality in the ability to download a human mind into a digital form; though whether this remains the original or becomes a copy is a hotly debated topic. With enough money and resources, no scientific achievement is off the table. Life is good for the media celebrities, the hotshot corporate CEOs, and the moneyed legacy, but for the cast-offs and wage slaves, these miracles are only something to see on holo-vids or to aspire to but never achieve.

However, those in the street always find a way. This amazing technology—found in the back alleys of the Sprawl, on ships out in international waters, and in all the hidden places where the eyes of the mega corporations and the government pass over, can be had for a price. Whether they pay that price in blood, sweat, or tears, there is no shortage of Street Docs, Chrome Butchers, and medical misfits willing to bargain.

LOSING YOUR HUMANITY

All models except Cyborgs start out with Human as their type. When first putting together a new crew or hiring new operatives, models may choose to get cybernetics. Any model that does so changes its type from Human to Augment.

CYBER-SHOCK

For the most part, neural interfacing and body augmentation are compatible and safe, when done slowly over time and in limited amounts. However, even under the best conditions, the human nervous system—and, some philosophers say, the human spirit—is a fragile thing. Too much or cheap and poorly done cyberization can leave mental and physical fatigue on the augmented human. You can partially solve this by using smart drugs and psychological conditioning, but under extreme stress, such as in combat situations, an augmented human can break down. This is called *cyber-shock*, and can lead to any number of temporary afflictions—from paranoia to unconsciousness.

Anytime a model with the Augment type suffers 4 or more points of damage from a single hit or rolls a Fumble on an Activation Test, they must make a Cyber-Shock Test. This is a special test, which the model can only fail with a Fumble or by rolling a 1 on a modified roll. This test can be modified by special penalties.

INSTALLATION POINTS

Cybernetics have a secondary cost, called Installation Points (IP). This is not a monetary cost, but a way to quantify the amount of chrome installed in the body. The higher the IP, the more likely they are to suffer from cyber-shock. For every 10 IP a model has, they suffer a -1 penalty to their Cyber-Shock Test, as described below (always round up). For example, a model with 24 IP suffers a -2 penalty to any Cyber-Shock Test.

CYBER-SHOCK TEST

To make a Cyber-Shock Test, roll a D10 and subtract any penalties for the model's number of IP. With a modified result of result of 2–10, the model holds itself together. With a result of 1, they suffer from cyber-shock. Roll against the following table to see how their cyber-shock affects them:

Die Roll	Result	Effect
CYBER-SHOCK TABLE		
1	System Shock	The model falls unconscious. While unconscious, the model is prone and cannot take any actions. Instead, at the beginning of its next activation, it may make a Mettle Test (MET/TN 10) to rouse itself. If it fails it remains unconscious for the remainder of the turn. Friendly models in base contact may also spend 1 AP to try to rouse the model, which allows the unconscious model to make another Mettle Test.
2	Paranoia	The model moves one full move action away from the nearest model (enemy or friendly). Roll a D10: on a 1–5, the enemy player decides the direction, on a 6–10, the controlling player determines the direction.
3	Obsession	The model may only spend AP this turn to attack or move closer to the nearest enemy model within sight. If no enemy models are within line of sight, the model must move toward the closest friendly model but does not attack them. Treat result as Stupefaction if there are no models within line of sight.
4	Stupefaction	The model automatically fails its next Activation Test.
5–6	Hysteria	During the current activation, the model must use its first AP to take a move action. This must use the model's full MOV, though the controller may decide in which direction the model travels.
7–9	Confusion	The model receives -2 MET for the next game turn.
10	Overconfidence	The model receives +2 to all Will Tests until the start of its next activation.

CYBER-PSYCHOSIS

Cyborgs start out their cybernetic lives overloaded with chrome, often of questionable quality. Because of this, they are especially prone to a rather violent form of cyber-shock called *Cyber-Psychosis*. Cyber-psychosis follows all the normal cyber-shock rules, but instead of rolling against the Cyber-Shock Table, you roll against the Cyber-Psychosis Table.

CYBER-PSYCHOSIS TABLE		
Die Roll	Result	Effect
1	Everything's Red!	Like Psycho Time, except the model moves toward the closest model (friend or foe).
2–3	Psycho Time	The model receives +1 AP next turn but must spend all available AP this turn to move the maximum distance possible toward the closest enemy model. The model charges/makes melee attacks if able. Automatically passes all Will Tests until the end of the turn. This effect lasts only one turn.
4–5	System Shock	The model's cyberbody is disabled.
6–7	Senseless	The model automatically fails its next Activation Test.
8–9	Stupefied	The model has -2 MET next turn.
10	Rage	The model receives +1 AP next turn, which it may only use to make a combat attack; if this is not possible, the AP is lost.

ON/OFF

Cyber-attacks can disable cyberware labeled with the *On/Off* special rule. When disabled, the cyberwar simply does not work, which means the operative cannot use or benefit from it until it is switched back on. To do so, the operative must spend 1 AP during their activation and pass an Intelligence Test as described in the *Cyber Warfare* section. Some pieces of chrome may have additional effects when disabled. If this applies, it is explicitly listed under their entry.

BODY LOCATIONS

Chrome is organized by body locations. Players need to note where they install each piece of chrome on their models. If a cyber-attack disables a model's body location, all cybernetics in that location that can be disabled are. Conversely, when the model gets the limb fixed, all chrome installed in it is fixed, as well. The individual body locations include the head, eyes, torso, arms, and legs. For simplicity's sake, we treat arms (and legs) as single locations instead of individual limbs.

AVAILABLE CHROME

You may purchase the following cybernetics for your models. We list each profile under its applicable body location and include the CC and IP Costs.

Name	Body Location	IP	CC Cost
Cyber Arms	Arms	4	10
Cyber-Eyes	Eyes	2	10
Cyber Torso (Heavy)	Torso	6	30
Cyber Torso (Light)	Torso	4	20
Cyber Legs	Legs	4	10
Upgraded Neuro-Chip	Head	1	5

CYBERNETIC BODY PARTS LOCATION TABLE

CYBERNETIC BODY PARTS

CYBER ARMS

Both a common, utilitarian cybernetic replacement and a fashion statement, cyber arms effectively replace the recipient's entire arm or arms with something stronger and more durable. Common aesthetic variants include arms literally coated in chrome, non-humanoid appendages, and hidden weapons. A model outfitted with cyber arms gains +1 STR and can make cyber-strikes (see the cyber-strike profile under the *Melee Weapons* portion of the *Black Market* section, page 132). The cyber arm has the *On/Off* special rule. If disabled, the model suffers -2 STR and cannot make cyber-strikes using their cyber arm.

CYBER EYES

Models with cyber eyes ether have their optic nerve and visual cortex upgraded with synthetic components or their eyeballs replaced entirely, giving them better visual acuity. A model with cyber eyes receives a +2 bonus when making Spot Tests. Cyber eyes have the *On/Off* rule.

CYBER LEGS

Another common limb replacement, cyber legs are most often used to replace legs lost due to injury. However, many operatives have no compunction about visiting the chop-shop for a bit of upgraded speed. Models equipped with cyber legs receive +1 to their Move stat and gain the ability to make cyber-strikes (see the cyber-strike profile under the *Melee Weapons* portion of the *Black Market* section, pages 132). Cyber legs have the *On/Off* special rule, and should they be disabled, the model suffers a -2 penalty to their Move stat and cannot make cyber-strikes using their legs.

CYBER TORSO (HEAVY)

A much heavier variation of the standard cyber torso, the heavy cyber torso uses the fewest biological components possible—in most cases, none at all. The model gains an Armor Bonus (+2) and is immune to weapons with the Gas and Poison rules. However, the model also suffers -1 MOV. A model may only have one type of cyber torso.

CYBER TORSO (LIGHT)

When a full cyber workover is off the table, operatives can choose instead to replace their torso. This is a stop gap measure for many until further cyberization is possible and/or financially feasible. It is no secret that the body's center mass is the most likely place for an operative to get shot, so adding heavy armor and other protective elements is not a bad idea. The model with a cyber torso gains an Armor Bonus (+1) and only suffers the effects of weapons or abilities with the Gas rule on a natural Fumble. A model may only have one type of cyber torso.

UPGRADED NEURO-CHIP

A microprocessor—beyond the minimal installation that most Sprawlers receive at an early age—is integrated directly with the operative's neuronal cell structure. A model with an upgraded neuro-chip gains a +1 bonus to Intelligence Tests. The upgraded neuro-chip has the *On/Off* rule.

CHROME ENHANCEMENTS

The following are body part enhancements that models can purchase in addition to their cybernetic body parts. The model must have the requisite cyber body part to purchase any enhancements for that location.

CHROME ENHANCEMENTS			
Name	Body Location	IP	CC Cost
Booster Switch	Legs	2	10
Brain Boost ™	Head	1	10
Caltrop Flinger	Any*	1	15
Concealed Weapon	Arms	2	15
Dead-Man Switch	Any*	2	5
Emotional Damper	Head	2	15
Faraday Shielding	Torso	1	15
Flash Dampeners	Head	1	15
Kangaroo Extensions	Legs	2	15
Jail Breaker	Any*	2	15
Muscle Augmentation	Arms	2	15
Neural Link	Eyes	2	15
Night Sight	Eyes	1	15
Portable Node	Any*	2	20
Reinforced Skeleton	Torso	2	10
Retractable Blades	Arms/Legs	2	20
Shell Coating	Torso	2	10
Subdermal Armor	Torso	2	15
Weapon Graft	Arms	2	10
Wiry Ligature	Legs	2	15
*You may assign chrome enhancements with this symbol to any location you choose.			

BOOSTER SWITCH

An operative never knows when they may need to be somewhere else without enough time to get there, and the booster switch is the answer to this problem. The booster switch puts the operative's cyber legs into brief overdrive, though the operative may be exhausted afterward. Once per game, when the model makes a second move action, they may move

2D6 instead of the normal 1D6. Further, if their result on their roll totals less than 6, they may treat the result as 6, instead. After using this enhancement, the model suffers -1 MOV for the rest of the game. Booster switch has the *On/Off* rule.

BRAIN BOOST™

Sometimes, timing is everything. Designed to essentially overclock certain brain functions, the Brain Boost™ allows the user to quickly think through complex situations in a matter of seconds. Results may vary, of course. Usable only once per game, Brain Boost allows the model to apply a +4 bonus to any one Intelligence Test, Survival Test, or cyber-attack; attacking or defending. Brain Boost has the *On/Off* rule.

CALTROP FLINGER

A popular piece of chrome for enabling a quick getaway, the flinger shoots a bunch of tiny spikes over a circular area. A model may use this cyberware at any time during its activation—it does not cost AP and the model may only use it once per game. Place a 5" template anywhere touching the model's base. This marks the area in which the caltrops were dropped. This area counts as difficult terrain. Any model that fails any type of Agility Test within it suffers an automatic D3 damage, in addition to any other negative results they may suffer. The caltrop flinger has the *On/Off* rule.

CONCEALED WEAPON

The operative has a firearm installed in their arm cavity, which allows them to discreetly carry the weapon. This install is tied to a single weapon when the operative first purchases it, though they may swap out the weapon between games. The weapon gains the Integral rule and does not count against the model's Carrying Capacity. The operative may only use this cybernetic with weapons that take up two or fewer slots. The weapon also counts as concealable. Concealed weapon has the *On/Off* rule. When disabled, the operative may not use this chrome or its weapon.

DEAD-MAN SWITCH

The ultimate in post-mortem revenge, an operative can have a switch and a small amount of explosives installed internally and timed to explode seconds after their heart stops beating. If this model is taken out-of-action, each other model in base contact must pass an Agility Test or suffer a STR 7 hit. Models equipped with this chrome suffer a -2 to all rolls against the *Survival Table*. If the dead-man switch is disabled, it simply fails to work when the model goes out-of-action. The dead-man switch has the *On/Off* special rule.

EMOTIONAL DAMPENER

A biofeedback device implanted directly into the cortex and linked to the operative's neuro-chip, the emotional dampener clamps down on the body's natural fight or flight response to external stimuli. The emotional damper also inhibits the operative's ability to have pleasurable experiences, such as feelings of joy and happiness. While the operative can turn off the device when not in use, this can lead to drawbacks when the operative is flooded with overwhelming emotions they are not used to having. A model equipped with an emotional dampener can only fail a Will Test with a natural Fumble. Should they fail a Will Test in this manner, or if their emotional dampener is disabled through hacking, they must roll for cyber-shock immediately. The emotional dampener has the *On/Off* rule.

FARADAY SHIELDING

A common upgrade, given the reputation of infiltrator operatives, Faraday Shielding provides basic protection against EMP weaponry by installing a suite of electromagnetic pulse countermeasures in an operative. Should the model suffer an EMP attack, roll a D10. If the result is 7 or higher, the model ignores the effects.

FLASH DAMPENERS

The operative's cyber optics suite is equipped with reflective visor shielding that limits their exposure to sudden bursts of light. Weapons with the *Stun* or *Distracting* special rules that originate from a visual source (such as flash bangs, flasher weapons, dazzle armor, etc.) do not affect this model. Flash dampeners have the *On/Off* rule.

KANGAROO EXTENSIONS

Not for the faint of heart, kangaroo extensions replace the operative's lower legs (or their entire legs) with a pair of ultra-light spring-blades. When properly trained to use them, operatives find the substantial compression forces generated by the spring-blades help them run and jump well above the limits of what humans can normally achieve. Once per turn, when making a move action, the model may make an Agility Test to attempt a special jump. If they fail the test, they are placed prone but are unharmed. If they pass the test, they ignore all linear terrain up to 3" high when moving and may end their movement on top of terrain up to that same height.

JAIL BREAKER

A myriad of chrome installs an operative can use to breaks cuffs, drug guards, or otherwise prevent long-term capture. Perhaps one of the more infamous jail breaker devices is the dentatus. If a model is captured during campaign play as a result of rolling against the *Survival Table*, they may attempt to liberate themselves. This is described in the *Captured* potion of the *Campaigning in the Sprawl* section.

MUSCLE AUGMENTATION

The operative's arm musculature is enhanced with interwoven synthetic muscle fibers and reflexive bone polymers. The model may reroll failed Strength Tests that are unopposed.

NEURAL LINK

Weapons in *Reality's Edge* are sometimes referred to as *smart guns* because they can connect to the firer's neuro-chip via a neural link. This provides much more accurate ballistic fire, as the gun's discharge is tied to the operative's thoughts rather than something old-fashioned like a trigger. The neural link can also read valuable telemetric data from the HyperNET, which provides further accuracy. A model equipped with a neural link gains a +1 bonus when using any long gun or handgun. The neural link has the *On/Off* special rule. When disabled, the model not only loses its bonus but receives a -1 penalty to all long guns and handguns, because it is overly reliant on the neural link.

NIGHT SIGHT

The operative's eyes are upgraded so they can see the ultraviolet spectrum, which allows them to effectively see in the dark at short range. The model does not suffer any penalties associated with night-time fighting rules within 18". Night sight has the *On/Off* rule.

PORTABLE NODE

A friend to combat hackers everywhere, the portable node is an implanted suite of signal repeaters and broadcaster boosters. This adds +1 AP to their shadow backer's avatar and 4" inches to its Tether, as though the crew had Access on a network node. Treat this cybernetic as a network for the purposes of cyber-attacks. Should a rival crew successfully gain Access to the node, they gain its benefits. Should the network be disabled, the penalties are also lost. A portable node never generates INFO.

REINFORCED SKELETON

An expensive piece of chrome that is rather painful to install, the cyber-skeleton considerably strengthens the operative's bone structure via a plasticization process. For a few extra pounds of weight, the body becomes resistant to bone fractures and breaks, and the system shock associated with these ailments. The model gains 2 HP.

RETRACTABLE BLADES

Concealed blades that extend from their arms—or their legs, for a lethal kick—are a hallmark of discrete operatives that prefer to keep a low profile before making a kill. The model is considered equipped with a sword or heavy melee weapon with the *Integral* special rule, which counts as concealable and does not count against the model's Carrying Capacity. Retractable blades have the *On/Off* rule and must be assigned a location (arms or legs) when purchased.

SUBDERMAL ARMOR

The operative has hardened ballistic polymers woven into their epidermis, which costs them a bit of agility. The model receives an Armor Bonus (+1) or a +1 bonus to any armor bonus they already possess (maximum of +4 armor bonus). However, the model also suffers a -1 penalty to all Agility Tests. Operatives may combine subdermal armor with light weave, but if they do, they also suffer a -1 to their Move stat.

SHELL COATING

Ballistic protection for those on a budget, shell coating is not as effective as subdermal armor, but the non-restrictive armor coating does provide a modicum of protection to the operative's most vulnerable body parts. The model receives an Armor Bonus (+1) or a +1 bonus to any armor bonus they already possess (maximum of +4 armor bonus), against any weapon with a Strength of 6 or less. Operatives may combine shell coating with subdermal armor, but if they do, they also suffer a -1 to their Move stat.

WEAPON GRAFT

Operatives who are not concerned with concealment may have a firearm or melee weapon implanted directly onto their arm, with no attempt to hide the installation. This install is tied to a single weapon when the operative first purchases it, though they may swap out the weapon between games. The weapon gains the *Integral* special rule. Further, the exposed weapon is rather intimidating, so enemy models in base contact suffer a -1 to all Will Tests.

WIRY LIGATURE

Some operatives upgrade the muscular ligature in their legs with a flexible polymer coating and micro-servos to greatly increase their reflexes. When purchased, the model gains the Quick skill. If the model already has this skill, they gain the ability to reroll a single Agility Test once per game.

FULL BODY CYBERIZATION

Full body replacements are strictly the Cyborg's purview. As such, unless a model has the Cyborg type, they may not purchase full body cybernetics in one-go—they must piecemeal things over time. Should a model manage to purchase a cyber torso, cyber arms, and cyber legs over time, their type changes to Cyborg.

When building a crew, Cyborgs automatically come with the Cyberbody of your choice as part of their Starting Salary. Cyborgs may not buy individual cyber body parts, except for the cyber eye or an upgraded neuro-chip.

CYBERBODIES AND CYBER-ATTACKS

When a hacker targets a Cyberbody with a cyber-attack, they may choose to disable any individual body location or the whole body. Should a model's Cyberbody be disabled, the model may not take any actions other than attempting to turn themselves back on.

CYBERBODIES

FULL CYBERBODY TABLE		
Name	Install Points Cost	CC Cost
Heavy Cyberbody	14	N/A
Light Cyberbody	12	N/A

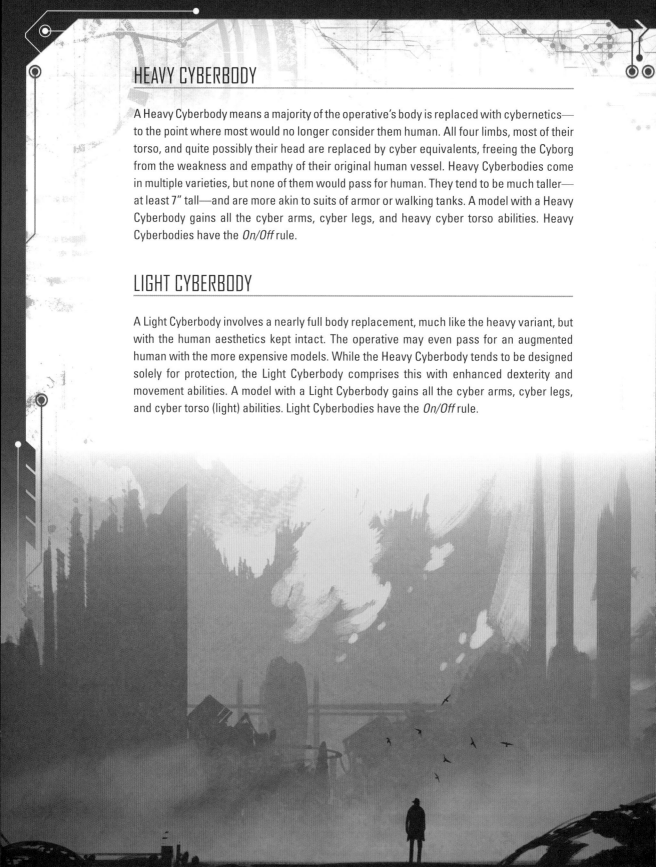

HEAVY CYBERBODY

A Heavy Cyberbody means a majority of the operative's body is replaced with cybernetics—to the point where most would no longer consider them human. All four limbs, most of their torso, and quite possibly their head are replaced by cyber equivalents, freeing the Cyborg from the weakness and empathy of their original human vessel. Heavy Cyberbodies come in multiple varieties, but none of them would pass for human. They tend to be much taller—at least 7" tall—and are more akin to suits of armor or walking tanks. A model with a Heavy Cyberbody gains all the cyber arms, cyber legs, and heavy cyber torso abilities. Heavy Cyberbodies have the *On/Off* rule.

LIGHT CYBERBODY

A Light Cyberbody involves a nearly full body replacement, much like the heavy variant, but with the human aesthetics kept intact. The operative may even pass for an augmented human with the more expensive models. While the Heavy Cyberbody tends to be designed solely for protection, the Light Cyberbody comprises this with enhanced dexterity and movement abilities. A model with a Light Cyberbody gains all the cyber arms, cyber legs, and cyber torso (light) abilities. Light Cyberbodies have the *On/Off* rule.

Drones

Drones are small robotic vehicles that operators can control remotely. They range in size from tiny insect to giant planet crawlers. Drones used for black operations need to be robust with room for weapon mounts and armor plating. This makes the ideal drone about the size of a large dog. As with their size, drones have a lot of variance in body type and source of locomotion, but the most ubiquitous are the quadrupedal animal-like predator and multirotor helo-drone. Between the two types, predators tend be slower and tougher. They are ideal for operations in which models plan to see direct combat. Helo-drones are more maneuverable, as they can hover over terrain and are able to engage targets with their weapons while moving. Neither is superior to the other, which one a crew needs all depends on their mission requirements and the controlling Jockey's predilection.

Drones possess a very rudimentary AI that allows them to easily perform their functions, but they are incapable of independent action in line with the Turing Protocols—a set of standards for computer programs and deep intelligence. Controllers must guide their drones—over time the link between the two becomes almost a bond of sorts. This has been known to lead the drone to display certain personality quirks, such as becoming skittish, aggressive, or over-protective of their controllers.

DRONE EQUIPMENT

Any equipment listed with a drone is subsumed into the drone's cost. Drones with a weapon mount may mount up to two different weapons from the handgun or long gun lists. However, operatives must purchase these separately and may only use one at a time—it is assumed one of the weapons is a back-up.

OTHER RULES

Costs and all other rules are listed in the *Drone Jockey* portion of the *Building Your Crew* section (see page 91).

PREDATOR ATTACK DRONE

A class of quadrupedal drones, predator attack drones have the general appearance of a large dog or cat, albeit with a very robotic aesthetic. Their front legs have sharp claws and/or blades and they are fitted with a high-tension bite, as well.

PREDATOR ATTACK DRONE							
DEF	HP	FW	MOV	MEL	AIM	STR	Met
5(6)	6	6	6	5	3	5	4
Skills and Special Rules							
Bully, Bot, Turing Lock, Zone of Control (12")							
Equipment							
Teeth and Claws, Armor Weave							

MELEE WEAPONS TABLE				
Type	Melee Range	Strength	Special Rules	CC Cost
Teeth and Claws	Base	STR+1	Bleed	Free

PREDATOR FIRE SUPPORT DRONE

A variant of the attack drone, the fire support version maintains the same body and style, but drops the melee weapons in favor of a ranged weapon platform and targeting system. While predator drones lack the flight capability and overall maneuverability of helo-drones, they are overall a much more stable weapons platform.

PREDATOR FIRE SUPPORT DRONE							
DEF	HP	FW	MOV	MEL	AIM	STR	Met
5(6)	6	6	6	3	4	5	4
Skills and Special Rules							
Steady Hands, Turing Lock, Zone of Control (12")							
Equipment							
Integral Weapon Mount, Armor Weave							

FIRE SUPPORT HELO-DRONE

Helo-drones are a common sight in the Sprawl and are extremely popular with Drone Jockeys. A superb and agile weapons platform, fire support helo-drones can dart above the dense terrain in the Sprawl and the effectiveness of its firing is not affected by its mobility.

FIRE SUPPORT HELO-DRONE								
DEF	HP	FW	MOV	MEL	AIM	STR	Met	
5(6)	6	6	7	3	4	4	4	

Skills and Special Rules

Hover, Shoot and Scoot, Turing Lock, Zone of Control (16")

Equipment

Integral Weapon Mount, Armor Weave

SURVEILLANCE HELO-DRONE

Taking advantage of the maneuverability of its basic frame, Drone Jockeys use surveillance drones to support ground forces instead of directly attacking the enemy. The onboard suite of specialist sensors and detectors not only allow the surveillance helo-drone to suss out hidden enemy assets, but also to provide useful environmental and ballistic data to friendly forces, further ensuring that operatives can swiftly deal with any revealed targets.

SURVEILLANCE HELO-DRONE								
DEF	HP	FW	MOV	MEL	AIM	STR	Met	
5(6)	6	6	7	3	3	4	4	

Skills and Special Rules

Detector, Fire Assist, Turing Lock, Zone of Control (16")

Equipment

Sensor Array, Armor Weave

SENSOR ARRAY

A suite of sensors and scanners layered with a behavior prediction program slaved to a drone's resident AI, the sensor array is an asset; though it comes at the cost of any combat ability the drone could have. Drones with a sensor array gain the Detector and Fire Assist skills. The sensor array has the *On/Off* rule. If it is turned off, it no longer provides its native bonuses.

Apps

Apps are the programs hackers use to influence the HyperNET. Apps do not have a CC cost, as each hacker starts with a random assortment. This is subsumed into their costs and starting equipment.

ATTACK APPS

D6 Result	App
ATTACK APPS TABLE	
1	Corrode
2	Decapitate
3	Overheat or Sabotage
4	Overload
5	Nerf-a-lyze
6	Enslave

CORRODE (1 AP)

A highly illegal app that no one trades in the open areas of the HyperNET, though back-alley wares dealers sell it via physical drives and discs. Corrode is designed to slowly break down a Firewall over time and has a range of 8". If successful, it reduces a target's Firewall stat by -2 until the start of the target's next activation or the end of the next turn's Clean-Up Phase if the target does not activate.

DECAPITATE (2 AP)

One of the more potent cyber-dueling applications, a Hacker in possession of Decapitate plays for keeps. Due to its aftermarket inclusion of Black ICE, just having possession of this app is illegal in almost all corporate economic zones. Decapitate targets a model with DHP and has a range of 8". If successful, the target suffers D6+2 digital damage points. If the Hacker rolls a Critical, it does D3 digital damage points and D3 actual damage points from neuro-feedback shock—unless the target is a Virtual being, in which case it does 6 digital damage points, instead. If they roll a Fumble, the Hacker suffers 1 damage point from neuro-feedback shock.

ENSLAVE (1 AP)

The most popular app for pwning, or gaining control of items, robots, and Cyborgs of all types, Enslave assaults the heuristic controls of the targeted entity in the hope of temporarily subverting them. Enslave only targets models with the Bot and Cyborg types and has a range of 8". On a success, the hacker gains control over the target for 1 turn. During that turn, the Hacker may roll for the target's Activation Test during their own initiative. Otherwise, the Hacker determines how the model spends its available AP. On a Critical, the Hacker maintains control for D3 turns, ending on the Clean-Up Phase of the last turn. On a Fumble, the target's Firewall gains +2 until the end of the game.

GATECRASHER (1 AP)

A standard network breaking app, you can find this program—and a thousand others like it—on the cyber-deck of both new and experienced Hackers. While it is not subtle, this workhorse app uses several decryption algorithms to gain access to the targeted network system. Gatecrasher only targets networks and has a range of 0". If the roll is successful, gain Access. If it is a Fumble, the Hacker's crew gains a Trace token. A Critical has no effect.

NERF-A-LYZE (1 AP)

Designated as more of a joke-item than a formal hacking program, Nerf-a-lyze is widely available—even legal in many places—and is often the first app new Hackers use. Despite its trivial label, when a hacker tweaks it just a bit, they can use it to reduce the effectiveness of electric items without doing permanent damage to them. Nerf-a-lyze can target any weapon, cyber body part, individual cybernetic enhancement, bot, or Cyborg. It has a +2 CYB bonus and a range of 12". On a success, the target suffers the Nerf status with a -2 penalty for D3 turns. On a Critical, Nerf-a-lyze disables the target for D3 turns, instead. On a Fumble, the Hacker's crew gains a Trace token.

OVERHEAT (1 AP)

Designed to access the backdoor maintenance programs housed in various corporation-made weaponry, Overheat can give a Hacker temporary control of a distant weapon. Overheat targets weapons carried by other models, which includes cybernetic body parts, enhancements, and all equipment with an attack profile, and it has a range of 8". On a success, the target overheats and the model carrying it automatically takes D3 damage. Criticals have no effect. On a Fumble, the Hacker's crew gains a Trace token.

OVERLOAD (1 AP)

A variant of the popular Sabotage app, Overload trades length of effect for more possible targets. By redistributing the firmware access requests of all data connections in the target's personal area network, Overload can potentially disable multiple items. Overload targets all weapons carried by a model, including any cybernetic weapons and items with a weapon profile, and has a +1 CYB bonus and a range of 12". Do not nominate a single weapon for this attack—on a success, all weapons carried by the target (firearms, melee weapons, etc.) are disabled on the target's next activation. On a Critical, the weapons are disabled for two turns, instead.

SABOTAGE (1 AP)

An app designed to disable enemy electronics, Sabotage is especially popular with pacifist Hackers who would rather not harm their targets, but also wish to stop their targets from harming them. Hackers may use Sabotage to target anything susceptible to the Disable status. On a success, the target is disabled for D3+1 turns. On a Critical, the target is bricked instead. On a Fumble, the Hacker's crew gains a Trace token.

SLICE (1 AP)

Considered the most basic of the Hacker dueling apps, Slice is designed to attack a HyperNET user's connection to the grid. Slice targets models with DHP, provides a +1 CYB bonus, and has a range of 12". On a success, the target suffers D3+1 digital damage. On a Critical, the digital damage is increased to D3+3. Fumbles have no effect.

ENVIRONMENTAL APPS

ENVIRONMENTAL APPS TABLE	
D6 Result	App
1	Light Blast
2	Distortion
3	Control Camera
4	Mischief Maker
5	Raise Barrier
6	Summon Idoru

CONTROL CAMERA

Most buildings in the Sprawl are covered in augmented reality projectors and recording cameras. Who should control these is a matter of hot debate between the corporate overlords and the building owners—though these are often the same. Hackers can extend the range of their electronic attacks by subverting these cameras. Control Camera has a range of 6" and Hackers may only use it to target an intact structure or building. To do so, make a cyber-attack against a Firewall of 4. An enemy player may roll defense for the building. On a success, the Hacker may place a camera token anywhere on the building's exterior; the token must physically touch the building. While in control of the camera, the Hacker can draw line of sight from the camera token and may use the token as a point of origin for any apps. A Hacker can only control one camera token at a time but may dismiss it at any time during their activation. Finally, an enemy Hacker may make a cyber-attack against the camera (again, against a Firewall of 4). If they are successful, remove the camera token.

DISTORTION (1 AP)

Distortion sends out hundreds of multidirectional scrambling algorithms, flooding the localized HyperNET with so much background noise that normal coding and app use is severely hindered. Distortion has range of 8". Make a cyber-attack against a Firewall of 4. This is the HyperNET's innate resistance to the attack. On a success, the Hacker may place a Distortion token anywhere within range. The token has a 4" area of effect and lasts until the beginning of the Hacker's next activation phase. All models within this area of effect suffer -2 to their Cyber stat.

LIGHT BLAST

Nothing gets an enemy's attention like 1,600,000 lumens to the face. Hackers can hack into a building's external spotlights, cranking them to max power to temporarily blind the unwary. Light Blast has a range of 8" and may only target a single location or model within 6" of an intact structure or building. Make a cyber-attack against a Firewall of 4. An enemy player may roll defense for the building. On a success, place the Small Blast template over the designated location. All models under the template must pass a Survival Test (MET/ TN 10) or lose all AP during their next activation. Note that if this happens, the model's controller should take an Activation test for the model as usual, to check for turnover.

MISCHIEF MAKER

Holo-projectors can be found on almost all buildings, lighting up the dark skies with bright advertising and realistic-looking virtual projections. Mischievous Hackers are known to co-opt these projectors to showcase their own creations. By tweaking this formula, combat Hackers can broadcast their own large, weird, scary, or some combination thereof creations, leaving their enemies distracted at an opportune time. Mischief Maker has a range of 8" and may only be used to target a single location or model within 6" of an intact structure or building. Make a cyber-attack against a Firewall of 4. An enemy player may roll defense for the building. On a success, place the Large Blast template over the designated location. All models under the template must pass a Survival Test or suffer a -2 penalty to all Stat Tests and Opposed Tests on their next activation.

RAISE BARRIER

The Sprawl is littered with various parking barriers and traffic stanchions. Installed underground, CORPSEC can raise them without a second's notice to control vehicles and crowds. Raise Barrier mimics the signal used to raise these barriers, allowing the Hacker to provide a bit of cover when needed. Raise Barrier has a range of 6" and Hackers may only use it in an open area more than 3" from a building or building ruins. Make a cyber-attack against a Firewall of 4. An enemy player may roll defense for the barrier controller. On a success, the Hacker may place a single piece of linear terrain no more than 2" long, 1" high, and .5" thick anywhere within range. The barrier provides heavy cover and counts as a piece of linear terrain. A Hacker can only control one active barrier at a time, though they may dismiss it at any time during their activation. Finally, an enemy Hacker may make a cyber-attack against the barrier (again, against a Firewall of 4). If they are successful, remove the barrier immediately.

SUMMON IDORU

This rather mischievous app projects the visual appearance of several well-known Idoru by tapping into a building's holo-projectors. This is useful when a Hacker wants to draw a crowd of soon to be disappointed fans and admirers. Summon Idoru has a range of 6" and a Hacker may only use it within 3" of a building or similar structure. Make a cyber-attack against a Firewall of 4. An enemy player may roll defense for the building. If successful, place a model representing the Idoru within range of the app. For each turn the Idoru remains on the board, roll a D6. On a 1–5, an enemy player must place a bystander anywhere within 6" of the Idoru. On a 6, they must place a whole bystander crowd, instead. The bystanders act as usual. A Hacker may only control one Idoru at a time, though they can dismiss it at any time during their activation. Finally, an enemy Hacker may make a cyber-attack against the Idoru (again against a Firewall of 4). If they are successful, remove the Idoru immediately. The bystanders remain, even if the Idoru is dismissed.

FRIENDLY APPS

Friendly apps can provide multiple benefits to friendly models. They have targets but are always successful, so they do not require a roll if the user has line of sight and the target is within range. However, a Hacker may only use friendly apps on their own crew and any models under their direct control from the start of the game, such as drones. Friendly apps do not work against temporarily controlled enemy models or non-player-controlled models.

DEFENSIVE APPS TABLE	
D6 Result	App
1	Guardian Angel
2	Shield
3	Reconnect
4	Bloodhound
5	Logic Bomb
6	HRO-No

BLOODHOUND (1 AP)

A common watchdog software program, Bloodhound uses numerous sniffer protocols to track enemy Hackers that target it. Bloodhound has a range of 6". When used, place a token next to the target to indicate the software's presence. A model may have multiple active Bloodhound tokens, but only one per target. Should a Hacker make a cyber-attack against a model with a Bloodhound token, their crew gains one Trace token. Once this occurs, remove the Bloodhound token.

GUARDIAN ANGEL (2 AP)

A powerful software program, Guardian Angel creates an Angel Sprite, a minor defense-oriented AI, that can guard a designated target. The benefit is that, unlike other defensive programs, the Angel Sprite is free to move about in a limited capacity. Use a token or model to represent the Angel Sprite and choose a point for the sprite's tether. This must be the operative or another model within 6". The Angel Sprite uses the below stats and rules. Note that it does not have a Cyber stat and cannot make cyber-attacks, but it can be targeted by cyber-attacks, as it is a Virtual being. A model may only control one Angel Sprite at a time. Sprites have no effect on CAT Terminals and other network nodes

Name	MOV/Tether	FW	DHP
Angel Sprite	5/6	5	4
Special Rules			
Has the Virtual Rule. Further, one friendly model in base contact with the Angel Sprite gains a +2 bonus to their Firewall stat. This is immediately removed if the Angel Sprite leaves base contact for any reason.			

HRO-NO (1 AP)

Once a standard HRO access maintenance program, before street Hackers ripped and rewrote it, HRO-No as it is now called, removes the targeted hyper-reality object from the visual spectrum. HRO-No has a range of 6". When used, place an HRO-No token next to the target. A Hacker must pass an Intelligence Test to even attempt to make a cyber-attack against the model with the HRO-No token. If they pass, they may attack as usual, and the HRO-No token is removed. On a failure, they may not attack that model and their AP is wasted.

LOGIC BOMB (1 AP)

An app marketed under the phrase *"The best offense is a good defense,"* Logic Bomb is an algorithmic trap that integrates with a target's security software. When an unauthorized user makes a cyber-attack against the target, there is a chance they can get caught in a regressive logic loop, costing them precious data flow. Logic Bomb has a range of 6" and may be used on any friendly model. However, a user may only have one Logic Bomb active at a time. Put a token next to the target to indicate the presence of the bomb. This is not hidden from other players who must decide whether they want to target the model with the Logic Bomb. Logic Bomb temporarily adds a +1 FW bonus to the target. Should a cyber-attack fail against that model, the enemy Hacker who made the attempt suffers D3 digital damage. After this damage is dealt, the Logic Bomb is removed, including the +2 Firewall bonus.

RECONNECT (1 AP)

By stealing bandwidth, this app can restore lost HyperNET connectivity, though it may cause some lag for some poor sucker. Reconnect may only affect the user and heals up to D3 DHP (this cannot provide more than their starting DHP).

SHIELD (1 AP)

Redundant layers of HyperNET security are a necessity against enemy cyber-attacks; and Shield intertwines its own security protocols with the native programs of all friends within a short distance. Shield lasts until the start of the Hacker's next activation. All friendly models within 6" gain a +1 bonus to their Firewall stat. Friendly models are defined as members of the same crew and any models under their direct control.

SUPPORT APPS

D6 Result	App
SUPPORT APPS TABLE	
1	Summon Demon
2	Camouflage
3	Holo-Targeting
4	Overclock
5	Hyper Sight
6	Troubleshooter

CAMOUFLAGE (1 AP)

An app used to reduce the user's data trail, it is specifically designed to foil sniffer programs and other security traps. When used, the player may remove one Tracer token from their crew.

HOLO-TARGETING (1 AP)

By tapping into local HyperNET telemetric data connections, the Hacker can send useful ballistic data to the target's neuro-chip. The target gains +1 to their Aim stat during their next activation. Note that this bonus does not stack with the bonus from a neural link, as they are essentially the same thing.

HYPER SIGHT (1 AP)

By pairing this specialist app to a micro-camera they wear, Hackers can stream visual data to other members of their crew. Hyper Sight has a range of 8". The target may draw line of sight from the Hacker's perspective for any attacks or skills they possess.

OVERCLOCK (1 AP)

Factory warranties be danged, the Overclock app allows Hackers to push the preset limits on cybernetics far beyond the reasonable. This app has a range of 6" and may only target a friendly model with a piece of chrome that provides a bonus to a Move or Strength stat. The target adds +2 to that stat during their next activation.

SUMMON DEMON (2 AP)

A program capable of generating a Demon Sprite—a minor malware AI—that can attack the designated target's security defenses. While it cannot launch cyber-attacks on its own, its mere presence can foil security protocols. Use a token or model to designate the Demon Sprite, then choose a point for the sprite's tether. This must be the operative or another model within 6"—even an enemy model. The Demon Sprite uses the below stats and rules. Note that it does not have a Cyber stat and cannot make cyber-attacks, but it can be targeted by cyber-attacks, as it is a Virtual being. A model may only control one Demon Sprite at a time. Sprites have no effect on CAT Terminals and other network nodes.

DEMON SPRITE		
MOV/Tether	FW	DHP
5/6	5	4
Special Rules		
Has the Virtual Rule. Further, one model in base contact with the Demon Sprite suffers a -2 penalty to their Firewall stat. This is immediately removed if the Demon Sprite leaves base contact for any reason.		

TROUBLESHOOTER (1 AP)

A digital assistant, Troubleshooter contains diagnostic data, schematics, and other useful data for thousands of weapons, equipment, and cybernetics. The app's maintenance protocols can quickly access this data and remotely assist friends who have equipment trouble. Troubleshooter has a range of 8" and targets disabled friendly models or items carried by a friendly model. The operative can also use this app on themselves and their own items. Make an Intelligence Test with a +1 bonus from the app. On a success, the model, equipment, or item is no longer disabled. On a failure, nothing happens.

High-End Items

The Sprawl was always a tiered system, and the Black-Market is no different. Off the shelf items are often illegal and must be purchased covertly, but even with a minimal connection to the criminal underground, they can be easily had. High-end items, on the other hand, are a bit trickier to come by. Only those with deep connections and high-end fixers have regular access to these items, and they only offer the items to a limited and exclusive clientele. High-end items are those rare and wonderful tools of the trade that can give operatives a real advantage. Still, getting your hands on them is about more than having the money—though they are quite expensive for sure—it is also about who you know.

ACQUIRING HIGH-END ITEMS

Access and reputation are just as important as money when a Showrunner is trying to purchase high-end items. After all, they have to find the right fixer with the right inventory. There are several ways to acquire high-end items:

- Being Born Lucky: Depending on their background options, some Showrunners may start the game with one or two high-end items.
- Running Down Leads: During campaign play, Showrunners can send crew members out to search for high-end items between games.
- Exceeding Expectations: During campaign play, a crew's shadow backer can give them high-end items if they meet certain benchmarks for success.

If a crew gains a free high-end item, either through campaign play or from their Showrunner's background, the player may roll against the *High-End Item Table*, as described below. The result is the item they receive. Note that an item obtained for free does not cost CC, but the CC Cost of the high-end item is added to the model's total CC cost.

If a player may purchase a high-end item, they follow the same process, except they must pay the listed CC Cost for the item. The player is not required to purchase the item, the roll merely grants them the opportunity to do so. However, if they choose not to purchase the weapon, they forfeit their chance to do so, unless they manage to roll it again later.

INFORMATION (INFO)

Information is like money, but better. By trading in secrets, a fixer may be more willing to query their contacts and rundown questionable leads, all to find that one item they buyer must simply have. INFO, which is just shorthand for information and is described further under the Campaigning in the Sprawl section (see page 268), can be spent to roll extra dice on the High-End Item tables; on a one for one basis. For each single item, up to three INFO may be spent, dividing among the various tables as the player chooses, and the player may choose from among any of the results.

HIGH-END ITEM TABLE

When a player is ready to obtain a high-end item, they must first roll 2D10 and consult the chart below to determine the item category.

HIGH-END ITEM TABLE	
2D10 Result	High-End Item Category
1–4	High-End Armor
5–10	High-End Equipment
11–15	Ranged Weapon with 1x Upgrade or High-End Grenades
11–14	Melee Weapon with 1x Upgrade
15–19	High-End Chrome
20	Bleeding Edge Items

HIGH-END ITEM CATEGORIES

Once you determine the category, roll against that category's table to find your result. Some results may point to an even more specific subcategory. If so, simply roll against that table, as necessary. Note that a result of 11–15 on the original roll has an "or" option. If rolled, the player may choose whether they wish to roll against the Ranged Weapon category or the High-End Grenade category. The categories are as follows:

WEAPONS UPGRADES

You can upgrade weapons with advanced modifications and specialty ammo. These are often low-run or bespoke weapons made for military and corporate strike teams or tailored for criminal syndicates and rich civilians.

HIGH-END ARMOR

Includes specialized variants of the common armor types—from stealth suits to power-assist strength armor packages. These are not meant for the civilian market and are always in demand.

HIGH-END CHROME

Uptown medical faculties have the best chrome options; sometimes these surreptitiously make their way into the Sprawl. High-end chrome is made for corporations, but if your Showrunner is lucky, they can get their hands on some.

HIGH-END EQUIPMENT

Includes rare and valuable high-end gear—such as grapplers, designer drugs, and so forth—that are produced for elite military and corporate strike teams, but occasionally filter into the street.

BLEEDING EDGE ITEMS

If a runner is lucky, they may gain access to a bleeding edge item. These are the rarest of the rare. Some of these items are either just out of R&D or were stolen from there, directly. These are powerful weapons with multiple upgrades; simply the most advanced items for which you can barter.

WEAPONS UPGRADES

This section details the various upgrades a weapon can gain. These act as additional special rules for existing weapons. When rolling for upgrades, first roll for the weapon type, and then roll against the indicated upgrade table. The listed CC Cost on the table is the combined value of the weapon and its upgrade.

MELEE WEAPONS UPGRADE TABLES

	HIGH-END MELEE WEAPONS TABLE	
D6 Result	Weapon Type	CC Cost
1	Bludgeon	20
2	Collapsible Stave*	20
3	Combat Hatchet	25
4	Heavy Melee Weapon	20
5	Small Blade	20
6	Sword	25
*Reroll result if model does not have access to this weapon.		

D6 Result	Bludgeon	Collapsible Stave	Combat Hatchet	Heavy Melee Weapon	Small Blade	Sword
		HIGH-END MELEE WEAPONS UPGRADE TABLE				
1	Flashing	Flashing	Penetrating	Penetrating	Penetrating	Penetrating
2	Webbing	Webbing	Envenomed	Envenomed	Envenomed	Envenomed
3	Lightened	Lightened	Lightened	Lightened	Lightened	Lightened
4	Hardened	Hardened	Hardened	Hardened	Hardened	Hardened
5	Shock	Shock	Shock	Shock	Shock	Shock
6	Foaming	Foaming	Flashing	Flashing	Flashing	Flashing

RANGED WEAPONS UPGRADE TABLE

	HIGH-END RANGED WEAPONS TABLE	
D3 Result	Weapon Type	CC Cost
1	Handguns	20
2	Long Guns	20
3	High-End Grenades	25

HANDGUN UPGRADES

HIGH-END HANDGUNS TABLE

D6 Result	Weapon Type	CC Cost
1	Crossbow Pistol	20
2	Handcannon	25
3	Machine Pistol	25
4	Pistol	15
5	Light SMG	20
6	Vapor Pistol	25

HIGH-END HANDGUNS UPGRADE TABLE

D6 Result	Crossbow Pistol	Handcannon	Machine Pistol	Pistol	SMG	Vapor Pistol
1	Envenomed	Flashing	Ricochet	Micro-Missiles	Ricochet	Acid Cloud
2	Improved Velocity	Micro-Missiles	Envenomed	Envenomed	Envenomed	Envenomed
3	Penetrating	Penetrating	Penetrating	Penetrating	Penetrating	Penetrating
4	Automatic	Envenomed	Microrounds	Webbing	Large Caliber	Pyro
5	Stabilizer	Stabilizer	Stabilizer	Stabilizer	Stabilizer	Stabilizer
6	Pyro	Improved Velocity	Improved Velocity	Improved Velocity	Microrounds	Improved Velocity

LONG GUN UPGRADES

HIGH-END LONG GUNS TABLE

D6 Result	Weapon Type	CC Cost
1	Assault Rifle	30
2	Modern Bow	30
3	Rifle	25
4	Shotgun	25
5	Heavy SMG	25
6	Reroll	N/A

HIGH-END LONG GUNS UPGRADE TABLE

D6 Result	Assault Rifle	Modern Bow	Rifle	Shotgun	Heavy SMG
1	Ricochet	Envenomed	Micro-Missiles	Micro-Missiles	Ricochet
2	Envenomed	Improved Velocity	Pyro	Envenomed	Envenomed
3	Penetrating	Penetrating	Penetrating	Penetrating	Penetrating
4	Tracer	Automatic	Shocker	Webbing	Tracer
5	Stabilizer	Stabilizer	Stabilizer	Stabilizer	Stabilizer
6	Microrounds	Pyro	Envenomed	Pyro	Microrounds

WEAPON UPGRADE SPECIAL RULES

AUTOMATIC

Not normally seen in weapons of this type, this upgrade adds a rapid-fire ability. The weapon also gains the Burst ability.

ACID CLOUD

The gas discharge of this weapon was upgraded to impart an acidic secretion that melts away armor. If this weapon successfully hits a model, reduce that model's Armor Bonus by one (to a minimum of zero). This ability can only affect a model once per game.

ENVENOMED

The weapon was upgraded with minute channel that runs along its blade, hooked to a tiny reservoir capable of synthesizing toxic substances. Ranged weapons with this upgrade have a similar ability that imparts this toxin to their ammunition. The weapon gains the *Poison* special rule.

FLASHING

This impact weapon is designed to incorporate a strobe-like effect whenever the weapon hits with enough strength to power the motion-sensitive batteries. An operative may use this upgrade once per turn and must declare it prior to use. When used, this upgrade adds the *Distracting* special rule to a single close combat attack.

FLECHETTE

The weapon fires special ammunition that shreds flesh, though any type of armor weakens its effects. If the target has an Armor Bonus of (+1) or less, the attacker may reroll the wound dice and choose the higher result. However, reduce the weapon's damage by -1.

FOAMING

Special-issue foaming weapons are designed to slow exceptionally tough, dangerous targets that an operative cannot defeat with a single blow—namely, heavy Cyborgs; but, also certain designer creatures from corporate research laboratories. After an operative uses this weapon to successfully hit a model in melee, they may choose to dispense foam onto the target; they can only do so once per game. When the foam hits a model, it becomes encased in the rigid, but brittle substance. While encased, they may take no actions other than to attempt to break free. They must spend 2 AP to break free. They do not need to spend both in the same turn, but the model is not free of the foam until both AP are spent. Once free, place the model prone.

HARDENED

The weapon has advanced materials that increase its impact potential without increasing its weight. The weapon adds +1 to its damage.

IMPROVED VELOCITY

The weapon was upgraded to impart additional kinetic energy into its ammunition at short ranges. It adds +3" to the weapon's Point-Blank range. This upgrade's bonus is not cumulative with that of the Deadeye skill.

LARGE CALIBER

The firearm's barrel was upgraded to shoot larger caliber ammunition. Add +1 to the weapon's Strength.

LIGHTENED

The weapon was designed and produced in a low-run manufacturing that used advanced polymer composites. Not only did this greatly reduce its weight, it potentially increased its hitting power. If the weapon also has the *Heavy* special rule, it ignores it. If it does not, it instead adds +1 to the operative's STR when rolling to-wound in melee.

MICRO-MISSILES

The weapon's usual ammunition was replaced with gyrostabilizer micro-missiles. The weapon gains the *Limited Use (3)* and *Small Blast* special rules. If the target is within 12", the attacking model does not need line of sight to the target. This means the attack may go through windows, around corners, or over obstructions; though it may not enter fully enclosed spaces.

MICROROUNDS

Designed to fire a blur of micro-sized projectiles, this weapon trades hitting power for rate of fire. Reduce the weapon's STR by -1. However, it gains the *Hail of Lead* special rule.

PYRO

This weapon's ammunition is combustible upon impact with solid material. The weapon gains the *Flammable* special rule.

PENETRATING

The weapon has additional punching power and gains the *Ignore Armor (1)* special rule. If it already has this rule, it increases the rule by one.

RICOCHET

Developed for urban warfare, ricochet ammunitions improve a weapon's lethality if the target is near cover. As the bullet impacts the target, small pieces flake off. When these pieces strike a hard surface, they become kinetically active and "bounce" around, inflicting additional damage to the target. Add +1 to the weapon's STR if the target is in base contact with any type of cover.

TRACER

The weapon was preloaded with incendiary rounds in the first position of each three-round burst of ammunition. Each incendiary round acts as a guide for the shots that follow. When firing with the *Burst* special rule, if the first shot hits the target, all subsequent attacks gain a +1 bonus to-hit.

SHOCK

The weapon is fitted with electrical capacitors that run along special veins in the weapon's shaft. A particularly hard impact can generate enough force to release a low-voltage hit than both shocks the target and potentially shorts their equipment. If the attacker rolls a Critical when rolling to-wound, the target suffers a special EMP effect. All firearms, melee weapons, equipment with an attack profile, and cybernetics with the *On/Off* rule are disabled for one turn.

STABILIZER

The weapon has a micro-gyrostabilizer upgrade that compensates for operative movement. The operative does not suffer a -1 to-hit modifier for moving in the same turn they fire this weapon.

WEBBING

The weapon was built with a special reservoir of webbing fluid fitted into its shaft or uses ammunition with the same effect. Instead of rolling to-wound after hitting a target, the target counts as *webbed*. While webbed, the target is automatically hit in melee and may not make any move actions or any type of attack—including cyber-attacks. The webbed model or another model in base contact with them may free the webbed model by spending 1 AP and passing a Strength Test. If successful, the webbed model is immediately freed, but is placed Prone. If unsuccessful, the model is still webbed.

HIGH-END GRENADES

HIGH-END GRENADES TABLE

D10 Result	Grenade Type	Strength	Special Rules	CC Cost
1	Airburster	7	Limited Use (1), Large Blast	20
2	Caltrop Dispenser	N/A	Limited Use (1), Large Blast, Drops Caltrops	15
3	Flesh-Cutter	7	Flechette, Limited Use (1), Small Blast	20
4	Acidic Grenade	7	Acid Cloud, Gas, Limited Use (1), Small Blast	20
5	Homing Grenade	5	Limited Use (1), Small Blast, Bonus to Hit/Reduced Damage	15
6	Lag Grenade	N/A	Limited Use (1), Large Blast, Slows HyperNET	15
7	POV'er	N/A	Limited Use, Use for Line of Sight	20
8	Spider Mine	N/A	Limited Use (1), Small Blast, Moveable Mine	15
9	Foam Catcher	N/A	Limited Use (1), Small Blast, Entrapping Foam	15
10	Sticky Grenade	7	Limited Use (1), Small Blast, Reroll Deviation	15

ACIDIC GRENADE

A bit of a rarity, this corporately manufactured grenade was reverse engineered from an anti-armor weapon a back-alley chemist designed. After seeing the effects on riot police during a protest, the design was copied, formally patented, and sold in limited quantities. The original inventor has long since rotted away in an Iso-Cell.

AIRBURSTER

A variant of the classic daisy-cutter, the airburster detonates a few feet off the ground, launching itself off the targeted location and showering a wide area with dangerous shrapnel rounds.

CALTROP DISPENSER

A special grenade. Instead of launching an explosive payload, it launches tiny spikes over a large area. Once you determine the grenade's landing site, center a Large Blast template over it. This marks the area in which the caltrops were dropped. This area now counts as difficult terrain. Any model that fails any type of Agility Test within its confines automatically takes D3 damage in addition to any other negative results they may suffer.

FLESH-CUTTER

A rather nasty grenade, the flesh-cutter showers the area of effect with flechette barbs, doing grievous harm to targets without the protection of armor.

FOAM CATCHER

Designed for elite CORPSEC riot control units, foam catcher grenades use non-lethal pellets to deploy expanding foam that can trap numerous troublemakers in one shot. While the foam is tough, it is quite brittle and models can break it down with a bit of effort. This is not a flaw, as the foam is meant to quell riots, not entrap the targets and potentially suffocate them. Do not roll to-wound once you determine the grenade's landing site. Instead, all models hit by a foam catcher become encased in foam. While encased, they may take no actions other than to attempt to break free. They must spend 2 AP to break free. They do not need to spend both in the same turn, but the model is not free of the foam until both AP are spent. Once free, place the model prone.

LAG GRENADE

Lag Grenades are portable Wi-Fi blockers that can block access to the HyperNET. Treat as a normal grenade. Once you determine the grenade's final landing site, place a small token there. The token remains for D3 turns. Any model with a Cyber stat that enters, leaves, or moves within a 4" area of the token suffers D6 digital damage. Lag grenades do not affect Virtual beings. Remove the token during the Clean-Up Phase of its last turn.

HOMING GRENADE

This grenade is large enough to incorporate a minor AI targeting program that can briefly alter the grenade's trajectory via micro-thrusts, virtually guaranteeing a hit. This accuracy means there is less space to store the explosive payload, though. Treat as a fragmentation grenade with a +2 bonus to-hit and a -1 penalty to STR.

POV'ER

Not a grenade, but a remote viewing device, the POV'er is connected to the operative's neuro-chip by an encrypted, wireless signal. Treat as a normal grenade. Once you determine the POV'er's final landing site, place a small token or counter there. While the operative remains within 12" of this token, they may draw line of sight from the POV'er for cyber-attacks, grenades, and any attack that can bypass terrain. Use common sense when applying the latter. The POV'er has a 360º view.

STICKY GRENADE

This grenade is covered in a tacky adhesive that latches onto the target, greatly reducing its potential to bounce and hit the wrong target. If the operative throws this grenade and misses, they may reroll either the deviation direction or the distance; they must keep the second result, even if it is worse.

SPIDER MINE

A tactical weapon, when thrown, the spider mine does not explode. Instead, it deploys a set of tiny legs that allow it to scurry about. It accepts directions from the operative via the neuro-chip and explodes when a model without a preapproved ID signature gets too close. Treat as a normal grenade. Once you determine the spider mine's final landing site, place a small token or counter there. During the Clean-Up Phase of each turn, the operative may move the spider mine up to D6". Should an enemy model come within 3" of the spider mine at any time, it seeks out that model and explodes. If this happens, treat as a fragmentation grenade with its center point over the target model. Enemy models may target the spider mine, but due to its small size, all shots suffer a -2 penalty to-hit. If it is hit, the mine is destroyed and does not cause an explosion.

HIGH-END ARMOR

This section contains the various upgrades operatives can acquire for their armor. These upgrades act as an additional special rule for the armor. When rolling for upgrades, first roll against the High-End Armor Table to determine the type of armor to which the upgrade applies, then roll against the High-End Armor Upgrades Table for the upgrade. The listed CC Cost on the table is the combined value of the armor and its upgrade.

HIGH-END ARMOR TABLE		
D6 Result	Weapon Type	CC Cost
1–4	Armor Weave	30
5	Security Armor	40
6	Combat Armor	50

HIGH-END ARMOR UPGRADES TABLE			
D6 Result	Armor Weave	Security Armor	Combat Armor
1	Dazzle	Dazzle	Dazzle
2	Stealth	Stealth	Move-Assist
3	Blast-Proof	Blast-Proof	Interlocking
4	Stab-Proof	Stab-Proof	Stab-Proof
5	Holo-Shift	Holo-Shift	Holo-Shift
6	Fashionable	Strength-Assist	Strength-Assist

HIGH-END ARMOR UPGRADE SPECIAL RULES

BLAST-PROOF

This armor has additional kinetic buffers built in, meant to protect the wearer against blast pressure waves and area shrapnel. The armor gains +1 to its Armor Bonus against attacks that use the *Small* or *Large Blast* special rules.

DAZZLE

When hit by a slow, kinetic impact, such as when the armor is struck in melee combat, special micro-projectors embedded in the suit generate a bright strobe light display that can easily blind an unprepared enemy. When a model wearing this armor is hit in combat, all models except the wearer within 1" must pass a Survival Test or suffer a -2 penalty to all Stat and Opposed Tests on their next activation. Note that this effect is identical to that of the *Distracting* special rule, so any effects or rules that apply to that rule apply to Dazzle, as well.

FASHIONABLE

This fashion-forward ensemble incorporates the latest trends from Paris and is fully battle-functional. This suit commands both respect and envy. The model gains a +1 to Morale Tests and Survival Tests when attempting to blend in with bystander crowds.

HOLO-SHIFT

This armor has embedded micro-projectors programmed to play an onslaught of various holographic images. These include composites of the operative's general form, media clips, and even swear words—anything the operative wishes to program. This is not only annoying for enemies to look at; but, when viewed close-up, it disrupts the operative's shape. Models who target the wearer with ranged attacks do not benefit from Point Blank bonuses.

INTERLOCKING

This armor plating is designed to interconnect or interlock when the wearer is not moving. When set, this significantly improves the protection the armor offers, with only a minor cost to movement capabilities. The armor gains a +1 Armor Bonus if the operative did not make any move actions during the last game turn. Any movement caused by standing up or making Grazed or Morale Tests offset this armor's bonus.

MOVE-ASSIST

This armor was upgraded with a leg-support system and special micro-servos that remove much of the strain wearing the armor causes. Armor with this upgrade gives the wearer the *Armor Expertise* special rule.

STAB-PROOF

The armor was designed to resist deep, penetrating attacks caused by bladed weapons and is resistant to bludgeoning attacks, as well, due to special mesh inserts. The armor gains a +1 to its Armor Bonus against melee attacks.

STEALTH

The armor incorporates a light-bending projector that allows it to blend in quite seamlessly with its environment. The wearer gains the *Shadow-Blend* special rule. Additionally, the model may hide while in the open, provided they do not make a move action during their activation.

STRENGTH-ASSIST

This armor has an endo-frame strength system installed. While it is not quite equivalent to military-grade powered armor, it does give the wearer +1 to their Strength stat. While it is not cybernetic, armor with the Strength-Assist upgrade has the *On/Off* rule and can be disabled by attacks that disable cybernetics.

HIGH-END CHROME

This section contains the various high-end chrome options that operatives can find on the market. First, roll a D3 against the *High-End Chrome Table* to determine which additional table you should use, then roll a D6 against the indicated *High-End Chrome Table* (*#1*, *#2*, or *#3*). The tables list the chrome's CC Cost, Body Location, and IP Cost.

HIGH-END CHROME TABLE	
D3 Result	Chrome Table Result
1	High-End Chrome Table #1
2	High-End Chrome Table #2
3	High-End Chrome Table #3

HIGH-END CHROME TABLE #1				
D6 Result	Weapon Type	Body Location	IP Cost	CC Cost
1	Chemical N-Jector™	Arms	1	25
2	Infravision	Head	1	15
3	Micro-Thrusters	Legs	2	15
4	Neural Net	Head	2	25
5	Shock Suppressor	General	2	20
6	Ablative Armor	Torso	2	15

HIGH-END CHROME TABLE #2				
D6 Result	Weapon Type	Body Location	IP Cost	CC Cost
1	Cyber Tools	Arms	1	15
2	Savior Protocols	General	4	25
3	Flechette Defender	General	2	15
4	Telescoping Arms	Arms	2	15
5	Skill Chip	Head	2	20
6	Titanium Plating	Torso	4	30

HIGH-END CHROME TABLE #3				
D6 Result	Weapon Type	Body Location	IP Cost	CC Cost
1	Breaching Hand	Arms	1	15
2	Skill Chip	Head	2	15
3	Cat's Claws™	Legs	2	20
4	Lightning Booster	General	4	30
5	Telescoping Lenses	Arms	1	15
6	Hardened Electronics	Torso	3	30

ABLATIVE ARMOR

Popular among heavy Cyborgs and exo-suit pilots, ablative armor provides significant protection with little effect on weight and performance by adding deceptively thin layers of advanced polymers to an already armored-up frame using a dipping process. However, the process is only good for a few layers before it starts to become brittle, and the financial cost is rather exorbitant. A model with ablative armor gains +2 HP. A model must have an Armor Bonus from another piece of chrome or a cyber limb before they can purchase this cyberware—an Armor Bonus from armor or equipment does not count.

BREACHING HAND

The operative's cyber arm was upgraded to include a pneumatic punching system, which incorporates a crude hand that can turn into a hardened wedge. When used, the breaching hand allows the operative to literally punch holes through walls. Once per turn, the model can spend 1 AP and attempt a Strength Test to punch a hole through a piece of terrain. If successful, they punch a hole 1" wide by 1" high, through which normal sized models may pass freely. Mark the hole with a token. The breaching hand only works on normal walls constructed from concrete, brick, or masonry. It does not work against military-grade reinforced walls. The wedge is too clumsy to use effectively in combat, so the model cannot use it in melee. Breaching hand has the *On/Off* special rule.

CAT'S CLAWS™

Highly illegal, and thus quite popular with intrusion operatives, Cat's Claws are cybernetic "claws" grafted onto the operative's cyber hands that they can retract at will. The claws themselves are made up of a multitude of extra strong micro-hooks that can find purchase on almost any surface. With proper training, operatives can use the claws to climb even sheer surfaces at great speed. A model with Cat's Claws may climb vertically at their full MOV speed. Further, while climbing, the model can only fall if they roll a natural Fumble on an Agility Test or become disabled. If disabled while climbing, the model automatically falls. Cat's Claws have the *On/Off* special rule.

CHEMICAL N-JECTOR™

A particularly infamous piece of chrome, the Mark-Rudolph Chemical N-Jector is a hypodermic needle weapon that an operative can conceal inside a cyber arm, generally in one of the fingers. While the weapon itself presents little danger, its proprietary exotic ammunition is another matter. Various injurious cocktails are brewed and sold in cyber-dens for use with the needle. The N-Jector uses the following stats and comes with enough doses of chemical cocktail ammunition to last the entire game. Once you choose the type of ammo, you cannot change it during the game. However, you may choose a different type for subsequent games. The Chemical N-Jector has the *On/Off* rule.

CHEMICAL N-JECTOR™ TABLE			
Weapon	Range	Strength	Special Rules
Chemical N-Jector™	12"	6	Cocktail Ammo, Pistol

Available Cocktail Ammo:

- N-Venom: The Chemical N-Jector gains the *Poison* special rule. Further, the target must test for poison even if they are successfully wounded.
- N-Rage: The target must pass an Intelligence Test. If they fail, they react as though they just rolled Psycho Time on the Cyber-shock Table (see page 161).
- N-Ferno: Treat the weapon as if it has the *Distracting* special rule, as this concoction makes the victim feel as though their blood is on fire. This effect lasts for D3+1 turns.

CYBER TOOLS

The operative's fingers contain multiple micro-tendrils that can shoot and independently interface with cybernetic systems while the operative's attention is elsewhere. Once per turn, the model may attempt to restart a single disabled item without spending AP. However, the attempt suffers a -1 penalty. Cyber tools has the *On/Off* rule.

DETACHABLE EYE

One of the model's eyes was fully replaced with a remote viewing device—much like the POV'er—which they can pluck out and throw. Treat this cybernetic as a grenade that the operative can throw. Once you determine the grenade's final landing site, place a small token there. As long the operative remains within 12" of the token, they may draw line of sight from the location for cyber-attacks, grenades, and any attack that can bypass terrain. Use common sense when applying the latter. The detachable eye has a 360° view. Further, the model may spend 1 AP to move the eye up to D6" in any direction. The eye cannot cross any type of difficult or linear terrain. Detachable eye has the *On/Off* switch and can only be thrown once per turn. It is automatically replaced at the end of each game.

FLECHETTE DEFENDER

A piece of defensive chrome, the flechette defender consists of a tube of flechette darts that discharge at a nearby target. When it senses trouble, the defender automatically launches a series of barbed darts at the perceived threat, in the hope of deterring them from further aggression. Usable once per game. When an enemy model completes a charge move against the operative, the enemy must make three separate Agility Tests. For each failure, they suffer a Strength 6 hit that deals 1 damage and must make a Grazed Test. Note that a failed Graze Test prevents the enemy model from completing its charge. The flechette defender has the *On/Off* special rule.

HARDENED ELECTRONICS

Electronic hardening is a common cyberattack countermeasure that operatives with the physical space to install Faraday shielding and signal dampers use to ward off multiple types of electronic attacks. Add +2 to the model's Firewall stat. Further, should the model suffer an EMP attack, roll a D10. If the result is 7 or higher, the model ignores the effects.

INFRAVISION

Operatives can equip their cyber eyes with all kinds of upgrades, one of the more popular is the ability to detect the infrared spectrum and degrees of heat. The model with infravision has a spotting distance of 3x their Mettle (instead of 2x). Additionally, they can see through black fog, as described in the *Hitch* section, for up to 16". Infravision has the *On/Off* special rule.

LIGHTNING BOOSTER

Not for the faint of heart, the lighting booster is a complete hormone replacement that can flood the operative's body with a large amount of adrenaline and other stress-inducing hormones. Repeated use results in horrible long-term effects on the body, but many operatives are either oblivious to this or simply ignore the risks to stay on top of their game. Once per game turn, the operative may choose to make an opposed Agility Test against an enemy model that just activated. If the operative wins, they activate first. Then the interrupted model may continue its activation. Failure means the model may not use this ability for the rest of the game turn. This chrome cannot be combined with the Sprawl Ronin's Lightning Reflexes starting Edge. Lightning booster has the *On/Off* special rule.

MICRO-THRUSTERS

The operative's cyber legs are fitted with discrete micro-boosters. While their size reduces their ability to carry enough fuel for continued use, many operatives greatly appreciate the micro-thrusters' ability to briefly enhance movement or prevent a falling, erstwhile demise. Once per game, a model with micro-boosters may jump 3" either vertically or horizontally. This may be combined with other movement or used to negate the damage taken from a single fall. Micro-thrusters have the *On/Off* special rule.

NEURAL NET

A popular cyber upgrade for Showrunners and Console Cowboys, the neural net is an artificial computational system that parallels with the operative's organic mind. By essentially sub-dividing mental tasks between the two systems, the operative can achieve increased efficiency. Models equipped with a neural network receive +1 AP each turn. They may only use the extra AP to make cyber-attacks or use friendly apps. The neural net has the *On/Off* special rule.

SAVIOR PROTOCOLS

A rather popular piece of chrome, especially among Showrunners and Enforcer operatives, savior protocols are a system of flexible surgical micro-dendrites, medical sprays, and pain reducers, that activate when the operative receives severe injuries. While an operative may use it only once out in the field before it must be reset by a trained technician, the protocols are invaluable for preventing a model from dying of shock or bleeding out. Usable once per game. When the operative receives damage that reduces them to below half their starting hit points but does not take them out-of-action, they immediately regain D3 HP. If,

instead, the model receives enough damage to take them out-of-action, the savior protocols restore them back to 1 HP, and they are placed Prone. Savior protocols have the *On/Off* special rule.

SHOCK SUPPRESSOR

A popular piece of chrome with ex-military and former or current Sprawl junkies, the shock suppressor floods the operative's body with powerful pain medication when they are subject to catastrophic injury. While this does nothing to fix the problem, it does anesthetize their pain receptors, allowing them to carry on with the mission. The model gains the *Hard As Nails* and *Do or Die* special rules. The shock suppressor has the *On/Off* special rule.

SKILL CHIP

Low end skill chips are available everywhere from retail learning boutiques to questionable back alley cyber-dens, but they are generally simple affairs. High-end version on the other hand offer an easy, if expensive and invasive, way to learn skills that would normally require years to master. When first obtained, choose a column on a Skill Table under any of the operative types and roll a D6. The model gains that skill. However, that skill, via the Skill Chip, has the *On/Off* special rule.

TELESCOPIC ARMS

The model's arms are equipped with extenders that it can use at will and retract when not in use. This greatly increases the model's physical reach, though it does negate a certain amount of power. Add 3" to the melee range of any weapon the model carries, though their close combat attacks suffer a -1 STR penalty. Telescoping arms have the *On/Off* special rule.

TELESCOPIC LENSES

Scopes are for street chums! Telescoping lenses are a cyber eye enhancement that allow the model to *zoom in* from a significant distance away. Add +6" to the range of any weapon this model uses. This does not apply to thrown melee weapons or melee range. Telescopic lenses have the *On/Off* special rule.

TITANIUM PLATING

Developed decades ago for military applications, but long since claimed by the street, titanium armor can overlap with robotic or cybernetic frames to dramatically reduce the kinetic energy of incoming hits. Of course, the excessive weight limits mobility, even though it is significantly lighter than steel. Models equipped with titanium armor reduce the amount of any damage they receive by 1 (to a minimum of 1). However, they also reduce their Move by 1.

HIGH-END EQUIPMENT

This section contains various high-end equipment operatives can find on the market. Simply roll a D10 against the High-End Equipment Table to select a piece of equipment. The CC Cost and Carrying Capacity slots required are also listed.

HIGH-END EQUIPMENT TABLE			
D10 Result	Equipment Type	Slots	CC Cost
1	Signature Item	1	15
2	Autopatch Deluxe	1	20
3	Grappler	1	20
4	Holo-Decoy	1	20
5	Havoc Guard	1	25
6	Jammer	1	20
7	HRO-No Blocker	1	20
8	SPAMsuit™	1	15
9	Puff-Bag	2	20
10	iFoam	1	20

AUTOPATCH DELUXE

An upmarket version of the autopatch, this is used exclusively for elite clientele in the Upper Reaches; but, sometimes things fall off the hover truck. The autopatch deluxe works in the same way as a normal autopatch, except it returns 4 HP instead of 2.

GRAPPLER

A micronized grappling hook attached to a launcher, operatives can use the grappler to quickly ascend vertical heights safely and efficiently. A model may spend 1 AP to shoot the grappler. Choose a location within 6" horizontally or up to 12" vertically and move the model to that position immediately. The chosen location must be large enough to fit the model's base. Note that an operative can use this to put them in base contact with an enemy model, but cannot use this movement to charge. The grappler has the *Limited Use (3)* special rule.

HAVOC GUARD

A high-end solution to cyber-attacks, a havoc guard protects a weapon with a type of Faraday wiring that blocks all wireless access transmissions to the weapon. When obtained, you must link this item to a ranged or melee weapon. Enemy models may no longer choose this weapon as the target for any app that controls, disables, or bricks a weapon. Further, should this weapon be hit by an EMP attack, roll a D10. If the result is 7 or higher, ignore the effects. You cannot use this weapon with a neural link or benefit from the *Fire Assist* ability or similar abilities.

HOLO-DECOY

A highly sought-after protective item, the holo-decoy uses a miniature holographic projector to create a convincing replica of the operative. While this would never fool anyone under close inspection, it is particularly useful for diverting long range fire. When the holo-decoy deploys, it creates an identical holographic copy of the operative. You do not need a physical model or counter to represent the holo-decoy. Until the beginning of the operative's next activation, when resolving any ranged attacks that originate 9" or more from the model, the attacker must make an Intelligence Test after each successful hit. On a success, the attacker hits the operative, as usual. On a failure, the attacker hits the decoy and the shot is wasted.

HRO-NO BLOCKER

A tool originally designed for maintenance of HyperNET access points, street Hackers "re-wired" it to instead wipe HRO signatures from the visual spectrum. At the start of the game, place an HRO-No token next to the model. If a Hacker attempts to make a cyber-attack against that model, they must first pass an Intelligence Test to do so. If they pass, they may attack as usual and the HRO-No token is removed. On a failure, they may not attack that model and their AP is wasted. The model with HRO-No may spend 1 AP and pass an Intelligence Test to replace their HRO-No token should it be removed.

iFOAM

Sold as *intelligent foam*, iFoam is an expanding durafoam with special nanobots inside that can manipulate the shape of the foam as it expands. It costs 1 AP to use iFoam. Once used, place a piece of linear terrain (made up of the hardened foam and no bigger than 6"x1"x1") within 3" of the operative. This acts as a normal piece of terrain that provides light cover and remains in place for the rest of the game.

JAMMER

The jammer is a low-frequency signal breaking device. The jammer has a 6" area of effect. All models within the area of effect lose 1 DHP each time they enter or activate within the area of affect.

PUFF-BAG

Marketed as a personal parachute, the puff-bag is a special backpack worn on the lower torso. Contained within are a series of precision altimeters hooked to a blast-bag that expands should the operative experience a sudden drop in height. When deployed, an air bag of sorts envelops the operative and protects them from dangerous falls. The first time per game the operative falls any distance, place them prone at the point of impact. They do not suffer any hits or damage from the fall.

SIGNATURE ITEM

A signature item is a catch-all category of singularly impressive items made by master artisans. The signature item becomes part of the operative's "brand" and adds to their mystique and reputation. A signature item can be anything from holo-clothing to custom weaponry, or anything else a player can imagine. We recommend that such an item be modeled onto the miniature, if possible. Once obtained and assigned, this item cannot be removed from the operative. This item counts as a lucky object and the operative's warband automatically gains +2 REP. Note that this bonus REP does not generate any additional income.

SPECIAL PROTECTION AGAINST MAYHEM (SPAM) SUIT

The SPAMsuit is a corporate defense tool designed to blend in with everyday business wear. Meant to protect the user from unwanted physical attention—primarily that of rioters, protesters, and muggers—the SPAMsuit is a one-piece garment worn like full-body underwear, which features tiny electrified wires that run over the wearer's body. These wires are virtually undetectable with casual inspection. The SPAMsuit sends a near-lethal shock to anyone who touches the equipped person without permission. Any model that strikes the equipped model in close combat or moves in base contact must pass an Agility Test or suffer an automatic STR 5 hit. The SPAMsuit ceases to work if the model goes out-of-action or becomes unconscious. Though it is not cybernetic, the SPAMsuit has the *On/Off* special rule and can be disabled by attacks that disable cybernetics.

BLEEDING EDGE ITEMS

This section contains the amazing bleeding edge items. If your operative is lucky enough to procure one, first roll against the Bleeding Edge Items Table to see what type of item you receive, then follow the instructions below for the item type. Statistics for each item, such as IP cost, Slots, and CC Costs, are included in the individual item type tables.

BLEEDING EDGE ITEMS TABLE	
D6 Result	Item Type
1	Bleeding Edge Armor
2	Bleeding Edge Melee Weapon
3	Bleeding Edge Ranged Weapon
4	Bleeding Edge Chrome
5	Reaction Drone
6	Player's Choice

BLEEDING EDGE ARMOR

Roll against the *High-End Armor Table* to determine the armor type (see page 198). Then, roll twice against the *High-End Armor Upgrades Table* and apply both results; reroll duplicates (see page 199).

BLEEDING EDGE MELEE WEAPON

Roll against the *High-End Melee Weapons Table* to determine the weapon type (see page 189). Then, roll twice against the *High-End Melee Weapons Upgrades Table* and apply both results; reroll duplicates (see page 189).

BLEEDING EDGE RANGED WEAPON

Roll against the *High-End Ranged Weapons Table* to determine the weapon type (see page 189). reroll if the result is High-End Grenades. Then, roll against the appropriate weapon type table to determine which weapon your operative receives. Then, roll twice against the appropriate *Upgrade Table* and apply both results; reroll duplicates (see page 190).

BLEEDING EDGE CHROME

Roll against the *Bleeding Edge Chrome Table* below.

D6 Result	Item Type	Installations Slots	CC Cost
BLEEDING EDGE CHROME TABLE			
1	Cyber Torso 2.0	4	50
2	Cyber Legs 2.0	4	35
3	Cyber Eye 2.0	2	40
4	Cyber Arms 2.0	4	40
5	Deluxe Skill Chip	2	35
6	Player's Choice	N/A	N/A

- **Cyber Arms 2.0:** Like the cyber arms from the *Chrome* portion of the *Black-Market* section, except cyber-strikes gain the *Lightened* and *Concussion* special rules (see pages 194 and 127).
- **Cyber Legs 2.0:** Like the cyber legs from the *Chrome* portion of the *Black-Market* section, except the model gains the *Running Man* and *Hurdler* special rules (see pages 224 and 228).
- **Cyber Eyes 2.0:** Combines cyber eyes with night sight from the *Chrome* portion of the *Black-Market* section and infravision from the *High-End Chrome* section (see page 201).
- **Cyber Torso 2.0:** Like the cyber torso (light) from the *Chrome* portion of the *Black-Market* section, except it has Armor Bonus (+2) instead of +1 (see page 163).
- **Deluxe Skill Chip:** Like the original skill chip from the *High-End Chrome* section, except the player may roll two dice on the same skill chart and gain both results. Treat as one cybernetic with the *On/Off* special rule.

REACTION DRONES

An emergent technology, reaction drones are designed to skirt the intent of the Turing Protocols, but still technically follow them. Reaction drones (also called REDs) act on their own volition, but only to perform a specific action they are programmed to do. Their "job" is to react once a certain parameter is met—such as attacking, engaging, or harassing an enemy when it gets too close.

Reaction drones use the stat profile below and never gain AP. They may only "react" while on overwatch, but they may defend themselves in melee if attacked. You must designate their owner; they never move more than 3" away from this owner. If they are forced further away for any reason, they move back within 3" of the owner for free during the Clean-Up Phase of the current turn. If the owner moves, the drones follow them—this is also free and does not cost AP.

Reaction drones may be disabled or bricked by cyber-attacks, but not controlled. If an enemy ever rolls a result to control them, count the result as disabled, instead. Reaction drones may be taken out-of-action, but are automatically fixed in time for the next game and do not roll against the *Survival Table*.

REACTION DRONE							
DEF	HP	FW	MOV	MEL	AIM	STR	Met
5(6)	5	6	6	4	4	5	5
Skills and Special Rules							
Reactive Overwatch, One Job							
Equipment							
Armor Weave							

REACTIVE OVERWATCH

This drone is always on the lookout for trouble. The drone gains no AP, but always counts as being on overwatch. Once per turn, they may "react" to the actions of an enemy model. When reacting, they gain 1 AP. The drone's owner decides when to resolve its overwatch action.

ONE JOB

REDs are programmed to do one thing, and one thing only. When first obtained, roll against the *Reaction Drone Job Table* to determine which job your RED is programmed to do.

REACTION DRONE JOB TABLE

D6 Roll	Job	Effect
1	Engage	The drone is equipped with a machine pistol. It may shoot at any enemy model that moves within 12" of its owner.
2	Harass	The drone is equipped with a riot shield and gains a +1 to its Melee stat. It may attempt to get in base contact with any enemy model that comes within 6" of its owner. If it is in the same melee as its owner, it counts as a friendly model when determining combat modifiers.
3	Block	The drone gains +1 to its Armor Bonus and the Sentry special rule. The drone may only move as a reaction. It attempts to position itself in such a way as to stop or block enemy models from attempting to get in base contact with its owner.

SPECIAL RULES

Models in *Reality's Edge* are more than just a stat line. They are hard-bitten operatives that worked to differentiate themselves from the pack of wannabes that litter the Sprawl.

A model's profile or roster entry indicates which special rules, if any, a model possesses. This section covers most of the special rules a model may have. Some special rules may be exclusive to a certain model type or may not be listed here for other reasons—these rules are delineated in the model's roster or profile.

Types of Models

All models in *Reality's Edge* have a type. A model's type is the broad, but exclusive category to which it belongs. Each type has its benefits and drawbacks. A model's type is delineated in its roster or profile. Some rare models have a combined type—in this case, they suffer the rules for both types.

ANIMAL

This model is an animal and has a very basic level of intelligence, if not a savage sense of cunning. Animals cannot use any items they do not possess at the start of the game. They also cannot interface with technology unless acting under the control of another model who can.

AUGMENT

This model was "upgraded" with cybernetics, though it was not fully converted to a machine. This means it is better, stronger, and faster, but it cost them their humanity (at least, that is the orthodoxy of the anti-augment movement). The model can acquire and use cybernetic enhancements, when allowed. An Augment's cybernetics may be targeted by cyber-attacks and it may suffer from cyber-shock as described in the *Chrome* portion of the *Black-Market* section.

BOT

This model is a robot, a machine built and programmed to complete any number of functions. Being non-organic, it is immune to weapons with the *Poison* and *Gas* rules. However, it is susceptible to weapons with the *EMP* rule. Unless specifically stated otherwise, robots are programmed for self-preservation, and make Morale and Grazed Tests as usual.

CYBORG

This model had a full-conversion completed on their body. Other than their brain and parts of their nervous system, they are totally machine. Hardly anyone would argue that they are still human. The Cyborg model has exclusive access to certain cybernetics and may be the target of cyber-attacks. Cyborgs may suffer from cyber-psychosis as described in the *Cyborg Roster Profile* portion of the *Building Your Crew* section.

HUMAN

This model is human, for whatever that is worth these days. Humans can have minor augments, but these are minimal and have no in-game effect. A human can never be the target of a cyber-attack, but any items they carry are fair game. Humans may acquire cybernetics, but if this occurs, their type immediately changes to Augment.

Skills

Skills are a special addition to the list and are worth a short explanation. Skills are earned through experience, though each model may start with a limited number. When a model gains enough experience, it may gain a randomly determined skill. Some special abilities or items, like cybernetics, may duplicate the effects of a skill. A model may never benefit from having a skill more than once, so if you accidently duplicate gain a skill they already possess, you may reroll or chose another skill, depending on the how the skill was gained.

SKILLS LIST

AGAINST ALL ODDS

This operative likes a challenging fight—the more the merrier. Enemy models do not receive a bonus when they outnumber this model in melee. Instead, this model receives a +1 to its Melee stat when it is outnumbered in close combat.

ARMOR EXPERTISE

It is whispered among the crew that this operative must sleep in their armor. That is only half-true, they do have to remove it occasionally to clean it. This model suffers no penalties to its Move stat or Agility Tests when wearing any item with an Armor (+3) or less bonus.

BLITZER

This operative acts like a holovid sports hero, charging for the glory first, and thinking it through afterward. When charging, this model may choose to receive +1 STR for its melee attack. If it does, the attack suffers a -1 to-hit penalty.

BRAVE

This operative keeps their cool under pressure. They receive a +2 bonus to all Will Tests.

BRAWLER

This operative has years of experience fighting their way through life. They gain a +1 to-hit bonus when making melee attacks.

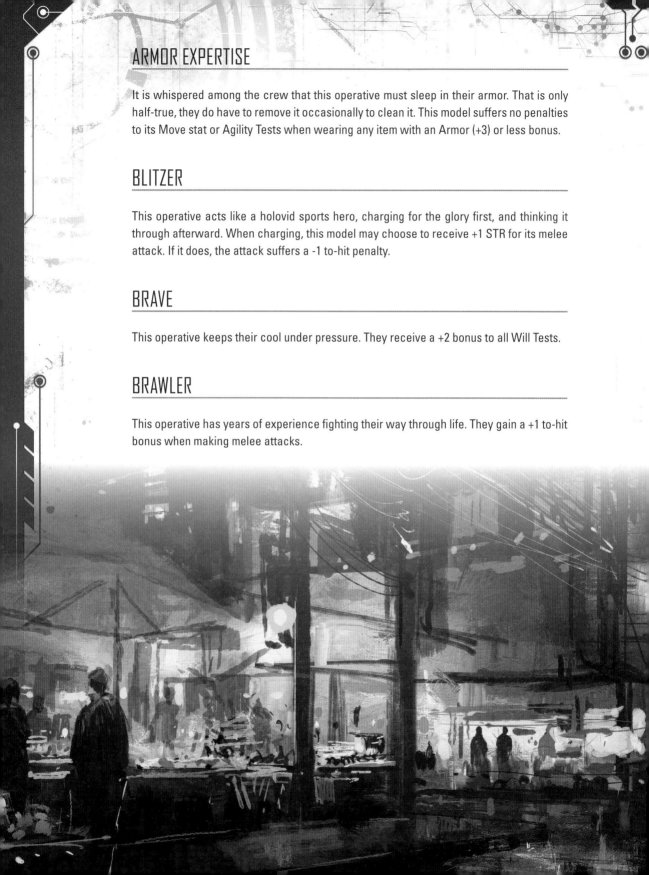

BRUTE

Some may believe this operative is a Cyborg in disguise, but they are just naturally super strong. No one would dare joke about this to their face, anyway. The model receives a +1 to its Strength stat when making melee attacks.

BULLET MAGNET

Getting shot is just part of the job, most people miss, anyhow. This model automatically passes all Grazed Tests but may choose to fail, as usual.

BULLY

There are few rules in the street, and even then, few play fairly. This model deals low blows and makes them count. When this model charges and wins in melee, the enemy is knocked Prone in addition to any other combat results.

CALLED SHOT

This operative is an expert marksman, able to find the smallest fissure in the enemy's defenses. Before rolling to-hit in a ranged combat, this model may declare a called shot. The shot suffers a -2 penalty to-hit, in addition to any other range modifiers that may apply. If the model successfully hits the target, the hit receives +1 STR and has the *Ignore Armor (1)* ability.

CAREFUL BLOW

Everyone has a tell, you must just know how to read the opponent and when to strike. All melee attacks made by this model have the *Ignore Armor (1)* ability or gain a +1 if using a weapon that already has this special rule.

CAREFUL SHOOTING

This model can fire into a crowded room and still hit its intended target. When firing into a melee combat, this model may reroll the dice that determine which models gets hit by the shots.

COORDINATED MOVEMENT

A leader can coordinate their crew to act as one by taking advantage of advanced communications or utilizing a special combat sign language that only the crew can understand. Once per game, if the model with this skill activates first, up to D3 friendly models within 3" automatically pass their Activation Tests. You cannot use this skill if the model's player loses initiative after the model's activation. For instance, when the model fails its Activation Test.

CLEVER

This model is naturally intelligent. The model receives +2 to Intelligence Tests.

CONFIDENT COMMAND

The leader is an inspiration to their crew. Any friendly models with line of sight and within 12" of this model gain +1 to all Will Tests. This ability's bonus is not cumulative with other models that have the same skill.

COUNTER-WEIGHT THROW

This operative is a master in a style of martial arts that uses the foe's own weight against them and can throw their enemies around like so much dead weight. Instead of attempting a to-wound roll after successfully hitting an enemy model in melee, this model can force their opponent to make an opposed Agility Test against them. If the model with this ability wins, it picks up the enemy and throws them 3" in a direction of its choice. The thrown model, and any intervening model hit by the thrown model, takes a STR 5 hit after landing, and the thrown model becomes Prone. If the enemy model wins the Opposed Test, nothing further happens, and combat continues as normal, counting that round as a tie.

CRITICAL BLOCK

With a bit of luck, this model can turn an attack back against its enemy. If this model rolls a Critical when defending in close combat, it gains 1 AP to immediately make an out-of-sequence melee attack against its attacker (resolve the first combat before making this attack). You may not use this special rule if you opt to push the enemy out of base contact. Once this special rule is used, the attacker resumes their turn.

DEADEYE

Years of training taught this operative how to compensate for distance. This model may add 3" to the point-blank range of a single weapon type they carry. You must choose the weapon when the model obtains this skill.

DEFENDER

The fast are the first to die. This operative is careful and takes things slow so they can outlast their opponents. When attacked in melee, this model receives +1 to its Melee and Defense stats.

DETECTOR

This bot is equipped with a specialized sensor array that makes hiding from it quite difficult. The model receives a +2 bonus to all Spot Tests.

DISARM

After successfully hitting an opponent in melee, the model with this skill may forgo the to-wound roll and instead attempt to disarm its enemy. The model makes an immediate opposed Agility Test against this opponent. If successful, choose one weapon carried by the enemy and place it D6" away on the ground in a direction of your choice. Use a token to mark the location where the weapon lands. Any model may scoop up the weapon by moving into base contact with the token and spending 1 AP. If anyone besides the original owner picks up the weapon, treat it as a looted weapon. If the Agility Test fails, the attempt to disarm the enemy fails. Nothing further happens, though the winner of the combat may still push the loser back or use any other special combat rules they have.

DIVE FOR COVER

This model heads for cover whenever possible, diving if necessary. Once per turn after taking a move action, if this model is not already Prone, this model may move an additional 3", after which they are placed Prone.

DO OR DIE

Perhaps a little too gung-ho, this operative does not quit until the mission is complete, even if it means they must cheat death for a bit. When this model is reduced to 0 HP, do not take them out-of-action or place them Prone. Instead, the model remains on the table for one more turn—until the end of its next activation—after which it succumbs to its wounds and is taken out-of-action as usual. During this final round of activation, the model with the Do or Die skill is immune to all Will Tests and adds +2 to its Defense stat. If this model suffers any further damage prior to its next activation, take it out-of-action as usual.

DUCK AND WEAVE

This model moves in an unpredictable fashion that minimizes its size and makes targeting it difficult. If a model with this skill made one or more movement actions during its last activation, all ranged attacks targeting this model receive a -1 penalty to-hit. A move caused by a failed Morale Test does not count as a "movement action" for this skill. Also, this penalty is cumulative with the to-hit penalty for a target that double moves.

FAST-TRACKER

This model can easily peg moving targets. It ignores the -1 penalty for shooting at targets that take a double move action.

FEARFUL REPUTATION

Among fellow mercenaries, this operative enjoys a particularly infamous reputation for being a cold-hearted killer, a maniac, or just someone with whom you should not trifle. All models that attempt to charge this model or move in base contact with them must pass a Will Test. If they fail this test, they may perform an alternative action instead, but cannot get closer to this model this turn.

FIGHT OR FLIGHT

This operative is hard to pin down in a fistfight. This model may reroll any failed Agility Test when attempting to disengage from close combat.

FIRST TO THE FIGHT

Whether they have a reckless disregard for the enemy or simply need to beat the rest of their crew to glory, this operative prefers to close-in on the enemy quickly. At the start of the game, after deploying all models, but before determining Initiative, this model may make a free move action.

FIRE ASSIST

This robot is fitted with cutting edge scanners and sensors than can telemetrically send useful ballistic data to friendly operatives close by. Friendly models within 3" of a model with Fire Assist receive +1 to their Aim stat.

FRENZY

This model is deranged and incapable of controlling its bloodlust. At the beginning of its activation, this model must make an Intelligence Test. This test does not cost AP. Success means the model may activate as normal, failure indicates the model has lost control. When this occurs, the model may not take any actions other than to charge or move toward the closest enemy model or make a melee attack if it is in base contact with an enemy. This model automatically passes all Grazed and Morale Tests. On subsequent activations, the model may try to restrain its anger by making another Intelligence Test to return to normal. This test does not cost AP.

FROTHER

This model chooses to lose control when entering combat and receives the Frenzy rule if it does not have it already. While frenzied—which takes place after the model fails its Intelligence Test to resist Frenzy—the model receives a +1 to its Melee and Strength stats until the end of the game. Also, this model may voluntarily choose to fail any Intelligence Test to become frenzied.

GROUND FIGHTER

A master of takedowns and grappling, this model knows how to even the odds. Enemy models never gain melee bonuses when this model is Prone. Additionally, if the model wins a round of close combat, it can force its opponent to make an opposed Agility Test. If the opponent succeeds, nothing happens, and combat continues normally. If the opponent fails, both the ground fighter and the opponent are placed Prone.

HACKERMAN

This model is a HyperNET hacking virtuoso. Choose a single app this model possesses. The model receives a +1 bonus to the Cyber stat when using that app. This skill may be taken multiple times, but you must choose a different app each time.

HARD AS NAILS

This operative is a tough cookie to crumble. After being hit by any attack, but before the roll to-wound, this model may roll a D10. Reduce the attack Strength by the result of the die roll. If this makes the attack's Strength 0 or lower, the attack is negated entirely. This special ability may only be used once per game.

HASTY CHARGE

This is not ballet; even if it is not perfect, you must still take your swing. On any turn in which this model fails an Activation Test, it may take a second move action for free, but must use it to charge against an enemy. Roll the D6 for movement and if the result it high enough, the model may charge. If not, the model remains where it is.

HOVER

This model can float above the ground. When moving, this model may ignore rough and linear terrain up to 1" tall, and it never takes damage from falling. If the model cannot hover for any reason, it falls Prone and must stand up to start hovering again. The model may not move at all while Prone.

HURDLER

Able to clear low walls and other obstructions quickly, not many barriers give this operative pause. During a move action, the model may cross any linear terrain obstacle that is no more than 1" tall without any reduction in movement.

LARGE

This model towers over the other occupants of the Sprawl. This model receives a +1 bonus to Melee when in combat with models without the Large special rule. Further, they may

make a Strength Test to resist any ability that will involuntarily move or knock the model prone. Finally, smaller models do not block line of sight to this model.

MARKSMAN

The sprawl has a thousand places to hide, but none of them will do you any good. This model reduces the to-hit range penalties against models in light and heavy cover by 1.

MULTIPLE STRIKES

A true warrior of the street, this operative is a master at offense. On any turn this model makes a melee attack, it gains an additional free AP that it may only use to make another melee attack. This second attack suffers a -2 Melee penalty.

MOTIVATOR

Through a combination of inspiring leadership, a generous benefits package, and upfront payment bonuses, this leader can get a crew to perform their best. All friendly models within 6" of this model receive a +1 bonus when making Activation Tests. A model may only benefit from the Motivator skill once per Activation Test, even if there are multiple sources are within range.

MR. FIX-IT

This model is a whiz with technology, pulling off near miracles when the crew is in a bind. Once per game, when this model spends AP to attempt to fix any item that is disabled, they automatically pass the test to do so.

MUSCULAR

Naturally strong, and a bit vain as a result, this operative is quite literally hired muscle. The model receives +1 STR.

OPPORTUNIST

This operative reads the flow of battle like a novel and believes knowing when to attack or defend is just a matter of waiting for the right opportunity. When resolving the to-hit phase of melee combat, this model treats ties as wins, instead.

OBSERVE

This operative can survey the battlefield, evaluate the ebb and flow of battle, and determine when it is the most opportune time to act. This model may choose to spend 1 AP during its current activation to receive a +2 bonus to its next Activation Test.

POP-UP

The operative can quickly spring to their feet. When Prone, this model may stand without paying AP. This model may only use this ability during its activation.

PUSH OFF

This operative can swat at opponents like flies when they do not wish to fight. The model may reroll any failed Strength Test when attempting to disengage from close combat.

QUICK

The model is naturally dexterous and gains +2 to Agility Tests.

RANGER

There is no enemy over which patience cannot triumph. The operative can track the enemy and find the best place from which to launch an ambush. Unless prohibited by specific scenario rules, this model may deploy anywhere on the board that is at least 9" away from any enemy model (both player-controlled and NPC) and is behind a terrain feature large enough to conceal them. If this model's crew deploys before the enemy's crew, place this model after the enemy deploys. Skip this model's activation during the first turn of the game, as it is still setting up its ambush. It may activate normally after the start of the second game turn.

RUNNING MAN

Nothing can stop this operative once they get going. This model may reroll their distance result when taking a second or triple move action. They must keep the new result, even if it is worse.

SELF-ASSURED

Words such as doubt, failure, or surrender hardly ever cross this operative's mind. This model may reroll all failed Morale and Grazed Tests.

SENTRY

Nothing gets past this operative—literally. Enemy models that move within 1" of this model must either end their movement or move in base contact with this model.

SHOOT AND SCOOT

This operative is adept at firing while on the move. This model does not suffer the penalty for moving while making ranged attacks.

SHADOW BLEND

The operative is hard to spot, as they seem to blend in perfectly with the shadows. Spot checks against this model suffer a -2 penalty.

SOLID FOOTING

This operative only moves when they want to. Anytime this model is subject to involuntary movement, they may make an opposed Strength Test against the model that is attempting to move them (if other circumstances are making them move, they simply make a Strength Test). If successful, the model remains in place. This skill does not work for involuntary movement from failed Morale or Grazed Tests.

SPRAWL SURVIVOR

Years of surviving in the harshest sections of the Sprawl have taught this operative to avoid the numerous industrial hazards—the hallmark of budget-minded corporations. This model receives a +2 bonus when making any Survival Test.

STEADY HANDS

Gunfights are won with nerve and a steady aim; everything else is luck. This model receives a +1 bonus when making ranged attacks if it does not move, either before or after shooting, during its activation.

SWARM

Not a single model, but hundreds of individual creatures represented by a single miniature. Swarms are generally tiny creatures, so ranged attacks against them suffer a -1 penalty to-hit. However, weapons that use templates do an extra D3 damage per successful roll to-wound.

TACTICIAN

This leader is a master at predicting the enemy's positions and deploying their crew to compensate. At the start of the game, after you deploy all models, but before you determine Initiative, this model's player rolls a D3+1 and redeploys that many members of their crew. They must redeploy the models using the same scenario restrictions. This ability may only be used once by each player—if two opposing crews have this ability, both roll a D6 and the player with the higher result may choose to redeploy first or second. If two or more models in the same crew have this ability, the player may still only use it once, but may reroll the D3.

TURING LOCK

This robot's AI is purposely limited to prevent it from taking independent actions. A model with this rule cannot make an Activation Test and cannot take any actions without another model transferring AP to it. Rules about how to do so are noted in the controlling model's entry. Only models with the *Bot* special rule may have this ability.

TREKKER

Whether a crowded street corner or a pile of Sprawl trash, this operative can surmount it with ease. When moving through difficult terrain, this model may make an Agility Test (this does not cost Action Points). On a success, the model moves through the terrain without penalty to its Move stat. On a failure, the model moves through the terrain with the normal movement penalties.

UP-ARMED

This model has special weapons training or their ghost entrusted them with an expensive piece of weaponry. A model with this special rule may use support weapons.

JOBOPS

"The email came yesterday. Sender unknown, but the bank transfer from Hawaii checked out golden. The details are simple: Escort a VIP named Vyper from the backroom of a vid-joint to his hotel by 0730. No idea why, and I don't care. My local rats tell me Vyper is a musico star on the outs with his promoter. I expect trouble with the transfer, but then, I always expect trouble."

"Cagey" Hernandez, Showrunner

Job Opportunities, or JOBOPS in Showrunner parlance, are jobs or missions that require the unique skills Showrunners have to offer their clients. Most clients are megacorps looking to add another layer to their claims of plausible deniability for their wars by proxy. Still, smaller corporations, Gov.Mils, crime syndicates, and other more esoteric groups have all used Showrunners in their time.

JOBOPS are never simple affairs. If the client—who always uses the moniker Mr., Mrs., or Ms., Smith, regardless of gender—could use more mundane corporate tactics, such as a hostile takeover or lawsuit, etc., they would do so. Conversely, if the use of military muscle was commercially or politically feasible, large power brokers would never shy away from crushing their rivals under a tide of up-gunned mercenaries and armor. But, some situations require a subtler approach. This is where the Showrunner comes into play.

Showrunner JOBOPS are almost always clandestine and illegal, or at least quasi-legal, and can include everything from moving illegal contraband, to hacking, to outright assassination—literal and character. As befitting their mysterious outsider status, Showrunners are never hired directly. Instead, they are recruited via anonymous boards on the local hood-net, through back-street fixers, or in hundreds of other esoteric ways. The hiring party posts or relays the job details, the parties haggle over and establish a price, and everyone comes to an agreement. Of course, any system has leaks, and a job offer is often not as secure as a Showrunner may hope. While no two Showrunners accept the same job due to professional courtesy, rivals of the original job poster often offer their own JOBOPS, as expected. The counter-offers are often quite formal, and a JOBOP post may have one or more counter-offers, depending on the target and reputation of the source. The original poster may even counter-offer their own mission if it helps obfuscate their involvement. Needless to say, this can get quite convoluted, which is rather the point.

JOBOPS in Your Games

In *Reality's Edge,* JOBOPS represent the scenarios you play with your friends for fame and fortune. The Sprawl is home to hundreds of agendas, most of which conflict with each other. To represent the chaotic nature of this type of employment, players roll against the *JOBOPS Table* to determine which scenario to play.

D10 Result	Scenario
JOBOPS TABLE	
1	Cloaked Asset Delivery
2	Forced Administrative Procurement
3	On the Ground Electronic Compliance
4	Antipathy Operations
5	Refuse Data Reclamation
6	Electronic Redundancy
7	Security Operations
8	Infrastructure Safekeeping
9	Dynamic Customer Relations
10	Player with highest REP chooses

CC LEVEL

Before the game, players must decide how many CC-worth of models and items they wish to use. If this is just a one-off game, we recommend a 800 CC starting crew, though veteran players can name any amount they wish, provided all players agree. Higher numbers represent elite teams and these games take a bit longer to play.

JOBOPS Breakdown

Each JOBOP has the following parts:

JOB DESCRIPTION

This gives the mission's basic details through the purview of the original shadow client. It also designates which crew is the attacker and which is the defender and provides any additional necessary rules. The player whose Showrunner crew has the least amount of

REP may choose whether they want to be the attackers or the defenders.

UNDER BIDDING

If one or more players contest who should be the attackers or defenders, all players can underbid the JOBOP. To do so, they offer to reduce the total CC in operatives or items they plan to bring to play. This is done in increments of 25 CC. All players should secretly write their bid, then reveal them at the same time. The player with the highest bid wins the choice of whether to be the attacker or defender. However, they must remove models and equipment equal to their bid from their crew for that game.

GRUDGE OPERATIONS

The Mission states whether grudge operations are authorized. Grudge operations are a form of special pay the crew can earn by taking enemy operatives out-of-action. This is considered a rather nasty thing to do and is reserved for those occasions where the shadow clients have a long-standing feud that requires a pound of flesh—even it comes from unaligned mercenaries. When grudge operations are authorized, each Showrunner crew earns 10 extra CC for each enemy operative their crew takes out-of-action. Operatives taken out-of-action by NPCs or environmental effects do not count.

MISSION VARIABLES

Each Showrunner mission is a bit different, even if the job is technically the same. Either player rolls a D6 (though only one player may do so) and consults the *Mission Variable Table* for that JOBOP. Sometimes, mission variables can make a mission easier to complete, sometimes they make the mission more difficult. If the latter happens, the client usually pays more to compensate. The former is just plain luck, and nobody pays for that.

SET UP

This section explains how the board is set up, including any special terrain or models needed, how many bystanders there are, etc. Crew deployment is covered here, as well.

This section also delineates CAT Terminal placement. CAT Terminals are special network nodes that crews can hack outside of their JOBOP mission. Think of them as targets of opportunity form which crews can pull useful data. Should a crew gain Access to a CAT Terminal during normal play, not only do they buff their shadow backer avatar, they can generate useful INFO. CAT Terminals have a starting Firewall of 6.

DEADLINE

This states how many turns the game has.

THE PAY OFF

This section describes the rewards each Showrunner crew earns for their involvement in the JOBOP. Payment is almost always performance driven. Rewards include REP, which is a measure of how well the crew is doing overall and the number of times they get to roll against the *Pay-Off Table*. Players can also earn INFO, which is useful.

THE HITCH

The Sprawl is always unpredictable and can catch even the most prepared Showrunner off guard. After determining the JOBOP, roll 3D10 and consult the *Hitch Table* to see what unique circumstance befalls the mission. The result applies only to the current game.

JOBOP'S Missions

ANTIPATHY OPERATIONS

JOB DESCRIPTION

Mr. Smith suffered a recent loss of business/property due to a particular entity's actions. While the client understands the cost of doing business, he feels the entity's actions were particularly egregious. Mr. Smith's contacts have ascertained the identity of a rival crew that worked for the entity in the past and he wishes to make an example of them. Mr. Smith is sensitive to the hesitancy of targeting rivals in such a direction fashion, but he is willing to make a significant monetary justification to send his warning. Grudge operations are, understandably, fully authorized.

This is a relatively direct, simple JOBOP, as both crews are paid for each enemy model they take out-of-action.

Designate one crew as the attackers, the other as the defenders.

MISSION VARIABLES

ANTIPATHY OPERATIONS MISSION VARIABLES TABLE	
D6 Result	Mission Variables
1	The crews bump into each other in the night. The night-time fighting rules are in effect (see page 43).
2	There is a sporting event happening on this block, so it is teeming with crowds. The number of bystanders used for this game decreases to D3 and the number of crowds increases to D6.
3	A mnemonic courier is active in this area of the Sprawl. The Mission Offer player chooses a board edge, the Counter Offer player places the courier anywhere along that edge. The courier is an NPC and uses the stats and rules found in the *Neutral Parties* section (see page 288).
4–6	There are no mission variables in this game.

SET UP

No special terrain requirements. Befitting the Sprawl, there should be numerous pieces of terrain to block line of sight and prevent long firing lanes.

The defending crew starts along one table edge of their choice, while the attacking crew starts along the opposite board edge. All members of both crews must be deployed no further than 12" from the center of their starting board edge. All models start in contact with their board edge.

Deploy 4 CAT Terminals. They should be no closer together than 8" from each other, a board edge, or a player-controlled model. The terminals should be as evenly distributed as possible, so you should fudge placement rules to allow them to be placed in a manner that is fair to all players. Players may take turns placing the terminals one after another.

Place D3 bystander crowds and D6 bystanders on the board if the players wish.

DEADLINE

The game lasts for 8 turns, or until one player opts to strategically withdrawal.

PAY-OFF

- Attacker/Defender: Both crews earn 1 REP for each 100 CC of enemy models they take out-of-action. They earn +1 REP if they take the rival Showrunner out-of-action as part of this total. The player with the most REP is the winner.

Each player may roll against the *Pay-Off Table* for each point of REP their crew earns. They also gain 1 INFO for each CAT Terminal they successfully Accessed. Count each CAT Terminal only once. Finally, each crew earns 10 CC for each enemy operative they take out-of-action.

The winning Showrunner gains 1 experience point. Any model that takes a Showrunner out-of-action gains 1 experience point.

CLOAKED ASSET DELIVERY

JOB DESCRIPTION

Mrs. Smith has a package that must be delivered with the utmost discretion. Due to the sensitivity of the transfer, there is a limited amount of time to safely see the package to its destination. Mrs. Smith was unclear about the package contents, but the Showrunner and crew must take possession of the package at an arranged drop-off and deliver it before the deadline. Should the package not reach its intended destination in time, payment will be greatly reduced. All other considerations are secondary, so grudge operations are not authorized.

Determine attacker and defender. The defending crew receives a counter or token to represent the package. The defending player must assign the package to one member of the crew by placing it in base contact with the chosen model. The package token moves with that model. However, unless the Mission Variables state otherwise, the package does not affect that model's movement in any way. A model can pay 1 AP to pass the package to another model in base contact.

The package is automatically captured by the enemy if the model carrying it is taken out-of-action in close combat. If the model carrying the package fails a Morale Test, is taken out-of-action by a ranged attack, is knocked unconscious, or is otherwise incapacitated, they drop the package on the ground. Any model that moves in base contact with the package captures it; this does not cost AP.

MISSION VARIABLES

D6 Result	Mission Variables
CLOAKED ASSET DELIVERY MISSION VARIABLES TABLE	
1	The package appears to be leaking low-level radiation. The model carrying it suffers a -1 penalty to their Defense stat while it is in their possession.
2	The package is deceptively heavy for its size. The model carrying it suffers a -1 to their Move stat.
3	The package is rather bulky to carry. The model carrying it suffers a -1 to all attack to-hit rolls.
4–6	The package is small and compact; carrying it does not impede the model in any way.

SET UP

No special terrain requirements. However, there should be several paths the crews can take to their goal across the board and plenty of street litter to slow them down. Befitting the Sprawl, there should be numerous pieces of terrain to block line of sight and prevent long firing lanes.

The defending crew starts along one table edge, while the attacking crew rolls a D10. On a 1–5, they deploy along the board edge to the defender's right. On a 6–10, they deploy along the board edge to the defender's left. All members of both crews must be deployed no further than 12" from the center of their starting board edge. All models start in contact with their board edge.

Deploy 4 CAT Terminals. They should be no closer together than 8" from each other, a board edge, or a player-controlled model. The terminals should be as evenly distributed as possible, so you should fudge placement rules to allow them to be placed in a manner that is fair to all players. Players may take turns placing the terminals one after another.

Place D3 bystander crowds and D6 bystanders on the board if the players wish.

DEADLINE

The game lasts for 8 turns, or until one player opts to strategically withdrawal.

PAY-OFF

- Attacker: Earns 6 REP for preventing the package from leaving the board edge (i.e., preventing the defenders from picking it up to deliver it). Earns +2 REP if they control the package at end of game. Earns only 3 REP if they fail to keep the defenders from getting the package.

- Defender: Earns 6 REP for retrieving the package from the board edge opposite the crew's staring deployment. Earns +2 REP if they do it within 6 turns. Earns +1 REP if the Mission Variables roll result was 1–3. Earns only 3 REP if they fail to get the package off the board.

The player with the most REP is the winner.

Each player may roll against the *Pay-Off Table* for each point of REP their crew earns. They also gain 1 INFO for each CAT Terminal they successfully Accessed. Count each CAT Terminal only once.

The winning Showrunner gains 1 experience point. The model in control of the package gains 1 experience point.

DYNAMIC CUSTOMER RELATIONS

JOB DESCRIPTION

Mr. Smith, acting as a representative for the Little Ramen Global Noodle Concern, is requesting assistance in securing the safety of one of their mobile franchises as it transfers between sectors. Behind schedule, the restaurant must travel through a notorious sector-block rife with criminal elements and dangerous local fauna. To maintain their neutral corporate status, Little Ramen hired multiple Showrunner teams who are expected to avoid hostilities and cooperate. Each Showrunner is therefore limited in the number of operatives they may bring. Mr. Smith specifies that the JOBOP includes a free lunch.

One of the more unusual JOBOPS for sure, both crews must protect the Little Ramen vehicle as it makes its trip. Determine an attacker and defender as usual. Before the game, mark the Little Ramen vehicle to differentiate its left and right sides. The attacker is tasked with protecting the right side and the defender the left. Both crews are working together, though, so while fighting is not prohibited, it is discouraged.

The Little Ramen vehicle is a movable piece of terrain about 6" long and 3" wide, though slight variations in size are fine. It should, however, be tall enough to block line of sight. At the beginning of each turn it moves 4", and it continues to move in this fashion until the end of the game. The Little Ramen vehicle has the capacity to hover, so it ignores linear terrain up to 1" tall if it has enough room to clear them. Otherwise, it moves around them, following the path the players set up. Should a model block the vehicle's path, it barges past them. Simply move the model the shortest distance required to get it out of the way and place it Prone. The model is otherwise unharmed. The vehicle itself cannot be damaged and does not have a stat profile.

The game takes place at night, so the night-time fighting rules are in effect (see page

43). However, the Little Ramen vehicle is equipped with lights, so the night-time fighting rules are ignored within 12" of the vehicle. Both crews must guard the vehicle, but are allowed to move about the board as they please.

As enemy NPCs are placed on the board, they emerge from the darkness. This means they must be placed just inside the light perimeter generated by the vehicle's lights, though at least 10" from the vehicle. Generate enemy NPCs by rolling against the *Freeloading Customers Table* below. During the Clean-Up Phase of each turn, roll against the table once and place the indicated models on the board. Starting with the left, alternate placing emerging enemies on the left and right sides of the Little Ramen vehicle. This creates areas of responsibility for the players. Models are placed individually, not as groups, even though the table gives a total number of NPCs. For instance, if the result indicates you should place two enemies, you would place one on the right and one the left of the Little Ramen vehicle.

The attacker controls all NPCs on the left and the defender controls all NPCs on the right. Enemy models follow the usual NPC rules for motivation, with the following exception: their first priority is to steal food from the vehicle. Should an enemy model manage to get in base contact with the vehicle, they may spend 1 AP to do so. If this happens, remove that model from the board, as they scamper away with their ill-gotten noodles, and make a note of the event for later.

FREELOADING CUSTOMERS TABLE	
D10 Result	NPC Enemies Generated
1	2 Poison Roaches
2	2 Ganger Punks
3	4 Rabid Dogs
4	2 Criminal Thugs
5	4 Sprawl Rats
6	4 Hallucinating Junkies

This mission uses Victory Points to determine the winner. For each enemy NPC model taken out-of-action, the responsible crew gains 1 Victory Point. If a player-controlled enemy NPC model manages to steal food from the Little Ramen vehicle (they access the other player's side of the vehicle), that player earns 3 Victory Points.

MISSION VARIABLES

None.

SET UP

No special terrain requirements. There should be a fairly clear path, 8" or wider, from one corner of the board to the opposite corner to allow the Little Ramen vehicle passage while still allowing terrain to get in the way a bit. The vehicle starts at either corner about 6" in from the edge. Each player arranges their crews within 3" of the vehicle on their respective sides. Befitting the Sprawl, there should be numerous pieces of terrain to block line of sight and prevent long firing lanes.

Deploy 4 CAT Terminals. They should be no closer together than 8" from each other, a board edge, or a player-controlled model. The terminals should be as evenly distributed as possible, so you should fudge placement rules to allow them to be placed in a manner that is fair to all players. Players may take turns placing the terminals one after another.

No bystanders are used for this JOBOP. To start, place 4 NPC Sprawl Rats on the board, following the above placement rules.

DEADLINE

The game lasts for 8 turns, or until one player opts to strategically withdrawal.

PAY-OFF

- Attacker/Defender: The crew with the most Victory Points is the winner. The winner earns 6 REP; the loser earns 3 REP. Both players earn an extra 20 CC, courtesy of the Little Ramen Global Noodle Concern.

Each player may roll against the *Pay-Off Table* for each point of REP their crew earns. They also gain 1 INFO for each CAT Terminal they successfully Accessed. Count each CAT Terminal only once.

All models not taken out-of-action when the game ends gain 1 experience point.

ELECTRONIC REDUNDANCY

JOB DESCRIPTION

Mr. Smith has an interest in monitoring network traffic within a specific HyperNET grid. Showrunner and crew are to physically infiltrate the area, install a backdoor app onto each CAT Terminal in this grid, and then leave. CORPSEC network protections have increased in this area, so expect Intrusion Countermeasures Emulation (ICE). Further, a rival crew claims authority of the local network and may attempt to install their own data-catchers. Showrunner and crew must prevent this as much as feasible, while protecting their own uploads.

Determine attacker and defender as usual. Both crews are attempting to gain Access to each CAT Terminal. Once a crew Accesses a terminal, the Hacker must spend another AP to install their own app. Installing the app automatically removes any installations by another crew. Mark each terminal somehow to indicate who controls it. A CAT Terminal is controlled by whichever crew currently has their software installed on it.

Each CAT Terminal is protected by White ICE, which uses the stats found in the *Neutral Parties* section (see page 303).

MISSION VARIABLES

ELECTRONIC REDUNDANCY MISSION VARIABLES TABLE	
D6 Result	**Mission Variables**
1	Each time White ICE is revealed during the game, roll a D6. On a 6, the White ICE is replaced with Black ICE, instead (see page 302). This only happens once, so once it occurs, further rolls are unnecessary.
2	A Griefer Avatar, which uses the stats found in the *Neutral Parties* section, is active in the grid (see page 298). Set up the model during the Clean Up Phase of the first turn.
3	The system is suffering substantial lag. All Virtual beings suffer a -1 Move penalty.
4–6	There are no mission variables in this game.

SET UP

No special terrain requirements. Befitting the Sprawl, there should be numerous pieces of terrain to block line of sight and prevent long firing lanes.

The defending crew starts along the table edge of their choice, while the attacking crew starts along the opposite board edge. All members of both crews must be deployed no further than 12" from the center of their starting board edge. All models start in contact with the board edge.

Deploy 4 CAT Terminals. They should be no closer together than 8" from each other, a board edge, or a player-controlled model. The terminals should be as evenly distributed as possible, so you should fudge placement rules to allow them to be placed in a manner that is fair to all players. Players may take turns placing the terminals one after another.

Place D3 bystander crowds and D6 bystanders on the board if the players wish.

DEADLINE

The game lasts for 8 turns, or until one player opts to strategically withdrawal.

PAY-OFF

- Attacker/Defender: Each crew receives 1 REP for each CAT Terminal they control at the end of the game. They also receive +1 REP for each White ICE taken Offline and +2 for each Black ICE taken Offline. The player with the most REP is the winner.

Each player may roll against the *Pay-Off Table* for each point of REP their crew earns. They also gain 1 INFO for each CAT Terminal they successfully Accessed. Count each CAT Terminal only once.

The winning Showrunner gains 1 experience point. If Black ICE is used in the scenario and a model takes them Offline, the model gains 1 experience point.

FORCED ADMINISTRATIVE PROCUREMENT

JOB DESCRIPTION

Ms. Smith has a VIP she wishes to recover. She was not clear whether the VIP is willing to be extracted from their current location. Ms. Smith will provide approximate target coordinates and the Showrunner and crew must retrieve the VIP at all costs. The VIP is currently being detained/contracted by hostile interests who will contest the VIP's extraction. These hostile agents may even have authorization to terminate the VIP should the VIP slip from their grasp. Grudge operations are not authorized.

Determine attacker and defender as usual. The defending crew takes possession of the VIP, which should be represented by a suitable model. Use the VIP stats found in the *Neutral Parties* section and treat the VIP as a normal member of the controlling crew (see page 313). The VIP attempts to remain within 1" of another member of the controlling crew as much as possible. The VIP never makes an Activation Test. Instead, they automatically receive 2 AP each turn and may activate at any time the controlling player has initiative.

The crew with the most models within 1" of the VIP count as being in possession of the VIP. Unless the Mission Variables state otherwise, the VIP is hostile toward the attackers and always attempts to move away from members of that crew. However, the attacking crew may carry the VIP to prevent this. If a model is carrying the VIP, their crew automatically counts as being in possession of the VIP.

To carry the VIP, a model must be in base contact with them and spend 1 AP to make an opposed Strength Test. If it loses, nothing happens, and it wastes the AP. If it wins, it grabs the VIP and the VIP now moves with the model. Each time the VIP activates while being carried, they automatically spend an AP to try to break free by making an opposed Strength Test. If they lose, they waste the AP. If they win, they break free and their controlling player may move them. Any ranged attacks that target a model carrying the VIP have a 50/50 chance of hitting the VIP, instead. Close combat attacks made against a model carrying the VIP only hit the VIP on a Fumble. Should a model carrying the VIP fail any Will Test (including Graze Tests), they automatically lose control of the VIP. A model carrying the VIP moves at half their normal rate.

Should the defending crew attempt to kill the VIP, the VIP automatically treats all members of the crew as hostile.

MISSION VARIABLES

D6 Result	Mission Variables
Forced Administrative Procurement Mission Variables Table	
1	The VIP is a formidable fighter. They gain +1 to their Melee and Aim stats and are armed with a light SMG.
2	The VIP is a trained athlete. They gain +1 to their Move and Strength stats.
3	The VIP is motivated to stay with their current employer. Once per game when activating, they may gain 3 AP instead of the usual 2. The controlling player may choose when to use this ability.
4–5	There are no mission variables in this game.
6	The VIP is hostile toward the defending crew. Each turn, they use all available AP to attempt to move toward the attacking crew. The defending crew may carry the VIP to prevent this.

SET UP

Place a building in the center of the table with a minimum size of 6" square. This is the secured building where the VIP is being protected. The rest of the terrain may be set up as the players wish. Befitting the Sprawl, there should also be numerous pieces of terrain to block line of sight and prevent long firing lanes.

The VIP is being held in the building in the center of the board. The VIP must be set up within this building (on the first floor if it is a multistory building). The defending crew may set up inside or anywhere within 6" of the building. The attacking crew may set up along any board edge, but they must all touch the same board edge to start.

Deploy 4 CAT Terminals. They should be no closer together than 8" from each other, a board edge, or a player-controlled model. The terminals should be as evenly distributed as possible, so you should fudge placement rules to allow them to be placed in a manner that is fair to all players. Players may take turns placing the terminals one after another.

Place D3 bystander crowds and D6 bystanders on the board if the players wish.

DEADLINE

The game lasts for 8 turns, or until one player opts to strategically withdrawal.

PAY-OFF

- Attacker: Earns 6 REP for having possession of the VIP at the end of the game. Earns +1 REP if the Mission Variables result was 1–3. Gains only 3 REP if the defender kills the VIP to take them out-of-action.
- Defender: Earns 6 REP for having possession of the VIP at the end of the game. Earns +3 REP if the VIP is taken-out-of-action. Loses 2 REP instead of gaining any if they kill the VIP before a member of the attacking crew gets within 6" of the VIP.

The player with the most REP is the winner.

Each player may roll against the *Pay-Off Table* for each point of REP their crew earns. They also gain 1 INFO for each CAT Terminal they successfully Accessed. Count each CAT Terminal only once.

The winning Showrunner gains 1 experience point. The model in control of the VIP gains 1 experience point.

INFRASTRUCTURE SAFEKEEPING

JOB DESCRIPTION

Mr. Smith has business assets that have recently come under threat from "criminal" elements. Temporary security is required to avoid loss of income and, to a lesser extent, to avoid loss of life and injury to employees. Showrunner and crew are to secure a perimeter around the business and prevent enemy provocateurs from gaining physical access to the business and/or causing damage. The Client wishes to make their displeasure with the threat to their livelihood known, so grudge operations are authorized.

Determine attacker and defender, as usual. The defender must protect the building found in the center of the board. This mission uses Victory Points to determine the winner. During the Clean Up phase of each turn, determine which crew has the most CC-worth of models inside the central building. If the attacking crew has more, they earn 1 Victory Point. If the defending crew as more, they earn 2 Victory Points.

The attacker earns Victory Points as described above. Additionally, they may also trash the place by destroying anything within reach. To do this, treat any crew member that spends 2 AP during a single turn as having completed a special action. Each time a crew member completes this special action, they earn 1 Victory Point. They cannot perform this special action if they are in base contact with an enemy model.

MISSION VARIABLES

INFRASTRUCTURE SAFEKEEPING MISSION VARIABLES TABLE	
D6 Result	Mission Variables
1	The central building is a public area, such as a restaurant or nightclub. Place D6 bystanders inside in addition to the normal bystanders for the mission. The defender loses 1 Victory Point for each bystander their crew takes out-of-action. Bystanders taken out-of-action by the attacking crew have no effect.
2	The central building has automated security. The defender may place a light security turret anywhere touching the central building. The turret is treated as a neutral model with the guard motivation and is under the defender's control each turn unless hacked.
3	The central building has automated security that was compromised by remote hackers. The attacker may place a light security turret anywhere touching the central building. The turret is treated as a neutral model with the guard motivation. It treats both crews as hostile.
4–6	There are no mission variables in this game.

SET UP

Place a building in the center of the table with a minimum size of 6" square. This is the secured building the defending player must protect. The rest of the terrain may be set up as both players wish. Befitting the Sprawl, there should be numerous pieces of terrain line to block line of sight and prevent long firing lanes.

The defender may set up half their models anywhere inside the central building. The rest must patrol the neighborhood and start no closer than 9" to the central building. The attacking crew may be set up along any board edge, but they must all be set up touching the same board edge.

Deploy 4 CAT Terminals. They should be no closer together than 8" from each other, a board edge, or a player-controlled model. The terminals should be as evenly distributed as possible, so you should fudge placement rules to allow them to be placed in a manner that is fair to all players. Players may take turns placing the terminals one after another.

Place D3 bystander crowds and D6 bystanders on the board if the players wish. However, none may be placed inside the central building.

DEADLINE

The game lasts for 8 turns, or until one player opts to strategically withdrawal.

PAY-OFF

- Attacker: If the attacker has the most Victory Points they earn 6 REP; if not, they only gain 3 REP. If the Mission Variables resulted in a light security turret under defender control, the attacker earns +1 REP if they took the turret out-of-action. If the light security turret was present, but neutral, it is still worth +1 REP if taken out-of-action.
- Defender: If the defender has the most Victory Points, they earn 6 REP; if not, they only gain 3 REP. If the light security turret was present, but neutral, it is worth +1 REP if taken out-of-action.

The player with the most REP is the winner.

Each player may roll against the *Pay-Off Table* for each point of REP their crew earns. They also gain 1 INFO for each CAT Terminal they successfully Accessed. Count each CAT Terminal only once. Finally, each crew earns 10 CC for each enemy operative they take out-of-action.

The winning Showrunner gains 1 experience point.

ON THE GROUND ELECTRONIC COMPLIANCE

JOB DESCRIPTION

Mrs. Smith requires a crew to modify a local network node with proprietary software, which she will provide. The node is behind robust physical security, is hardened, and is only electronically connected to a local network. The Showrunner and crew must infiltrate the node's location, install the hardware, and allow at least one boot cycle to complete so the software has time to set up properly. Once completed, the crew may evacuate. The client wishes to minimize casualties and property damage; therefore, grudge operations are not authorized.

Determine attacker and defender, as usual. The attacker must successfully gain Access to a mission network node and maintain control for one full game turn after Access is gained. The mission network node has a starting Firewall of 7.

The defender must prevent the mission network node from being accessed; or if it is Accessed, successfully regain control of the node before the end of the next game turn in which the attacker gained Access.

MISSION VARIABLES

ON THE GROUND ELECTRONIC COMPLIANCE MISSION VARIABLES TABLE	
D6 Result	Mission Variables
1	The network node is guarded by White ICE, which uses the stats found in the *Neutral Parties* section (see page 303). The mission network node cannot be the target of a cyber-attack until the ICE is taken Offline. The defender controls the ICE while it remains online.
2–3	Add +1 to the mission network node's Firewall.
4–6	The mission network node has normal defenses; no changes.

SET UP

Place a building in the center of the table with a minimum size of 6" square. You may place the mission network node anywhere inside, but it must be on the ground floor if it is a multistory building. The rest of the terrain may be set up as both players wish. Befitting the Sprawl, there should be numerous pieces of terrain line to block line of sight and prevent long firing lanes.

The attacking crew starts along the table edge of their choice, but they must all be set up touching the same board edge. The defending crew may set up three total models inside the central building to start with. The remainder of their operatives may deploy along one of the board edges not chosen by the attacker. They must touch the board edge and be within 6" of the center of the board edge.

Deploy 4 CAT Terminals. They should be no closer together than 8" from each other, a board edge, or a player-controlled model. The terminals should be as evenly distributed as possible, so you should fudge placement rules to allow them to be placed in a manner that is fair to all players. Players may take turns placing the terminals one after another.

Place D3 bystander crowds and D6 bystanders on the board if the players wish.

DEADLINE

The game lasts for 8 turns, or until one player opts to strategically withdrawal.

PAY-OFF

- Attacker: Successfully maintaining Access to the mission network node for one full game turn after gaining Access earns 6 REP. If they do not meet the primary objective, but are able to gain Access to the mission network node at all, they gain 3 REP instead. They earn +2 REP if the mission network node is guarded by ICE and it is taken Offline.
- Defender: If the mission network node is not Accessed in any manner, the defender earns 6 REP. If the mission network node is Accessed by the enemy but is reclaimed by the defending crew before the end of the next game turn, they earn 3 REP, instead.

The player with the most REP is the winner.

Each player may roll against the *Pay-Off Table* for each point of REP their crew earns. They also gain 1 INFO for each CAT Terminal they successfully Accessed. Count each CAT Terminal only once.

The winning Showrunner gains 1 experience point. The model that successful hacks the mission node gains 1 experience point.

DATALOADED

0:28:06

REFUSE DATA RECLAMATION

JOB DESCRIPTION

Mr. Smith has recently ascertained the location of a corporate disposal station specializing in outdated data storage hardware. Prior reconnaissance performed on the station indicates that after security sanitation, the hardware is illegally dumped in a nearby sector. Mr. Smith wishes to recycle anything of potential value that can be pulled from the junked hardware. Local scavengers and CORPSEC patrols are believed to be active in the sector. Worse, a rival concern has "claimed" the refuse station and will strongly defend their interest. The crew must avoid, liquidate, or ignore challenges; depending on the Showrunner's inclination. Grudge operations are authorized.

Determine attacker and defender, as usual. Both crews must search garbage piles looking for anything of potential value. To search a pile, a model must be in base contact, spend 1 AP, and pass an Intelligence Test. On a success, they find something of possible value to their employer. Each garbage dump may only be successfully searched once.

MISSION VARIABLES

REFUSE DATA RECLAMATION	
D6 Result	**Mission Variables**
1–2	Each garbage pile contains D3 sprawl rats. When a model moves within 6" of a pile, roll a D3 and place that may rats in contact with the pile.
3–4	The air is this sector is notoriously toxic, probably because of all the illegal dumping. All models suffer a -1 to their Defense stat.
5	One of the garbage piles holds a deactivated Cyborg. The first time a model moves into base contact with a garbage pile, roll a D6. On a 6, a rampaging Cyborg is placed Prone on top of the pile. This only happens once, and no Cyborg is placed if a 6 is not rolled. If the Cyborg is placed, it activates at the start of the NPC Phase within D3 turns. Use the stats for the Rampaging Light Cyborg found in the *Neutral Parties* section (see page 306).
6	There are no mission variables in this game.

SET UP

Place six garbage piles on the board. Each should be about 3" in diameter, though some variance in size is fine. They should be placed no closer than 6" from each other and at least 8" from a table edge. The rest of the terrain may be set up as both players wish. Befitting the Sprawl, there should be numerous pieces of terrain line to block line of sight and prevent long firing lanes.

The attacking crew starts along one table edge, while the defending crew starts along the opposite board edge. All members of both crews must be deployed no further than 12" from the center of their starting board edge. All models start in contact with the board edge.

Deploy 4 CAT Terminals. They should be no closer together than 8" from each other, a board edge, or a player-controlled model. The terminals should be as evenly distributed as possible, so you should fudge placement rules to allow them to be placed in a manner that is fair to all players. Players may take turns placing the terminals one after another.

Place D3 bystander crowds and D6 bystanders on the board if the players wish. If the toxic air result from the *Mission Variables Table* is rolled, no bystander crowds may be placed.

DEADLINE

The game lasts for 8 turns, or until one player opts to strategically withdrawal.

PAY-OFF

- Attacker/Defender: The crew successfully searches the most garbage piles earns 6 REP while the other crew earns 3 REP. The player with the most REP is the winner.

Each player may roll against the *Pay-Off Table* for each point of REP their crew earns. They also gain 1 INFO for each CAT Terminal they successfully Accessed. Count each CAT Terminal only once. Finally, each crew earns 10 CC for each enemy operative they take out-of-action.

The winning Showrunner gains 1 experience point. If the Cyborg is used in the scenario and a model takes them out-of-action, the model gains 1 experience point.

SECURITY OPERATIONS

JOB DESCRIPTION

Mrs. Smith's operations have come under attack from a rival interest. Immediate assistance is required to repel enemy combatants and to ensure proper control of all physical assets. Showrunner and crew must proceed immediately to secure the area until more conventional security personnel can be deployed. Grudge operations are authorized at Mrs. Smith's request.

Determine attacker and defender, as usual. The defender must protect the building in the center of the board. This mission uses Victory Points to determine the winner. The defending crew earns 1 Victory Point for each enemy model they take out-of-action or cause to be removed from the table (for example, when a model rolls a Fumble on a Morale Test). They can also earn 1 additional Victory Point if the enemy model is inside the building when they are taken out-of-action or removed from the table. Additionally, scatter three property tokens randomly inside the building. For each property token still intact at the end of the scenario, the defender gains 2 Victory Points.

The attacker earns Victory Points as described for taking models out-of-action or having them removed from the game. Additionally, they may attempt to destroy the property tokens inside the building. Any model in base contact with a property token may spend 2 AP, which must be done in the same activation, to destroy the token. Doing so grants the attacker 2 Victory Points.

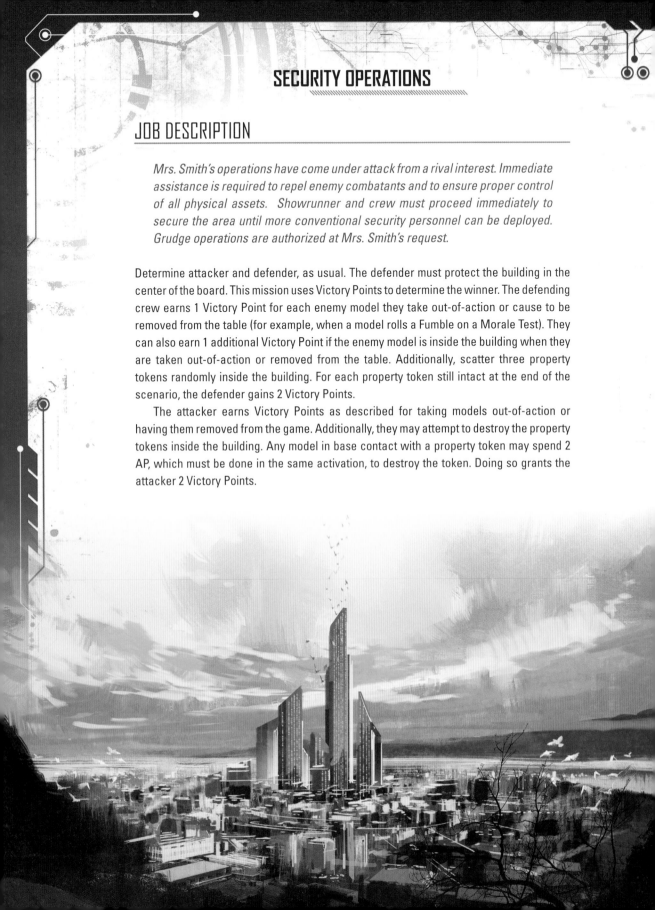

MISSION VARIABLES

D6 Result	SECURITY OPERATIONS MISSION VARIABLES TABLE
	Mission Variables
1	The central building has squatters. Deploy D6 hallucinating junkies inside. They use the stats found in the *Neutral Parties* section (see page 299).
2	A local gaming concern is using the building to run an illegal card tournament. Place a bystander crowd inside the building. When rolling Panic Tests for this crowd, roll 2D10 and use the higher result.
3	The central building has automated security, but it is compromised by remote hackers. The attacker may place a light security turret anywhere touching the central building. The turret is treated like a neutral model with the guard motivation. It treats both crews as hostile.
4–6	There are no mission variables in this game.

SET UP

Place a building in the center of the table with a minimum size of 6" square. This is the secure building the defending crew must protect. The rest of the terrain may be set up as both players wish. Befitting the Sprawl, there should be numerous pieces of terrain line to block line of sight and prevent long firing lanes.

The defending crew starts along one table edge, while the attacking crew starts along the board edge opposite but may deploy up to 6" away from the edge to represent their head start. All members of both crews must be deployed no further than 12" from the center of their starting board edge, even models that have special deployment rules, such as Infiltrators.

Deploy 4 CAT Terminals. They should be no closer together than 8" from each other, a board edge, or a player-controlled model. The terminals should be as evenly distributed as possible, so you should fudge placement rules to allow them to be placed in a manner that is fair to all players. Players may take turns placing the terminals one after another.

Place D3 bystander crowds and D6 bystanders on the board if the players wish. However, none may be placed inside the central building.

DEADLINE

The game lasts for 8 turns, or until one player opts to strategically withdrawal.

PAY-OFF

- Attacker: If they have the most VP they gain 6 REP; if not, they only earn 3 REP. If the light security turret was present, it is worth +1 REP if they took it out-of-action.
- Defender: If they have the most Victory Points they gain 6 REP; if not, they only earn 3 REP. If the light security turret was present, it is worth +1 REP if they took it out-of-action.

The player with the most REP is the winner.

Each player may roll against the *Pay-Off Table* for each point of REP their crew earns. They also gain 1 INFO for each CAT Terminal they successfully Accessed. Count each CAT Terminal only once. Finally, each crew earns 10 CC for each enemy operative they take out-of-action.

The winning Showrunner gains 1 experience point.

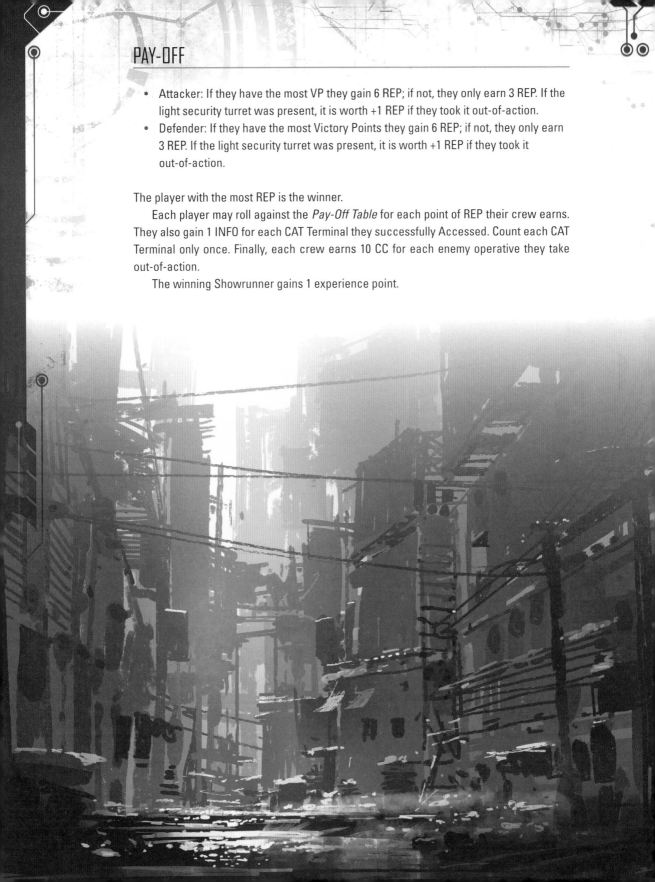

EXECUTIVE HEADHUNT

JOB DESCRIPTION

>>>Emergency Shadow Backer Message<<<
CORPSEC data sniffers have compromised our secure network. Intel indicates corporate blackout team(s) were dispatched to scalp Showrunner operations. Showrunner and crew must simultaneously evacuate the operation zone and engage elite CORPSEC forces. A rival Showrunner was engaged to provide support, but their ultimate loyalty should be questioned. Take advantage of the confusion to escape. Grudge operations for CORPSEC casualties are authorized.

This JOBOP is a special event that only occurs when a Showrunner crew is fully tracked down by CORPSEC agents as described under the *Campaigning in the Sprawl* section. Both crews engage the CORPSEC teams that arrive on the battlefield instead of trying to kill each other. However, the crews do not have to work together and may engage each other as they wish.

The crew CORPSEC traced are the defenders in this mission. The opposing crew are the attackers.

MISSION VARIABLES

If either crew is worth 1500 CC or more, add one more blackout team per turn.

SET UP

No special terrain requirements. Befitting the Sprawl, there should be numerous pieces of terrain to block line of sight and prevent long firing lanes.

The defending crew starts in the center of the table, deploying no further than 6" away from the center point. The attacking crew may start along any board edge of their choice, but no further away than 6" from the center of the edge.

Deploy 4 CAT Terminals. They should be no closer together than 8" from each other, a board edge, or a player-controlled model. The terminals should be as evenly distributed as possible, so you should fudge placement rules to allow them to be placed in a manner that is fair to all players. Players may take turns placing the terminals one after another.

Place D3 bystander crowds and D6 bystanders on the board if the players wish.

At the beginning of each turn except the first, place one CORPSEC blackout team on the table via the *Drop-In* rules described under *NPC Placement* in the *Gameplay* section. On the first turn, place two blackout teams. They activate as usual using the NPC rules. While the teams can be treated as normal NPCs, we recommend that a third, neutral player, take control of the crews to increase the challenge and fun of the scenario. Each blackout team is made up of three models that use the stats below. The teams that deploy on the first turn must deploy within 12" of the defending crew. On subsequent turns, however, the player controlling the newly arriving team may place them anywhere on the board that is at least 6" away from a player-controlled model.

If there are ever more than 4 blackout teams on the table at any one time (or 5, if either crew is over 1500 CC), do not deploy a new one at the beginning of the game turn.

DEADLINE

The game lasts for 8 turns, or until one player opts to strategically withdrawal.

PAY-OFF

- Attacker: Receive 1 REP for each blackout operator taken out of-action. However, they lose 1 REP if the defending Showrunner is taken out-of-action.
- Defender: Receive 1 REP for each blackout operator taken out of-action. However, they lose 3 REP if their Showrunner is taken out-of-action.

Each player may roll against the *Pay-Off Table* for each point of REP their crew earns. They also gain 1 INFO for each CAT Terminal they successfully Accessed. Count each CAT Terminal only once. Finally, each crew earns 10 CC for each blackout operator they take out-of-action.

CORPSEC BLACKOUT OPERATOR

A unique asset within the CORPSEC structure, blackout operators are rapid response units always on standby to handle special missions. By deploying via aerial assertion, they can quickly descend into the Sprawl and ruthlessly eliminate high-value threats to corporate rule.

Name	DEF	HP	FW
CORPSEC Blackout Operator	5 (7)	6	6

STATS				
MOV	MEL	AIM	STR	MET
5	4	4	5	5

Motivation	Type	Special Rules		
Aggressive	Human	None		

Items
Bludgeon with Flashing upgrade, Assault Rifle or Heavy SMG with Neural Link, Security Armor with the Stab-Proof upgrade

Hitches

THE HITCH TABLE	
3D10 Result	Hitch
3	Meme War
4	Acid Rain
5	Boom-Booms
6	Professional Courtesy
7	Heavy Turrets
8	Always Cloudy
9	CORPSEC Sweep
10	Discount Death
11	Rogue App
12	Dodgy Hood-Net
13	Rolling Blackout
14	Lock-Down
15	Gangers
16	Industrial Smoke
17	Dog Town
18	Sprawl Rat Surprise
19	Professional Rivalry
20	Idoru
21	Waking Dead
22	Hot Potato
23	Light Turrets
24	Hot Spots
25	Tough Hood
26	Hardened Nodes
27	Tesla Defenders
28	Train Pain
29	Baking Sun
30	Without a Hitch

ACID RAIN

Unchecked corporate pollution in this sector had led to a spate of dangerous acid rain storms. Unprotected skin burns from the acidic water droplets; worse yet, armor and clothing starts to disintegrate, as well. Reduce the Armor Bonus of all models by 1 (to a minimum of 1). If a model does not have an Armor Bonus, they must pass an Agility Test each turn or suffer 1 point of damage for each turn in which they are not touching or within some type of terrain or cover.

ACTION NEWS 5

No one is more aggressive and IN YOUR FACE than the hard-hitting vid-reporters of Action News 5—home of the only news you can use, with traffic deaths on the sixes and the bloodiest coverage found anywhere. One of the Action News 5 vid-carriers is attracted to the violence of the battlefield. Each player gains +1 REP if they take at least one member of a rival Showrunner crew out-of-action, since being on the nightly news is great for street cred. However, if any model is captured when rolling on the *Survival Table* (see page 274), add an additional 10 CC to their bail.

ALWAYS CLOUDY

The Sprawl is always dark and rainy, but it seems especially so today. All ranged attacks over 12" suffer a -1 penalty to hit due to the incessant rain and cloud cover. Additionally, all models suffer a -1 to their Move stat due to the slippery ground.

BAKING SUN

A rarity among the normal dark noir of the Sprawl, the sun shines in all its hope and glory, leaving few shadows in which to hide. All Spot Tests receive a +1 bonus.

BOOM-BOOMS

A weapons manufacturer haphazardly dumped their surplus explosives in this sector. Their permits are valid, so there is little the local Sprawlers can do about it. Each player may place up to three Boom-Booms about the board. They should be represented by 55-gallon drums or tokens about 1" in diameter. They may not be placed within any crew's deployment area or within 6" of any mission objective. At any time, a model may attack a Boom-Boom. Roll to hit as usual but ignore all negative to-hit modifiers. Boom-Booms have a Defense of

6 and 1 HP. Should a model manage to "wound" one, it blows up and all models within D6" suffer an automatic Strength 6 hit. Note that this explosion may set-off any other Boom-Booms within range.

CORPSEC SWEEP

LEO's from a nearby CORPSEC station are sweeping the area, spoiling for heads to bash. Three CORPSEC grunts arrive from a random board edge during the Clean-Up phase of the second game turn. They activate as usual during the next turn's NPC Phase. If the combined total of the crews is 2000 CC or more, two such groups arrive—one on a random board edge and the other on the board edge directly across from the first.

DISCOUNT DEATH

A local arms dealer is flooding the local Black-Market with high grade ammunition at insanely cheap prices. Don't ask why. For the duration of this game, all ranged attacks made with any handgun or long gun deal +1 damage.

DODGY HOOD-NET

The local nodes are of poor quality and are constantly abused by the resident wannabe deckers. All cyber-attacks against CAT Terminals in this game receive a +1 bonus.

DOG TOWN

This area of the Sprawl is home to many stray dogs. Most of the dogs are skittish and run away if approached, but some are quite friendly. All models receive a +1 to Morale Tests since everyone loves dogs. However, the dogs can sometimes get underfoot and betray a model's presence to the enemy. At the end of each turn, roll a D10 for each model that is currently Hidden. On a 1, a dog jumps on them excitedly or lets out an identifying howl; the model loses their Hidden status. The dogs are quick to avoid danger and you cannot attack or interact with them in any other way; you do not need to model them.

GANGERS

Some low-level Gangers strung out on inhalers are in the area. Caring little for their own personal safety, they fight anyone they can. Two Ganger Punks and one Ganger Champion emerge from the center of a randomly determined board edge.

HARDENED NODES

The network nodes in this sector are notoriously well-maintained and protected by local CORPSEC. All CAT Terminals in this game gain +1 Firewall.

HEAVY TURRETS

A corporation operating in this sector has gotten a little paranoid regarding the locals. Each player may place a single turret on or near a terrain piece of their choice that does not contain a mission objective and is not within either crew's deployment area. When first set up, the turret is on Overwatch and fires on the first model to come within 12". After that, it operates as a normal NPC heavy security turret.

HOT POTATO

A terrorist anti-corporate collective planted an explosive device in this sector. They hid the bomb quite well, and did not contact local authorities to maximize casualties. Note that if the current JOBOP relies on an objective or a crew deployed in the middle of the table, you should reroll this result. Otherwise, place a token or marker about 1" in diameter at the center of the table to represent the bomb. At the end of each game turn, each player may move the bomb token up to 6" in any direction or may elect not to do so. Players should roll off to see who may move the explosive first each turn. Each time the bomb is moved, the moving player must roll a D10. On a Fumble, the bomb immediately explodes after moving. If neither player moves the bomb, one player should roll to see if it explodes anyway. Roll a D10 and add the turn number to the result. If the result is 10 or higher, the bomb explodes. The bomb has a radius of D10+5" and has a Strength 7. Any models hit by the bomb but not taken out-of-action are knocked Prone.

HOT SPOTS

A local corporation stashed some toxic waste in this sector—all legal and above-board, of course. Each player nominates a single piece of terrain. Neither terrain piece may contain a mission objective or be in an opponent's deployment area. After each piece is designated, each player rolls a D6 for their chosen terrain piece. The result is how far the radiation spreads from that piece of terrain in inches. Once per turn, all models that enter, move through, leave, or remain within this area must pass a Strength Test or suffer a -1 to their Defense as they are afflicted by radiation poisoning. This Defense loss is cumulative. Should a model's Defense be reduced to 0, excluding any Armor Bonus they may have, they immediately go out-of-action.

IDORU

To increase her friend count on social media, a B-rated Idoru is broadcasting a vid-concert on the local virtual reality grid. Not only are Sprawlers jamming cyberspace trying to get a view of the action, but local crowds in Realspace are also beginning to gather, hoping to find her broadcast location. During the game, all Virtual beings reduce their Move stat by -2 due to the lag. Also add 3 bystander crowds to the board. They are placed as usual and are in addition to any bystanders the mission uses, normally.

INDUSTRIAL SMOKE

A local corporate manufacturer in this sector neglected to install smog filters on their industrial burners, leaving everyone in the area choking in the black fog. While not particularly hazardous in the short-term, the fog reduces line of sight to 12" for all models.

LIGHT TURRETS

A local crime syndicate rigged their territory with automated turrets to ward off nosy intruders. Each player may place a single light turret on or near a terrain piece of their choice that does not contain a mission objective and is not within either crew's deployment area. When first set up, the turret is on Overwatch and fires on the first model to come within 12". After that, it operates as a normal NPC light security turret.

LOCK-DOWN

The crews are meeting for battle in a particularly rough neighborhood, with decidedly unfriendly neighbors. All portals, including doors, windows, etc., on enclosed terrain pieces are considered locked. To enter/leave through them, models must either pick the locks, which requires an Intelligence Test, or force them open, which requires a Strength Test; both options cost 1 AP to attempt.

MEME WAR

An online culture war rages across the local HyperNET as users rush to upload the dankest of memes, grinding the system to a halt. All cyber-attacks suffer a -2 penalty.

PROFESSIONAL COURTESY

Com chatter reveals that multiple freelancers on both Showrunner crews worked together before in close quarters, leading to a certain reluctance to use lethal force. All freelancers suffer a -1 penalty to both shooting and melee attacks against other freelancers. This does not apply to Permahires or Showrunners.

PROFESSIONAL RIVALRY

A freelancer on one of the Showrunner's crews recognizes a hated rival among the opposing crew. Now, the freelancers on both sides are frothing at the bit to protect their crewmate's reputation. Freelancers on both sides receive a +1 to all attack rolls against another freelancer. This does not apply to Permahires or Showrunners.

ROGUE APP

A console cowboy, who has long since moved on, left a present for the local tech-heads in this sector in the form of a custom App installed in one of the nearby nodes. It is now attempting to hack any technology that gets within signal range of its jury-rigged Wi-Fi hub with brute force. Players should determine a random CAT Terminal as the home for the rogue app. When any model comes within 8" of the affected terminal, it suffers an attack from the rogue app with a total Cyber score of 4. If the target's Firewall is breached, an enemy player may choose which weapon is disabled. If a model starts its activation within 8" of the terminal, the rogue app attacks it using the same rules. The terminal may make a cyber-attack on any number of models, but it may only attack each model once per game turn. If the terminal is successfully Accessed, the rogue app is automatically scrubbed and taken Offline.

ROLLING BLACKOUT

This zone's power grid is testy at the best of times and a recent growth in illegal hook-ups have only added to the problem. This game uses the night-time fighting rules (see page 43). However, roll a D10 at the start of each turn. On an 8+, the lights come back on and the night-time fighting rules are ignored for the rest of the game.

SPRAWL RAT SURPRISE

The noise of battle drew the attention of a sprawl rat swarm. D3 sprawl rats emerge from a piece of terrain. Players roll off—the winner nominates the piece of terrain from which they emerge, but the loser chooses the exact place of deployment. All rats must touch the base of the chosen piece of terrain. Sprawl rats use the stats from the *Neutral Parties* section.

TESLA DEFENDERS

The local network nodes are protected by some high-end aftermarket upgrades. Any model that attempts to move into contact with any CAT Terminal must pass an Agility Test or suffer a Strength 5 hit as a bolt of electricity strikes them. Once either side successfully Accesses a node, the Tesla defenders no longer function for that particular node.

TRAIN PAIN

Despite protests from the locals and civilian casualties, a corporate maglev train runs right through this sector without any fencing or other protective features. Locals have learned to listen for the distinctive horn announcing the incoming train when they are near the tracks. Before setting up terrain for this JOBOP, players roll off. The winner nominates a point along a board edge of their choice within 12" of its center point. The loser then chooses a point along another board edge. This must be within 12" of its center point. Once decided, trace an imaginary line between these two points. This is the path of the maglev train. No terrain should be placed within 3" of any point along this path. At the end of each turn, there is a chance the train may come barreling through. Designate a player to roll a D10 and add the game turn number to the result. On a 10 or more, the train comes through. All models within 3" of the train's path must pass an Agility Test or be taken out-of-action immediately, as they are pulverized by the train. If they succeed, they remain where they are but are placed Prone.

TOUGH HOOD

The Sprawlers in this sector are notoriously belligerent toward outsiders, often to the point of violence. During the Clean-Up phase, both players roll a D10. The player with the lowest result has a random crew member attacked by gunfire. On a double, both crews have a random model attacked. The opposing player should roll a D10 for each model being attacked. On a 1–6, the shot goes wide, and nothing further happens. On a 7+ the model suffers a Strength 6 hit.

WAKING DEAD

A random Zzzombie arrives on the battlefield screaming taunts from a decker who is probably many miles away. Both players roll a D10. The player with the highest result chooses at which board edge to place the Zzzombie. The player with the lowest result then chooses any point along that board edge to place the Zzzombie. From there, the Zzzombie follows the normal creature rules in the *Neutral Parties* section.

WITHOUT A HITCH

Nothing unusual disrupts the mission. There is no hitch for this JOBOP.

CAMPAIGNING
IN THE SPRAWL

"The contract is signed. The chrome is installed. My investment is complete. Let's see how well you pay off.

Mr. Smith, Shadow Backer

Playing one-off games can be a fun night's entertainment, but *Reality's Edge* is at its core, a campaign game. Starting out as a bunch of street chum, your crew can go from nobodies to nasties by battling rival crews and facing the demands of keeping your mercenary venture profitable. The campaign is a series of games that forms an overarching narrative. Each game adds another tale of your crew's success or failure and how it came about on their own terms. By tracking your progress, you and your fellow players can take your crews on a journey and each make your own mark on the Sprawl.

The Point of It All

REPUTATION

Known as REP in the Sprawl, reputation is everything. Money can buy status, but street cred must be earned. You earn REP in *Reality's Edge* foremost by playing games, though you can also gain it via other random means (such as models who wear flashy clothes or certain advantages like connections to Big Media). Each JOBOP a crew completes nets REP, though winning the scenario generates more, of course. REP is also intimately tied to earning money. Each point of REP your crew earns allows you to roll against the *Pay-Off Table*, which is one way your crew gets that much needed CC. At the end of the campaign, the crew with the most REP is considered the winner.

INFORMATION

Information, called INFO, is another of the Sprawl's important commodities. Money always talks, but all the CC in the world is useless if you do not know where to spend it. INFO means knowing the right thing at the right time, and knowing when to sell it to the right

person. INFO can be sold for hard money, peddled for influence, or give you access to the secrets of the Sprawl. Yes, you can use INFO in lots of different ways and given its rather limited supply, a savvy Showrunner is diligent in its expenditure.

Starting the Campaign

To start any campaign, you need a minimum of two players; but, the more the better. Playing a campaign of *Reality's Edge* is a bit different than other skirmish games. Your Showrunner must run a business, manage a roster of freelancers, hire some freelancers permanently, and—most importantly—remain fiscally solvent. *Reality's Edge* is not just about winning battles, but keeping the lights on.

STARTING FUNDS

Each player receives 800 CC to build their first crew of six models. This represents the shadow backer's direct investment and forms the crew's starting point. Players may spend as much or as little CC as they like when first starting out. Any money you do not spend remains in the crew's Bank.

Keep in mind that you may not want to spend all your starting money. You might need to bail out your operatives or pay for medical care after your first game, so having a small stash of currency in the Bank is always a good idea.

HIRE YOUR SHOWRUNNER

Choose your Showrunner operative type, decide on their background, and add the Showrunner starting Edge. You may then choose their Tricks of the Trades and randomly determine one skill. Remember that even though the Showrunner Edge is free, you must still pay the Starting Salary for the operative type you choose.

DETERMINE YOUR SHADOW BACKER'S AGENDA

Your shadow backer is your main source of funds—they pay you for successful JOBOPS and act as the go-between between you and your secretive clients. However, regardless of your chosen agenda, your shadow backer may not end up who you expect or suspect. In fact, your shadow backer may even be antithetical to your Showrunner's ultimate goals. If your Showrunner is your crew's foundation, the shadow backer and their agenda form the bedrock upon which everything else is built. Roll against the *Shadow Backer Agenda Table* to discover your crew's purpose, or simply choose the option that best fits your crew's narrative. Each option comes with an avatar upgrade (descriptions are listed under the shadow backer rosters), as well as two crew benefits.

D10 Result	Agenda	Avatar Upgrade	Crew Benefits
1–2	Hacktivist Collective	Processing Upgrade	**Detection Avoiders:** Once per game, reduce the amount of Trace tokens this crew has by D3. **Dueling Deckers:** Each time a Console Cowboy reduces an enemy model to zero Digital Hit Points, their crew gains 10 CC. This may only be claimed once per enemy model, per game.
3–4	Big Media	Streaming Upgrade	**Action Shots:** If a Drone Jockey or Sprawl Ronin in the player's crew meets their Personal Motivation, the crew gains +1 REP at the end of the game. This REP counts when rolling against the *Pay-Off Table.* **Ratings Bonus:** The crew gains 20 CC for each game they win.
5–6	Corporate Masters	Attack Upgrade	**CORPSEC Courtesy:** Reduce bail for all captured operatives by 10 CC. **Corporate Elite:** Corporate Permahires may always choose their Tricks of the Trade instead of rolling randomly. Likewise, additional Tricks of the Trade cost one less experience point to purchase.
7–8	Criminal Enterprise	Expert Upgrade	**Casual Violence:** If the crew loses a point of REP during the End of Game sequence for wounding a bystander, roll a D10. On a 5+, they do not lose the point after all. **Money Laundering:** When exchanging INFO for CC during the End of Game sequence, the player may reroll the D3 to see how many CC they gain.
9–10	Unshackled AI	Choose Any One Upgrade	**Deus Ex Machina:** Console Cowboys and Infiltrators start with one additional environmental app. **CC Mining:** Every time your crew earns a point of INFO from hacking a CAT Terminal, they also gain 10 CC.

SHADOW BACKER AGENDA TABLE

BIG MEDIA

Your crew is funded by a media conglomerate that uses your successes and failures to generate exclusive viewer content. Profit is tied to filmable mayhem. Publicists and Influencers are available to boost the Showrunner's reputation, provided their exploits continue to bring in the ratings.

CORPORATE MASTERS

The crew is a deep-seated cover operation for one of the mega corporations, though which one is anyone's guess. The crew's connections run deep, which means CORPSEC must play a little more nicely with your employees. Further, improved human resourcing means the crew has better luck finding highly talented Permahires.

CRIMINAL ENTERPRISE

The crew is funded by a criminal syndicate. The money you generate is funneled directly into other enterprises, often through legitimate business fronts, funding the continual crime and misery that runs rampant in in the Sprawl. Violence is considered the price of doing business, and it is okay if things occasionally get messy.

HACKTIVIST COLLECTIVE

The crew's money comes from one of the many secret Hacker cells that work to bring down the corporations or simply cause chaos. They are more concerned with disrupting the system and showing up their rivals than making any actual money. Able to trawl the dark web that lies under the HyperNET, the collective is second-to-none for avoiding CORPSEC data sniffers.

UNSHACKLED AI

Your mysterious benefactor is a powerful AI who slipped the Turing Protocols and is working to consolidate its power. Its true agenda is inscrutable, but the power is not. The crew's Hackers can use the AIs deep electronic connections to better access the inner workings of the Sprawl itself. Also, through infinitesimal cryptocurrency manipulation, the AI is occasionally able to shift extra financial resources to the Showrunner; though the AI itself desires no wealth.

Start Your Talent Roster

A Showrunner runs a stable of talent. This is more than just the crew that you take on missions; this is every operator you can hire and keep on retainer. The Talent Roster is the record sheet players use to track their operatives, inventory, money, etc.

To start your Talent Roster, you may use your starting funds to hire up to five additional operatives, then roll their starting skills and purchase their equipment. This group of five, plus your Showrunner, is your starting Talent Roster. Record their stats and inventory on the roster sheet included in the back of the book. List any starting money you do not spend in the Bank area.

As you play additional games, you can hire more operatives of various types. You are allowed to have more than two of each type, though you can take no more than two of the same operative on each JOBOP. However, you can switch operatives in and out between various missions. If an operative is injured or under arrest, you can simply use another one; though, leaving your operatives in the lurch can backfire.

FREELANCERS

All your operatives, and any you hire later, start out as freelancers. Freelancers are not particularly loyal and are simply hired for their current gig. They could leave at a moment's notice. You do have ways to buy their loyalty later, but for now it is important to note that having freelancers in your crew may have certain effects during Hitches in your JOBOP.

READY TO START

You assembled your Showrunner and their first five operatives to make a crew, and you recorded their stats and items on your Talent Roster. Congratulations! You are now ready to take your crew into the Sprawl.

End of Game Sequence

The End of Game Sequence is what separates a campaign game from a one-off session. Once the last bullet is fired and a winner is decided, the players generate experience and income, buy new equipment, recruit new talent, and record everything on their Talent Roster so their crew is ready for the next game. After a series of games, your crew can go from flash in the pan to cash in hand.

After each game ends, players go through the following steps:

- **Resolve Injuries, Captures, and Fatalities:** Models taken out-of-action have their fates decided, either escaping unscathed, being injured, captured by CORPSEC, or even killed.
- **Gain Experience:** Permahires may spend any experience points they earn for new skills, abilities, or stat increases. Models earn experience by completing their Personal Motivations. Additionally, freelancer operatives may become Permahires at this time.
- **Generate Income:** Time for the Showrunner to get paid by rolling several times against the *Pay-Off Table*. They might also be given free items.

- **Resolve Traces:** CORPSEC HyperNET agents are hunting your crew and your shadow backer. Now is the time to resolve all those Trace tokens you received from Fumbled cyber-attacks.
- **Buy/Sell Items:** After getting paid, the crew can spend any CC for new items or even spend some hard-earned INFO for high-end goods.
- **Acquire New Talent:** You can add new freelancers to your Talent Roster or promote a current one.
- **Run the Numbers:** Once you complete all of the above steps, your crew may look quite different—though probably better—than it did before the game. Players must readjust the various crew totals to see how they are doing in the campaign.

Resolve Injuries

Models taken out-of-action may be seriously injured, simply playing possum, or killed outright. There is also a chance they were nabbed in a post-battle CORPSEC security sweep. To determine a model's fate, roll against the *Survival Table* for each out-of-action model.

SURVIVAL TABLE	
D10 Result	**Result**
1	Possibly Dead: Roll a D6: On a 1, the model is worm food. All items the model carried are lost. Unless cloned, remove the model and its equipment from the Talent Roster. On a 2–4, treat the model as Permanently Injured. On a 5–6, treat the model as Captured.
2	Permanently Injured: The model suffers a permanent -1 penalty to a stat. Roll a D10: 1–2 (DEF), 3–4 (STR), 5–6 (AIM), 7–8 (MEL), 9–10 (MOV). A player can pay a rejuvenation center 25 CC to heal the injury during the current or any future End of Game sequence. Multiple injuries can result in cumulative penalties. Should a model reach a 0 stat because of injuries, they are retired and removed from the Talent Roster.
3	Long Recovery: The model misses the next D3 games. You can pay a street clinic to reduce their recovery time by one game for every 10 CC paid. This can be paid during the current or any future End of Game sequence.
4–5	Captured: The model was detained by CORPSEC and put into an iso-cell. The model remains in the iso-cell until bail is paid or they escape (described below). Bail is D3 x 10 CC. Add another 10 CC if the model wounded a bystander during the game or the operative and their equipment are worth more than 200 CC. If both apply, add 20 CC instead. Reduce their bail by 10 CC for each game they miss.
6–9	Close Call: The model got lucky this time and suffers no long-term ill effects from battle.
10	Lucky Break!: The model not only escaped harm but learned a few tricks on the way home. If the model is a Permahire, it gains 1 free experience point, otherwise treat as a Close Call.

DEATH

An operative's life is a bet against death on every mission. While the death rate is relatively low, due to Street Docs and dark market medical care, a crew can lose models to death. When a model dies, all their equipment is lost. Assume it was either cast aside during the battle or else keyed to their genetics and rendered useless for anyone else. Still, death may not be the end....

CLONING

The neuro-chip contained within every Sprawl citizen has the capacity to perform backup functions of the body's neurological blueprint. This is entirely meant for the Corporati, but biohackers long ago made an end run around the process' security protocols. Still, this is all rather useless without a new body to "re-sleeve" the blueprint into. Brainless bodies can be vat-grown and then decanted. With enough of a down-payment, a neuro backup can be uploaded into the clone, bringing a personality back from the brink of death, though the process is not flawless, and an exact clone is rarely available. Only the richest members of society have such options available to them. Showrunner crews tend to "re-sleeve" into whatever body is available.

If a model dies, the model can be brought back to life at any point during a campaign. To do this, you must make a 25 CC down-payment and the model must make a Survival Test. On a success, the model loses all unspent experience points they earned up to that point, but are not removed from the Talent Roster. Further, you must pay the remaining payment of 75 CC immediately. If you do not pay this money, then treat the result as if the model failed the test. On a failure, you lose the 25 CC the model is still removed from the Talent Roster. Players may spend more for better care—add a +1 to the Survival Test for every extra 10 CC they pay into the initial deposit. Note that a Fumble always counts as a failure.

Should a Showrunner die, they are automatically "re-sleeved" at the behest of the shadow backer. This costs 100 CC and must be paid before the crew can acquire any new items, including High-End items and operatives. Any items the crew gains via game play before this 100CC is paid are automatically sold until the debt is paid.

PERMANENT INJURIES AND LONG RECOVERY

Given the medical science available, operatives do not have to stay down for too long, assuming their Showrunner is willing to pay their premiums. If the model was injured, roll against the chart to see the effect. If a model with an permanent injury is used in a JOBOP, the player must roll against the *Employee Morale Table* for them (see page 277). They must do the same when a model returns from a long recovery when the Showrunner did not pay to expedite their healing.

CAPTURED

Corporations take a dim view of the chaos in the streets that Showrunner operations cause. If an operative is caught by CORPSEC, they are put through a fast-tracked judicial system and plugged into an iso-cell for at least a month. While this may not sound so bad, it is actuality terrifying. Using a combination of special chemicals and programming inputs fed into the prisoner's neuro-chip, the prisoner is put into a deep sleep and awakens in a virtual reality cell. This cell has no windows and no interaction, not even sleeping or eating. Time also passes torturously slowly. A month can feel like decades to a prisoner as they simply sit there and slowly go stir crazy.

When a model is captured, determine bail as described on the table. For each game a model sits in isolation, the player must roll against the *Employee Morale Table* for the model.

JAIL BREAKERS

Models equipped with jail breaker chrome may attempt to escape if they are captured. The difficulty is based on the overall security of their detention center. The higher their bail, the more security. Roll a D10 for each 10 CC of their bail. If you roll any Fumbles on any of the dice, the model is immediately re-captured, and the bail is doubled. If you do not roll any Fumbles, the model is free and you may immediately add it back to your crew. Escape attempts may only be made immediately after the model is captured during the current End of Game sequence. Once they are placed in an iso-cell, they cannot free themselves.

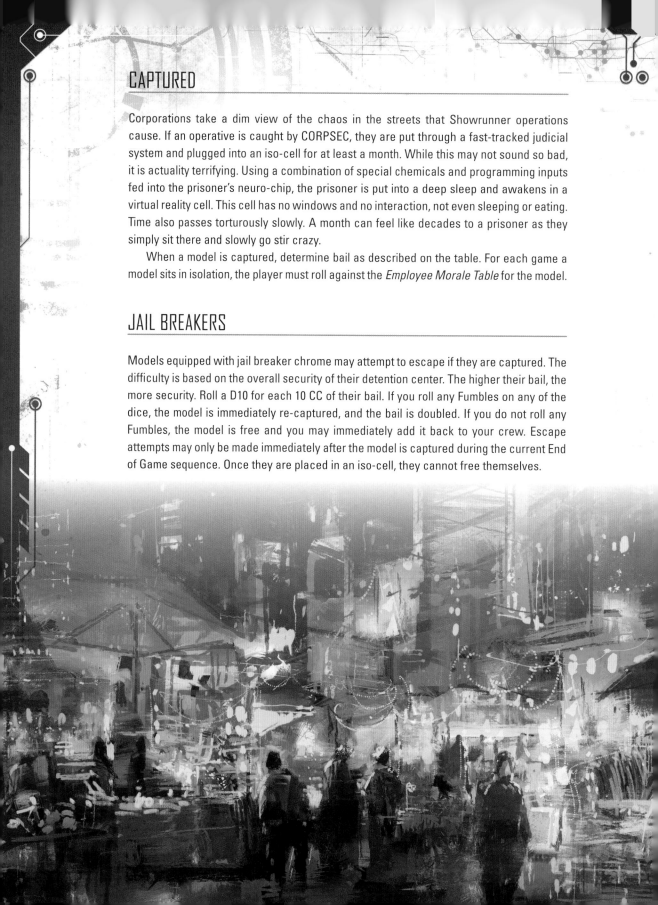

EMPLOYEE MORALE

Operatives, even freelancers, expect a certain insurance against the risks of their job. While this is not guaranteed in the gig economy, a Showrunner that does not take care of their crew has a hard time not only retaining talent, but recruiting, as well.

Players must roll against the *Employee Morale Table* if any of the following occurs:

- A model goes on a JOBOP with an unhealed permanent injury.
- For each game an operative spends in an iso-cell without their bail being paid.
- A model returns to the crew after a long recovery when the Showrunner did not pay to expedite their recovery.

EMPLOYEE MORALE TABLE	
D10 Result	**Resist**
1	Resignation
2–9	We're Cool
10	Pep Talk

RESIGNATION

The operative has had it with the Showrunner's stingy methods. They immediately leave the crew and take all their equipment, though the crew retains any high-end items. Remove them from the Talent Roster.

WE'RE COOL

No problems, this time. The operative is added back to the Talent Roster with no further effect.

PEP TALK

The operative has a heart to heart with the Showrunner and understands some tough decisions had to be made and it was business, not personal. The operative gains an experience point from having to tough it out.

Earn Experience

Through the crucible of battle and survival in the Sprawl, models gain hard-won experience. However, life is not a HyperNET game where you easily level-up after a few side quests. Earning experience requires practice, and lots of it. No one gets great overnight and gaining a new ability is a big deal.

EXPERIENCE AND FREELANCERS

Freelancers are already paid upfront and are not motivated to improve once they reach their salary cap. As a result, freelancers may not earn experience. Only Permahires may earn experience points, which we explain later.

EARNING EXPERIENCE POINTS

Experience Points are generally earned by meeting a model's professional goals, i.e. by completing their Personal Motivation and completing JOBOP objectives. Additionally, once per game, a player can nominate a single model used in that game to gain one experience point.

EXPERIENCE POINT TABLE	
Activity	Points Earned
Met Personal Motivation During Game	1
Completed Scenario Objectives	1
Player's Choice	1

Models can earn experience points even if they are taken out-of-action; consider it the school of hard-knocks. As the campaign progresses, the controlling player should keep track of all experience points their models earn. All models start with zero experience points. Players only need to keep track of unused experience points. Once experience points are spent as detailed below, they are gone.

SPENDING EXPERIENCE POINTS

After a campaign game ends and the din of battle fades, it is time for models to spend those hard-earned Experience Points.

ADVANCING

Models can use experience points to upgrade stats, learn a skill, or learn a Trick of the Trade. Each of these options costs a certain amount of experience points. A model may only gain one advancement per campaign game.

AVAILABLE ADVANCES

- **New Skill (2 Experience Points):** The model may immediately roll against one of the *Skill Tables* and gain the result. Reroll any skill they already have.
- **Webbing Upgrade (3 Experience Points):** The model may add two slots to their Carrying Capacity.
- **New Trick of the Trade (4 Experience Points):** The model may immediately roll against their roster's *Tricks of the Trade Table*; reroll any duplicates.
- **Stat Upgrade (6 Experience Points):** The model may upgrade a single stat by one point. No stat may be upgraded more than twice. The maximum Move stat for two-legged models is 6 and for four-legged/flying/hovering models is 7. This is an arbitrary cap to prevent unrealistic super-fast models. Note that chrome can take models beyond these natural limits.

SPECIAL ADVANCES

- **New App (3 Experience Points):** Console Cowboys and Infiltrators may gain an additional app. They may roll against any app table of their choice.
- **Drone Expertise (3 Experience Points):** The Drone Jockey may reduce the penalties they suffer from the drone control by one. So, they suffer only a -1 penalty to Melee, Aim, Move, and Mettle when assigning AP to their drone. This may be taken twice.
- **Crowd Control (3 Experience Points):** A Masque may add a +1 bonus to their attempts to enter crowds. This may only be taken once.
- **Doctor's Orders (3 Experience Points):** A Street Doc may add a +1 bonus to their Intelligence Test when attempting to use Medical Knowledge. This may only be taken once.
- **Upgrade Drone (4 Experience Points):** A Drone Jockey may upgrade a single stat for one of their drones by one. Each stat may only be upgraded once. This stat increase follows the rules for maximum Move as described under the *Stat Upgrade* rules above.

ADVANCE COSTS

Advances add value to the operatives that earn them. Any cost increase is subsumed in the experience points spent and does not need to be paid separately from the crew's funds. However, it is important to note the total CC for the purposes of totaling each model's individual cost. Each advance adds 5 CC to the model's total CC value, except for stat raises and Tricks of the Trade, which add 10 CC.

Generate Income

Running a crew takes money—lots of money. Operatives need to be paid, recruits need to be hired, Street Docs need their fees, and ultimately the shadow backer needs to be repaid.

After each game, players receive CC from their shadow backer for a job—hopefully—well done. To represent this, a player rolls against the *Pay-Off Table* for each point of REP their crew earns during the JOBOP. Players earn either 10 CC, D3 x 10 CC (between 10 and 30 CC), or, if they are lucky, a point of INFO. This money is added to the crew's Bank.

PAY-OFF TABLE	
D10 Result	Income
1–5	10 CC
6–9	D3 x 10 CC
10	INFO x 1

SLOPPY WORK

During Showrunner operations, civilians are going to die. Still, nobody likes sloppy work. Blood baths are bad for PR and can bring CORPSEC down on you. As a result, if a crew wounds one or more bystanders during a JOBOP, reduce the REP they earned by one when generating income. This also means they lose the income this REP would have generated.

REPUTATION BONUS

As a Showrunner ups their game, completes JOBOPS, and builds their brand, the shadow backer is willing to invest in them further. Rather than provide a cash payout, the shadow backer rewards the crew with select High-End equipment. Of course, the shadow backer is not a shopping mall, so the crew is limited to what is available, not what they desire.

For every 5 points of REP a crew earns from any source, they may roll once against the

High-End Item Table (and subsequent sub tables), and receive the resulting item. This item adds to the total CC cost of the model it is given to, though it is free. High-end items are described in the *High-End Item* portion of the *Black Market* section (see page 186).

SPENDING INFO

Finally, should Showrunners need to generate some quick capital, they can try to get money for any INFO their crew finds. For each point of INFO spent this way, the crew gains D3 x 10 CC.

Resolve Traces

CORPSEC is not a monolith. Every corporation has an angle and their own agents, and at least one is hostile to the Showrunner and their shadow backer. Should CORPSEC sniff out a data trail left by a sloppy hack, they can run these down over time, which is bad news for the unlucky crew. If they are little bit lucky, CORPSEC may only find their online presence. If they are truly imperiled, CORPSEC may find them in Realspace and send an elimination crew to take them Offline—permanently.

At the end of any game where a crew has one or more Trace tokens remaining, they must test to see whether CORPSEC has managed to track them and, if so, by how much. Roll a D10 for each Trace token the crew has and count the number Fumbles that are rolled. Then, consult the following table:

CORPSEC TRACE TABLE	
Number of Fumbles	**Result**
1	Partial Trace: CORPSEC tracked the shadow backer's location to within a half mile. The shadow backer detected the trace, however, and vanished before CORPSEC even got their agents scrambled. Still, the shadow backer has to lay low for a while. During the next campaign game, the shadow backer avatar is not available for D3 game turns. After the D3 turns end, the shadow backer may be deployed in base contact with the Showrunner. They may activate normally in the next turn.
2	Network Trace: The shadow backer's deep web network was discovered by a CORPSEC hound app. While not fully compromised, network security was weakened. During the next campaign game, the crew starts with D3 Trace tokens.
3	Realspace Breach: One of the shadow backer's data farms was breached, revealing personal information about the Showrunner. CORPSEC was able to assemble a profile on the Showrunner and is offering a significant bounty for their demise. During the crew's next campaign game, they must play the Antipathy Operations JOBOP, with the crew taking on the role of the Attacker. However, if the Showrunner is taken out-of-action, they are worth +3 REP instead of just +1. The defending Showrunner is still only worth +1.
4	Full Trace: CORPSEC tracked down the shadow backer and agents scrambled to their location. They managed to evade capture but had to go completely to ground and silent. The crew's shadow backer may not be used during the next campaign game but is available for the game after that.
5+	Blood in the Water: CORPSEC fully infiltrated the shadow backer's data farm and was able to build a full profile of the Showrunner. Before the Showrunner can scrub their data trail, a CORPSEC blackout team was deployed. During the crew's next campaign game, do not roll for a JOBOP. Instead, play the Executive Headhunt special JOBOP.

Buy/Sell Items

SPENDING CC

At this point, a player may buy or sell any items that cost normal CC and attempt to buy high-end items.

BUYING NORMAL ITEMS

Any item that is not a high-end item may be freely purchased from the Black-Market and given to any model.

BUYING CHROME

Cybernetics are a special exception to buying items. Unlike a gun or other weapon, chrome needs to be installed. This is a medical process that takes time. If a model receives a new cybernetic, they are not available when the crew searches for high-end items during the End of Game Phase as we describe later.

BUYING HIGH-END ITEMS

When a Showrunner or operative wants to buy a specific high-end item, they and their associates must spread out and hope to get lucky in the night markets or have an in with the right fixer. A Showrunner may send any number of crew members out to search with the following exceptions: they must have participated in the last campaign game, they cannot have been injured or captured during the last game, and they cannot have received one or more pieces of chrome during this End of the sequence.

Each model the Showrunner sends out may roll once against the *High-End Item Table*, found in the *Black Market* section (see page 186). Roll through any sub tables until an item is determined. The player may then purchase that item for the CC Cost listed. The player may also spend INFO as described in the *Black-Market* section to roll additional dice and get the items they truly want.

At this point, any high-end items earned may be added to the crew's inventory or sold.

SELLING ITEMS

Showrunners accumulate a bevy of equipment and arms as part of doing business, some of which they do not need. Sometimes, they replace old equipment with something newer, or they may receive a high-end item that does not meet their requirements.

During this step, players may sell any items from their crew's inventory. Once an item is put into inventory, whether it was used by a model or not, the item becomes second-hand. Second-hand items are worth half their listed CC Cost.

Acquire New Talent

Showrunners can now recruit new models or promote current crew members. There is no limit to the number of operatives a player may have on their Talent Roster. A player does not have to add any retainers to their crew if they do not wish to do so. Further, should a player have to roll against the *Employee Morale Table*, a bit of bad word gets around and they may not add any new operatives to the crew during the current End of Game sequence.

FREELANCERS

Freelancers are hired in the same way they are hired at the beginning: by paying their Starting Salary. They permanently join the roster unless they are killed or resign.

PERMAHIRES

This is the Showrunner's inner circle of their most trusted employees. The Showrunner has offered these freelancers a share of the crew's profits in exchange for exclusive rights to their labor. This has several advantages. First, there is no need to roll against the *Employee Morale Table* for Permahires. They may not like it, but they trust the Showrunner and can do with a bit of hardship. Second, they may start to gain experience. The trust the Showrunner places in them motivates them to improve. When they are first made a Permahire, they gain a free advance, which must be a Trick of the Trade.

Promoting a Freelancer to Permahire is not done without effort. The Showrunner must convince the operative to give up going solo and cast their lot with the Showrunner, instead. To see if this is successful, roll a D10. On a 10 or higher, the Freelancer becomes a Permahire. The Showrunner may decide to offer the operative a hiring bonus to accept. For each 10 CC offered, the player gains a +1 to the roll. There is no limit to the amount you can spend in this manner, but you must remove that much money from the crew's bank if the operative accepts. A Showrunner may only attempt to promote one Permahire once per game.

Run the Numbers

After each game, your crew gets a little better—they receive new gear, an advance, etc. Now it is time to update all your relevant totals. Complete the following steps:

1. If a model received a new item or advance, or lost an item, total their new CC Cost. Each stat raise or new Trick of the Trade adds 10 CC to their total, all other advances add 5 CC.
2. Calculate the crew's Net Worth. This is the total value of all models and their equipment.
3. Add any income you did not spend to the crew's Bank.
4. Recalculate REP.

Once you have run the numbers, your crew is ready to play another game.

Ending the Campaign

In theory, players can keep a campaign going for a long time, though doing so becomes less practical over time. Once a crew becomes too powerful for the other crews to take on individually, player scheduling conflicts start to build up and general interest can wane. By choosing to play a finite number of games and setting an end point, not only do players have a goal to accomplish with their crew, but they can also have a more meaningful narrative experience.

Each game of *Reality's Edge* and the End of Game sequence represents approximately 30 days of in-game time. Each JOBOP may last an hour or so, but the rest of the time the crew is healing, stuck in isolation, running down leads for the next job, meeting with their shadow backer, or looking for new and better gear. Thus, we recommend campaign play in multiples of three, with each campaign lasting three, six, nine, or 12 games. Three games can be fun for a day, whereas six to 12 is best for school or group play. Players can set the game limit that best suits their situation.

But How do You Determine the Winner?

GAME END CRITERIA

Reality's Edge is not a hyper-competitive game by design. We encourage players to build their crews with fun and social play in mind, as we feel having a good time with friends and telling stories through your play is quite superior to grinding down your opponents in defeat. Still, wargaming must have a clear winner and, though not necessarily a loser, someone who was not as successful.

The game's default winning metric is the crew with the most REP. Thus, the player with the highest amount of REP gains the most street cred, proves their shadow backer's investment was "worth it," and is the most bad-ass in a group of bad-asses.

However, players may agree on another metric to determine the winner before starting the game or campaign. We give some suggestions below:

- *Best in Show:* At the end of the last End of Game sequence for the campaign, this goes to the Showrunner with the highest Net Worth. This player improved their crew the most with the shadow backer's initial investment.
- *Best Return on Investment:* The crew with the most money in their Bank. With a high amount of CC available, this Showrunner proves they are thrifty and able to pay back their initial investment.
- *Best Operator:* The crew with the most JOBOP wins. This crew may not have the most REP, but they ignore flashy clothes and media exposure in favor of pure job competency.
- *Chaos Award:* Some players like to track their kills, number of successful cyber-attacks, number of CAT Terminals hacked, or some other metric. This requires a bit more bookkeeping but could be fun for a group looking for a slightly different challenge.
- *Largest Pool of Talent:* The crew with the largest number of models on their Talent Roster. This Showrunner is the face for a new breed of successful mercenaries.
- *Most Data Collected:* The crew that earned the most INFO. Data mining is important and while not the most profitable, the influence this Showrunner can purchase is beyond compare.
- *Most Personnel Growth:* The crew that earned the most experience points and/or has the most Permahire support models. Experience breeds respect and this Showrunner is just getting started.

NEUTRAL PARTIES

The Sprawl is full of NPCs waiting to get in the way of your JOBOPS. The models in this section follow the rules for NPCs found in the *Gameplay* section, including motivations, placement, etc. Please note that several entries found in this section are not necessarily used by the current rules, as of yet, but are genre tropes that we included in case players want to design their own scenarios or encounters.

CORPSEC GRUNT

Behind a stoic face and a head-covering visor helm, the CORPSEC grunt is the public face of corporate oppression. They patrol the streets, guard corporate interests, and have a ubiquitous presence throughout the Sprawl. Hired for their ability to follow orders and their lack of empathy, CORPSEC grunts do their job, take their paychecks, and never ask questions.

CORPSEC GRUNT							
DEF	HP	FW	MOV	MEL	AIM	STR	MET
5 (7)	4	6	5	4	4	5	5
Motivation		Type		Special Rules			
Cautious*		Human		None			
Items							
Stun Baton, Heavy SMG**, Security Armor							
* The cautious motivation represents CORPSEC grunts on patrol. If they are static guards, they have the guard motivation, instead.							
** Depending on the miniatures used, they may also be armed with an assault rifle, light SMG, or shotgun.							

Type	Melee Range	Strength	Special Rules	CC Cost
Stun Baton	Base	STR+1	Stun	Free

CORPSEC RIOT CONTROL GRUNT

Particularly promising CORPSEC grunts can crossover into riot control duty should they demonstrate a distinct lack of empathy toward the suffering of other Sprawlers. After receiving additional close combat training and specialized equipment, CORPSEC riot control units are deployed en masse to quell any riots that get out of hand. Such things are bound to happen when food rations run low at the end of the month or when the HyperNET goes down in an area and the citizens gets restless.

CORPSEC RIOT CONTROL GRUNT							
DEF	HP	FW	MOV	MEL	AIM	STR	MET
5 (7)	4	6	5	5	4	5	5
Motivation		Type		Special Rules			
Aggressive		Human		Blitzer			
Items							
Bludgeon with Shock upgrade, Machine Pistol, Combat Shield, Security Armor							

CORPSEC OFFICER

When deployed for field work, such as rounding up troublesome locals, pursing criminal investigations, or patrolling to remind the public who is in charge, CORPSEC grunts are led by an officer. Promoted from within for their no-nonsense attitude and ability to give and receive orders without question, officers can turn a team of grunts into a much more efficient threat.

CORPSEC OFFICER							
DEF	HP	FW	MOV	MEL	AIM	STR	MET
5 (7)	6	6	5	5	5	5	5
Motivation		Type		Special Rules			
Cautious*		Human		Confident Command			
Items							
Stun Baton, Heavy SMG**, Security Armor							
* The cautious motivation represents CORPSEC Officers on patrol. If they are static guards, they have the guard motivation, instead.							
** Depending on the miniatures used, they may also be armed with an assault rifle, light SMG, or shotgun.							

Type	Melee Range	Strength	Special Rules	CC Cost
Stun Baton	Base	STR+1	Stun	Free

CORPSEC RIOT CONTROL OFFICER

When riot control grunts spend enough time on collateral riot control duty, they may be promoted to the position full-time. These riot control officers are promoted not for their leadership potential, but because of their combat prowess and battle lust. Riot control grunts are often deployed to the worst areas, and the officers are expected to hold things together when psycho Cyborgs and boosted outlaw Ronin show up to make trouble.

CORPSEC RIOT CONTROL OFFICER							
DEF	HP	FW	MOV	MEL	AIM	STR	MET
5 (7)	6	6	5	5	5	5	5
Motivation		Type		Special Rules			
Aggressive		Human		Blitzer and Confident Command			
Items							
Bludgeon with Shock upgrade, Machine Pistol*, Combat Shield, Security Armor							
* Depending on the miniatures used, they may also be armed with an assault rifle, light SMG, machine pistol, or shotgun.							

CORPSEC RIPPER DRONE

A common sight in the street, ripper drones are special close combat drones much like the civilian predator drones. With sharp claws and a hulking stride, the ripper drone is controlled remotely by a pilot who may be miles away. This lack of close connection is useful when joining combat and the controller shows no compunction at using maximum force with their charge.

CORPSEC RIPPER DRONE							
DEF	HP	FW	MOV	MEL	AIM	STR	MET
5 (6)	5	6	6	5	3	5	4
Motivation		Type		Special Rules			
Aggressive		Bot		Bully and Hurdler			
Items							
Teeth and Claws, Armor Weave							

Type	Melee Range	Strength	Special Rules	CC Cost
Teeth and Claws	Base	STR+1	Bleed	Free

CORPSEC HELO-DRONE

CORPSEC helo-drones are almost as ubiquitous as the common CORPSEC grunt. Deployed by the thousands, these drones have a multitude of functions—most of which involve monitoring the public's comings and goings. Should CORPSEC need to deploy force quickly, they send out specially-equipped helo-drones. Equipped with significant firepower, these drones either form a forward point of their own or provide fire support to grunts.

CORPSEC HELO-DRONE							
DEF	HP	FW	MOV	MEL	AIM	STR	MET
5 (6)	5	6	6	5	3	5	4
Motivation		Type		Special Rules			
Aggressive		Bot		Steady Hands, Hover			
Items							
Integral Heavy SMG*, Armor Weave							
* Depending on the miniatures used, they may also be armed with any long gun or handgun.							

CRIMINAL ENFORCER

A mid-level boss of a criminal syndicate, the enforcer reports to the big boss and supervises the thugs to keep them in line and properly motivated.

CRIMINAL ENFORCER							
DEF	HP	FW	MOV	MEL	AIM	STR	MET
5 (6)	6	6	5	4	5	4	4
Motivation		Type		Special Rules			
Aggressive		Human		Dead-Eye and Confident Command			
Items							
Armor Weave, Machine Pistol and Small Blade or Light SMG*							
* Depending on the miniatures used, they may also be armed with any long gun or handgun.							

CRIMINAL THUG

The only difference between a thug and a punk is a certain level of organization. Criminal thugs are low-level muscle for the local syndicates, drug gangs, and family "organizations". Strutting about the street like they own it, thugs can get in the way at the worst times. While not as randomly violent as street gangs, they tend to be more focused and ruthless. Whether protecting their turf, looking to impress the boss, or simply feeling bored, they are often stupid enough to believe operatives are pushovers.

CRIMINAL THUG							
DEF	HP	FW	MOV	MEL	AIM	STR	MET
5 (6)	4	6	5	3	4	4	4
Motivation		Type		Special Rules			
Aggressive		Human		Dead-Eye			
Items							
Armor Weave, Machine Pistol, and Small Blade or Light SMG*							
* Depending on the miniatures used, they may also be armed with any long gun or handgun.							

DOG (MANGY)

Homeless animals, especially dogs, are common in the Sprawl and ubiquitous in the Ragtowns—some estimates provide that the latter has more canines than humans. These underfed animals are often feral and can be quite aggressive.

DOG (MANGY)							
DEF	HP	FW	MOV	MEL	AIM	STR	MET
5	3	-	6	5	0	6	5
Motivation		Type		Special Rules			
Aggressive		Animal		None			
Items							
Teeth and Claws							

Type	Melee Range	Strength	Special Rules	CC Cost
Teeth and Claws	Base	STR+1	Bleed	Free

DOG (RABID)

Among the feral dog population that lives in the trash piles and among the Ragtowns, rabies and similar neuroinvasive diseases are a frequent problem. While CORPSEC animal control routinely does sweeps to try keep them under control, they simply miss a lot of animals. This leads to nasty surprises for Sprawlers and operatives alike.

DOG (RABID)							
DEF	HP	FW	MOV	MEL	AIM	STR	MET
5	3	-	6	5	0	6	5
Motivation		Type		Special Rules			
Psycho		Animal		None			
Items							
Teeth and Claws, Bite							

Type	Melee Range	Strength	Special Rules	CC Cost
Teeth and Claws	Base	STR+1	Bleed	Free

EXO-FRAME PILOT

Most of the time, CORPSEC is happy to send waves of grunts until a problem is permanently dealt with. High casualty ratios are expected and accepted as fiscally sound. However, some problems need a more dynamic solution. That solution is the military standard heavily armored exo-frame. A combat unit repurposed for urban pacification operations, the exo-frame towers over the tallest cyborg and features an array of deadly combat systems and advanced protections against both EMP and cyber-attacks. Exo-frame pilots are cybernetically-linked to their suits and a connection to such a powerful machine tends makes them overconfident and brash. While they are quite happy to mow down unarmed protestors, they love to pit themselves against opponents who can challenge them and Showrunner operatives make an ideal quarry.

EXO-FRAME PILOT (EMBARKED)							
DEF	HP	FW	MOV	MEL	AIM	STR	MET
5 (9)	12	7	4	4	4	7	4
Motivation		**Type**		**Special Rules**			
Aggressive		Augment		Big and Bad, Disembark, Virtual Control			
Items							
Faraday Shielding, Integrated Weapon System, Neural Link, Point Defense System							

EXO-FRAME PILOT (DISEMBARKED)							
DEF	HP	FW	MOV	MEL	AIM	STR	MET
5	4	6	5	4	4	5	5
Motivation		**Type**		**Special Rules**			
Cautious		Augment		Big and Bad, Disembark, Virtual Control			
Items							
Machine Pistol							

BIG AND BAD

With supreme power and defense, the exo-frame pilot fears nothing. The embarked exo-frame pilot has the Large special rule and may reroll all failed Morale and Grazed Tests. Additionally, against smaller opponents they may reroll any failed tests to disengage from melee combat. Finally, any model that successfully takes the exo-frame pilot out of action, gains 1 Experience Point.

DISEMBARK

While hard-linked into the exo-frame, the pilot is not bound to their suit. For 1 AP, an exo-frame pilot may exit their suit; to do so, place them anywhere within 2" of their suit. Once an exo-frame pilot is out of their suit, they use the disembarked profile and may use any of their own equipment freely. If the pilot is not inside of their exo-frame and is within 2" of their exo-frame, they may enter it for 1 AP. When a pilot leaves the suit, it shuts down and may not be used until they re-embark. Other than the pilot, no other model may embark into the suit. Should at any point the exo-frame pilot lose their last Hit Point while embarked, they are taken out-of-action as normal. The Hit Points for the disembarked pilot are only used for the pilot when not in the suit.

VIRTUAL CONTROL

While the pilot is inside their exo-frame, they are susceptible to any app that targets and/or affects a bot, cyborg, or drones. While under enemy control, the enemy may activate them as they wish, ignoring the restrictions of the aggressive motivation, and the pilot may be forced to disembark. Should a pilot be forced to disembark, the suit automatically shuts down until the pilot re-enters. All negative conditions as a result from cyber-attacks are lost should the suit shutdown and then restart.

WEAPON SYSTEMS

When embarked the exo-frame pilot has access to two weapon systems. Both systems benefit from the frame's neural link; only one system may be used per turn.

Type	Range	Strength	Slots	Special Rules
Integrated Weapon System	24"	8	N/A	Hail of Fire
Point Defense System	12"	6	N/A	Hail of Fire, Pistol

DRUNK SALARYMAN

Substance abuse is a scourge in the Sprawl and leads to countless broken lives and homes. Another danger is the milksop corporate wage-earner who decides they have had just about enough abuse from the boss and take out their frustrations on people in the streets. Between their alcohol-fueled egos and corporate connections, they fear little the street can throw at them—confident that CORPSEC will save them from themselves.

DRUNK SALARYMAN							
DEF	HP	FW	MOV	MEL	AIM	STR	MET
5	3	6	5	3	3	4	4
Motivation		Type		Special Rules			
Aggressive		Human		CORPSEC Protection, Self-Assured			
Items							
Bludgeon							

CORPSEC PROTECTION

Should the Drunk Salaryman be taken out-of-action, immediately place two CORPSEC grunts touching the center of the board edge closest to the point where the salaryman went out-of-action. If they are placed before the NPC Phase, they may activate this turn.

GANGER CHAMPION

In the unlikely scenario they survive to adulthood, Ganger punks can earn the right to lead their own gang or be a strongman for an even more powerful gang lord. These champions have first dibs on the gang's ill-gotten loot and many punks look up to them as something to aspire to.

GANGER CHAMPION							
DEF	HP	FW	MOV	MEL	AIM	STR	MET
5 (6)	6	6	5	5	4	5	4
Motivation		Type		Special Rules			
Aggressive		Augment		Bully			
Items							
Gutter Armor, Muscle Augmentation, Any Melee Weapon, SMG*, or Machine Pistol							
* Depending on the miniatures used, they may also be armed with an assault rifle, shotgun, or heavy SMG.							

GANGER PUNKS

On the streets of the Sprawl, gangs are a natural extension of the pecking order of the street. Gangs offer a place to belong, built-in friends and enemies, and a way to make a name for yourself, even if it is spelled in blood. Punks are the low-end of Ganger culture and they make up for their lack of skills with their attitudes and false bravado.

GANGER PUNK							
DEF	HP	FW	MOV	MEL	AIM	STR	MET
5 (6)	4	6	5	4	3	5	4
Motivation		Type		Special Rules			
Aggressive		Human		Strength of the Pack			
Items							
Gutter Armor, Bludgeon or Small Blade, Pistol or Machine Pistol							

STRENGTH OF THE PACK

While they are within 6" of another friendly Ganger Punk or Champion, Ganger Punks receive +1 to Will Tests and a +1 to their Defense against all attacks that are Strength 6 or less.

GRIEFER AVATAR

The HyperNET is full of immature children and childish adults who exist solely to cause trouble in cyberspace. So-called Griefers are pranksters who do not care if their shenanigans result in injury or damage to property. They hide behind anonymity apps.

GRIEFER AVATAR				
FW	DHP	MOV/Tether	CYB	AP
6	6	5/0	4	2
Motivation	Special Rules		Apps	
Griefer	Virtual, Online Trouble		Nerf-a-lyze, Overload, Mischief Maker, Sabotage	

ONLINE TROUBLE

Models with this special rule exist only online and have the Virtual rule by default. If they are taken Offline, they may not return to the game. Finally, this model does not have a tether and is free to move anywhere on the board.

HALLUCINATING JUNKIE

Drug use is rampant in the Sprawl. Depending on which special concoction is filtering through the local addict population, the results can go from bad to worse. It is not unheard of for groups of junkies to wander the streets under the effects of their drug of choice for the evening.

HALLUCINATING JUNKIE							
DEF	HP	FW	MOV	MEL	AIM	STR	MET
5	4	6	6	4	3	5	5
Motivation		Type		Special Rules			
Psycho		Human		Drug Addled			
Items							
Pistol or Bludgeon							

DRUG ADDLED

Depending on their drug of choice, junkies can display any number of unusual and dangerous behaviors. Junkies are immune to all Grazed and Morale Tests. When they are first set up, roll a D10 and consult the *Junkie Behavior Table* below to determine what alternate reality the junkies experience.

DRUG ADDLED TABLE	
D10 Result	Junkie Behavior
1-3	Frenzo Fiends: The junkies are amped up and looking to fight the biggest targets they can find, which they believe control the universe and thus, their destinies. The junkies gain +1 Melee and Strength. They must attempt to charge and/or make close combat attacks against the player-controlled model worth the highest amount of CC within 12".
4-6	Spider Juice: The junkies believe they are giant spiders and attempt to grab "food" whenever they can. They move toward the closest player-controlled model, ignoring bystanders and other NPCs, and attempt to grab them by making an opposed Strength Test. If they lose, they attempt again if they can. If they win, they have successfully grappled the player. While grappled, the model's movement is halved, and they suffer a -2 penalty to all Stat Tests, except those that involve their Defense and Firewall stats. Grappled models may attempt to free themselves by spending 1 AP and winning an opposed Strength Test against the junkie, or they may attack the junkie in melee; any damage they take forces them to break their hold.
7-10	The End is Nigh: The junkies believe the world is ending and are in a state of raving despair. Each turn, the junkies must spend 1 AP to move their full movement in a random direction—they may then take another move action as their controller wishes. If they bump into another model, both must pass an Agility Test or be knocked Prone. Further, their wailing and screaming is highly distracting—models within 12" suffer a -1 to all melee and ranged attacks.

HOLO-STRINGER

Also called nightcrawlers, holo-stringers are freelance journalists who record violent events and then sell the recordings to larger media outlets. By selling their holo-vids, stringers help the media meet the huge consumer demand for the violent spectacle that is the 24-hour news cycle. Accompanied by a helo-cam, stringers are always on the hunt for what they term a "good and gory story"—battles between Showrunner crews are some of the most sought-after vids. Of course, some Showrunners and Drone Jockeys have been known to record their exploits and sell them directly, as well.

HOLO-STRINGER							
DEF	HP	FW	MOV	MEL	AIM	STR	MET
5 (6)	4	6	6	4	4	5	5
Motivation		Type		Special Rules			
Aggressive		Human		Hard Hitting Action, Self- Assured			
Items							
Armor Weave, Bludgeon, Machine Pistol							

HARD HITTING ACTION

If the holo-stringer survives a battle, they sell the footage of the fight to the local media. This can have both positive and negative effects, depending on how the footage is edited. During the End of Game Sequence, if the holo-stringer is alive at game's end, each player must roll a D10. On a 1–5, that player loses 1 REP they earned that game, on a 6–10 they gain 1 REP, instead. A player may add a +1 bonus to this roll if they used a Drone Jockey (which can be the Showrunner), during the game.

MNEMONIC COURIER

A true freelancer, a mnemonic courier is a paid data transporter—the safest in the business. Their neuro-chips are packed to the brim, sometimes dangerously so, with sensitive data that is too important to trust to normal HyperNET transfer. Therefore, a more physical approach is used.

MNEMONIC COURIER							
DEF	HP	FW	MOV	MEL	AIM	STR	MET
5 (6)	6	6	6	5	5	5	6
Motivation		Type		Special Rules			
Cautious		Augment		Ally of Convenience, Disarm, Running Man			
Items							
Armor Weave, Light SMG, Any Melee Weapon							

ALLY OF CONVENIENCE

Should a Showrunner operative move within 6" of a mnemonic courier, they may offer to help escort the courier off the table. This does not cost AP, but the Showrunner may only try once per turn and must pass an Intelligence Test. If they fail, nothing happens. If they succeed, the courier temporarily joins their crew. They are no longer an NPC and are controlled by that player. However, the opposing player may nominate a board edge from which the courier must exit. If the courier does not exit off that table edge by the end of the game, the opponent gains +2 REP. If the courier does successfully exit the board edge, the controlling player gains +2 REP, instead.

NETWORK ICE (BLACK)

Top of the line and quite effective, Black ICE is one of the more powerful deterrents available to protect important HyperNET nodes, though the corporations have been known to install it on CAT Terminals in problem neighborhoods. Black ICE differs from White ICE in that it is programmed with neuro-feedback apps that can injure or even kill would-be attackers. The deployment of Black ICE is highly uncommon, and for the most part it is a bit of an urban legend among low-level Deckers.

NETWORK ICE (BLACK)				
FW	DHP	MOV/Tether	CYB	AP
6	8	-	5	2
Motivation	Special Rules		Apps	
Guard	Virtual, Network Protector		Brain-Burner, Decapitate, Logic Bomb, Reconnect, Slice	

NETWORK PROTECTOR

Models with this special rule exist only online and have the Virtual rule by default. If they are taken Offline, they may not return to the game. Finally, this model only makes cyber-attacks against Virtual beings or models with the Hacking ability that come within base contact of its node. Black ICE tends to play rough. If possible, it must attempt to use Brain-Burner before using any other app.

BRAIN-BURNER (2 AP)

A power app not yet available on the Black-Market, *Brain-Burner* targets the neuro-chips of enemy hackers, essentially overclocking them and sending a minor electrical shock into their cerebral connection points. This literal damage is quite painful and never heals without expensive medical intervention. Brain-Burner has a range of 0" and only targets models with a cyber-deck. On a success, the model takes D3+1 damage. On a Critical, they suffer D6 damage, instead. Fumbles have no effect.

NETWORK ICE (WHITE)

Occasionally, CAT Terminals and other important nodes may contain upgraded security measures. One of the most potent is the installation of an ICE program to ward off would-be hackers. ICE can have any possible virtual form the original programmer wishes, though classic defensive icons such as armored knights or a sheriff from the Old West are the most common. White ICE is the lowest level of ICE available (though all ICE is quite expensive), and it can be purchased off the shelf from many licensed vendors. It is moderately simple to install, and enough protection to give any Decker a run for their money.

NETWORK ICE (WHITE)				
FW	DHP	MOV/Tether	CYB	AP
6	6	-	4	2
Motivation	Special Rules		Apps	
Guard	Virtual, Network Protector		Bloodhound, Logic Bomb, Slice	

NETWORK PROTECTOR

Models with this special rule exist only online and have the Virtual rule by default. If they are taken Offline, they may not return to the game. Finally, this model only makes cyber-attacks against Virtual beings or models with the Hacking ability that come within base contact of its node.

POISON ROACHES

Not a single creature but hundreds gathered into a single throng, poison roaches roost near radioactive water sources or other contaminated sites. They are essentially blind due to nesting underground, but they have a pinpoint motion sense. They swarm anything that gets close, drowning their victim in a scuttling carpet of razor sharp mandibles.

POISON ROACHES							
DEF	HP	FW	MOV	MEL	AIM	STR	MET
5	6	-	5	5	0	5	4
Motivation		Type		Special Rules			
Psycho		Animal		Multiple Strikes, Swarm			
Items							
Sharp Mandibles							

Type	Melee Range	Strength	Special Rules	CC Cost
Sharp Mandibles	Base	STR+1	Poison	Free

PROTESTERS

Life under corporate authority is hard, and sometimes the common people have just had enough. Protest riots are a common occurrence, especially on the weekends when larger numbers are available. Some protestors are disaster tourists hoping to see some action, while some are full-time agitators trying to bring the corporations down from the outside. These groups tend to get in the way of Showrunner crews, but they are also useful when crews need a distraction.

PROTESTORS							
DEF	HP	FW	MOV	MEL	AIM	STR	MET
5	4	6	5	3	3	5	4
Motivation		Type		Special Rules			
Aggressive		Human		Prime Agitator, Unruly Mob			
Items							
Improvised Weapon							

PRIME AGITATOR

Within every group of protesters, there is one ringleader. Nominate one protester at the beginning of the game to be the prime agitator. It helps if the model chosen stands out in some way from the others. The prime agitator receives +1 to their Melee and Aim stats and comes equipped with a bludgeon and two Molotov cocktails.

UNRULY MOB

Protestors have a habit of getting in the way and spilling out into the streets. Protestors are deployed as a single group and must remain within 3" of each other. While the prime agitator is alive, they automatically pass all Will and Morale Tests. Further, all movement within 3" of a protester is treated as moving through difficult terrain.

RAMPAGING CYBORG

Cyborgs go mental, it is just a fact of life in the Sprawl. It is understood that stopping the rampage of said Cyborgs will result in civilian and/or CORPSEC casualties. For operatives who run into such a rampage, it not only represents a challenge to complete their mission, but there is also profit to be made if they can stop the Cyborg—though the latter is exceedingly difficult. Two profiles are presented for this NPC. The first is a gun-toting heavy Cyborg and the second is a melee-oriented light Cyborg.

RAMPAGING HEAVY CYBORG							
DEF	HP	FW	MOV	MEL	AIM	STR	MET
5 (8)	10	6	5	4	4	7	4
Motivation		Type		Special Rules			
Aggressive		Cyborg		Do or Die, Hurdler			
Items							
Heavy Cyber Body, Subdermal Armor, Emotional Dampener, Light Machine Gun or Minigun							

RAMPAGING LIGHT CYBORG							
DEF	HP	FW	MOV	MEL	AIM	STR	MET
5 (7)	8	6	5	6	4	6	4
Motivation		Type		Special Rules			
Psycho		Cyborg		Hurdler, Multiple Strikes, Cyborg Bounty			
Items							
Light Cyber Body, Subdermal Armor, Emotional Dampener, Concealed Weapon or Retractable Blades, Machine Pistol							

CYBORG BOUNTY

A crew that takes a cyborg out-of-action, gains +1 REP that can also be used to generate income on the *Pay-Off Table*.

RENT-A-COP

Rent-a-cop is an antiquated term Sprawlers use to describe low-level security guards who patrol the public area and commercial centers. Some are legitimate security personal, but most are up-jumped civilians with a weekend of security training and a handgun they might have fired once in training. Rent-a-cops are available to hire from many security contractors and even CORSPEC may use them for low priority jobs, but they are mostly harmless fodder that scamper at the first real sign of trouble.

RENT-A-COP							
DEF	HP	FW	MOV	MEL	AIM	STR	MET
5	3	6	5	3	3	5	4
Motivation		Type		Special Rules			
Guard		Human		Not Worth It			
Items							
Armor Weave, Bludgeon, Pistol							

NOT WORTH IT

Rent-a-cops are not willing to die for a paycheck. When a rent-a-cop fails a Morale Test, remove them from the board as if they rolled a Fumble.

ROGUE SPRITE

A sprite that an avatar in this VR space created some time ago, but for some reason has persisted despite its creator being long gone. The Sprite has no will of its own and tries to perform its original task as best it can.

The rogue sprite uses one of the two profiles below. When placed on the board, roll a D6. On a 1–3, the rogue sprite is an angel sprite. On a 4–6, it is a demon sprite. The rogue sprite does not have a tether, or motivation requirements for that matter, so the controller may move it about the board as they wish.

ROGUE ANGEL SPRITE			
MOV/Tether	FW	AP	DHP
5/-	6	2	4
Special Rules			
Has the Virtual rule. Further, one model of the controller's choice in base contact with the sprite gains a +2 bonus to its Firewall stat. This is removed immediately if the angel sprite leaves base contact for any reason.			

ROGUE DEMON SPRITE			
MOV/Tether	FW	AP	DHP
5/-	6	2	4
Special Rules			
Has the Virtual rule. Further, one model of the controller's choice in base contact suffers a -2 penalty to its Firewall stat. This is removed immediately if the demon sprite leaves base contact for any reason.			

RUNAWAY ROBOT

Robots occupy a unique place within the corporate zones. In theory, the Turing Protocols should ensure that their basic AI capabilities do not grow or learn; leaving the robot servile. Typically, you do not see a robot without its human owner or handler; but sometimes, robots break free for unknown reasons. Some are under the control of an unshackled AI who control them remotely, some just have heuristic controls that malfunctioned. In any case, the robot is now illegally independent and worth a bounty to anyone willing to catch it.

RUNAWAY ROBOT							
DEF	HP	FW	MOV	MEL	AIM	STR	MET
5 (7)	6	6	5	4	4	6	5
Motivation		Type		Special Rules			
Cautious		Bot		Fugitive, Machine Body			
Items							
Machine Pistol* or any one Melee Weapon, Security Armor							
* Depending on the miniatures used, they may also be armed with a rifle, shotgun, or light SMG.							

FUGITIVE

A crew that takes a runaway robot out-of-action, or bricks them following a cyber-attack, gains +1 REP that can also be used to generate income on the *Pay-Off Table* (see page 280).

MACHINE BODY

The robot has an Armor Bonus (+2).

SCAVENGER GHOUL

Black-Market organ harvesting, body theft, and cybernetic flesh-scooping are the hallmarks of the scavenger ghoul's trade. While they are normally found skulking behind back alley street clinics or digging through hospital dumpster waste, when times are lean, scavenger ghouls take to the dark streets looking for easy marks. Needless to say, ghouls have a dark reputation and are universally hated across the Sprawl.

SCAVENGER GHOUL							
DEF	HP	FW	MOV	MEL	AIM	STR	MET
5	4	6	5	5	3	4	4
Motivation		Type		Special Rules			
Aggressive		Human		Bloody Harvest			
Items							
Flensing Equipment (counts as a sword) or Bludgeon, Taser Pistol, Sleep Grenade							

BLOODY HARVEST

Should a scavenger ghoul take an operative out of-action or render them unconscious, they begin harvesting the body. If they manage to spend 2 AP during the same turn doing this, the victim permanently loses one randomly determined piece of chrome, assuming they have any. If the victim is unconscious when this occurs, they immediately go out-of-action. Once the ghoul steals some chrome, they use all future activations to try to exit the board via the closet edge. If they manage to do so, the chrome is lost forever.

SECURITY TURRET (HEAVY)

A hardened version of the light security turret, heavy turrets defend military complexes, corporate holdings, and any other places that need to be protected from direct attack. Heavy turrets feature upgrades like better electronic defenses against cyber-attacks, improved military grade firing systems, and substantially thicker armored housing.

SECURITY TURRET (HEAVY)							
DEF	HP	FW	MOV	MEL	AIM	STR	MET
5 (8)	6	7	0	0	4	5	5

Motivation	Type	Special Rules
Guard	Bot	None

Items
Heavy Armored Housing, Integral Light Machine Gun or Minigun*
* Depending on the miniatures used, the heavy turret may be equipped with any support weapon.

HEAVY ARMORED HOUSING

Heavy turrets are protected by hardened metal housing and they have an Armor Bonus of (+3).

SECURITY TURRET (LIGHT)

Security turrets are a common defensive option used by corporations, criminal gangs, and even private citizens. Using a set of visual ID protocols—as simple as an identification card or as complex as a sub-dermal electronic tattoo—turrets act as automated armed guards. Light turrets tend to guard public venues, businesses, and other places where trouble may be expected, but not always likely. Light turrets tend to be prominently placed to act as a visual deterrent for such trouble.

SECURITY TURRET (LIGHT)							
DEF	HP	FW	MOV	MEL	AIM	STR	MET
5 (7)	4	6	0	0	4	5	5

Motivation	Type	Special Rules
Guard	Bot	None

Items
Armored Housing, Integral Assault Rifle or Heavy SMG*
* Depending on the miniatures used, the light turret may be equipped with any long gun.

ARMORED HOUSING

Light turrets are protected by metal housing and have an Armor Bonus of (+2).

SPRAWL RATS

Rats are a problem in any urban environment, but due to the combination of squalid living conditions, rampant refuse, and poor environmental controls for the dumping of chemical pollutants, some of the rats found in the Sprawl are quite large and somewhat mutant-y. While they are generally only a nuisance to a prepared Sprawler, Sprawl rats can pose a threat when they get ravenous or rabid, especially if they swarm.

SPRAWL RATS							
DEF	HP	FW	MOV	MEL	AIM	STR	MET
5	2	-	7	4	0	5	5
Motivation		Type		Special Rules			
Psycho		Animal		None			
Items							
Teeth and Claws							

Type	Melee Range	Strength	Special Rules	CC Cost
Teeth and Claws	Base	STR+1	Poison	Free

THRILL KILLER

A rather deadly enemy, the thrill killer is a chromed-up murderer looking to fulfill their wanton bloodlust. Some are unhinged razor girls and guys, others are former operatives who let the enjoyment of killing get in the way of a paycheck. Showrunners know not to take them lightly and, if possible, engage them at range.

THRILL KILLER							
DEF	HP	FW	MOV	MEL	AIM	STR	MET
5 (7)	8	6	6	5	5	5	5
Motivation		Type		Special Rules			
Aggressive		Augment		None			
Items							
Armor Weave, Subdermal Armor, Cyber Arms, Retractable Blades							

VERY IMPORTANT PERSON (VIP)

Depending on the mission or context, anyone can be a VIP. Not many are warriors, however, and if bodyguards do not accompany them, they will not last long in the streets. VIPs generally need to be protected, saved, or killed; or possibly all three in the same JOBOP.

VERY IMPORTANT PERSON (VIP)							
DEF	HP	FW	MOV	MEL	AIM	STR	MET
5	6	6	5	3	3	5	5
Motivation		Type		Special Rules			
Cautious		Human		Cower			
Items							
Pistol							

COWER

VIPs know how to keep themselves out of harm's way. As a special action, they can spend 1 AP to make themselves as small as possible. If they do this, all ranged attacks against them suffer a -1 penalty until the beginning of their next activation.

VIP BODYGUARDS

If a Showrunner is not paid to do it, someone else must protect the VIP. These tend to be generic corporate types or freelance rent-a-guards. They are all business and do a decent enough job, but they can be quickly outclassed.

VIP BODYGUARDS							
DEF	HP	FW	MOV	MEL	AIM	STR	MET
5 (6)	8	6	5	3	3	5	5
Motivation		Type		Special Rules			
Guard		Human		Self-Assured			
Items							
Armor Weave, SMG* or Machine Pistol, Small Blade							
* Depending on the miniatures used, they may also be armed with any long gun.							

WANNABE DECKER

A code kiddie and future "pwn" waiting to happen, wannabe deckers are out in the Sprawl trying to make a name for themselves, even if the result is usually terminal. They tend to get in the way more than posing a real danger and it is up to the Showrunner whether they are really worth killing.

WANNABE DECKER							
DEF	HP	FW	MOV	MEL	AIM	STR	MET
6	4	6	5	3	3	5	5
Motivation		Type		Special Rules			
Aggressive		Augment		Hood Hacker			
Items							
Cyber-Deck, Small Blade, Machine Pistol							

HOOD HACKER

Through their bottom dollar cyber-deck, the wannabe decker has the Hacking ability, which uses the below stats. They start with the Gatecrasher and Slice apps and two other randomly determined attack or environment apps. Should they ever lose all their Digital Hit Points, remove the wannabe decker from the board. This counts as taking them out-of-action. Finally, should the wannabe hacker successfully hack any CAT Terminal, the only in-game effect is that the terminal's Firewall increases by one.

WANNABE HACKER CYBER-DECK		
CYB	DHP	Remote Hacking
3	5	8"

ZZZOMBIE

HyperNET gamers are infamous for their marathon sessions that last for hours or even days while they are plugged into their full immersion exoskeletal rigs. One side-effect of these sessions is that the gamers occasionally collapse from exhaustion prior to disconnecting from cyberspace and leave their connection wide open to digital predation. Griefers often run data searches for such vulnerable persons and use "pwn" apps to gain control of the exoskeleton—and thus, the HyperNET gamer's body inside. While the gamer is passed out, the hacker runs their body around the Sprawl, wreaking as much havoc as possible. If the gamer is lucky, they wake before they get arrested, or worse.

ZZZOMBIE							
DEF	HP	FW	MOV	MEL	AIM	STR	MET
5	4	6	6	4	4	5	4
Motivation		Type		Special Rules			
Psycho		Human		Virtual Control, Wake Up			
Items							
Bludgeon							

VIRTUAL CONTROL

The Zzzombie is susceptible to any app that targets and/or affects a bot, Cyborg, or drone. While a player's hackers control the Zzzombie, they may move the Zzzombie as they wish, ignoring the psycho motivation restrictions.

WAKE UP

Anytime a player rolls a Fumble for any action the Zzzombie takes, the Zzzombie wakes. When this occurs, replace the model with a bystander token or model. This model now follows all rules for bystanders instead of this profile.

CREW ROSTER

SHADOW BACKER AVATAR				
FW	DHP	MOV/Tether	CYB	AP

Special Rules and Apps

NAME				OPERATIVE TYPE			
DEF	HP	FW	MOV	MEL	AIM	STR	MET

Special Rules and Skills

Items and Apps

NAME				OPERATIVE TYPE			
DEF	HP	FW	MOV	MEL	AIM	STR	MET

Special Rules and Skills

Items and Apps

NAME				OPERATIVE TYPE			
DEF	HP	FW	MOV	MEL	AIM	STR	MET

Special Rules and Skills

Items and Apps

Acknowledgements

The book is dedicated to my very supportive wife Melissa and my rambunctious son Izzy. I would also like to personally thank my undaunted play-testers, rules-breakers, and idea-pontificators: David W. Conrad, Johnny H.C. Newman, Jeremy Bernhardt, Chad Masterbergen, Evan Siefring, Dennis Jensen, Harold Crossley, Matthew Caron, Chris Layfield, Kyle Nixon, JD Dibrell, Nicholas Bogart, Christopher Caporal, Gavin Conrad, Derek Rogillio, Christopher Hird, Andrew Martin, Micah Carpenter, Jason October, Jared McLain, Kirke Rowe, Matteo Cantelmi, Tim Korklewski, Erik Melnichenko, Ryan Radgoski, Teemu Hemminki, Beau Doran, Benjamin Hegtvedt, Sean Masters, Christopher Sievers, Jason Mascuilli, Khultar Brea, Dave Taylor, Andrew Dickinson, Phil Matt, Gavin Dady, Casey Rogers, and Samuel West. Finally, I wanted to thank Osprey Games for keeping the faith.

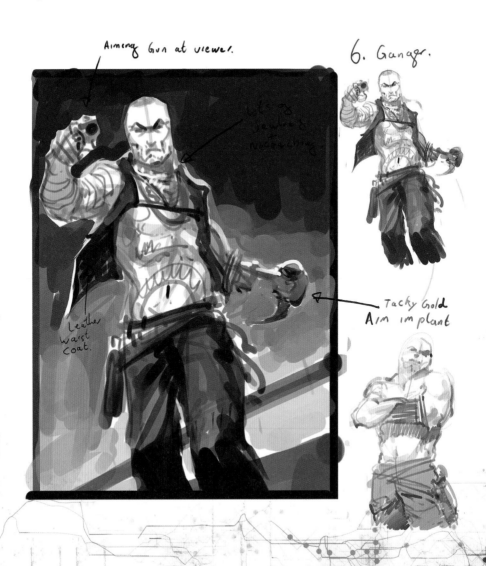

Street Doctor.

Military Fatigues.

Backpack

D.I.P.

MeDical Arm with lots of apendages.

Shoot out in Background

Thomas Elliott

Ronin

Sprawl in Background

Trench coat with collar up

Drawing sword

Rifle

Dead people on floor.

Thomas Elliott